NOT YOUR
AVERAGE VIXEN

 A CHRISTMAS ROMANCE

USA TODAY BESTSELLING AUTHOR

KRISTA SANDOR

Candy Castle Books

FREE 15-MINUTE QUICK READ ROMANCE

LIP LOCK LOVE-A STEAMY SHORT STORY

A crash course in kissing can't be that bad? Or can it?
Lip Lock Love is a short & steamy quick-read with all the feels.
Tap the cover to get your free ebook!
https://BookHip.com/XKMAVR

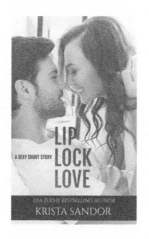

1

"*M*iss, we'll take four chocolate peppermint eclairs, two dozen of the classic French Madeleines, and a dozen of those adorable Rudolph the Red-Nosed Reindeer sugar cookies. Are those new? I don't remember seeing those darling decorated cookies last year," a rosy-cheeked woman donning a candy cane pin asked as she held the hand of a little girl with pigtails.

Bridget Dasher brushed her long bangs out of her eyes with the back of her wrist, then nodded to the woman who, along with her pint-sized companion, was sandwiched between a sea of bakery patrons, all eager to procure holiday treats the week before Christmas. But before she could answer, Gaston Francois, the chef and owner of Gaston Francois Pâtisserie, Dallas's most acclaimed pastry shop, nudged his ample belly forward. He pushed her to the side, causing her to nearly fall over onto one of the assistant bakers sliding a fresh tray of fragrant macarons into the display case. The oblivious man took no notice as he thrust onto his tiptoes. At five one, the master chef could barely see over the counter. But what he lacked in height, he'd made up for in ego, pomp, and pageantry.

"*Mais oui*! But, of course, madame! Who doesn't love the red-nosed reindeer?" the man replied, his thick French accent as syrupy as his smile.

Bridget pressed her lips together in a forced grin when the woman with the macarons leaned over and whispered into her ear.

"Weren't you the one who suggested the Rudolph cookies? They're selling like hotcakes. You should open up a bakery of your own, Bridget. Everybody knows you're the one who makes this place tick."

"It's a team effort," she replied under her breath, her pasted-on smile still in place.

She knew damn well that the only team in this shop was Team Bridget, busting her ass to churn out pastry perfection and make this place run like clockwork. But Gaston Francois had a fancy degree from Le Cordon Bleu. The only credentials she could tout were a childhood spent baking alongside her grandmother and a few online business courses she'd taken over the years.

Who was she to open up her own shop?

No, the smart thing to do was play it safe. She had a job that paid the bills. That had to be enough.

"*Brigitte!*" came the chef's high-pitched squeal, sending an avalanche of piercing pinpricks through her body.

She used to love the sound of a French accent until she started working here six years ago.

Had it been six years?

She stood there, frozen in place, and stared out at the mass of people whose lives seemed to teem with purpose and resolve.

She had purpose, right? She had Lori, her little sister, who, at twenty-five, only three years her junior, wasn't exactly little anymore. But Lori was all she had. Warmth infused with pride smoothed out the needling pinpricks at the thought of her bubbly, bright-eyed sis. An Ivy League grad and an accomplished attorney practicing in Boston, Lori had attained every goal she'd set. And, in the space of a week, she could add happily married woman to her list of accomplishments.

The little girl whose hair she used to braid was on the cusp of starting a life with the man she loved.

Bridget swallowed past the lump in her throat. It was just excitement and nerves. She'd taken on the role of wedding planner for her hardworking legal eagle of a sister. And, of course, she'd insisted on making the wedding cake and planning a bevy of activities for the entire wedding party over the week leading up to the nuptials.

But it wasn't like she'd had months to pull the event together. Lori and Tom's whirlwind romance started barely five months ago. And when her sister told her that she and Tom wanted to get married over the winter holiday on Christmas Eve, like their parents had done thirty years ago at a charming mountain house located in the Colorado Rocky Mountains, the wedding countdown clock started ticking. And there wasn't a moment to lose.

"Hey, your last name is Dasher—like one of Santa's reindeer," the little girl with pigtails exclaimed, pulling Bridget from the past.

She tucked away the thoughts of her sister's Christmas wedding, then tapped her name tag.

"That's right! I'm up there with Dancer and Prancer."

"And Comet and Cupid and Donner and Blitzen," the girl added, counting off the reindeer on her fingers.

Bridget chuckled. "Don't forget Vixen. You don't want to leave her out."

The child's brows drew together. "Vixen's a girl reindeer?"

"Why not?" Bridget answered with a playful shrug.

If Santa did exist, she could only imagine the jolly man would be all about equal opportunity.

"I bet you really love Christmas, Bridget Vixen! Oops, I mean Bridget Dasher," the girl replied, her cheeks growing rosy as she giggled at her mistake.

The pinpricks were back. But this time, they had nothing to do with her French tyrant of a boss.

"I do," she replied, hoping the little girl didn't notice the thread of sadness woven around her words.

She wasn't lying. She'd always loved her last name—loved the connection to a time of year focused on family, friendship, and festivities. And she did love Christmas—the Christmases of the past where she wasn't working or separated from Lori. Christmases, from over a decade ago, when she'd gather around a twinkling Christmas tree with not only her sister, but her parents and her grandma Dasher.

How she missed them.

The little girl's gaze traveled to the cookie display, and she pressed her nose to the glass.

"Mommy, can I get an angel cookie, too?"

The woman peered into the case. "I didn't see those! They're precious! Yes, let's add a dozen."

Bridget removed the tray containing the decorated angels and angled it so the girl could get a better look. "The angels are my favorite. Have you ever made a snow angel?"

The girl nodded with gusto. "Yes! When we visit my nana in Minnesota for Christmas, it's not like Texas. There's lots of snow! As soon as we get there, I run outside with my cousin, and we make snow angels all over Nana's backyard," she replied, waving her arms and kicking her legs as if she were about to make one right here in the store.

Bridget chuckled. "I used to make them with my little sister when we were your age. My dad used to say that if you find a snow angel with no footprints leading up to it, you may have come upon one made by a real Christmas fairy. They like to make snow angels, too. He used to tell us that Christmas fairies would fly down from the North Pole, make a snow angel, then fly back to help Santa and his elves. And if you happened to catch one in the act, they'd grant you a Christmas wish."

"Wow! I never heard of a Christmas fairy," the little girl replied, wide-eyed.

Bridget leaned over the counter and waved the girl in. "Not many people know about them," she said with a conspiratorial wink, like her dad used to do.

"*Brigitte! Vite, vite!* Look at all these customers!" Gaston Francois squawked, cutting short her conversation with the child as he glanced greedily at the packed shop before snapping her apron tie between his meaty fingers and pulling her down a few inches.

She gasped as the beady man eyed her warily.

"And what are you doing working the counter? Why aren't you in the back, finishing up the wedding cakes? I'm running a business here—not a silly fairy cookie shop," he hissed.

Her gaze darted toward the cashier and the drove of staff, boxing cakes, cookies, and puff pastries as if their lives depended on it.

Working for the temperamental chef was no walk in the park. When she'd started as an assistant baker, she'd hoped to learn from the man. Instead, she'd found herself doing the work of not only a pastry assistant but also the manager and the head baker. She could barely recall the last time the man lifted a finger in the kitchen. If he did show up, he'd hide away in his office, gobbling down whatever delectable pastry she'd prepared that day.

She was quite literally the Cinderella version of fondant and frosting.

"Sorry, chef, it was so crazy up front, I thought I'd help out," she answered.

The shop was always busy, but the week before Christmas, it hummed, no, pulsed with a frenzied cinnamon-spiced, mistle-toe-infused buzz of sugary-delicious energy. And this year was no different—except for one thing.

Instead of working through the holiday like a freight train barreling down the track with no end in sight, by this time tomorrow, she'd be boarding a plane headed for the snow-capped mountains of Colorado for Lori's wedding.

A week of holiday bliss, away from the demanding glare of Monsieur Gaston Francois, celebrating with Lori, Tom, and members of Tom's immediate family. It wasn't a large group, but she'd have her hands full cooking, baking, and coordinating all the activities she'd set up.

That was who she was. The doer. The planner. The one behind the scenes making it happen.

"You!" Gaston ordered, pointing at a gangly teen, sweeping up the bits of powdered sugar and cookie crumbs.

The blood drained from the kid's face. "Yes, chef?"

"Assist this woman and her daughter. *Brigette* needs to tend to the cakes."

"Merry Christmas, Bridget Vixen," the little girl said with a wave, again, mixing up the reindeer.

"Same to you. And keep an eye out for the Christmas fairies when you're in Minnesota," she added, then glanced at her scowling boss before making a beeline toward the back of the shop.

The swinging door closed behind her, but not a second had passed before she was hit with another barrage of people who needed her.

"How many plum tarts for the Holbert order?"

She caught the eye of a young man whipping up a batch of

frosting. "Four dozen," she answered, plucking a tasting spoon, sampling the creamy vanilla confection, then nodding her approval.

"Do you want me to make another batch of the chocolate Bûche de Noel cakes?" another baker called.

She assessed the table, lined with the French yule logs. "Let's make another dozen. We've only got a few left in the case."

A part-timer waved to her from the back of the kitchen with the bakery phone in her other hand. "Mrs. Miller's on the line. She wants to pick up her daughter's wedding cake an hour early."

Bridget glanced at the clock. "Then it's a good thing I finished it last night."

"That's in fifteen minutes! Are you sure?" the woman pressed.

"It's ready, and I'll make sure to greet Mrs. Miller myself," Bridget replied when her phone pinged in her apron pocket.

"Is that your boyfriend calling?" Della, a sassy sixteen-year-old seasonal hire, chimed from where she stood, sliding a batch of puff pastry into one of the industrial ovens.

"I doubt it. Garrett is pretty busy at the hospital," she replied as unease rippled through her chest.

When was the last time she'd actually seen her boyfriend?

They'd texted a few times this week, but with work and wedding planning, she'd barely had a second to herself over the last month.

"Dating a fancy doctor," the teen clucked, but Bridget frowned.

This young lady needed to learn that, in the kitchen, the focus was on the food. Her grandma Dasher had instilled that in her from day one. But it wasn't a gloomy attention to task that she'd prescribed—quite the opposite. Grandma Dasher believed in the magic of positivity.

Always bake with love.

And how had she infused her confectionary creations with the emotion?

By singing and dancing.

Oh, how they had loved to dance as the sweet scent of a soufflé or a lemon tart lured Lori to join them in the kitchen—especially during the holidays. They'd sway to Bing Crosby crooning "White Christmas," laughing and twirling in the warm, cozy space.

Bridget schooled her features. "Watch what you're doing, Della. You do not want to burn anything in this bakery. Especially with chef right up front," she warned, gesturing with her chin toward the door leading to the bakery's retail area.

The teen cringed, then saluted her acknowledgment before turning to observe the delicate pastry as it grew crisp in the heated oven.

"And don't forget to dance," she added.

The girl huffed as she did a little shimmy, followed by a twirl." I know. I know. Always follow Grandma Dasher's advice. Dancing spreads good karma to whatever you're baking."

Bridget suppressed a grin. Her grandma Dasher would be proud. But before she could fall back into her memories, her phone pinged again. She pulled it from the apron pocket, and now she couldn't hold back her smile.

"I'll be in the alley taking a five-minute break," she announced to the bustling staff before heading out the back door.

She sat down on a crate, then answered the call. "Hey, little sis! How's Colorado?"

"Birdie, Kringle Mountain House is amazing. It's exactly how I remembered it when we used to come here with Grandma, Mom, and Dad. I can't believe I'm getting married here! There are so many big changes on the horizon."

All the anxiety Gaston Francois had whipped up inside her melted away at the sound of Lori's voice. Her sister still called her by her nickname, Birdie—given to her by her parents, who said when she was a wee little thing, she'd pop her head out of the crib like a little bird. Lori was the only one who called her that now—the two syllables a salve for her heart.

"So, you made it in okay last night? Tom's family, too?" she pressed.

"We sure did. And the SUV they sent from Kringle Mountain House was right there, waiting for us outside the airport. I needed to make a quick pit stop on the way. But we arrived here safe and sound. They're calling for some snow, quite a bit of snow, from what the mountain house staff says," Lori reported.

A smile—a real smile—stretched across Bridget's face. Her plans to give Lori and Tom the perfect Christmas wedding would only be better with the addition of a Rocky Mountain winter snowstorm.

"That's great news! I've arranged for you all to ski today and tomorrow. You'll have loads of fresh powder! Kringle Mountain House should still have a lift to bring you up to the ski runs."

"It's there. I can see it from my room," Lori answered with a touch of nostalgia to her words.

Bridget nodded, grateful the staff had given Lori and Tom the room she'd selected for them. The mountain house only had five rooms—exactly what they needed—no more and no less—to accommodate Tom's immediate family for an intimate mountain wedding.

"You've got the schedule of events and activities I emailed to you, right? I sent a copy to the Kringle Mountain House caretakers, too."

"Oh, yes, Birdie, super baker and wedding planner extraordinaire, I got it. It's so kind of you. You've thought of everything and have already done so much."

A heavy beat of silence passed between them.

"What is it?" she asked, sensing something was weighing on her sister's heart.

Lori released a shaky breath. "After Mom and Dad died, back when we were girls, and then when we lost Grandma Dasher two years later, you've been my rock. I don't know what I would have done without you. And now, I'm getting married, and I'm..." Lori trailed off, her voice thick with emotion.

Bridget twisted the hem of her apron and blinked back tears. While most eighteen-year-olds were going to parties and preparing for college or a gap year to travel the world, she'd started working two jobs to make sure her fifteen-year-old sister had everything she needed. She'd become Lori's legal guardian and a single parent before she'd even lost her virginity.

"I want you to know that Tom and I are so grateful, Birdie."

Bridget swallowed past the emotion. It made sense that Lori would be feeling sentimental and reflecting on their parents and grandmother. They'd spent their last Christmas as a family at Kringle Mountain House. And truth be told, she could hardly believe she'd be back there after all this time.

"Hey, what are big sisters for?" she answered, trying to keep it light. But not even she was immune to the onslaught of memories. She could picture her grandmother, feel the papery skin of her cheek the moment before the kind woman took her last breath a decade ago.

Take care of your little sister, Birdie. You're all she has now.

"I didn't mean to get all mushy," Lori said, clearing her throat.

Bridget dabbed away the moisture welling in her eyes with the edge of her apron. "Well, I fly in tomorrow, and we can be all sorts of mushy when I get there. I know that Grandma, Mom, and Dad would be so happy for you."

Another sliver of silence stretched between them before her

sister spoke.

"Birdie?"

"Yeah, Lori?"

"Are you sure you don't mind that I'm getting married here?"

Bridget wasn't expecting that.

"Mind? I think it's wonderful! We always said that whoever got married first would have to do it like Mom and Dad did at Kringle Mountain House."

"There's something else." Lori paused.

"What?"

"I have a bad feeling about something, Birdie."

Bridget's stomach turned to stone.

"Is it Tom? Did something happen? Did you have a fight?" she pried.

"No, nothing like that," her sister replied, lowering her voice.

"Then, what, Lori?"

"I'm worried about Scooter. Tom's on the phone with him now."

"Who?" Bridget shot back.

There wasn't any Scooter on the guest list.

"He's Tom's best friend, and he's going to be his best man. I texted you the details. Tom had asked him, and he'd been waiting on the guy's answer. He finally agreed. Tom's over the moon, but I'm not so sure about it."

"Is Scooter the lunch from hell guy?" Bridget asked, vaguely remembering the mention of the man.

Lori huffed an audible breath. "Yep, that's him. About a month ago, he flew up from New York City to have lunch with Tom and me. The man gave me the cold shoulder and didn't speak to me the entire time. He answered any question I asked him with a grunt, and then he got a call and left the restaurant before our entrées had even arrived! But he had time to slip the waitress his card and tell her to call him when she got off."

Bridget gasped. "Now, I remember. What a sleazeball! What does Tom say about him?"

"Just that Scooter's a good guy with a complicated past. They've been friends for years. I'm trying to be kind and patient and give the guy another chance. He is Tom's best friend, and my fiancé has a heart of gold. But I won't lie. It's not easy, and I'm concerned he may have ulterior motives."

"What does this Scooter do again?" Bridget asked. She needed some intel on this creep.

"He and Tom went to law school together, but now he runs a business where he buys and sells companies. He's a successful guy—a hard-nosed businessman from the sound of it."

"What do you think his ulterior motives are?" she pressed.

"For one thing, Tom says that Scooter's not sold on the institution of marriage at all. And I get the feeling that he thinks I'm wrong for Tom or doesn't approve of me. I don't know! I'm worried about what he might say or what he might do once he gets here."

Bridget clenched her jaw as anger coursed through her veins.

Who the hell was anyone to judge her sister's character? Smart, kind, and dedicated, women didn't get better than Lori! And she wasn't about to let anyone—let alone some douchebag named Scooter—wreck her sister's happiness. She'd made a promise to her grandmother that she'd take care of Lori, and she wasn't about to sit back and allow some jerk with an agenda to ruin her little sister's wedding.

Hell to the no!

But she couldn't unload on the guy—not to Lori. As much as she wanted to have a bitch fest and roast the guy's testicles, it wouldn't do any good. This guy was Tom's friend, and she had to defuse this now and put her sister's mind at ease.

Not to mention, she felt like there was something else

weighing on her sister's heart. But managing this Scooter was priority number one.

"Lori, honey, I've only met Tom once, but it was clear as day that he loves you. He could barely look away from you. It was like watching Mom and Dad."

"Love at first sight," Lori said, the wistful lilt of nostalgia replacing the worry in her voice.

"Love at first sight," Bridget repeated. She closed her eyes. "Dad said the moment he walked into the lecture hall and saw Mom finishing up teaching her class, he knew right then and there that he was going to marry her."

"Like me! When I got hired on at Abbott and Associates. Tom walked into my office on my first day to introduce himself, and I don't think I've ever been the same since," she answered, her tone growing dreamy.

Her sister's romance with Tom was right out of a storybook. He'd swept Lori off her feet. The guy sent her flowers and took her on romantic getaways. And he'd done something she'd never expected. He'd asked her for Lori's hand in marriage. The two of them had only been dating three months, but when he and Lori had flown down to Texas for a visit, the man was as genuine as they come.

"Is there something else you want to tell me, Lori?" she asked, her sister sixth sense kicking in.

For a beat, neither woman spoke.

"Look at me, blabbering on about Tom. How's Garrett? Is he still able to come with you to the wedding?" Lori replied, shifting gears.

Bridget blinked. Was it odd that sometimes she forgot that she was dating someone?

Garrett was in the last year of his surgical residency and worked almost as much as she did. They were...fine. Compatible. Not the stop-the-presses kind of love like her parents or

Lori and Tom had. No, what she had with Garrett was comfortable. The sex was...adequate. Or at least, that's how she'd remembered it. With the holidays, she'd been working hundred-hour weeks, and he'd been equally busy at the hospital. They didn't have a whole lot of time to tear each other's clothes off. Well, they'd never done that. But who does that, really?

Bridget chewed her lip.

When was the last time they'd even kissed, not to mention slept together?

Worry settled in her belly, but she ignored the sensation.

It was all good.

Yep, totally fine.

The last time she'd stopped by his place, she'd seen a gift bag tucked away in Garrett's closet. Upon closer inspection, she'd found it contained a sexy fire-engine red bra and pantie set.

It had to be her Christmas present.

You don't buy sexy underwear for someone you're not attracted to. Maybe there was more to them? Maybe attending her sister's wedding together would catapult their relationship to the next level—whatever that may be.

"Bridget, Mrs. Miller's here!" Della called, poking her head out the half-opened door.

"Lori, I need to get back to work. Try not to give Scooter a second thought. I'll handle him."

"He's supposed to be flying in the day of the wedding, so, hopefully, he won't have time to do anything too outlandish."

"That's right!" Bridget affirmed. "Don't give him a second thought. You enjoy Kringle Mountain. I'll see you soon!" she said, injecting extra cheer into her voice. The last thing she wanted was for her sister to worry about anything the week of her wedding.

"Do you want me to get the cake?" Della asked, poking her head out again.

"No, I'll get it," she answered, ending the call.

She hurried inside and headed for the refrigerated room that held all the orders. And there it was—a gorgeous five-tiered cake.

The Millers had recently fallen on hard times. They'd been loyal customers for years. But when Peggy Miller put in the cake order for her daughter and saw the price, she'd asked for something less elaborate, citing her financial hardship.

But Bridget had offered to make the cake at half-price. It was the right thing to do. Her grandma Dasher had sold baked goods from her dusty West Texas home. And more times than Bridget could count, she'd witnessed the woman not only charging a fraction of the cost but outright giving away her culinary creations, especially around the holidays.

Following her grandmother's baked-goods dance superstition, she twirled to give the cake one last round of love. Then, carefully, she slid the cake out of the refrigerator and headed for the front where Gaston Francois looked ready to blow a gasket.

"Where have you been? We cannot have Madame Miller waiting," the little man barked.

"I apologize for the wait," she said, setting the cake on a side table as the mother of the bride assessed the marzipan masterpiece.

"It's perfect!" the woman exclaimed as tears came to her eyes. "And thank you for giving me a discount. This cake will be the centerpiece of the wedding."

"You're very welcome. It was my pleasure," she answered, smiling at the grateful customer.

"Discount?" Gaston hissed, his fat cheeks growing red.

Bridget threw the man a nervous glance, then turned back to Mrs. Miller. "And I altered the recipe. I glazed the cakes with a simple syrup before I frosted it. It'll keep it moist and delicious for days," she added, silently thanking her grandma Dasher for teaching her that trick.

The woman lifted the cake box into her arms. "My daughter is going to love it. You're an angel, Bridget Dasher."

"Merry Christmas, Mrs. Miller," she said as a blanket of warmth enveloped her body.

There was nothing better than seeing her confectionary creations bring people happiness. She turned to her boss, but instead of being happy with a satisfied customer, Gaston glared at her, red-cheeked and seething.

"What's wrong, chef?" she asked.

"You did not charge her full price?"

"No, chef. Mrs. Miller recently lost her job, and her husband's been ill."

"This is not a food bank, *Brigette*."

She should have expected this. The man was a miser.

She gave him a placating smile. "I'm happy to pay the difference out of my wages. Now, I better get back to work."

Gaston turned a deeper shade of red. "You're not getting back to anything."

"I'm not?" she replied, her voice barely a whisper.

This was not good.

Gaston Francois's beady gaze darkened. "You dared to change my recipe?"

Oh no!

She tried to swallow, but her mouth had grown dry.

"Not changed, enhanced," she sputtered.

"Enhanced?" he growled.

"Clients had commented that the cakes were a bit dry, that's all. I decided to try something new," she rambled, then smacked her hand over her mouth.

Altering a master chef's recipe was the culinary kiss of death.

She'd only made a tiny tweak, but it was still a change.

The little man cocked his head to the side as a slippery smirk pulled at the corners of his mouth. "You like to try new things, *Brigette*? Like giving away my cakes and *enhancing* my recipes that were perfected at Le Cordon Bleu? You, a girl with no formal training. No credentials."

She stared at him. There wasn't a right answer—not after what she'd admitted.

"I—" she began, but the chef raised his meaty index finger, silencing her.

"Now, you can *try* getting a new job, *Brigette.* You are fired!" he snapped.

"Fired?" she cried. Her voice, a shrill scrape of a sound, cut through the hum of the shop.

The chatter stopped as all eyes fell on her.

"You, broom boy! Get *Brigette's* things," Gaston called, puffing up like an inflated peacock.

She looked on as the gangly teen ran through the door leading to the back of the shop, then returned with her backpack.

The chef grabbed the bag from the boy and thrust it into her chest. "I will not have anyone stealing my profits or modifying my recipes! You're through here. And I'll make sure every pastry shop in the state hears about this betrayal."

She couldn't be labeled as a pastry pariah! And like Gaston reminded her, it wasn't as if she had a fancy degree to fall back on. All she'd ever been was an amateur baker.

She glanced around the shop as judgmental glares tore into her at every angle.

What would she do now?

She was the play-it-safe sister. The keep-your-head-down, do-what-it-takes sister. She didn't have the luxury of dreaming big.

A hot rush of humiliation threaded with embarrassment heated her cheeks. With her gaze trained on the floor, she turned toward the door as the crowded shop parted, making way for the disgraced employee. She squinted as the midday sun nearly blinded her as she exited the shop, and the door to Gaston Francois Pâtisserie slammed behind her.

The final harsh goodbye.

"What happened in there?" she whispered.

She started down the sidewalk—a zombie sprinkled in flour and bits of fondant. Garrett's place wasn't far from here. She could go there. He'd be at the hospital, and she needed somewhere close by to process the lightning-fast demise of her baking career. If you could call it a career. And she sure as hell wasn't ready to endure the forty-minute bus ride home. No, she'd go to Garrett's, get her bearings, think of something to say to Gaston, then go back to the shop and plead her case. He could have a change of heart, right?

In an hour or so, he'd cool off. He'd see that he'd acted rashly. They'd work it out. He was a passionate Frenchman. These things happened. But the more she kept trying to convince herself that it was going to be okay, the less okay she felt.

No job meant no income. She'd spent the last of her savings on Lori's wedding. At least, she didn't have to worry about her soon-to-be depleted bank account impacting her sister's big day.

She rounded the corner and arrived at her boyfriend's townhouse. Taking the front steps two at a time, she fished her keys from the bottom of her bag and unlocked the door.

"You need a minute to make a plan. You're a planner, Birdie. You'll figure this out," she said, shutting the door when a shriek from inside rippled down from the second floor.

"Garrett?" she called as another sound, a low, purring groan, echoed through the space.

Was he sick? Did he fall, or was he hurt?

She sprinted up the steps, flung open the bedroom door, then stilled. A woman sat on the bed, facing away from her and wearing a fire engine red bra.

"Who are you, and what are you doing in my lingerie?" she called.

She took another step into the room and discovered her boyfriend lying flat on the bed while being straddled by the lingerie thief.

And then the penny dropped.

"Oh my God," she said on a tight exhale as the second sucker punch of the day landed straight into her gut.

"Bridget!" Garrett called. His disheveled brown hair, guilty eyes, and the giant hickey on his neck confirmed what she already knew.

She scrambled out of the room, listening to her cheating boyfriend and his lingerie-stealing floozy break out into panicked whispers.

Tears, hot and angry, welled in her eyes. She ran out of the townhouse, leaving the door wide open.

"Bridget! Stop, please!"

She released a ragged breath, then turned to find her boyfriend, no, her ex-boyfriend, standing on the sidewalk with a sheet wrapped around his waist.

Quite a *cheater-esque* choice. But when you've been caught mid-thrust, one's options must be limited.

"Bridget, I'm sorry. I..." the man trailed off.

"I somehow fell into bed with another woman, who happens to be wearing the lingerie I bought for my girlfriend? Is that what you were trying to say?" she offered, crossing her arms.

He glanced away. "It's not your lingerie."

"I saw it in your closet weeks ago, Garrett. I know it's supposed to be my Christmas gift."

"I didn't buy it for you, Bridget," he answered, still not meeting her eye.

And the punches kept coming.

"I see," she answered as a dull numbness took over.

She stared at the person she'd been dating for the better part of two years. This should have stung. This betrayal should have cut right through her heart. But all she could think about was how Garrett's absence at the wedding would screw up her seating arrangement.

"I need to text Lori," she said, reaching for her phone.

He let out an incredulous bark of a laugh. "You catch your boyfriend in bed with another woman, and all you can say is that you need to call your sister? I guess it's fitting. That is what it's like dating you."

She narrowed her gaze. "What does that mean?"

He shook his head. "It's always your sister. Harvard law. Hired on at a prestigious firm. Dating the man of her dreams. I feel like I know more about her than I do about you. That's probably why..."

"Why what? You might as well say it. That little afternoon delight session I walked in on sealed the deal that it's over between us," she replied, forcing her tone to remain even.

Garrett ran a frustrated hand through his hair. "Maybe that's why you never go after what you want. Maybe that's why you're still a bakery assistant. You're so busy thinking about Lori and butting into her life that you don't have a life of your own."

The admission might have hurt if she hadn't heard it before.

A muscle ticked in her jaw. "I have a perfectly fine life. Well, I did until I walked in on my boyfriend cheating on me."

"You know we've been over long before today. Every time I've seen you over the last few months, all you talk about is your sister's wedding. I want a girlfriend, not some woman fixated on someone else's life."

How dare he?

She took a step forward. "This wedding is important. Lori and I are recreating the wedding our parents had thirty years ago. It's not something you can hand off to an event planner. I need to be this involved. If you'd cared about me, you would have understood that."

The guilt in Garrett's eyes dissolved into pity. "It's not your wedding, Bridget."

A thread of longing twisted around her heart—a feeling she'd grown used to disregarding.

"I know that," she answered, now the one looking away.

"Do you? Or have you been hiding behind this maternal guise of caring for your sister to shield yourself from anyone who might care for you or stop you from grasping at any opportunity that came your way? You're the most stifled, stuck person I know. I feel sorry for you," he said, looking at her as if she were the last puppy left at the pound.

The thread tightened its grip on her heart, twisting and tormenting. But she'd become a pro at dismissing its selfish pleas.

"Is this your way of blaming me for the lingerie-clad woman in your bed?" she asked, unwilling to let his words shake her resolve.

"Bridget, you're a nice girl, but..."

You're a nice girl, but...

She didn't have to listen to what came after those five words because she'd heard them before, littered in the trail of her past relationships. And what did it matter anyway? Garrett, like all the rest, had no sense of duty. He'd never been tasked with ensuring another's happiness. He'd never made a solemn promise to put another person before himself.

Grandma Dasher had entrusted her sister's happiness and

wellbeing to her. If someone couldn't understand that, then that person didn't understand her.

"I'm sorry, Bridget. I didn't want it to end like this," he said, his words floating in the air as she turned and headed for the bus stop.

No job. No boyfriend.

But she hadn't lost everything. She stared down at her phone, then clicked the text icon.

Birdie: Hey, little sis. I caught Garrett in bed with another woman. But don't worry about me. I'm okay. He was like all the rest. I'm relieved, actually. Now, I won't have anyone to distract me from making sure the best man is on his best behavior.

Within seconds, three flashing dots appeared, signaling her sister's reply.

Lori: I'm sorry about Garrett, Birdie. It's his loss—you know that. I love you!

Bridget gathered her resolve. She'd figure out her life. She'd find another job—somewhere.

But now wasn't the time to worry about that. No, she'd made a promise—a promise more important than a crummy job or a philandering boyfriend.

Only one thing mattered, and that was making sure Lori's wedding went off without a hitch.

She thought back to the little girl with the pigtails and her sweet slip of the tongue.

Merry Christmas, Bridget Vixen!

There had to be a little vixen in her somewhere—a little badassery hidden beneath the surface. She lengthened her stride and added a little swing to her step.

For Lori, she'd be the vixen.

The dragon slayer.

A woman on a mission.

This Scooter better watch out. Birdie was on her way.

2

SOREN

*S*oren Rudolph assessed the half-dozen men and women seated around the table in his spacious office overlooking the southern end of Central Park. Prime NYC real estate. Nothing less would do—not for the city's top private equity firm.

"Report," he ordered, leaning back in his chair.

Six four and built like a Greek god, he was used to having all eyes on him. But behind his chiseled features and appraising cat-like eyes was a mind that never stopped.

Sure, it was a quarter past seven in the evening the week before Christmas. The brake lights of rush hour traffic thirty stories below reflected off the towering skyscrapers, signaling the end of the workday. But not for him. Not for the real movers and shakers in this city.

Those with their eye on the prize were interested in one goal.

Making cold, hard cash.

Lots of it—and at any cost.

He'd started Rudolph Holdings seven years ago, and in that short amount of time, he'd become the king of asset stripping. Like a wolf searching out the weakest sheep in the flock, his corporation would purchase vulnerable companies. If they were able to turn a profit, adding to his bottom line, they were safe. But if they faltered, if they exhibited even a hint of weakness, it was off to the chopping block. He'd squeeze everything he could from the failed venture. There were wimps and whiners out there who labeled his business practices as callous and cruel, but he didn't give a damn.

This endeavor required one to mute their feelings and cast away any inkling of sentiment.

If there were ever a person built for this life, it was him.

At thirty years old, even with a law degree and an MBA under his belt, he might be considered young and inexperienced in some circles. But what he lacked in age, he more than made up for with his sharp business acumen and acute intelligence.

Some said he had a sixth sense. He didn't. He relied on the facts. The data.

Suckers trusted their gut. Losers put their faith in feelings and intuition. Winners pushed that mushy bullshit aside and trusted the numbers.

"Sir, in the past six months, Rudolph Holdings has acquired several factories and a chain of boutique bakeries. Despite the bakery closing locations in smaller cities and resort towns, it's operating at a loss and has been bleeding cash for the last nine months. We sent out a final notice last week, alerting the owners to the situation," a young man said with a nervous twitch.

Soren suppressed a grin. He reveled in his power—in his ability to make men and women alike quiver in his presence.

He leaned forward. "I want a full assessment of the bakery chain: property information and an estimate of key assets. Let's do what we do best. Take them apart and get top dollar for every sellable component."

"And the staff, sir?" the man added, running his index finger under the collar of his dress shirt.

Soren stared at the man. A new hire.

"The staff?" he repeated, his voice low.

"Yes, how should we proceed with the employees," the newbie asked as beads of sweat lined the guy's upper lip.

Soren rose to his feet and paced the length of the office. "You're new here."

"Yes, sir, I'm Cory. I was hired a month ago."

"Let me give you a tip, Cory."

The young man wiped his wrist across his sweaty lip. "I'd appreciate that, sir."

Soren stared out the window at the park he'd visited a million times, but never with his parents. No, they had no interest in him. Petty affairs and private jets headed to Monte Carlo or the Italian Riviera took priority for his aloof mother and playboy of a father.

He turned and pinned the man with his piercing green gaze. "We don't concern ourselves with the employees."

The new hire opened a folder and glanced at a piece of paper. "We don't? I figured they had families, and it's so close to Christmas. I thought we could be charitable and give them some more time."

Jesus Christ!

A muscle ticked in his jaw. "Time to do what? Cost us more money?"

Cory swallowed hard. "I didn't think of it that way, sir."

"If you want to be successful in this business, you need to start thinking of it that way. Charity doesn't pay the bills. It simply draws out the inevitable. We go in for the fast kill—precise and lethal. We don't fuck around. Do you understand?"

The man nodded emphatically. "Yes, Mr. Rudolph, I do."

"You all know what you need to do. Get to work," he said, addressing the group as his phone buzzed an incoming call.

He slipped it from his pocket and nearly cracked a smile, but he maintained a neutral expression as he dismissed the employ-ees. Once they were down the hall and out of eyesight, he glanced at the only framed photo he kept on a shelf near his desk. The corners of his lips tipped into the ghost of a grin as he took in the image of two gangly fourteen-year-old boys with their arms slung over each other.

He tapped the phone icon and answered the call.

"Is the funeral still on?" he asked in lieu of a greeting and was met with the easy laughter of his best friend, Tom Abbott.

"Scooter! You've got to stop referring to my wedding as a funeral. I'm grateful as hell that you finally agreed to be my best man this morning, but..."

"But what?" he threw back playfully.

"But flying in the night before the wedding then leaving right after won't give you any time to enjoy the mountain. Come and stay for the week. We can hit the slopes. Eat delicious food. Drink good beer."

"All this with your fiancée present, right?"

Fiancée.

He hated the sound of the word.

He and Tom were a twosome. Two men on a mission to live their lives to the fullest. That is, until Tom—in what he could only describe as a crushing lapse of judgment—added a fiancée to the mix, throwing off the delicate balance of their friendship. How were they supposed to pick up women and drop everything to go cliff diving in Australia with a fiancée in tow?

"Tell me you've come to your senses, and we can catch a flight to Ibiza. Think of it, Tommy. Sand, sun, and more pussy than you'd know what to do with," he answered but was met with a heavy silence.

Tom had been his best friend and partner in crime since they'd met at boarding school in Boston when they were freshmen in high school. They'd even gone to college and law school together. For the better part of the last sixteen years, there were inseparable.

And when it came to women, they were unstoppable. With his all-American, boy next door blond hair and blue-eyed vibe, Tom contrasted with his dark and brooding personality to create the perfect chick magnet.

But they'd never had more than a fling. Neither had ever dated anyone seriously. Who wanted the old ball and chain?

It was the perfect setup. Nothing tied them down.

They'd traveled the world. They'd run with the bulls in Pamplona, summited Everest, and had spent every Christmas together since they were fourteen. Before his first Christmas with the Abbotts, he'd planned on staying in his dorm room at boarding school for the entire winter break.

The beauty of having divorced parents who detested each other and couldn't give a shit about their kid meant that he could tell his mom he was going to stay with his dad, then tell his dad that he was going to be with his mom.

By fourteen, he'd had his fill of waking up on Christmas morning to a housekeeper.

Upon hearing his plan, Tom had dragged his moody ass to the Boston suburbs to spend the holiday with his family.

And from that moment on, he'd found the one place where he could be himself.

The Abbott's had welcomed him with open arms and were the closest thing to family he'd ever known.

He wasn't about to have some fiancée shifting the dynamic or changing the rhythm that had meant everything to him.

"Scooter, buddy, I told you. Lori's the one for me. When you know you know," Tom replied with a dreamy quality to his voice that made him want to hurl.

Soren frowned. "Don't give me that love at first sight bull-shit," he shot back.

"It's not bullshit. And you know that means something coming from me. I wouldn't lie to you, Scooter."

Soren huffed. "And the prenup? Has she signed it?"

"You know I don't want one."

Soren shook his head. "You're a damn lawyer, Tom. You should know better."

His friend chuckled. "You sound like Lori. She drew one up the other day at work, but I threw it in the trash. I'm the one saying no to a prenup. I don't want it, and I don't need it. I love Lori and—"

"And what, Mr. Pussy Whipped?" he grumped.

Tom paused, not taking the bait. "Not all marriages are like your parents. Think of my mom and dad."

That's exactly what he was thinking about. Tom's parents, Grace and Scott, treated him like another son. Tom's grandfather, Franklin Goodwin Abbott, who they affectionately called Judge because the man had served in the family courts for over fifty years, taught him how to fish alongside Tom. He even enjoyed spending time with Tom's Uncle Russell, who could be best described as a balding, leisure suit Larry wannabe Casanova. The guy might have had game once upon a time, but he and Tom always got a kick out of taking him out to the bars over the holidays to watch him get shot down by women half his age.

Then there was Tom's ballbuster of an older sister, Denise, who gave him shit like an older sister should. And Denise's wife Nancy wasn't one to be left out either when it came to the playful ribbing. Their kids, Cole and Carly, called him Uncle Scooter, for Christ's sake! Soren Christopher Traeger Rudolph, the hard-nosed, money-making womanizer, allowed two children to call him Uncle Scooter.

Why? Because they loved him.

He opened his desk drawer and peered at a picture that five-year-old Cole and eight-year-old Carly had drawn for him. A picture of a stupid Vespa scooter, and it was a damned treasure.

Denise and Nancy had gotten married ten years ago, which, along with having the kids, had altered the holidays. But he and Tom had taken on the role of uncles together.

It was always him and Tom.

And he sure as hell wasn't about to allow a shake-up to the status quo. More than that, he had to think of Tom. Marriage was nothing to take lightly. He was moving too fast. He wasn't in his right mind.

"Come on, Scooter. If I can't lure you out for the week, promise me that you'll be on good behavior when you do get here," Tom said, exasperation coating his words.

His fiancée must have put him up to this call.

Soren closed the drawer containing Cole and Carly's picture as a sly expression graced his features.

"Hey, if this love of yours is as strong as you say, it can survive anything, right?"

Throwing Tom's love logic back at him was a jackass lawyer move. But he was starting to feel something deep within him.

His past, percolating in his chest.

Before he spent the holidays with the Abbotts, he'd been utterly alone.

"Scooter?" Tom pressed.

Soren tapped his fingers on the desk. "I agreed to be your best man. Isn't that enough?"

"And I'd like my best man with me for the week. You've celebrated every Christmas with us since we were fourteen. You'd be here right now if there wasn't a wedding."

"I prefer your parents' place in Massachusetts," he shot back.

"Well, tough guy, this year, the Abbotts are in Colorado."

"For an entire damned week," Soren mumbled.

Tom groaned. "Again, Scooter, you've always spent a week

with us. Plus, Birdie's got the whole week planned with activities, dinners, and all sorts of good stuff. It's going to be a blast."

Soren bristled. The thought of prearranged plans left a bitter taste in his mouth. He'd lost count of the camps and daycares his parents had enrolled him in when he was a boy to get him out of their hair. Nannies who were charged with his well-being dragged him all over the city. Neither of his parents ever asked about his day, his likes, his dislikes. They'd breeze in and out of his life like leaves in the wind.

"I make my own schedule," he replied, shaking off the memories.

"Scooter! Dude! It's my wedding," Tom pleaded.

"You're not married yet, and who the hell is this Birdie. And what the fuck kind of name is that?"

"Birdie is Lori's sister. I told you about her."

Soren frowned. He'd become accustomed to zoning out of the conversation when it turned to Lori. In fact, he was damned ready to have his friend back and talk about something other than this woman.

"Scooter, you need to get on board with the wedding. My whole family loves Lori. Even Denise. And you know what she's like."

Soren stared out into the city, twinkling with holiday lights. "*S, C, T, R*," he said softly.

"Scooter," his friend replied. "I was sure you were going to hate me after Denise saw your initials on your luggage and started calling you Scooter."

"Stupid fucking name," he replied with a grin.

"It's been your nickname for sixteen years. You know you love it," Tom teased.

His best friend wasn't wrong.

He did love the silly moniker. He might not be an Abbott, but when Tom's sister anointed him Scooter, a twisted childhood logic took over. In his heart, this naming, this connection bound them together. It made him a part of them. Tom's entire family called him Scooter. They used the nickname with such love, in his darkest moments, all he'd have to do was whisper the word, and instantly, he was home.

Soren Christopher Traeger Rudolph was a calculating businessman who regularly stripped companies of their livelihood. He dismantled and demolished.

His life as Scooter was the only redeeming part of him.

"Why the rush to get married, Tommy?" he asked, changing tack. "We're thirty. We're young. We've still got places to go and people to meet. Beautiful women in need of having their brains screwed out. This is the time in our lives to indulge."

"We've been indulging for over a decade. Aren't you ready for more? And I've got to tell you, I have quite a bit of *more* on the horizon with her," Tom said, back to sounding like a whipped schoolboy.

"More on the horizon?" he repeated. She did have him watching chick flicks.

Soren undid the top button on his dress shirt, but it didn't alleviate the tightness in his throat.

"Scooter, I love Lori. It was love at first sight, and it's only gotten stronger. I wish you could understand what it's like when you lock eyes with someone, and you know that your life will never be the same."

"What the hell, man! Does she have you watching *The Notebook* on repeat?" he shot back, but Tom only chuckled.

"It's not a half-bad movie, Scooter."

Soren shook his head. His friend wasn't ready. This was simply a passing fancy. He'd met Tom's fiancée briefly at lunch before he'd rendezvoused with their waitress for a quick and dirty fuck in the restaurant's alley. It wasn't one of his classiest of moments. But when he saw the way Tom looked at Lori, he had to get out of there and blow off a little steam. The screw was mediocre and mindless. He'd wanted to get the image of Tom and Lori out of his head. But it didn't work. Nor did it quell the unease inside of him.

Lori was attractive and smart. Who wouldn't like her?

But to marry her—after only a few months of dating?

Hell no!

Tom was caught up in her. That's all. They worked together. They saw each other every day. It's no surprise he'd want to take her to bed.

But marriage? Actual marriage?

He knew his best friend. The man might have thought he was ready to pull the matrimonial trigger. But he wasn't.

A knock on his office door caught his attention as his assistant waved to him from the other side of the glass door.

"Tom, I have to go. Janine needs something. I'll see you in a few days."

"Thanks, man. Remember, I need you on best, best man behavior. No funny business and tell Janine that the Abbotts wish her a Merry Christmas."

Soren ended the call, not agreeing to anything, as he waved the woman in.

"Were you talking to Tom Abbott?" she asked, eyeing him closely.

"Not that it's any of your business, but yes," he answered, playing coy.

A smug grin bloomed across the woman's lips. "I know that face, Soren."

"What face?" he parroted back.

"Your *real* happy face."

"I don't have a *real* happy face. I have a face, Janine," he answered, careful to keep his features neutral. But he should know better, especially with this one. At almost seventy, the woman only kept getting sharper.

And she wasn't only his assistant.

Years ago, she'd worked as a nanny and happened to be the one person who, before he'd met the Abbotts, had bestowed genuine kindness upon him. She wasn't with him long. His mother had hired her a few days before his tenth birthday, then, out of nowhere, fired the woman a week before his eleventh. There was never any rhyme or reason to his parents' behavior, but he'd never forgotten Janine's compassion. When he needed an assistant years later, he'd found her, offered her triple what she was making as a secretary in a dentist's office in Queens, and that was that.

"I took care of finding the *exotic entertainers* you requested. They were happy to let me know they can accommodate both dates," she said with a disapproving glance at the iPad in her hand.

The strippers!

He'd forgotten that after his call with Tom this morning, he'd tasked Janine with acquiring strippers for some bachelor entertainment. When he agreed to be Tom's best man, and despite Tom telling him he and Lori had decided against the traditional bachelor-bachelorette parties, he took on the important job of planning a surprise event. Which, of course, needed to include scantily clad women. And he knew for a fact that Tom's Uncle Russ would be on board.

He bit back a grin. "Look at that! Janine, you're a gem. How many personal assistants out there could procure strippers in the middle of nowhere Colorado, on such short notice?"

She watched him from over her bifocals. "Are you sure that's what Tom would want?"

He chewed the inside of his cheek. Tom didn't know what he

wanted, and it was his job to help his friend see exactly what was at stake.

Janine ignored his silence and plowed on.

"You're scheduled to leave for Denver early in the morning on the twenty-fourth. I've notified the staff at Kringle Mountain House, and they've assured me that they'll send a car for you. Then the wedding will take place that evening. And I have you flying out the next morning."

He nodded when a flash of red grabbed his attention, and he caught a glimpse of a woman wrapped like a present in a slim-fitting ruby red pencil skirt.

"Is that my Christmas gift?" he asked with a teasing grin, checking out the redhead standing outside his office.

Janine balked. "It's Mr. and Mrs. Angel. They've come with legal counsel. I told them they could have fifteen minutes with you."

He crossed his arms. "Who are the Angels? Is this a Christmas joke, Janine?"

"They're the people who own the Cupid Bakeries."

"So, they're the ones who have been wasting my money," he answered, eyeing an older couple standing next to the curvy redhead.

The gentleman sported a white beard and was a dead ringer for Santa Claus, and his wife got in on the holiday action with a little red shawl. They looked like they'd just gotten off a shift at a holiday meet-and-greet at the mall.

"They've been calling all week, pleading for a time to meet with you," Janine continued.

He cleared his throat. "I have people who deal with this sort of thing."

"They asked for you, Soren. And look at them. They flew out here, hoping to speak with you. They told me that they built

Cupid Bakery from the ground up. And it's the holidays. A little goodwill toward men would do you good."

A little goodwill with that redhead would do him good as well. The siren of an attorney looked up and caught his eye through the glass wall. Her gaze traveled lasciviously down his body.

A quick meeting didn't sound so bad now.

"What do you say, Soren? Do you need me to brief you on the Cupid Bakery account?"

He crossed his arms. "Give me the basics."

Janine tapped the screen. "Okay, Cupid Bakery was a mom and pop venture that made it big back in the late eighties. They'd expanded from selling cakes and cookies out of their kitchen in Vermont to opening shops all over New England. A few years after that, they had locations in every major city across the US. But they didn't count on the big box retailers cutting into their profits. It seems that they hadn't pivoted, hadn't taken steps to brand themselves as a niche market."

He nodded, remembering this account. Sure, he could have done a deep dive into making them profitable again. But that wasn't his job. Quick and dirty. In and out. He wasn't a career counseling center. Rudolph Holdings provided funding to companies in crisis. But the reality of any company choosing to take his money was laid out right there in the contract in black and white. If the profits didn't roll in, the company was his to do as he pleased.

He sighed. "Fine, send them in."

Janine nodded, then headed out the door to speak with the couple and their smokin' hot attorney. Moments later, Mr. and Mrs. Angel entered his office, grinning ear to ear.

"Thank you for seeing us, Mr. Rudolph. I'm Ernie Angel, and this is my beautiful wife of sixty-two years, Agnes. And this young lady is Cindy Callahan. She's a lawyer from Los Angeles," the man said, shaking his hand.

"My grandparents are friends with the Angels, and I agreed to assist them with this issue," Cindy replied smoothly, offering him her hand.

"Are you in town for long?" he asked.

A devilish glint sparked in her eyes. "Just for the night."

Just for the night were four of his favorite words.

He held her hand for an extra second, and the woman drew her tongue across her top lip.

Yep, this one was a vixen for sure.

"We're here for the night, too. We'll head back to Vermont tomorrow," Agnes Angel said, ending his handshake with the attorney when she thrust a red box tied with a green bow toward him.

"What is this, Mrs. Angel?" he asked, passing the item to Janine.

"Chocolate peppermint cupcakes! They're our top seller this time of year. We thought that if you tasted them and got to meet us, you'd see that you simply can't close all of our bakeries," the woman replied warmly with one hell of a Mrs. Claus vibe.

He stole a glance at their vixen of a lawyer who gave him a resigned shrug. She had no skin in the game. Her family must have put her up to this. A good thing to know because this meeting wasn't going to end well for her clients.

He gestured toward the conference table. When everyone was settled in their chair, he steepled his fingers and glanced between Ernie and Agnes—still thrown by the Santa factor. But it didn't matter if Ernie resembled Kris Kringle, Elvis, or Peter Pan, their bakery business was over.

"Unfortunately, your company is failing," he said as plainly as he could.

He wasn't one to sugarcoat anything—not even for a pair of pleasant old people.

"It was heart-wrenching, but we closed a few of our bakeries across Colorado and Wyoming. We chose you specifically to help us," Agnes said, smiling sweetly.

He assessed the woman. It was no wonder the company was in shit shape. She and her husband didn't get it.

"We did help you, Mrs. Angel. Rudolph Holdings invested in your company. We gave you a generous injection of cash. You, in turn, promised to increase your profits by forty percent. You didn't. You lost money."

"But Cupid Bakery was started with love," Agnes offered.

He pinched the bridge of his nose. "Is that right?"

The damn origin story.

Why the hell did people think good intentions meant anything when it came to business?

"Oh, yes! When I saw Agnes for the first time, it was like Cupid's arrow hit me straight in the heart," Ernie Angel replied.

"And Cupid's a reindeer, just like Rudolph!" Agnes exclaimed.

He released the bridge of his nose. The last thing he wanted was to be compared to a fucking reindeer. What the hell kind of Frosty the Snowman, chestnuts-roasting-on-an-open-fire bull-shit logic was that?

"None of those things change your fiscal outlook," he said, starting to get a little freaked out by how they continued to smile at him.

Their business was over. There was no saving this company.

"Mr. Rudolph, Cupid Bakery is the cornerstone of every city where we have a location. We routinely give back to the community. With our bakeries across the country, we're a lifeline to food pantries. We believe in charity," Mr. Angel continued.

Soren leaned forward and held the man's gaze. "And I believe in profits. Guess what wins in the real world?"

The couple shared a knowing glance, but the smiles never left their faces.

"That's a very naughty list type of attitude. You should taste one of my cupcakes, Mr. Rudolph. That would bring some joy into your heart," Mrs. Angel replied.

Naughty list attitude? No wonder they'd lost a boatload of money. These two were nuts.

"Mr. Rudolph," Ernie Angel began, "would you consider an extension? There has to be something we can do to turn this around."

Soren glanced over at Janine, who replied with the hint of a nod. This woman had been trying to thaw his frosty demeanor for years. Why she thought for even a second that he was going to turn over a new leaf left him speechless.

He was who he was—a Rudolph who was the furthest thing from a benevolent red-nosed reindeer.

"It's just the two of you running the business, correct?" he asked the couple.

"Yes, Agnes and I do everything. Our children worked in the bakery when they were younger, but none of them expressed any interest in continuing on with the family business."

"So, there's no succession plan?" he asked, catching the attorney's eye.

"No, the Angels still operate the company as they did back in the eighties," she replied, then glanced at her polished nails.

No shit. And their profits showed this.

He turned back to the Angels. "You will receive a portion of the liquidation profits. Aren't you done working? What do you care about what happens with the business?"

Agnes gasped and pressed her hand to her chest as Ernie's rosy cheeks bloomed crimson.

"Mr. Rudolph, we might not have the cash flow to show it. But there are things more important than money," Ernie answered.

The vixen attorney crossed her legs and leaned forward just enough to reveal the hint of a lacy black bra beneath her satin blouse. His fingers ached to tear it off—to hear the pop of each creamy button scattering across the marble floor inside his office. He could have her buck naked and bent over his desk in a matter of seconds.

"Perhaps, Mr. Rudolph can be enticed to allow Cupid Bakery to continue business as usual until after Christmas. We could call it a holiday act of generosity," the woman purred.

His wolfish gaze traveled from her cleavage to her red lips— lips that would look good wrapped around his cock.

He sat back in his chair. "I can be generous when the mood strikes."

"I imagine you can," she replied, her eyes raking over his torso.

"Then you'll do it? You won't shut us down quite yet?" Agnes asked.

He blew out a tight breath.

A few more days wouldn't make much difference.

"My team will assess your financial standing on December twenty-sixth. I can't make any promises beyond that."

Mrs. Angel clapped her hands. "How wonderful! And perhaps, a Christmas miracle could make Cupid Bakery profitable again."

"That would certainly be a fascinating development, but I wouldn't hold my breath if I were you," he answered.

The last thing he needed was little old ladies pegging their hopes on Christmas miracles, but it wasn't his fault they hadn't done the work to turn a profit.

"I think this meeting has been a success. We appreciate your time," the attorney said, coming to her feet.

"Thank you, Mr. Rudolph!" Agnes gushed as Ernie took her hand and led her toward the door with the vixen lawyer a step behind them.

"See, I'm not always naughty," he said, sharing a glance with Janine, who was not amused.

"Oh no!" she replied, bending down to retrieve a hotel key card.

"Mr. and Mrs. Angel, did you drop your hotel room key?" she called.

Ernie Angel reached into his breast pocket and pulled out a key card. "Nope, it's not ours," he said, then headed down the hall with his wife.

"Miss Callahan, this must be yours. You must have forgotten it," Janine said, holding out the card.

The redhead didn't give Janine a second glance. "I didn't forget it. Room nine twenty-two at the Four Seasons."

"I'll take that, Janine," he said, plucking the card from his assistant's grip.

It looked like he would be riding that vixen tonight.

The attorney glanced back at him, then continued down the hall.

"I don't know why you bother with that, Soren. You should take a lesson from your friend, Tom, and find a nice girl," Janine said, tidying up a stack of files on the corner of his desk that didn't require tidying up.

"You know I'm not looking for an angel, Janine."

But he wasn't about to get into this with his assistant.

"Is there anything else we need to go over?" he asked, staring at the black key card.

"A few things," Janine answered, picking up her iPad.

He leaned against his desk, turning the room key in his

hand. First, he'd take that vixen hard and fast against the wall. Then, a long, slow fuck in the steam shower. And finally, she'd get down on her knees and wrap those red lips around his rock-hard cock.

"Your parents," Janine said, knocking the sex scenario right out of his head.

"What about them?" he bit out.

"I reached out to them. Well, their assistants."

He gave a bark of a laugh. Neither of his parents had a job. They were the epitome of trust fund trash.

"And?"

"Your mother will be in St. Tropez with her husband for the holidays."

"Fourth husband," he corrected.

Janine nodded. "And your father will be on a yacht, cruising the Mediterranean until the middle of January with his—"

"Fifth wife," he supplied as a muscle ticked in his jaw.

How little they'd changed over the years. At least, he knew to expect nothing from them. He made his own money. He had his own life.

"And what would you like to get Tom for a wedding gift? Goodness, things are going to be different," Janine said with a chuckle.

But he wasn't laughing.

"What do you mean by that?"

Janine opened the box of cupcakes. "Don't these look delightful? Would you like one, dear?"

"Do you think I look like this because I binge on boxes of sugar?" He frowned. "What did you mean when you said things were going to be different? I assume that you meant with Tom."

Janine closed the lid, then pinned him with her hazel gaze. "Tom is getting married, Soren. There's a chance his holiday plans will change. He'll have his wife and her family to consider.

And then, who knows if they'll decide to have children soon. This might be your last time celebrating Christmas with him and the Abbotts."

He would have fallen on his ass had he not been leaning against his desk.

The last Christmas with the Abbotts?

He'd considered Tom's fiancée a mere nuisance—an obstacle, something to placate. But the thought of his connection with the Abbotts becoming severed never entered his mind until Janine mentioned it.

Was she right?

He couldn't take the chance of finding out.

He glanced at the card key, then tossed it into the trash. There was no time for mindless escapades with a vixen now.

He cleared his throat. "Janine, there's been a change of plans. I need to leave for Colorado on the first flight out tomorrow. I'll be gone the entire week."

"Tomorrow?" she echoed, wide-eyed in disbelief.

"Yes, can you book the flight now?" he replied, then walked to the window.

The *tap-tap-tap* of his assistant checking airline schedules ticked like a clock counting down.

"I can get you on a flight tomorrow morning, but there's a weather advisory for Colorado."

He nodded, then glanced at the photo on his bookshelf. "That's fine. Book it. I need to get there as soon as possible."

Janine came to his side. "I'm proud of you, Soren. I'm glad you're going to spend the week with Tom and get to know his fiancée."

He grunted a non-reply, and she chuckled.

She wouldn't be proud if she knew her words had lit a fire inside of him—not to only take part in his best friend's wedding —but to make sure the damned thing got called off.

"s he looking at you?"

"I think so."

"Is he cute?"

Bridget glanced at the man sitting catty-corner from her in the bustling hotel bar. Dark hair. Broad shoulders. He cracked the hint of a smile when the bartender brought him his drink, and she would have sworn she saw a dimple hidden beneath a layer of sexy, dark scruff.

She crossed her legs, repositioned herself on the barstool, then angled her cell phone closer to her lips. "Yes, he's cute."

"Go for it, Birdie!" Lori cheered.

Bridget's heart beat like a drum. Nothing seemed real.

Getting fired.

Catching Garrett with another woman.

Twenty-four hours ago, her life had imploded.

But here she was, sipping wine like she could be anyone or anything.

The last time she'd felt like this was, well, never.

"You're there for one night, Birdie. All the weather reports say that the snow will let up and that the roads should be cleared by tomorrow morning. You'll be out of Denver and on your way to Kringle Mountain before you have to worry about bumping into him at the hotel breakfast buffet."

Bridget twisted the corner of her cocktail napkin. "What do you think I should do?"

"Flirt with him," her sister replied.

Flirt?

When was the last time she flirted?

She'd met Garrett when he'd come into the bakery to purchase a cake for a coworker's birthday. There was no flirting involved, not really. He was a nice enough guy. He came back the next day, then the day after that. For all she knew, the man kept things going as long as he did to ensure a steady supply of baked goods.

Then his words drifted back to her.

You're the most stifled, stuck person I know. I feel sorry for you, Bridget.

The last thing she wanted or needed was anyone's pity.

She shook off her ex-boyfriend's assessment of her character and stared down at her tattered napkin, embossed with the outline of the Rocky Mountains. She'd landed in Denver to find the city at a standstill. Mother Nature had blown into town with arctic temperatures and two feet of snow. There was no way she'd be able to make it to Kringle Mountain today, so she booked a night at the hotel adjacent to the airport. Lucky for her, they'd had one room left.

The bartender gestured to her empty glass. "Would you like another, miss?"

She wasn't a big drinker. A glass of wine, here and there. But what did she have to lose? She wasn't driving anywhere—nobody was. She nodded to the man, then took the chance to sneak another peek at the handsome stranger as he sipped a tumbler of whiskey and checked his phone.

She drank him in. It wasn't like her to swoon over a man. Who had time for that? But he'd rolled up the sleeves of his dress shirt, exposing tanned, muscular forearms. A curl of dark hair fell forward, and as he reached to brush it out of the way, he met her gaze.

One beat, then two. She focused on two intelligent, cat-like eyes staring into hers. Her mouth went dry, and she licked her lips. Could it be the altitude? She wasn't in Texas anymore. Even in the midst of a snowstorm, it was dry as hell in this city. But this rush of heat felt like a lot more than merely the effect of an arid climate. She pressed her thighs together, released a jagged breath, then broke their connection.

What was that?

The bartender returned with her Chardonnay, and she gripped the stem and took a long sip, trying to get her bearings.

"Birdie!" came an urgent voice. "Are you there, or did I lose you to that hotel hottie?"

She'd almost forgotten she was on the phone with her sister.

"I'm here. Sorry, I'm really in my head. I must be tired from traveling," she lied, still reeling from the intensity of catching the man's eye.

"Travel or not. Tonight, you're a woman of mystery. Tomorrow, you'll be on your way to my wedding. A nice one-night stand could help you unwind, big sis. The three orgasms I had with Tom have put me in a great headspace."

Bridget groaned. "I don't want to hear about my baby sister's multiple orgasms. I'm happy you're happy. Let's leave it at that."

Perhaps Lori was on to something. Blowing off a little sexual steam with a handsome stranger might be what the doctor ordered. And she needed to be on her A-game tomorrow. Once she arrived at Kringle Mountain House, nothing was going to stand in her way of Lori's wedding—especially not a killjoy named Scooter.

"Oh, and I should let you know that Scooter is going to be here for the week, too," Lori added.

Bridget ripped a corner off the poor napkin. "I thought he was flying in the day of the wedding and leaving the next morning."

"Nope, and Tom's thrilled that he changed his mind," her sister answered.

Lori tried to sound upbeat and supportive—that's who her sister was. But she could hear the worry in her voice.

Crap!

Now she would have to pull off this wedding and keep an eye on this asshat the entire time!

She took another sip of wine. "What made him change his mind?"

"I don't know. He texted Tom early this morning to tell him that he was catching a flight out today," she answered, sounding matter of fact as she went into lawyer mode.

But the strained tone betrayed her words.

Bridget started in on the cocktail napkin's opposite corner, twisting the paper as she tried to piece together what would have caused the best man's change of heart.

"Does he ski? Could he have seen the weather report and decided he wanted to get in a few days on the slopes?" she ventured.

Lori released a pained sigh. "Yes, he skis, but I'm not convinced that's the reason he's coming early."

Heat that had nothing to do with the wine warmed her cheeks. She'd managed Gaston Francois for six years. Granted, that didn't end well. But all she had to do was run a little interference with a jackass of a best man. This Scooter would be nothing compared to what she'd dealt with over the years.

"Don't give him a second thought. Do you think I'd let some jerk screw things up? I've always been in your corner," she said as a surge of determination accompanied the alcohol circulating through her bloodstream.

"Thank you, Birdie. I've got a lot on my mind," Lori said.

"Don't worry about the wedding. Everything is planned and ready to go." She paused. "Is there something else on your mind?"

"Um...no, no! It's an emotional time, that's all. It'll be good to see you, Birdie. It's been too long."

She wasn't wrong.

It had been ages since they'd had some one-on-one sister time. While they talked and texted every day, with Lori in Boston and her in Texas, they'd only seen each other a handful of times in the last several years. But now, she needed to be Lori's rock.

"All right, little sis," she began, channeling a pepped-up cheerleader. "Go enjoy yourself and knock out another orgasm with your fiancé—only spare me the details."

"Same goes for you! You don't have to be Bridget Dasher tonight. Find that sexy bar guy and have some fun," Lori replied, sounding more like herself.

"I could be a vixen," she said, thinking back to the little girl's slip of the tongue the other day.

Bridget Dasher. Not your average vixen—at least for tonight.

"Hell yes, you could," her sister agreed.

Bridget bit her lip. It had been ages since a man had made her toes curl.

Scratch that. No man had ever made her toes curl.

"Hey, Birdie, Tom just got back to the room, and I think we're going to go for orgasm number four," her sister whispered.

"Lori, you're killing me! Four orgasms in a day? I don't think I've had four orgasms in a month! God, maybe longer!"

Her sister giggled as Tom's muffled voice hummed in the background. It was good to hear her laugh. The last thing she should be doing the week of her wedding was worrying about some douche of a best man.

"I've got to go, Birdie, but I want to hear all about your night! Do not back out of this! You deserve to have some fun. Be the vixen!" Lori coaxed.

Be the vixen.

Bridget traced her fingertip around the rim of the wineglass. "I can't promise anything, but I'll let you know if something happens."

She ended the call, then took a sip of wine. This was it. She'd lift her chin, look his way, give him her best come-hither bedroom eyes, and demand her handsome stranger's attention —like the vixen she was. Or at least what she assumed a vixen would do. She was literally making it up as she went along.

Slowly, she turned and peered across the bar to find...

An empty barstool.

Her hotel hottie had vanished.

She shook her head and chuckled. Who was she kidding? When had she ever taken a chance like that? Still, a thread of longing wove its way through her heart. But before disappointment could set in and she could head up to her room to binge on late-night TV, the man seated on the barstool next to her placed his meaty hand on her leg.

She gasped at the contact, then found herself eye to eye with one of the smarmiest men she'd ever laid eyes on. Balding with a bad comb-over, the man licked his glistening lips as his gaze raked the length of her body.

"What do you think you're doing?" she cried.

The man grinned, revealing a mouthful of pearly whites speckled with salsa.

Who was this Mr. Smarmy Salsa man?

He licked his lips again. "That was a pretty hot conversation, baby."

"Baby?" she echoed, brushing away his hand.

Oblivious to her disgust, Mr. Smarmy Salsa leaned in and made an attempt to squeeze her knee. "All that talk about multiple orgasms got me so hot. I know when a girl is trying to seduce me. You've wanted to get my attention all night."

All night? She'd barely registered the guy was there. And what kind of creeper listened in on a woman's call.

"Get your hands off me," she ordered, twisting away from the man, but the salsa mouth-breather wasn't letting up.

"Come on, baby. You know you like the attention," he crooned, sliding his hand up her leg.

She batted him away, but the comfortable shirt dress she'd chosen to wear on the flight, which was perfect for travel, turned out to be terrible at deterring salsa-infused meatheads. And since it was nearly eighty degrees when she'd left Texas, she didn't even have on tights or pantyhose, and her bare skin crawled from his touch.

His salsa-sticky assault startled her, knocking her off balance. She reared back, attempting to get out of his grip when her barstool tipped, teetering dangerously on two legs. A rush of adrenaline sent her scrambling to stay upright. But just as she was about to fall flat on her ass, two strong hands caught her from behind. The stool crashed to the ground as her back made contact with a wall of muscle. She stilled, safe in her rescuer's embrace, and inhaled hints of soap and sandalwood. Strong, warm hands gripped her shoulders, then slid down the length of her arms, leaving a delicious trail of goose bumps in their wake. The frantic fight-or-flight frenzy set off by the salsa creep melted away. She took a breath, then another, matching her breathing with the stranger standing behind her.

She waited for her protector to continue on and leave her to fend for herself, but the man didn't move a muscle. Instead, his fingertips lingered on her forearms, leaving her breathless.

Slowly, she turned to meet the person who'd saved her from crashing to the floor and found...him.

She stared into his eyes. In the bar's dim light, they sparkled green-gold. Her hotel hottie held her gaze as everything disappeared. The clank and hum of the bar. The jazzy holiday tune playing over the speakers. It all vanished.

What was this? Some after effect of being manhandled, only to find yourself staring into the eyes of the sexiest man alive?

Could she have fallen? Maybe she fell over, hit her head, and this was a dream or a delusion.

She parted her lips to speak, but nothing came out. Her handsome hotel hottie watched her with an intensity that sent a ripple of heat between her thighs. All she could do was breathe and pray she wasn't concussed and lying on the floor of a hotel bar hallucinating.

"Hey, buddy!" Mr. Smarmy Salsa yapped. "We were having a conversation!"

Her handsome stranger didn't acknowledge the man. His cat-like gaze stayed locked with hers. "A table has opened up in the restaurant. I was wondering if you'd like to have dinner with me?"

"Dinner," she repeated, rendered near speechless.

Because, OMG, this was happening!

A wolfish grin pulled at the corners of his mouth as he knelt and retrieved her clutch.

"You don't want to forget this," he said, handing her the little purse.

She stared at his hand and couldn't stop herself from imagining what it would be like if he slipped that hand into her panties.

"Miss?" he said, snapping her back.

"Thank you," she replied.

Get ahold of yourself, girl!

She glanced at Mr. Smarmy Salsa. Bent over a fresh bowl of chips and another saucer of his signature dish, he'd switched from mauling her to hoovering more of the snack food. Ugh! That poor salsa!

"Are you hungry?" her rescuer pressed, killing all thoughts of the smarmy man.

His voice washed over her—a sensual rumble like the preamble to a dirty bedtime story. And again, she was speechless as she stared up at this Adonis of a man.

Maybe Lori was right. Perhaps, it would do her good to fall into bed with someone for a night of pure animal sex. A tempting opportunity for a reset and an escape all at the same time. And if there was a man who looked like he could deliver on that request, it was the handsome stranger standing in front of her.

He tucked a lock of her hair behind her ear.

This guy's sexual magnetism was off the charts, and he looked at her as if he were photographing her with his eyes— like he could see everything.

"You're blushing," he remarked with a sexy smirk.

She smoothed her dress. "This isn't my scene. I don't usually go to bars and find myself falling off of barstools. Thank you for catching me," she replied, praying that the words coming out of her mouth made sense. It took everything she had not to disintegrate into a million tiny pieces of swoon.

He smiled, and holy moly, there was that dimple.

"Where do you usually hang out?"

This man.

She gathered her resolve. If this was going to be her first one-night stand, she needed to play it cool. Tonight, she wouldn't be the protective older sister. She wouldn't be the girl who'd lost her job and her boyfriend all in the span of an hour. She wouldn't be a lonely twenty-eight-year-old woman with zero prospects.

Nope, not tonight.

Tonight, she was mysterious. Tonight, she could be anyone.

Goodbye, Bridget Dasher. Hello, Bridget Vixen.

She drew the tip of her tongue across the top of her lip. "I don't think you really want to know where I hang out."

His eyes raked boldly over her body as the electricity between them crackled.

Holy faking-it vixen! It worked. She was no expert on men, but her handsome stranger appeared to find her alluring.

"How about we make our way to the table," he said and gestured for her to walk ahead of him.

A tingle ran down her spine as he pressed his hand against the small of her back.

They left the bar, and he guided her into the dining area. He nodded to a hostess, and the woman showed them to their table, but not before giving her hotel hottie the once-over.

Bridget couldn't help herself from smiling as she rode this new wave of sexual confidence. She caught the woman's eye and shook her head.

Sorry, honey, this tall glass of sexy is all mine.

The woman instantly broke their connection and stared at the floor, and *wowie zowie!* Look who was the new alpha lady in town!

The hostess slinked away as her handsome dinner companion helped her into a U-shaped booth. While the restaurant was busy, their table, tucked away in a dim corner, felt miles away from the other diners.

A waiter set a glass of wine on the table along with a whiskey. "A Chardonnay for the lady and a whiskey neat for the gentleman."

She turned to find her hotel hottie watching her.

She cocked her head to the side. "You've already ordered?"

His powerful thigh brushed against her knee as he settled in beside her. "I did."

She took a sip of wine. And lo and behold, it was her favorite Chardonnay.

"How did you know what I was drinking?" she asked.

There was an air of arrogance about him that sent a dizzying current racing through her body.

"I asked the bartender."

Butterflies fluttered in her belly. "Why?" she pressed.

That sexy smirk was back, taunting her. "Because I knew you were going to have dinner with me."

She gazed at him through her lashes.

Don't blow it by saying something ridiculous, Bridget Vixen!

She lowered her voice. "What if I turned you down?"

Somehow, that sexy smirk of his got sexier. "Then I guess I would have rescued you from that jerk at the bar, then had my dinner alone. But I couldn't leave the bar until you did."

"Why not?" she asked, all eyelashes and silky-smooth tone.

She was getting the vixen act down pat!

He leaned in, and she inhaled hints of whiskey and sandalwood. "Because that guy had been trying to get your attention all night, and I didn't like it."

"Why not?" she repeated, pulse pounding. Her brain had turned to mush, and *why not* happened to be the only two words she was capable of verbalizing.

He'd been watching her, just as she'd been watching him.

Was she the predator or the prey?

His sexy smirk morphed into something deliciously wolfish. "Because I want you all for myself."

There was the answer.

Prey or not, she couldn't deny that this vixen business was exhilarating.

"Let me introduce myself. I'm—" he began, but she pressed a finger to his lips, silencing him. The contact rippled through her body.

She leaned in. "First names only. I'm Bridget."

She went to remove her finger from where it rested against his lips, but he gripped her wrist and pressed her finger back in place. Without missing a beat, the man opened his mouth and grazed his teeth slowly up her index finger. When he'd made it to the top, he licked the pad of her trembling digit.

Wowza!

A tremor passed through her body as the air around them became electrified. She arched a fraction closer to him. She was no virgin, but this kind of sexual energy was like a tornado trapped inside a hurricane, and she was walking straight into the storm.

"I'm Soren," he answered.

Soren.

What a perfect name. It sounded like a movie star or some mega mogul.

She stared into his eyes, mesmerized. She'd seen this man for the first time less than an hour ago. Now, she was cuddled up next to him in a darkened booth. He released her hand, still tingling from his tongue.

"I think you're a woman who likes to play, Bridget," he said, that wolfish grin turning carnal.

He slid his hand up her thigh. And, in what could only be described as the polar opposite reaction to what she'd experienced with the creep at the bar, she reveled in his attention. With his warm breath against her skin and the scorching heat radiating off his body, his strong, rough hand lit a path straight to the apex of her thighs. Instinctively, she parted her legs and allowed him access to her most sensitive place as her fantasy became a reality.

She gripped his thigh, needing to anchor herself to this man, to this moment. He rocked his palm against her as his middle finger teased her entrance.

"Soren," she breathed, her eyes fluttering closed.

"I've barely touched you, and you're already wet," he answered in a low growl, his whiskey sandalwood scent driving her wild.

Her nipples tightened into sharp peaks at the low, dirty rumble of his voice. But she wanted more. She opened her eyes and met his gaze. It didn't matter that they were in a crowded restaurant. It didn't matter that a waiter could arrive at any second. She was locked in, trapped by wanton attraction, and utterly enthralled with Soren's seduction.

He smiled, and that sexy wolfish grin sealed her fate. "Bridget," he purred, drinking her in.

Her name, flowing from his lips, sent her arousal ratcheting up another notch.

"Yes," she gasped.

He massaged her with deliciously slow strokes, kindling a flame deep within. And heaven help her, her toes curled as she rocked against his hand, back and forth, setting a sinfully slow pace.

"Do you know what I want to do to you?" he asked as the sweet torture of his touch left her breathless.

She squeezed his thigh harder as he teased her entrance.

"Tell me," she begged on a tight moan.

He pressed a kiss to her temple. "Bridget, you sexy as hell vixen, I'm going to make you come, right here, right now, right in the middle of this restaurant."

*H*e couldn't tear his gaze from his dinner companion as her sweet sighs got him rock-hard.

Who the hell was this woman—this alluring vixen?

Just as his plane landed in Denver, he'd received a text from Janine. Newsflash: the city was shut down thanks to a snowstorm. She'd reserved a room for him for the night—a godsend because he needed to work out the maddening buzz rushing through his body. The realization that there was a decent chance his relationship with the Abbotts was about to change had left him off-kilter—an unwelcome emotion that could only be numbed by sex.

Raw animal fucking.

And then, he caught a glimpse of the petite brunette, and he had to have her.

She was on the phone, engrossed in a conversation, which allowed him ample time to drink her in. Stunningly beautiful with long, chocolate brown hair, the light brought out hints of red and chestnut. He didn't usually notice bullshit things like this about anyone. But he couldn't get enough. Her smile. The way she nibbled at her lip—a nervous habit, but with her, it was endearing, even sweet.

He did not do sweet...or maybe he did?

When the jackass seated next to her began eyeing her, his inner caveman nearly had him flying across the bar to knock the guy into next week. Thank Christ, he was able to keep his cool. In reality, the jerk had actually done him a favor. The salsa slurper's pathetic attempt at hitting on his hotel bar beauty had sent her right into his arms. And now, his hand was inside her panties.

Not bad progress—not by a long shot.

He stroked her slick center as her soft moans fed his deepening desire, and her intoxicating cinnamon vanilla scent had his head spinning. He could eat her for dessert. And he would. He would feast on this woman. Her hand slid up his thigh and rested near his rock-hard cock as he slipped his finger deep inside her wet heat and cupped her sex. Her nails dug into his leg, clutching him as his body ached for her touch.

But they'd get to that later. Now, he was doing something he'd never done before. While no woman had ever complained after jumping in the sack with him, he'd never put another's pleasure above his own until now.

Until her.

He set a steady pace and worked her with the palm of his hand. Her legs parted another inch, opening for him, welcoming his touch, and he reveled in carnal victory as she bucked her hips against his firm grip. Her chest heaved as she rode his hand, swaying to the rhythm of their covert erotic escapades. He wanted to pull her onto his lap and make her come while her ass rubbed against his cock. His mind raced with all the ways he could please her, desperate to explore every inch of her body.

The breath hitched in her throat, and she stared up at him—all innocent eyes and trembling lips. Trapped between this world and the next, she teetered on the edge of release, her eyes burning with desire.

There was no other word to describe her other than to admit that she was absolutely magnificent.

She was heartbreakingly beautiful, and something deep within him knew that she wasn't the kind of girl who got off in restaurants with strangers. She wasn't the Cindy Callahan type —the type who, like him, took what they wanted without remorse.

But whoever she was, tonight, she wanted to play the vixen, and he wasn't about to deny her the experience.

Did she crave the escape as much as he did? Did she long to be tangled in a stranger's heated embrace, all sweaty limbs and quivering bodies, ripe with lust and raw with need?

"Yes!" she moaned, surrendering to his touch, the word going straight to his cock.

He needed to get some damn control over himself, or he'd lose it right alongside her.

"Easy," he whispered against the shell of her ear. "You don't want anyone to know what we're doing, do you?"

"What *are* we doing?" she asked on a tight breath.

Her brown eyes blazed with lust and something else, something more profound—a yearning he knew all too well. He couldn't look away from this beauty. He wanted to explore the graceful curve of her neck with his tongue and catalog every freckle on her ivory skin with his kisses. Even in the dim light, he could see the pink flush to her cheeks, like rose petals scattered across fresh, fallen snow.

He lowered his voice. "Did you forget? I'm making you come."

He slipped another finger inside her, determined to make good on his claim. Already, he felt a kinship with her body. She was close to meeting her release. Her grip on his thigh tightened as her sweet center clenched his fingers. It would be goddamn amazing to slide his cock into her tight, wet heat. To lay her down on his bed and cover her petite frame with his large, muscled body as he filled her to the hilt with his hard length. But he couldn't deny how much he liked watching as he owned her pleasure. He pressed his thumb against her sensitive bud, and her eyes fluttered open. Suspended in that moment, he held her, body and soul, as she spiraled over the edge. Her orgasm tore through her, and she dug her nails into his leg—the sweet bite of pain a delicious reward.

He could spend the rest of his life making this woman come, and it would be time well spent.

Then the restaurant disappeared. The hushed conversations and pockets of laughter vanished. The buzz of waiters and busboys disintegrated into thin air. His entire world consisted of two things: this woman and the overwhelming desire to give her pleasure.

She parted her lips, dissolving into orgasmic bliss, as a rich, sated moan, evidence of her unabashed pleasure, carried on her breath. But before anyone could hear her wanton cries, he pressed his mouth to hers and swallowed her heated exhalations.

Her lips were the final blow. Petal soft, they beckoned him.

Kiss me and never stop.

What was this fascination? It had to be his reaction to the possibility that the only redeeming part of his life could soon become nothing but a memory.

Casting away his fears, he focused on Bridget and the visceral desire that drove him to take more and allowed him to forget. He cupped her face in his hand and deepened their kiss. Their tongues met in a sensual dance, licking, exploring, and ravenous for more. Her fingertips trailed down his jawline as if she were smoothing out his rough edges, those ragged emotions he kept hidden deep within. She hummed a honeyed, sated sound, and despite being in the midst of a bustling restaurant, the warmth of her voice wrapped them in a cocoon of perfect seclusion.

"That was...wow," she whispered against his lips, and her raw honesty made him want to do it all over again.

Except, not here. They needed to go somewhere else, so he wouldn't have to stifle her cries of pleasure. And he wanted to see her—all of her.

He wanted to unwrap her like a Christmas present.

Jesus! This wasn't him. He was no romantic. But maybe that was okay. He could use a night to forget himself. A night to forget his worries. A night to be a man who wasn't on the brink of losing everything that mattered.

Gently, he slipped his hand out of her panties, drawing his wet fingers along her thigh. She watched him closely—those trustworthy chestnut eyes awash with satisfaction. He liked having her gaze trained on his every move. And with that thought, a wicked idea formed.

Without breaking their connection, he raised his hand to his lips, moist with her arousal, and sucked the tip of his middle finger.

Now, he was the one humming his delight—sampling a taste of what was to come.

"What are you doing?" she asked, her gaze locked on his mouth.

"You got to start with dessert. It's only right that I get a little taste," he replied and instantly was rewarded as his one-night vixen's eyes widened in a sensual state of awe.

She bit her lip, then gave him the hint of a naughty grin as she ran her hand up his inner thigh and palmed his thick, hard length. "I think we could arrange for you to have some dessert, too."

He could see the glimmer of wonder in her eyes—the titillating moment of being someone else. This was new to her. Despite being beautiful, she didn't realize her powers of seduction.

"You'll be skipping dinner? Shall I bring you the dessert menu instead?"

At the arrival of their waiter, Bridget gasped and tried to pull away, but he held her close.

He schooled his features. "We've changed our plans. We'll be ordering room service tonight."

Without missing a beat, he covertly slid her hand off his cock and laced their fingers together.

"We have?" she questioned.

He could see the wheels turning in her head. She'd played the vixen in public. But did she have it in her to take it up a notch?

His pulse raced.

Why the hell was he so determined for her to say yes?

He could have any woman he wanted. This place was crawling with singles on the lookout to hook up. But he only wanted her—this striking enigma.

He rubbed slow circles with his thumb on the back of her wrist. "Room service would be a better choice for us tonight."

A few tendrils of her dark hair had fallen forward, framing her face and kissing the apples of her cheeks. She tucked the locks behind her ear, still turning over the proposition. A muscle ticked in his jaw. He was a lion ready to pounce, and the anticipation was nearly unbearable.

Every cell in his body wanted her.

She met his gaze as her soulful dark eyes seared into him with the glimmer of a newfound confidence.

Now, it was his vixen schooling her features for the waiter. "I agree. This night definitely calls for room service."

Hell yes!

His inner caveman was prepared to throw her over his shoulder and sprint up the twenty flights of stairs to his penthouse suite. But he knew better. He nodded to the waiter, and the man stepped aside as he helped his petite vixen out of the booth. Hand in hand, he led her through the crowded restaurant and over to a bank of elevators.

"My room," he said, and it wasn't a question.

"What if I offered *my room*?" she countered, arching an eyebrow.

Two could play at this.

"What floor are you on?" he continued, biting back a grin.

She lifted her chin—a proud little thing. It made him want her even more.

"Five," she shot back, unflinching.

He allowed the corners of his mouth to tip into the hint of a self-assured smile. "I think you'll like my room better."

Janine knew his tastes and hadn't disappointed him in her choice of rooms. When he'd arrived, he'd been pleasantly surprised. There was no doubt that he'd be bringing back a conquest with him. That was without question. But now, he wanted her to see it.

"You seem pretty sure of yourself?" she parried back.

He held her gaze, which now, in the light, revealed not only a deep hue of brown but more of a rich mahogany.

God, help him. A man could get lost in those eyes if he weren't careful.

He took a step toward her. "I'm sure about this."

The banter between them, this spark that ricocheted back and forth, sent his pulse racing. He didn't have fun with women. He slept with them. He partied with them, but he didn't talk to them—not like this. What was the point? He didn't want anything more.

Not only that.

He wasn't capable of anything more. The vice that had gripped his heart since he was a boy tightened, but he ignored the yearning. Tonight, he didn't have to worry about Bridget wanting more. She would play her game, and he would play his.

What were the chances their paths would cross again? He was headed to some bullshit tiny mountain town that barely showed up on the map.

The elevator doors opened, and they entered the snug space.

He removed his hotel key card from his pocket, then swiped it through the card reader, triggering the button for the top floor to illuminate.

"What'll it be? Boring on five, or what I have to offer on twenty?" he asked, aching for their witty repartee to continue.

The best kind of trouble glittered in her eyes as she reached over and trailed her index finger along the column of buttons.

"Hmm, whatever will I pick?" she mused playfully.

He stared at her hand and took in her slender fingers. His cheek tingled where she'd stroked him, moments ago, as if she'd already worked her way into his muscle memory.

"We're headed to the top," she said, then pressed the button with that naughty glint dancing in her eyes.

But he didn't take the bait.

"Now we have more time," he remarked, feigning indifference.

Her brows drew together. "More time for what?"

"For this," he growled, pressing her against the elevator doors as they began their ascent to the twentieth floor.

She gasped, surprised by the quick movement, which gave him the perfect opportunity to claim her mouth in a scorching kiss. On the brink of losing all restraint, he devoured its softness, reveling in the sensation. Bridget dropped her purse onto the floor as she wrapped her arms around his neck and sighed into his mouth. The sensual sound sent a rush of urgency surging through his body.

He needed more of her. And he needed it now.

Gripping her ass, he lifted her into his arms. He had a good eight to ten inches on her, but in his embrace, they were eye to eye.

"Why can't I stop kissing you?" he whispered against her lips.

She entwined her fingers in the hair at the nape of his neck. "Because you're under my spell. You see, Mr. Twentieth Floor, I'm not your average vixen."

Sweet Christ, she sure as hell wasn't!

The elevator pinged their arrival, but he didn't move. With her flushed cheeks and lips red from his kisses, her angelic features had him mesmerized.

"No, you most certainly aren't." He glanced into the room. "Are you ready to leave the elevator, or would you like to stay here for a while?"

She glanced out the open doors. "Where's the hallway?"

He surveyed the suite. "Probably on the floor below."

She frowned, her brow crinkling into an innocent expression of confusion.

She cupped his cheek in her hand. "Where are we?"

"We're on the twentieth floor. You pressed the button," he deadpanned.

She ping-ponged her gaze into the spacious room, then back to him. "What's on the twentieth floor?"

He suppressed a grin. "Not a hallway."

The adorable crinkle to her forehead was back. "Is this whole floor your room?"

He gave a little shrug. "They call it a suite."

"Holy moly," she said with such awe in her voice he nearly chuckled.

When the hell was the last time he'd heard anyone utter something as hokey as holy moly?

Even Janine didn't drop that kind of exclamation.

But, somehow, it made his one-night vixen even more alluring.

Gently, he lowered her to the ground, retrieved her clutch from the elevator floor, then took her hand.

"I want to show you something."

They entered the darkened suite. Track lighting leading to the bedroom gave him just enough light to find what he was looking for.

He led her to the center of the room. "Close your eyes."

She glanced up at him. "Please tell me this isn't the part where you decide to drug me and harvest my organs."

She was teasing, but he could hear the trace of hesitation in her voice.

He tucked a lock of hair behind her ear. "We organ harvesters like to take off the week before Christmas. So, no, I won't be harvesting your organs tonight. But I can't make any promises about what I'll be doing next week."

She giggled. "Phew! Thank goodness for the holidays."

"You're a lucky lady. You should see what kidneys go for these days," he teased.

"Soren!" she chided. And there it was again—his name coming from her lips, and the two syllables had never sounded so lovely.

He squeezed her hand. "Now that you know that I'm not here to drug you and harvest your organs, could you please close your eyes?"

Her sweet as hell giggle echoed through the room. "You must get all the girls with lines like that."

This woman.

"Bridget," he said, lowering his voice, and she stilled.

She bit her lip. "I like the way you say my name."

He liked it, too—more than he should.

"Close your eyes, *Bridget*," he repeated, and this time, she complied.

He released her hand, then went to the opposite side of the room and pressed a button. A mechanical hum filled the dimly lit space as a curtain spanning the length of the suite opened. He stared at his one-night vixen, who remained still with her eyes closed as the glow from the city lit her in an angelic hue of warm golden light.

"Soren, can I open my eyes?" she asked, her teasing tone gone as the mood shifted.

It was as if she sensed that they'd moved past the witty banter stage and onto—to what? The part where they shared their darkest secrets? He swallowed hard, hating himself for how badly he wanted to open his heart to a complete stranger.

"Yes, you can open your eyes," he replied, fighting to keep the emotion from coating his words.

Observing her like a hawk, he watched as she blinked her eyes open, then gasped. Slowly, as if she were in a dream, she walked to the window and stared out at the city.

"Oh, Soren," she said on a faraway whisper as she pressed her hand to the glass.

He observed her expression of awe in the reflection as he came up behind her. "Have you ever been to Denver?"

She nodded, gaze trained on the city with the Rocky Mountains standing, dark and formidable in the distance. "Yes, years ago, and it's as beautiful as I remembered. The snow and the twinkling holiday lights make you feel like anything's possible, doesn't it?"

There was a thread of yearning in her words that wound around his heart. A parallel longing they each possessed.

What did she want? What were his one-night vixen's innermost desires?

He swallowed hard. He couldn't go there—not with her, not with anyone.

"Unbutton your dress," he said instead.

She held his gaze in the window's reflection as her slender fingers worked their way down, undoing each button in a seductive striptease. Every inch of revealed creamy skin set his body ablaze. And once she finished, he couldn't stop himself from trailing his fingertips along the nape of her neck, then peeling the garment from her body.

In a lacy nude bra and matching panties, she was the best early Christmas present he could ask for.

She caught her reflection in the window, then wrapped her arms around her body. "You're probably used to women wearing sexier lingerie."

With perfect breasts that begged to be licked and sucked, hips he wanted to grip as she rode his cock, and an ass that could stop traffic, how could she not grasp her own exquisiteness?

He pressed a kiss between her shoulder blades as he removed her bra, then dropped to his knees and slid her panties down her toned legs.

"You could wear a paper bag, and I'd still want you," he growled as he rose to his full height.

The mischievous glint returned to her eyes, and his cock twitched in his pants.

His vixen liked a little dirty talk.

"Your turn. Shirt first, then pants," she ordered without even the hint of unease.

He took a step back so she could take in the complete package. Slowly, he slipped out of his dress shirt, tossed it onto a chair, then removed his shoes before undoing his pants and adding them to the pile.

"Commando!" she said on a surprised yelp.

He grinned.

What was the point of underwear? It only got in the way.

She stared at him, and her greedy eyes devoured his reflection.

He took care of himself, and women liked the way he looked —that was a given. But he'd never gotten a rush out of a woman admiring his hard abs and muscled body until this little vixen showed up.

"Do you want me to take off my boots?" she asked, her voice a sexy rasp.

Buck naked in black high-heeled boots and lit only by the lights of the city; she was a goddess.

"They stay on, for now," he answered, taking his cock into his hand as he gave it one hard stroke, then two as he drank in the scene.

She glanced over her shoulder. "Are you going to stare at me all night?"

He could. He most certainly could, but his cock was done waiting for this woman. He slipped a condom out of his pants pocket, tore it open with his teeth, then rolled the sheath down his hard length, already weeping with desire.

He came up behind her, and they locked eyes in the window's reflection. She parted her lips and released a ragged breath as he slid his hands up the sides of her body before palming her ripe, round breasts.

She arched her back and pressed her ass against his cock, igniting a firestorm of desire. He leaned down and dropped a series of kisses on her bare shoulder before working his way to her earlobe.

"Everyone in this city will know that tonight, you are mine," he whispered against the shell of her ear.

She pressed her hand against the glass, and he covered it with his own, entwining their fingers together. But she wasn't here to only hold hands—and neither was he. Gripping her hip, he held her in place, lined up his cock, then thrust into her wet heat. He sucked in a sharp breath as he took it slow, stretching her, opening her, filling her to the hilt.

She cried out as her body inched forward, now pinned between him and the cool glass. The contrast between their heat and the window's cold bite sent a frenzied zing through his body. He slipped his hand from her hip down between her thighs, feeling his cock enter her slick, tight center. He'd never basked in this moment. He liked a good, hard fuck. He didn't slow down to savor the connection. It was like nothing he'd ever experienced. A mindfulness he'd never thought to employ.

Bridget squeezed his hand and rolled her hips, and a torrent of desire redirected his attention to his restless vixen.

"Soren, don't tease me," she whispered, raw need dripping from her plea.

"You need to know something about me," he said, rocking his hand against her tight bundle of nerves.

She gasped. "What's that?"

"I'm no tease," he answered, pulling back then rocketing forward.

His cock slid in and out with punishingly delicious thrusts. She welcomed his hard length into her body's tight embrace as the slap of skin on skin fused with the hum of the city below. The sounds and sensations twisted and tangled around him, heightening his arousal. Every thrust drove him higher. Every sigh, every moan, every heated breath intensified their connection.

And he couldn't get enough.

Wanting more and desperate to touch her very soul, he changed the angle of penetration and caressed her with his hand as he pistoned his hips, making love to her with a desperate ferocity. Their bodies rubbed against the cool glass, and the opposing sensations, coupled with the slick slap of their bodies, had him ready to commit himself to unrestrained oblivion. The desire within him twisted into a coil, aching with the need to explode.

Bridget's cries of passion rang out as her body gripped his cock in spasms of pleasure. She craned her neck, and his lips collided with hers in a frenzied kiss. He doubled his pace, and his body moved as if its sole purpose in life was to bring this woman unimaginable sexual gratification.

With her wild cries of passion urging him on, he joined her as a tidal wave roared through them, crashing and colliding in a storm of passion. He called out, repeating her name, unable to stop himself.

Bridget! Bridget!

Uninhibited and blissfully unrestrained, this was their night to forget the world, take unbridled passion by the reins, and ride that stallion all night long. Her body trembled beneath his, as the power of the pulsating rush receded, and they stilled as their audible breaths punctuated the silence.

She stared at the city, shrouded in a hazy holiday glow, hummed a sweet, satisfied sound, then tightened her grip on his hand—the hand that had remained laced with hers. She held him in place—a safe harbor offering refuge. He kissed her temple, and she leaned back, resting against him.

"Soren?"

Whatever she said next, whatever she'd asked for, it would be hers. Had she cast a spell on him, or was she a beautiful Christmas vixen, a gift from above sent to get him through the week?

"Yeah?"

"I don't know if my legs will be able to keep me upright much longer," she said with a sated sigh.

In all fairness, the intensity of his orgasm had taken a hell of a lot out of him, too.

"We can't have you collapsing," he replied.

Carefully, he pulled out of her, then removed the condom, and tossed it into a small trash bin. Then, before she could stop him, he scooped her into his arms.

"I didn't mean that you had to pick me up, but I'm not complaining," she said, resting her head in the crook of his neck as he brought her into the bedroom.

Gently, he laid her on the plush comforter, removed her boots, and covered her body with a blanket. "Are you hungry? We could order room service," he offered, suddenly feeling like an awkward teenager.

But she shook her head and reached for his hand, guiding him under the covers with her. She reclined onto her back as he rolled onto his side.

She brushed a dark curl from his forehead. "Would you think it was strange if I just looked at you?"

There it was again—that gentle, piercing honesty. He traced a line from her earlobe to the hollow of her neck.

"No, I don't think it's strange," he answered, unable to look away, unable to take his eyes off of her.

She smiled up at him. Her expression welling with such tender gratitude, he wished he could bottle the moment and keep it with him, close to his heart.

She blinked, then pressed her hand to her mouth as a yawn escaped. Her eyes grew heavy as they watched each other in the glow of the city as she hovered on the verge of sleep. And then, after a heavy blink, her eyes remained closed, and he listened to the sound of her breath, slow and steady, like the tide coming in and going out in a rhythmic lullaby. He stroked her cheek, and her lips curved into a smile.

"I can feel you looking at me, Soren."

Damn, he liked the way she said his name.

He twisted a lock of her hair between his fingers. "I thought you were asleep."

She opened her eyes, and the breath caught in his throat. It was as if he'd spent a lifetime adrift, and she was his anchor. A woman he knew nothing about had pierced his heart with her soulful brown eyes and her delicate lilt of a sweet, sated smile.

She stroked his cheek. "What is it?"

But he couldn't speak as Tom's words echoed through his mind.

I wish you could understand what it's like when you lock eyes with someone, and you know that your life will never be the same.

She frowned as worry flooded her mahogany gaze. "I should get back to my room."

He should let her go. No woman had ever spent the night with him—just sleeping. He'd made damn sure to structure his life around no strings attached sex. He'd never had the desire to wake up next to anyone. Not until Bridget, *not your average vixen,* crashed into his orbit.

He shook his head. He'd give in to the ache—the empty part of him that wanted, no, needed her with him tonight.

"You should stay here," he said, hardly able to believe he'd spoken the words.

"With you?" she pressed.

This wasn't him. He wasn't a sleepover, cuddle bug of a bastard. Once he'd gotten his fill, scratched that lustful itch, he was out the door without a backward glance. But this mystery woman was different. He'd felt it the moment he saw her. The honest hunger in her eyes. The unabashed need. The sincere, open desire. This one-night stand wasn't her norm. She wasn't like him.

She didn't plow through lovers like a steam train.

He'd never met anyone like her.

"Soren?" she whispered.

There it was again—she said his name, and angels couldn't have made the word sound sweeter.

He gathered her into his arms and tightened his grip on her body. "I want you to stay. I want you to fall asleep in my arms."

A dreamy smile pulled at the corners of her mouth as she nestled into him. "I'd like that," she replied with a whisper that washed over him like a prayer.

He'd give himself tonight. A night to pretend that someone like her could be his. A night to pretend he wasn't the lonely little boy on the cusp of losing everything that mattered.

He inhaled her cinnamon vanilla scent. Tomorrow, he'd get back on track. Tomorrow, he'd be ready to fight and fight dirty to make damn sure that his best friend didn't make the biggest mistake of his life.

*B*ridget closed her suitcase, then glanced around her hotel room. The morning sun streamed in through the window, and the storm that had dumped over two feet of snow yesterday had vanished like a thief in the night. She glanced in the mirror as a giddy euphoria took over.

She'd done it.

In the last twenty-four hours, she'd experienced not one, not two, not even three or four orgasms.

Nope, she blew past that when her handsome stranger rocked her world with seven—count them—seven mind-blowing, toe-curling, hot as hell orgasms.

In one single night!

If a vixen hall of fame did exist, she was pretty sure that having seven orgasms in one night would qualify her as one of the top one-night stand vixens out there.

After she'd fallen asleep in Soren's arms, she'd woken to find him not at all displeased when she'd reached beneath the covers and stroked his hard length. A very vixen thing to do. And it only got crazier from there. His hands, his mouth, his cock. Every part of this man sent her pulse racing.

Missionary, doggy-style, side by side, sitting, standing, and then, balanced on an ottoman, there didn't seem to be a bad way to spiral into sweaty sexual bliss with her hotel hottie.

No, not hotel hottie. He had a name. A beautiful name. A name she whispered to herself this morning in the shower and instantly had craved his touch.

Soren.

A name as delicate as it was powerful, she'd sensed the same quality about the man.

There were moments when he'd looked at her with such tenderness it nearly penetrated her soul. What was supposed to be a night devoted to unadulterated pleasure, at times, felt like more—like so much more.

When he'd said her name, it was as if she really were someone else. Someone confident. Someone ready to take charge of her life. Soren, with his smoldering eyes and electric touch, saw her. The *her* she could only dream of becoming.

Or—at least, he did for the night.

Because that was all she had to give. She was no vixen, not in real life, and that's why she had to leave the warmth of his embrace.

Thanks to waking on a baker's schedule at four thirty in the morning, she'd given herself five minutes to watch the man as he slept. And he was nothing short of glorious. Chiseled jaw. Rock-hard abs. A cock that put Garrett's in the category of itty-bitty cocktail wiener. Observing him was like appreciating a work of art.

But while his body was sinfully unreal, his eyes were the real masterpiece.

In his gaze, she'd seen him.

Sure, they'd just met, but in those unguarded seconds, his green eyes revealed such longing and such heart-breaking sadness, all she could do was allow it to wash over her. Like him, she knew those emotions far too well herself.

And that's where she'd left him—in bed, sleeping. But not before she'd swept a dark curl off his forehead and left a whisper-soft kiss on his cheek.

She glanced at the bed she didn't sleep in last night, then wheeled her bag to the door. Time to check out. Time for the fairy tale to end. She released a slow breath as the whispers of that plan-for-everything sister edged its way back into her mind.

But she couldn't get Soren out of her head.

Could there be a future for two people with such instant chemistry?

She could wait for him in the lobby, and...

No, she couldn't go back. That was the whole point. For one night, she'd pretended to be someone different. She'd slapped a strip of duct tape over the mouth of that broken, betrayed girl. Silenced her fears of inadequacy and became the woman any man would want.

And she'd done it. She'd put on the vixen mask, and now that sweet ache between her thighs was the only reminder of being screwed six ways from Sunday. Well, seven. But who's counting?

No matter the number, it had to be enough.

There was no other option.

She left the room and caught the elevator to the lobby. As if on autopilot, she checked out and headed toward the restaurant to grab a quick breakfast before the car arrived to take her to Kringle Mountain.

The dimly lit space where she'd had her first orgasm of the night looked nothing like what she'd remembered. The staff had rearranged the room for a breakfast buffet, and she stared at the booth she'd shared with her handsome stranger.

In her mind, it appeared darkened and secluded. But a

frown pulled at the corners of her mouth when she saw it in the light of day. No longer shrouded in a dim, hazy glow, the same booth that had hosted their naughty sexcapades now held a family of four happily munching on omelets and cinnamon rolls.

Was her night with Soren just a beautiful fantasy? A perfect holiday escape?

She scanned the buffet line, hoping to catch a glimpse of the man who'd kissed her with such intensity that her lips still tingled. But her Christmas hotel hottie wasn't there.

"Gone, like it was a dream," she whispered, dismissing the lonesome pang in her chest.

"Ms. Dasher?" came a curious voice.

She glanced up to see a man holding a sign with Kringle Mountain House printed in festive lettering. He had a beard as white as snow and sported a red flannel. Looking like Santa's lumberjack cousin, he gave her a friendly nod.

"Yes, I'm Ms. Dasher."

"I'm Dan. My wife, Delores, and I are the mountain house caretakers. I'm here to drive you up to Kringle Mountain."

She nodded, then glanced at the buffet table and spied a fruit display. "Give me one second, Dan."

While she and Soren had done some very interesting things with a bowl of strawberries and champagne they'd ordered late last night, she was famished from skipping dinner and needed some real nourishment. It was game time. From this point on, her top priority was to make sure that Lori's wedding went off without a hitch.

Goodbye, not your average vixen. Hello, ball-busting maid of honor.

She grabbed a banana from the table. "I'm all set, Dan. Thanks for coming to pick me up."

Rosy-cheeked, the man looked even more like Santa than

she'd initially thought. She was about to tell him this when her phone buzzed. She reached into her purse to find that she'd missed five calls.

All of them from her sister.

Dan led her out to an older model Range Rover that looked more apt for the Serengeti than the Colorado slopes, but it had to do.

"I've got one more to take up to the mountain house," he said as he loaded her luggage into the back of the vehicle.

She tried to smile, but a lump of worry hardened in her belly.

Five calls in one night was a lot.

She pressed play on the first message, but she could only hear sobbing. Finally, by the fifth and final call, her sister had calmed down.

"Birdie, Scooter sent strippers to the mountain house! Strippers! Tom promised me that he wouldn't let Scooter turn our wedding into a bachelor party gone wild! But the guy didn't listen to him!"

Bridget fumed, but now wasn't the time to call Lori back—not with the driver only a few feet away and another passenger coming. Instead, she switched to text and hammered out a message.

I'm on my way, little sis. I'll sort out everything when I get there. Don't you worry!

She dropped her phone into her bag and peeled the banana with a ferocity that the poor piece of fruit didn't deserve. She took an angry bite. Damn this Scooter! The bastard better be ready for a fight. He was about to incur the wrath of Bridget Dasher.

She took another angry bite, furious with this moron. Agitation prickled down her spine. They needed to get on the road. It was a good ninety-minute drive to Kringle, and if this Scooter was up to no good, she needed to be there to defuse whatever wedding bombshells he had up his sleeves.

Dan tapped the opened door. "I'll be right back after I find the other guest, Ms. Dasher. It turns out, the best man got snowed in, too."

"The best man is here? At this hotel?" she asked, her voice rising an octave. She knew he was coming early, but she hadn't even thought they'd be stuck at the same hotel.

"He sure is—a Mr. Rudolph. I'll be right back. Sit tight," the jovial man replied.

Now, like her Santa-double driver, her cheeks were as red as roses, but not because she was feeling anything close to jolly.

In fact, she was the epitome of the exact opposite of jolly.

Tom's best man was no best man. No, he was the worst man, and this stripper-sending creep was about to get an earful.

But her mouth fell open when Mr. Smarmy Salsa sauntered out of the hotel, trailing a few steps behind Dan.

She gritted her teeth. Of course, this salsa-eating freakazoid was the infamous Scooter. She narrowed her gaze, ready to tear this guy a new one. But Mr. Smarmy Salsa veered right, then slid into a waiting cab a few cars ahead of them.

She glanced at Dan. "Where's the best man?"

But she spoke too soon.

"I'm the best man," came the sexy voice that had whispered sweet nothings—and some very dirty nothings—into her ear last night.

Holy vixen catastrophe!

Wide-eyed, the man stopped a few paces from the car and stared at her.

"You're Birdie?"

Her gaze dropped to his satchel, and the black leather personalized luggage tag with the initials *S, C, T,* and *R* emblazoned in silver lettering.

"*S, C, T, R?*" she read, unable to look away.

"Soren Christopher Traeger Rudolph," he parroted back robotically.

She gasped. "Scooter?"

It was true!

Her handsome stranger was the playboy asshat with the stupidest nickname in the world!

"Let me take your bag, Mr. Rudolph," Dan said with a warm grin.

Soren handed over his suitcase and satchel but kept his gaze locked on her.

"We better get going," Dan added, oblivious to the fact that she had the worst luck in the entire universe and that the devil incarnate just handed him his suitcase.

Soren blinked as if opening and closing his eyes would make her disappear. And if she possessed a disappearing superpower, she would have gladly granted him his wish. Unfortunately, even a real vixen couldn't do that.

Dan got behind the wheel, and Soren, Scooter, whatever the hell his name was, slid into the back seat with her.

Her mouth opened and closed like a goldfish. What was she supposed to say? Remember that fun girl from last night? You know, the one that rode you like a cowgirl on the hotel's bearskin rug? Well, she's me, but I'm not her. I'm no vixen. I'm Lori's older sister, her greatest protector, and you, *Scooter,* are in a world of shit!

But one thing was crystal clear. She had to suppress any feelings of tenderness toward this man.

Starting now, he was public enemy number one.

"I can't believe that you're *Birdie,* Lori's uptight sister," Soren said under his breath, breaking into her thoughts.

She harnessed her resolve. "I can't believe you're the playboy stripper-sending schmuck, *Scooter.* Suck on that, creep!" she whisper-shouted, keeping her voice low so Dan couldn't hear them.

But when it came to sucking, all she could imagine were her lips wrapped around his glorious cock.

He laughed under his breath.

Oh, my God! Was he thinking the same thing?

The perfect-cocked creep!

She faced him head-on. "You don't know who you're dealing with, *Scooter!*"

He held her gaze, and for a fraction of a second, he was there. The man who'd made her body purr. The man whose eyes flashed with such broken yearning that she'd wanted to gather up all his broken pieces and put him back together.

And then, it was gone—he was gone.

His eyes went flat, and the emotion drained from his expression. "I'd say the same for you, *Birdie*."

Dan turned on the car, and holiday music flooded the cab.

"So, you're Bridget Dasher, the maid of honor. And you're Soren Rudolph, the best man. How fitting!" Dan remarked as he maneuvered the car into traffic.

"What's that supposed to mean?" Soren asked with a sharp edge.

But his New York jackassery didn't seem to bother Dan one bit.

"Dasher and Rudolph! You'll fit in perfectly at Kringle Mountain. We have many retirees in town who have dedicated themselves to the Christmas season. It's a great place, and it really comes to life this time of year. It is a shame that the local bakery closed a few weeks back, but I know the folks at Kringle Acres are mighty appreciative that you've agreed to supply them with homemade Christmas cookies, Ms. Dasher. And they're all looking forward to the spaghetti dinner tonight, too."

"What are you talking about? A spaghetti dinner at Kringle

Acres? What the hell is Kringle Acres?" Soren questioned with that city slicker chip still on his shoulder.

She plastered on a smile, then pinned the worst best man with her gaze. "We're talking about community service. The entire wedding party is putting on a spaghetti dinner for the Kringle Acres Retirement Community residents. Volunteering and community service were important to my parents. And it's on the wedding schedule. The schedule for the people who care about this wedding and are dead set on making sure that it's executed with military precision," she replied, all syrupy sweet.

Dan glanced over his shoulder. "I've got to say, Ms. Dasher, Delores was quite impressed with the emails you've sent. She said that you've got quite an eye for detail. You don't see that much in Kringle, these days. It's a pretty easy-going, go with the flow type of town. But don't you worry! That doesn't mean that Delores and I are slacking off. The chapel on top of Mount Kringle will be ready Christmas Eve for the wedding ceremony, and we were able to have all the baking supplies you requested delivered this morning."

"Is the gondola that will take the wedding party up to the chapel working? Last I checked, Delores said it was a little touch and go," she asked, ignoring the wedding crasher and focusing on what needed to get done.

While they were staying at the mountain house, the wedding was set to take place in the same tiny mountain chapel where her mother and father were married thirty years ago. The very same chapel that was only accessible by gondola.

"With enough Christmas spirit, I'm sure everything will be fine," Dan answered as if Christmas spirit had anything to do with the mechanical functioning of the transportation that provided the only way to get to the cozy chapel.

She started to ask the jolly man to extrapolate on this when Soren cut her off.

"You're baking?" he asked with a sour edge.

She sat back. "Yes, in addition to baking cookies for the residents of the retirement community, I'm making Lori and Tom's wedding cake."

"We'll see about that," he muttered, and her blood boiled.

He *was* there to disrupt the wedding! Lori's gut-feeling was right!

"I love this song. I'd bet that it's one of your favorites, too, Mr. Rudolph," Dan remarked, turning up the volume on a big band rendition of "Rudolph the Red-Nosed Reindeer" as they left the city and headed west toward a vast expanse of snow-covered mountains.

She glanced over at her scowling back seat companion. The man gave Dan a polite nod, but the guy was clearly not a fan of the song—which made sense. Rudolph, the Red-Nosed Reindeer was a benevolent, save-the-day kind of reindeer. The man seated next to her was more of a Grinch than a hero—no matter what his last name was.

Soren cleared his throat. "You killed your banana."

"What?" she shot back, giving him her best screw-you look, then glanced down to see that, yes, she'd strangled what was left of the poor fruit.

She'd forgotten she'd even been holding the half-eaten thing.

Before the banana mush could fall onto her lap, she popped what was left of it into her mouth. Dabbing at the corners of her lips with her fingers, she caught her *former* hotel hottie watching her.

If her mouth wasn't filled with the potassium-packed sweetness, she'd tell the banana peeper to peep somewhere else. But in his gaze, she didn't see the worst best man. Sadness flashed in his eyes before he looked away.

She swallowed the giant bite as Dan held up a little trash can, and she disposed of the peel.

Perhaps Soren wasn't so bad. Maybe there was something inside of him that she could appeal to? She'd swear she'd glimpsed a good man last night. She turned to him, then parted her lips, but before she could speak, he winced.

"Now, you've got banana in your teeth."

She gasped and pulled her sunglasses out of her bag to use their reflection as a mirror.

"Like that salsa guy last night. Only banana," he added with one *jerktastic* smirk.

She stared at her mirrored reflection, smiling like a game show hostess and shifting her jaw to check every tooth.

"No, I don't!" she shot back.

He shrugged—a cocky little movement. It made her want to slug him right in his beautiful face.

"My bad. I guess I was wrong."

She slid the glasses on and scooted as far away from this *Scooter* as possible.

What was the penalty for punching a smug worst best man in the presence of a Santa lookalike? It was the holidays. A time for kindness, leniency, and goodwill toward women and men who weren't giant wedding crashers. And her sister was a lawyer —a Harvard educated lawyer. She could get her out of jail.

Bridget huffed a frustrated breath.

No, no, no!

She was not about to take his bait and add any drama to this week. She was a steamroller—there to smooth out any rough patches—including a best man with the worst intentions.

She'd ignore him. She'd formulate a battle plan. But just as the thought materialized, so did one hell of a yawn.

"It appears you didn't get much sleep last night?" he said, all cool tone and detached sexiness.

"I slept fine," she replied as her treacherous body yawned again.

"I know you did. I watched you."

Her head whipped toward him, and she caught a glimpse of the witty, affectionate man who'd made her body hum all night. What was going on with this Dr. Jekyll and Mr. Hyde routine?

"You did?" she whispered, throwing a furtive glance toward Dan, who was *fa, la, la, la, la-ing* away to the Christmas music.

But just as quickly as Soren looked ready to offer her the world, his expression hardened.

"Yeah, you drool."

Her jaw dropped, and so did another yawn.

So, this was how it was going to be!

She wedged herself into the door and rested her head on the window.

Think of Lori. Think of Lori. Think of Lori.

She closed her eyes, but instead of her sister's face, she saw her grandmother. Yes, she'd channel Grandma Dasher. She'd dig deep and stand her ground. Her grandma Dasher was kind and soft-spoken, but she also had a steel spine and probably a touch of vixen.

Be the vixen.

The low rumble of the engine and the soothing hum of the road soon had her on the brink of sleep. She'd rest her eyes for a few minutes. She'd allow herself this tiny respite before the epic holiday wedding battle between Rudolph and Dasher commenced.

"*F*rosty the Snowman."

She hummed a happy little sigh as the song, good old "Frosty the Snowman," one of her childhood holiday favorites, played in the background. She snuggled in as warmth radiated around her body. This is what she needed. She patted the blanket, then twisted her fingers into the comforter. The music stopped and a peaceful sigh vibrated through her body. Only, she wasn't the one doing the sighing this time.

"Just look at you two! Like two chestnuts, cozied up and roasting on an open fire. Take your time. I'll bring your bags in."

"Thanks, Dan," she answered on a dreamy exhale at the same time as a voice, much lower than hers, offered the same reply.

She opened her eyes a sliver, but all she could see was black. She shifted a fraction as her sleep haze cleared and one very warm, very familiar hand rested on her shoulder. She held her breath and experienced the gentle rise and fall of her hotel hottie and now, mortal enemy, Soren, the worst best man, Rudolph's, chest as he slept peacefully.

She wiggled, trying to break free of his iron grip.

"Let go of me!" she shrieked.

The man startled, but instead of letting go, he tightened his grip.

"If you squeeze any harder, there's a good chance you'll end up with banana all over your fancy coat!" she warned, hating that it wasn't the fruit she was thinking about while wrapped in his strong embrace.

Immediately, his arms flew open, and she tumbled back, but not before grabbing onto his elbow and pulling him over to the other side of the car. He landed, sandwiched in next to her, and in a frantic tangle of limbs, she extricated herself from beneath Soren's large frame.

Not that he was crushing her. She'd spent a good deal of time under his toned, muscled body last night.

Washboards would be jealous of this man's abs.

And her banana had nothing on this hotel hottie.

Ugh! Stop!

She shook her head, trying—without much luck—to get this man's body off her mind.

"What were you thinking?" she cried, staring him down in an attempt to recalibrate her raging libido. He was no longer her sex machine, orgasm-inducing handsome stranger.

No, he was the devil.

He smoothed his coat. "For the record, you fell asleep on me."

She scoffed. "No, I wouldn't do that."

There was no way she'd migrated toward this moron, not even in her sleep, would she?

"Yeah, you did," he countered, looking all smug and handsome—the jerk!

She lifted her chin. "Why didn't you just push me back over to my side?"

That sexy smirk stretched across his cat-who-ate-the-canary

face as his equally sexy dimple made an appearance. "I tried. You kept coming back for more. Even in your sleep, you can't get enough of me."

Heat rose to her cheeks. This cuddle bug bastard was asking for it!

She glanced out the window as Dan disappeared into the mountain house with their bags.

Good! They were alone now. And this was the perfect time to lay down the law.

Vixen mode on.

She leaned in. "Maybe you can't get enough of me."

His cocksure expression vanished as a muscle ticked on his perfect chiseled cheek, and his tanned complexion grew rosy.

Ha! He was attracted to her!

It was time to strike while the iron was hot. She gripped the collar of his coat and pulled him in closer.

"This is your warning! Do not derail this wedding. And don't think I didn't hear about the strippers!" she hissed, her voice low and deadly.

That sexy smirk pulled across his smug lips. "Tom's not ready for marriage. I'm his best friend. It's my job to look out for him."

"The hell it is. Tom is lucky to have Lori. And news flash! He proposed to her. He's crazy in love with her," she shot back.

Soren pinned her with his gaze. "He's not crazy in love. He's confused."

Nearly a breath apart, she wasn't about to blink. "This wedding is happening. And I have a warning for you."

"Oh yeah? What's that?" he challenged, his breath tickling her lips.

Her pulse thrummed. Her entire body vibrated with frantic energy. It was as if every cell in her body ached for this man's touch.

"Do not mess with me, *Scooter*," she growled, channeling her badass pretend vixen.

"That's how it's going to be?" he growled back, that sexy rasp coating each word.

"My way or the highway, *Scooter*," she replied with a smirk of her own.

He twisted a lock of her hair between his fingers. "Call me Scooter one more time and see what happens."

He was playing with her. If he wanted to raise the stakes, that was his funeral.

She tightened her grip on his collar and met those cat-like green eyes head-on. Heat blazed in his eyes, and fire roared through her veins.

It was hardcore vixen time.

She moistened her lips with her tongue, then narrowed her gaze.

"Scooter."

They hovered there, eye to eye, their breaths mingling. She wasn't sure how much time had passed. It could have been a fraction of a second or, quite possibly, a quarter of a century. But as if a switch had flipped, she tightened her grip on his collar. His hands flew to her face, cupping her cheeks and sending electric sparks down her spine. Her body, which must not have gotten the memo that this slimeball was off-limits, melted into his touch as their mouths came together in an angry, ravenous kiss fueled by lust and loathing.

It was…glorious. Their tongues fought and retreated. Their lips crashed in a frenzy of furious passion.

"I don't like you, *Scooter*!" she breathed, then bit his lip.

"I don't like you either, *Birdie*!" he said, meeting her bite with one of his own.

She wrapped her arms around his neck, then wove her fingers into his dark shampoo-commercial-ready hair. Endorphins flooded her system in a dizzying state of complete make out mania. She'd never hate-kissed anyone. Before Soren, Scooter, whatever, making out with your adversary seemed like something only idiots did in rom-coms.

She wanted to construct a witty retort. She wanted to tell him just how much of an asshat a person would have to be to go to a wedding with the sole intention of stopping it. The whole "I don't like you" response reeked of seventh grade. She could do better. But as soon as this man's lips connected with hers, her brain turned into a gelatinous mound of mush.

He kissed a trail along her jawline, then combed his fingers into her hair, holding her at just the right angle. "This wedding is a mistake, *Birdie*. And I plan on making damn sure Tom knows it," he murmured against the sensitive skin below her earlobe.

She tilted her head, her treacherous body welcoming the heat of his touch. "Well, *Scooter*, unlike you, I put others' happiness and wellbeing above my own, and that especially includes my little sister. I am ride or die when it comes to her. So, you better not sabotage this wedding!" she threatened, followed by a dirty little sigh, which may have reduced the mafia hitman effect she was going for.

He stilled, and she pulled back, expecting to meet his gaze brimming with contempt or conceit. But something more akin to panic or possibly grief flashed in his green-gold eyes. But before she could blink, he had his asshat glare back. Still, she couldn't look away.

"Soren, why are you against this wedding?" she whispered, stroking his cheek just as she'd done when she'd left him this morning.

He closed his eyes, rested his forehead against hers, then released a pained sigh.

It didn't make sense. Tom's family had welcomed Lori with open arms. Why wouldn't his best friend feel the same way?

She was ready to ask him point-blank when a sharp knock on the window sent them jumping to opposite sides of the back seat like teenagers caught necking after curfew.

"Uncle Scooter? What are you doing in there?"

A little girl with a scrunched-up face stood beside a little boy wearing bright red bifocals.

"Did that lady have an eyelash stuck on her eyeball? Sometimes, when I have an eyelash stuck on my eyeball, Mommy has to get that close to fish it out," the boy commented, pressing his gloved hands to the glass to get a better look at them.

"It's all steamy in there," the little girl remarked, rubbing her mitten against the window above the boy's head.

Soren's gaze bounced between her and the children, who were watching them as if they were in a zoo enclosure.

"That's Carly and Cole," he said, losing the asshat vibe and looking downright flummoxed.

She nodded, completely cognizant that two little kids had caught them full-on sucking face.

"Tom's niece and nephew, right?" she replied, going for casual, which was not as easy as one would think after a make-out session that left her swaying side to side in a woozy kissing daze.

"Yes, that's right," he answered, still looking quite shell-shocked.

Before this awkward moment, their lives had intersected, first, in a rapture of anonymous sexual bliss, then as steadfast sworn enemies, once their veil on anonymity got blown to hell. And now, they were two people connected to these children, who continued to watch them like a science project gone wrong.

She waved to the kids and did her best not to look like a wannabe dirty girl vixen.

These two kiddos were just as Lori had described: Carly with her button nose, ash-blond hair in two braids, and Cole with his rosy cheeks and sparkling blue eyes. Her sister had told her all about Tom's family. She absolutely adored them, and from the sound of it, they adored her, too.

It was quite a distinguished group.

Tom's parents, Grace and Scott Abbott, ran their Boston-based law firm, Abbott and Associates, where Lori and Tom met and worked. Tom's sister, Denise, a social worker, was five years older than Tom. She and her wife Nancy were the proud parents of eight-year-old, Carly, and five-year-old, Cole.

Lori had spent many a weekend with them on the coast along with Tom's grandfather, who Lori described as one tough, lovable character. Franklin Abbott went by the moniker, Judge. Everyone, even the grandkids and the great-grandkids, called him by this name as a tribute to his forty-five-year career on the bench. Tom's uncle Russell would be joining them for the wedding, but Lori hadn't spent much time with him.

"Is your eyeball okay, lady?" the little boy called.

She nodded to the child, then turned to Soren.

"We should probably get out of the car," she said, smoothing a lock of her hair before gesturing to the door.

"Yeah," he answered with a minute shake of his head.

At least, this seemed as weird for him as it did for her.

He opened the door and barely had a foot out before the children pounced on him.

"Uncle Scooter rides!" Cole cheered.

"Me, first," Carly called, jumping into the man's arms.

"Uncle Scooter, do you want to see the snow angel I made?" Cole asked, pulling on Soren's coat sleeve.

The little girl pointed toward a small log cabin about fifty feet away from the large mountain house. "I made one in front of Dan and Delores's little log cottage. See, it's right over there. Dan says that there are lots of little cabins in the forest around here, but only theirs is warm enough to live in over the winter."

"Is that so?" Soren asked, glancing over his shoulder at her as she got out of the car.

It was as if he didn't know who to be. The cocksure asshat or Uncle Scooter—who, quite possibly, had one of the nerdiest uncle names out there.

"You're Birdie, Aunt Lori's sister!" the little boy said, materializing by her side.

This kid could really move.

"Yes, that's me. My name is Bridget, but Lori's always called me Birdie."

"I like Birdie better," the little girl chimed from Soren's arms.

"His name is Soren, but that's a stupid name, so we call him Uncle Scooter because scooters are cool," the little boy countered.

Bridget pressed her hand to her mouth to stifle a laugh.

"Hey, you know that's not how I got my nickname," Soren said with a playful edge.

"Yeah, I do. Mommy gave you the name a long time ago because you have a hard to remember name that spells Scooter," Cole conceded.

Bridget smiled at the little boy and made a mental note. If Tom's sister had given him that nickname, Soren and the Abbotts must have been close for quite a while.

"Guess what we were doing, Uncle Scooter? We were out looking for Christmas fairies," Carly said, answering her own question as Soren set her down.

He frowned. "I've never heard of a Christmas fairy."

"Aunt Lori says that Christmas fairies help Santa and the elves," Cole chimed as his sister nodded.

Bridget joined the trio. "That's right. My dad used to tell me and Lori that the Christmas fairies would fly down from the North Pole to make snow angels for the good little boys and girls to see. So, if you ever come upon a snow angel with no footprints leading up to it, that means that a Christmas fairy probably made it. And if you happen to see one, they may grant you a Christmas wish."

Cole nodded emphatically. "I'm going to find a Christmas fairy and get a Christmas wish! I've got new glasses, and I can see far, far, far away. I'm going to ask it what its name is, and then tell the fairy to tell Santa that I've been really good this year and that Carly's been really bad and should be on the naughty list."

"No way! You should be on the naughty list!" Carly threw back along with a handful of snow.

"Hey, easy! I'm sure neither of you are on Santa's naughty list," Soren corrected, separating the squabbling siblings.

She smiled at him, fascinated with the difference between the giant douche canoe, Soren Christopher Traeger Rudolph, and the light-heartedness of Uncle Scooter. But the man's expression darkened the moment he caught her watching him.

"And you shouldn't call Lori, Aunt Lori. She's not your aunt," he said, making damn sure to catch her eye as he corrected the children.

And boom! There it was. While he could play with kids and appear to be a decent human, he was still the devil. The devil who looked like sex on a stick dressed as if he were ready to model for Mountain Sports Weekly in his down jacket and dark jeans—but a wedding crashing devil, nonetheless.

"You're not our uncle, and we call you Uncle Scooter," Cole said, sharing a confused look with his older sister.

Soren's expression soured. "That's different."

"How?" Carly asked.

"Yeah, how?" Bridget echoed, goading the worst best man.

Soren pointed to a spot in the distance. "I think I saw a Christmas fairy. You guys better check it out. You wouldn't want to miss out on making a Christmas wish."

The kids took the bait and headed for a grove of evergreens.

As soon as the siblings were out of earshot, she marched over to the man and pushed up onto her tiptoes. It barely got her to his perfect chin. Damn his towering physique!

"This is your warning. Do not pull anything like that again!"

His eyes glimmered like a cheetah ready to pounce. "Like what? I'm not wrong. She's not officially their aunt *yet*."

She grabbed his coat—again—and yanked him down. Cheetah eyes or not, she was nobody's prey. And when it came to Soren, unlike every other man in her life, she seemed to have no qualms flashing her badass vixen ballbuster side.

His gaze flicked to where she crumpled his coat's down collar. "You'll owe me a new jacket if you keep this up."

"You'll be lucky to make it out of this mountain house with your coat," she shot back.

Confusion marred his perfect stupid face. "What the hell does that mean?"

She sucked her teeth. What did she mean?

"I don't know. But it sounded badass," she replied, doing her best to sound like a badass.

"It kind of did sound badass," he admitted as the crazy lust tractor beam pulled them in—again!

She closed her eyes and surrendered to their super-magnetic attraction. Perhaps it was the altitude, but once she was within kissing distance of this creep, she lost all rational control.

"Birdie! You're here!" came her sister's bubbly voice as she and Soren pulled apart like oil repelling water.

Lori came down the mountain house porch steps dressed in her ski gear and shielded her eyes from the bright midday sun. "Oh, and I see you've met..."

"Hello, Lori," Soren said, sounding as slippery as a snake—because he was a snake. A wedding disrupting snake. She needed to remember that.

"Scooter!" Tom called, emerging from the house.

Soren grinned up at his friend. But when Tom took Lori's hand, the man's expression dimmed a fraction. What was this? Kindergarten? Could Tom not have a fiancée and a best friend?

Tom leaned in and wrapped her in a friendly embrace as Lori attempted to hug Soren. The wedding crasher acquiesced with the most robotic hug ever recorded.

"It's good to see you, Birdie. This place is great. But Lori says it's changed a lot since the last time you two were here. What do you think?" Tom asked.

She hugged her sister, then glanced up at the majestic mountain house. Thanks to the hate-kissing-upon-arrival session followed by the whirlwind meet and greet with the pint-sized Cole and Carly, she hadn't had a moment to take in their destination.

"The house looks the same to me," she said, inhaling the crisp mountain air as she observed the weathered log cabin. With a large gathering area in the center, the guest rooms lined one side of the structure while the kitchen and mudroom used to store skis and other outdoor equipment ran along the opposite side.

"We're so happy that you both are here," Lori said, taking the high road with Soren—because that's who her sister was. A good person. No, a great person.

"But you look a little disheveled," Lori continued with a crease between her brows.

Bridget brushed an errant lock of hair behind her ear and pasted on her best *I wasn't just making out with anybody* grin. "I do?" she asked innocently.

Now, it was Tom eyeing them. "You guys look a little scruffy. Scooter, I don't know if I've ever seen you so…"

"So, what?" Soren asked, stone-faced.

"I don't know. You guys look like you've been roughed up," Tom replied, sharing a look with Lori.

No, no, no! Nobody could know about what they'd done last night or five minutes ago in the car.

Bridget glanced up at Soren, who must have been thinking the same thing. He gestured toward the children, who were tossing snow at each other between the trees.

"The kids, they wanted Scooter rides," he said with a nonchalant wave of his hand.

Good save! If she didn't hate the guy, she'd have thanked him for coming up with that excuse.

Lori cocked her head to the side. "Did they want Birdie rides, too?"

"Um," she began, because, unlike Soren, she was a terrible liar.

"I need a second with my sister," Lori said, hooking their arms and guiding her a few paces away from the guys.

"Birdie?" her sister whispered, stretching out the syllables.

"Lori," she replied, because when she was singsong echoing, she wasn't lying.

"You did it, didn't you?" Lori whispered.

Oh no!

"The hotel hottie! I can tell! You seem a little more high-strung than usual but in a good way. Does that make sense?" Lori pressed.

It made more sense than her sister would ever know. But there was no way she was going to tell anyone, let alone Lori, that the asshat of a best man had been the hotel hottie making her toes curl and her body sing with carnal delight all night long.

"Yes, I hooked up with the guy at the bar. It was nice," she said as placidly as possible.

"I think it was more than nice. You look positively sexed-up, you one-night vixen," Lori teased.

The sexual acrobatics she and Soren had engaged in last night flashed through her mind. Her sister would want details, and there was no way she was about to allow this line of questioning to continue.

"Enough about me. What about you? All those messages about..." she trailed off, praying Lori wouldn't catch her purposely changing gears.

"The strippers?" Lori answered with a pinched expression.

"Yeah, it was awful to hear you so upset."

Lori stared up at the sky. "I was upset, really upset, and I know Tom didn't want to have a pair of exotic dancers sent to the room. I just want our big day to mirror Mom and Dad's wedding, which I know didn't include scantily dressed bimbos."

Bridget chuckled. "Yeah, I don't see Grandma Dasher or Mom onboard with that."

Lori's expression softened. "They can't be here physically, but I feel like they are here. And I want this wedding to be for them, too. I have so much going through my head. My emotions are a little amped up. I'm sorry I left you all those messages."

She rubbed her sister's arm. It was an emotional time. The last time they'd stepped foot in the town of Kringle, they'd been girls accompanied by their parents and grandmother. Now, it was just the two of them.

Bridget swallowed past the lump in her throat. "That makes sense. And I get it. I feel close to them here, too. And I know they'd want this time to be special for you and Tom."

Lori glanced at Soren and Tom. "But now that Scooter is here, Tom thinks that he'll see how great it is having us all together, but I'm still not sure of his intentions."

Bridget squeezed her sister's hand. "That's what I'm here for. I'll take care of Scooter. Don't give the guy a second thought."

Lori leaned in, and the sisters embraced.

"Thank you, Birdie."

"And you can forget about having to deal with any more strippers, little sis," she added.

"Did somebody say strippers?"

Bridget looked up as Soren flashed a smug grin.

"I was disappointed I wasn't able to make it up yesterday for the entertainment," the jackass replied, his cat-like eyes glittering with mischief as the men joined them.

Tom ran a frustrated hand through his hair. "Scooter, I told you, Lori and I don't want that for our wedding. What were you thinking? Two strippers? Where'd you even find two strippers around here? This place is mostly locals and retirees."

Soren's expression grew somber. "I should apologize."

"I appreciate that," Lori replied as mischief continued twinkling in the asshat's eyes.

"It was supposed to be four. Two for me and two for Tom—for old times' sake," he added.

Hello, gag reflex! This man was abominable!

Tom shared a stunned look with Lori, then pinned Soren with his gaze. "What the hell are you talking about, Scooter? I've never been with a stripper, let alone two."

Soren nodded. "That's why I sent them. Think of all the things you and I still have to do."

"Jesus, Scooter! Luckily, Lori and I saw them come in. What do you think my family would have thought?"

"Russ would have been good with it," Soren replied with an aloof shrug.

"Scooter!" Tom exclaimed.

"And how'd you know they weren't staying here?" Soren pressed, gesturing to the mountain house.

"There are only five guest rooms in this place. It's just *family* staying here," Lori replied as Soren bristled at her explanation.

"Is there a problem, Scooter?" Tom asked.

Good! Tom was on Team Wedding and didn't appear to be swayed by Soren's antics. Still, counting today, there were four days until the Christmas Eve nuptials, and she had to stay vigilant. Anything could happen. And with this slippery best man, anything was possible.

Soren's expression grew pensive. "Of course not. You're my best friend. You've been my best friend for sixteen years. I'll always want what's best for you."

She shared a quick glance with her sister and tossed her a little wink that said, don't you worry. Birdie is on to this guy.

A slice of silence stretched between the men as they stood face-to-face. Were they having some silent BFF conversation? Was Soren a certified hypnotherapist on top of being a certified douche canoe? She was about to snap her fingers when a woman's cheerful voice cut through the silence.

"They're here!"

Bridget glanced up to see a line of adults, all dressed to hit the slopes, stream out of the mountain house.

"Birdie, it's so nice to meet you in person after exchanging all those emails with you these past few weeks. I'm Grace, Tom's mother. This is my husband, Scott, and my father-in-law."

"Call me Judge," the man said with a watchful nod.

"We adore Lori and are so happy to have you here, Birdie," Scott said with a welcoming grin.

Relief washed over her as she embraced Tom's parents and his grandfather. These were the people who mattered—and they loved her sister.

"Look what the cat dragged in!"

"More like the snowcat with all this fresh powder," Soren answered, kicking up a little snow as a woman who looked like a younger version of Grace emerged from the mountain house along with another woman.

"Birdie, this is my daughter, Denise, and her wife, Nancy,"

Grace said, introducing the pair.

"Scooter hasn't given you any trouble, has he? You've got to watch this one," Denise teased, clapping Soren on the shoulder.

Bridget caught the man's eye. "Nothing I can't handle."

A sly smirk pulled at the corners of his mouth. Damn that sexy expression!

"Lori, you didn't mention that your sister was as gorgeous as you are."

Bridget looked past the wall of Abbotts to see a man in an electric green ski jacket. Sporting a comb-over, he and Mr. Smarmy Salsa were on the same page when it came to grooming and cringe-worthy pickup lines.

"Behave, Uncle Russell," Tom said, shaking his head.

The man joined the group and gave her the once-over, not once, not twice, but three times before opening his arms for a hug.

Reluctantly, she indulged the man.

What would a wedding be without a creepy uncle?

"This place is wonderful. We rode the gondola up to the Kringle Chapel once the power came back," Nancy remarked.

Bridget frowned, and not only because Uncle Russ brushed his hand a little low during their brief embrace.

"The power went out?" she questioned.

Grace nodded. "Dan says when they get big storms, it's common for the mountain house to lose power temporarily, and that includes the gondola."

Bridget glanced past the ski lift and observed the enclosed gondola, sitting vacant. That gondola was the only way to the chapel, and she made a mental note to check with Dan to make sure it was good to go for the wedding.

"Oh, Birdie, the chapel still looks like it did when Mom and Dad got married here," Lori said as Tom wrapped his arm around her shoulders.

"We do wish your parents could be with us," Tom's grandfather offered.

Soren crossed his arms. "Where are they?"

"They passed away when Birdie and I were teenagers," Lori answered.

"I'm sorry. I didn't know that," Soren replied, his voice losing its cocky edge.

Bridget put on her brave face. "We went to live with our grandma Dasher in Texas after our parents passed away."

"Is she coming to the wedding?" he asked.

Her throat went dry. "No, she died of breast cancer two years after we lost our parents."

"Birdie was eighteen and became my legal guardian, and it's been the two of us ever since," Lori said, holding her gaze.

Grace pressed her hand to her heart. "Now, you've got us. And with Lori marrying Tom, Birdie, you'll be part of the Abbott family, too. And since you're family, I have to tell you that we were so sorry to hear about your breakup and that you lost your job on the same day, dear."

Bridget turned to her sister.

"I hope you don't mind that I told them. It's so awful and unfair, Birdie," Lori offered.

"Dumped and sacked all in one day?" Soren said—because, of course, he'd be interested in her humiliation.

Grace and Denise shared a sympathetic look. "Oh, Scooter, it's even worse than it sounds," Grace said as Denise nodded.

"Lori told us that you actually walked in on your boyfriend with another woman right after you lost your job. Those are two challenging life events to endure at the same time. We're all here for you, aren't we, Scooter?" Denise added.

Bridget stood there, frozen with mortification. This must be what it's like to have your life dissected in front of an audience on one of those midday self-help TV talk shows.

"Yep, we sure are," Soren answered, mock sincerity dripping from his reply.

Bridget glanced up at the steep mountainside. If there were ever a time for an avalanche to sweep her off the face of the earth, this was it.

She plastered on a grin. "Well, we can't dwell on that. We've got a wedding coming up, and you should be hitting the slopes. It's a perfect day to ski."

"That's what you've got on the schedule for us," Scott remarked as Soren rolled his eyes.

"You'll have to count me out," the judge said, glancing between her and Soren before waving to Dan as he emerged from the mountain house. "I'm not much for skiing these days, and I ran into an old colleague of mine in the village. So, Dan is going to drive me down to play some poker with him and the other old-timers at the Kringle Acres Retirement Community."

"Enjoy yourselves. We'll get settled and then start on baking the cookies for the spaghetti dinner. We can meet up at Kringle Acres," she said, opting to go all cruise director in hopes that everyone would forget that she was an unemployed loser who'd walked in on her boyfriend screwing another woman.

"We?" Soren repeated, confusion written all over his face.

She grinned up at him, playing to the audience. "Absolutely! We've got maid of honor and best man duties," she said to the group. "Scooter will be my right-hand man over the next few days, helping to make sure everything runs smoothly."

"And there's one more thing," Dan said, all-rosy cheeked as he joined the group.

"And what's that?" she asked, feeling pleased as punch to be able to drop this zinger on the wedding Grinch.

Dan gestured to the mountain house. "The best man will also be your roommate."

"*R*oommates?" he and Bridget exclaimed in unison.

This petite bull of a bridesmaid thought she had him cornered, but now, they'd both been thrown for a loop. Sure, he was going to have to play the part of the wedding assistant, but he'd figure out a way to lose her and get some alone time with Tom. Time to convince his best friend that this wedding was a mistake. And pretending to be Birdie's little helper would make everyone—including Tom—think that he was one hundred percent supportive of this hasty union until he could convince Tom that he wasn't ready to get married.

He had to be smart. He had to make Tom think that calling off the wedding was his idea.

But he figured he'd at least have his own room to plot and plan. Someplace to escape his nemesis's perfect curves and cinnamon vanilla scent.

Helping Bridget glue pinecones onto chandeliers or what-ever the hell kind of bullshit went into a mountain wedding was one thing. Spending twenty-four seven with her could...

It could damn well push him over the edge.

Those mahogany eyes lured him in and made him forget everything.

He'd broken every rule he'd made for himself last night. He couldn't help it. With her in his arms, he wasn't the aloof womanizer. He wasn't the ruthless businessman. He was different. Her kiss-swollen lips and rich brown eyes had given him a glimpse of life's true, vibrant palette with its bright, shining splendor and endless possibilities. He'd been living a black-and-white existence, but with her, anything seemed possible.

Sweet Kris Kringle! What the hell was wrong with him? He could not entertain this quasi-poetic and utterly sappy nonsense.

The chance of Soren Christopher Traeger Rudolph becoming a benevolent, doting boyfriend was about as likely as Cole and Carly capturing a Christmas fairy.

If anything, he was more of an Ebenezer Scrooge, and there was no way Bridget, or some aberration, could make him change his ways.

Hell no!

It wasn't real. She'd played the part of the vixen while he'd pretended to be...whole, complete. Two things he could never be. He wasn't built that way.

Last night was a mistake. He'd given in to that little voice inside of him that yearned for more. He wasn't capable of giving a woman his heart—if he even had one. Thanks to a miserable childhood void of warmth and kindness, the only connection he was capable of was the one forged with the Abbotts.

And it didn't matter if Bridget "*Birdie*" Dasher was the most alluring and disarming woman on the planet. He wasn't about to lose them. They were the closest thing to family he'd ever known.

This was war. And thanks to a career spent callously dismantling companies, he'd allow that side of him to take the Dasher sisters down and put the brakes on Tom's wedding.

Bridget cleared her throat. "I don't think I heard you correctly, Dan. It sounded like you said that Soren and I will be sharing a room."

That's what he'd heard, too, and also could use some clarification. He took in the crowd, watching their exchange, and forced himself not to react. He had to play it cool.

"That's exactly what I said, Birdie. There are five guest rooms in the mountain house. Tom and Lori are sharing room one. Denise, Nancy, and the children are in room two. Grace and Scott have room three, and the judge and Russell are in room four. That leaves room five which—"

"Which was going to be for Garrett and me," Bridget replied in a tight whisper.

Irritation pricked through his body at her response. "Is that his name? Garrett?" he asked a little more forcefully than he'd intended. Why did it bother him that some asshat cheated on her? What was it to him? But that didn't stop the drive to want to kick the guy's ass.

"Yes, I guess everyone knows why he's not here. I'd forgotten about the room situation. Everything's changed so fast," she said, trailing off, her gaze awash with bewilderment.

No shit, life had changed fast! Since meeting her, his entire life had turned upside down.

She caught his eye, and the woman looked as disoriented as he felt. But, damn, if he didn't want to kiss her until her eyes gleamed with unbridled passion like it did last night.

Enough! He could not let his mind go there.

Russ shuffled forward. "Scooter could room with the judge. I'd be happy to take one for the team and bunk in room five with Birdie—on the sleeper sofa, of course," Russ offered with a casual wave of his hand, but the guy's eyes were trained well south of Bridget's face.

He stared hard at the man. He'd always liked Uncle Russ. The guy was clueless and got shot down by women left and right, but he was harmless. Except now, the thought of Bridget sharing a room with him made him want to kick his ass—after he finished kicking the ass of her ex-boyfriend.

Jesus! He'd known Bridget for a day and already had two asses to kick, and he didn't even like the woman!

"No, I'll bunk with *Birdie*," he said in his best do-not-fuck-with-me voice.

"You will?" Bridget asked with that adorable crinkle to her forehead.

He had to stop noticing everything about her. It didn't help that he'd spent the better part of an hour watching her sleep last night. And then, did it again in the car before, like a total sleep-deprived sucker, he'd fallen asleep with her in his arms.

He schooled his features. "It's like you said. The best man and maid of honor duties start now, right? It'll be easier to get things done if we're in the same room."

She narrowed her gaze, sizing him up. "True."

He glanced around the group to find all eyes still trained on them.

"It's settled. Bridget and I will take room five," he said, hoping he looked decisive and not like a sap who'd spent twenty minutes cataloging the adorable smattering of freckles on her nose.

Dan clapped his hands. "It looks as if everything is coming together."

That was an understatement.

He did his best to appear like someone not plotting to ruin a wedding. "Dan's right. Let's get this day started. Have fun on the slopes. Birdie and I will take it from here."

"Are you sure you're okay with this arrangement, Birdie?" Lori asked with a brow crease that matched Bridget's.

The women did some weird eye thing before the hint of a playful grin pulled at the corner of his vixen's lips.

"We'll be fine. Like two chestnuts roasting over an open fire," she replied, quoting Dan in quite a precarious tone.

"Marvelous! We'll see you both for the spaghetti dinner at Kringle Acres in the village," Grace said, patting his cheek before hugging Bridget goodbye.

Denise and Nancy broke off from the group to gather the kids as a glum Russell trailed behind his family toward the ski lift. But Tom stopped, said something to Lori, then jogged back to where he and Bridget still stood.

Holy hell! Was it that easy? Could it be that just seeing each other in person had miraculously broken the Dasher spell and brought Tom back to his old self?

"I'm glad you're here, Scooter," Tom said.

He nodded as his pulse kicked up. "I'm always here for you."

Tom's features grew pensive. "Good, because I need you to do something for me."

"Anything."

His mind raced. If Tom needed to make a quick getaway, they'd need a vehicle. He spied an old pickup truck parked on the side of the mountain house. There! Knowing places like these, the keys were probably tucked above the sun visor.

Tom reached into his pocket, removed a small black velvet bag, then shook the contents into his palm.

Oh shit! The rings!

"Best man duties. I'm trusting you with these," he said, handing them over carefully.

Soren held his friend's gaze and remembered back to the day Tom dragged him onto the train to spend his first Christmas with the Abbotts.

"You're trusting me with the wedding rings?" he asked, trying not to sound like a fox who'd been given the keys to the henhouse.

Tom chuckled. "Yeah, of course, I am. You're my best friend, Scooter," the man finished with a pat to his shoulder before hurrying to join Lori at the ski rack.

He pulled his gaze from his best friend and stared at the gleaming bands.

This was not what he was expecting, not by a longshot.

"You better put them someplace safe," Bridget warned.

He nodded, hardly able to believe he held an essential piece to Tom's wedding in his hand. Without thinking, he put the rings back in the pouch, unzipped his coat's interior pocket, and tucked the bands inside.

"Hey, Birdie! Don't let Scooter slack off," Denise teased, throwing him a little wink as she helped Cole and Carly put on their skis.

"Don't you worry. I plan to make him work for it," Bridget answered.

Thrown off by Tom's request, he met her gaze. A man could get drunk off the confidence brimming in her eyes. She thought she had the upper hand—thought she was holding all the cards. He parted his lips, ready to knock her down a peg when a pat to his back caught his attention. He turned to see the judge, eyeing him closely.

Soren shifted his weight from foot to foot. The rings in his pocket weighed nothing, but a strange heaviness had set in.

"Have fun cleaning up in poker," he said, aiming for easy-going, but Tom's grandfather didn't move.

"There's something about you two," he said, wagging a finger at them.

Bridget blushed. She had to work on her poker face. Luckily, he was the king of suppressing his emotions.

"You're right, Judge. We both care about Tom and Lori and want them to live their best lives," he answered, leaning on his law degree with that statement. It wasn't a lie. He wanted Lori Dasher to have a nice life—far the fuck away from his best friend.

"Hmm," Judge replied, sharing a look with Dan.

When did these two become thick as thieves? Maybe it was an old guy thing.

The judge was a fascinating man. He'd spent his career in the family courts, which sounded like a goddamn nightmare. But the man's office was littered with thank you cards and photographs of people he'd married, adoptions he'd overseen, even divorcees, who couldn't stand each other but maintained a soft place in their hearts for the man.

There typically wasn't a jury in family court, and the judge alone is tasked with ensuring justice—something that Franklin Abbott took seriously. The man was unequivocally fair and unwavering in his deployment of justice, but he did it with compassion. When he'd taught him how to fish, the judge's steady demeanor, so different from what he'd experienced with his parents, had made him the man's biggest fan. He'd never met the judge's wife. The two had been high school sweethearts, and she'd passed away years before he'd met Tom. But the man still carried her high school photo in his wallet.

A sappy as hell move for most, but with the judge, it was the real deal. True love.

"I'll see you both at dinner. Thank you for planning such a festive week for us, Birdie. I can tell that you've put quite a bit of thought into our time here in Kringle," the judge added, then nodded to Dan as the men headed toward the old Rover.

Soren breathed a sigh of relief. If he could fool the judge, he could fool anyone.

He and Bridget waved as the pair made their way down the

snowy drive, headed for Kringle Village, and thought of that crinkled photograph. He couldn't imagine keeping any woman's picture with him all the time.

Or could he?

An icy breeze picked up, and a lock of Bridget's hair brushed against his arm.

And then it was just the two of them.

"Shall we," he said, gesturing to the mountain house.

The massive one-story structure looked like something kids would dream up with multiple boxes of Lincoln Logs at their disposal. Tucked into the side of the mountain with smoke coming out of the stone chimney, this place was the epitome of rustic chic and had a certain charm he couldn't quite put his finger on.

No matter. This would soon be the location where Tom came to his senses. He should look into flights to Bali or Australia. After his friend ended things with Lori, he'd need an adventure to get her out of his head.

"That was interesting," Bridget said with a surreptitious twist to her lips as they crunched through the snow toward the house.

He pasted on his cocksure smirk. "See, I can be nice."

She barked out a laugh. "No, you can't."

"I can't?"

His pulse quickened. Why did he like going back and forth with her?

He reached to open the door, but she pressed her back against it before he could pull it open.

"I know what you're doing, and I'm not falling for it, Scooter," she said with a determined edge.

He took a step closer and tipped her chin to meet his gaze. Barely an inch apart, it would take no effort for him to lift her into his arms and kiss her into oblivion.

"What is it that you think I'm doing, Birdie?" he asked

instead, his fingers twitching at the thought of gripping the globes of her perfect ass.

Sweet Jesus, this was hot!

She lowered her voice. "I see you playing the nice guy, and we both know that you're not a nice guy."

His fingertips grazed hers as electricity crackled between them. "You thought I was nice enough last night after I gave you, what was it, five orgasms?"

She looked away and murmured something under her breath.

He wove his fingers with hers, and the contact had him rock-hard.

"What was that? I didn't quite hear you, Bridget?" he continued, loving the sound of her name.

Her chest heaved with each punctuated breath. She felt it, too—this crazy charge between them.

She schooled her features. "Seven, I said seven! I had seven orgasms last night. Are you happy now? You shouldn't be. That whole orgasm business is over. From this moment on, I won't have any time for orgasms because I'll be watching you like a hawk."

"Is that right?" he purred.

She sucked in a sharp breath. "You bet your life, *Scooter*."

They were back to the Scooter and Birdie game.

He cupped her cheek in his hand and licked his lips. His one-night vixen looked good enough to eat.

"What if *I* plan on not letting *you* out of my sight, *Birdie*?"

Her bottom lip trembled, and he couldn't tear his eyes away. The cold air paired with the inferno blazing between them sent a delicious buzz through his body. Her eyes fluttered closed, and he leaned in, unable to stop himself when a sharp knock on the mountain house window broke the kissing spell. Bridget shrieked, then shoved him with the force of an NFL linebacker.

Surprised at his vixen's upper body strength, he lost his footing, hit the side of the steps, then fell into a mound of snow with a frosty thud.

"Are you two coming in, or do you plan on standing in front of my door all afternoon?"

He raised his hand to block the sun and got a glimpse of a smiling older woman with round wire-rimmed glasses and a coat covered in candy canes.

"Mrs. Claus?" he sputtered.

"No, dear, it's Mrs. Donner. I'm Dan's wife. You can call me Delores."

Jesus! More damn reindeer names. And, in his defense, the Claus remark was a knee-jerk reaction to a woman who looked like she'd been deployed from Christmas central casting.

"Are you okay?" Bridget exclaimed, hurrying to his side.

Worry creased her brow as she extended her hand to help him up. He knew she was sweet. He'd seen through her vixen facade, but it turned out that she was also genuinely kind—another reason he could never be with someone like her. Still, he hated how easily she could awaken that lost, lonely part of him that longed for more.

"You must be Birdie and Scooter! Come in. I've got the oven all preheated for you," the woman said warmly.

"You do?" Bridget asked as he came to his feet and stood beside her.

"It's on your schedule. I figured since you got delayed in Denver and lost a day, you'd want to get started baking right away."

Dammit! That's right! His one-night vixen had a schedule.

Delores gestured for them to follow her inside. He dusted the snow off his ass and trailed a few steps behind the women, then stopped in his tracks and couldn't hold back a grin.

This place was fantastic!

Antler chandeliers strung with white lights hung from exposed timber beams built into the pitched roof as the scent of evergreens and fresh-baked cookies wafted through the room. The main gathering space was part living room with plush seating and part dining room with a long rustic table running down the center. A decorated Christmas tree sat in each corner of the room, while stockings hung along the hearth. Everyone had a stocking with their name written in gold or silver glitter, and his Scooter stocking hung next to the one with Birdie written in swooping silver letters.

"It's…" he began, but Bridget cut him off.

"It's exactly how I remembered it," she said, her voice full of wonder.

Delores straightened one of the stockings. "Your sister had the same reaction when she'd arrived. She said your family loved coming here for the holidays."

Bridget nodded. "We did."

"And your parents were married at the Kringle Chapel?" Mrs. Claus's doppelgänger continued.

"Yes, they met when they were English professors at the University of Colorado. They'd invited my grandmother to spend their first Christmas here and chose to come to the Kringle Mountain House instead of staying in their cramped apartment in the city. They fell in love with this place and got married here a year later. But I haven't been back since I was a teenager."

"That's a lovely story, dear, and we're so happy to have you here celebrating not only Christmas but your sister's wedding. The town of Kringle may be a bit different now than what you remember."

Bridget walked down the center of the room, grazing her fingertips along the length of the rustic table as she stared at the mountains framed by the floor-to-ceiling windows lining the back of the mountain house, and he couldn't help remembering her doing the same thing last night when they'd entered his suite.

Was that only last night? It felt like the two of them had been tangled together for eons—not hours.

"It's perfect. It's absolutely perfect," she said, glancing over her shoulder at Delores as her eyes shined with emotion.

"Is this them, Mrs. D? Robin and Vespa?"

He turned to see a young man saunter in from the kitchen. In sunglasses, a red and white slouching Santa beanie sitting cockeyed on his head and zipped into an oversized hoodie covered in poinsettias, or some other green pointy plant, he was the poster kid for grunge Christmas. The guy lowered his shades to get a better look at them, then quickly slid his glasses back in place.

"It's Birdie and Scooter, dear," Delores corrected.

The young man nodded slowly. "But robins are birds, and Vespas are scooters."

Delores grinned at the guy as if he didn't seem totally out of his mind. "This is Tanner Baker. He works part-time doing odd jobs at the Kringle Mountain House and in the kitchen at Kringle Acres."

"Right on! And I also dabble in agricultural pursuits," the kid answered, sounding as if he'd spent the last decade locked in a room watching *Point Break* and mastering the tone and cadence of pseudo-surf speak.

Delores grinned at the guy. "Our young Tanner is a Colorado renaissance man. Are your brownies and gummy bears ready, dear?"

"Bears are done, and three more minutes on the Baker's delight brownies, Mrs. D," he answered, procuring a plastic bag teeming with gummy bears and popping one into his mouth.

"Very good, and please leave the oven on, dear. Our guests

are baking cookies for the residents at Kringle Acres."

Tanner popped another gummy into his mouth. "Sweet, let me know if you need me to hook you up with any special ingredients."

Bridget glanced between the peculiar pair, then looked up at him. Her questioning expression seemed to ask if they'd entered into an alternate universe.

He was wondering the same thing.

He gave her a little shrug. They were miles away from the closest major ski resort, and these out of the way towns were often packed with interesting characters.

Bridget turned to the holiday odd couple and pasted on a grin. "I think we should be fine, but thank you for offering. Dan said everything I'd asked for had been delivered. Did my baking equipment make it to you? I shipped it last week. I'll need it to make the wedding cake."

Delores nodded. "It did, but we don't have the refrigerator space here for you to make and store the wedding cake."

He bit back a grin. There it was—the first sign this wedding was doomed!

Bridget gasped. "But I have an email from you confirming the exact measurements of your freezer."

He crossed his arms, feeling pretty damn good.

Rudolph one. Dasher zero.

"Don't worry, dear. There is freezer space, just not here."

That adorable crinkle between her eyebrows made an appearance. "I don't understand."

Delores adjusted her Mrs. Claus glasses. "About a month ago, the little bakery in our town closed. But the power is still on, and everything works. You're welcome to use the facility to prepare the wedding cake. It's down the street from the Kringle Acres Retirement Community."

Dammit! A whole bakery at her disposal? God only knows

what she could do with an entire shop!

"But how will I get there?" she asked.

He stepped forward and nodded as if he cared. Well, he did, just not for the same reason she did.

"Take the truck. It's the red one parked outside. It's for guest use, and you're welcome to take it out whenever you need it," the woman answered, dashing his hopes to dash his Dasher's agenda.

Bridget glanced up at him, grinning like she'd won the lottery. But just as quickly as her victorious expression appeared, a somber countenance took its place.

"And you're sure it's okay for me to use the bakery? I don't want anyone to get in trouble," she pressed—the Goody Two-shoes.

Still, it was a good question. Who was Delores Donner to allow anyone the use of a closed down business? He shifted his weight nervously. There was still a chance her cake dreams would be crushed, but his gut seemed to think otherwise.

Delores chuckled. "I'm not only the caretaker of Kringle Mountain House. I'm also the mayor of the town. I've got a little pull," she said, removing a set of keys from her pocket and handing them to Bridget.

Shit.

"And you don't want to forget this. Here's the key to room five," Delores added, handing him a long antique key dangling from a Santa Claus key chain.

He placed the key into his pocket. "You guys are pretty serious about Christmas around here."

Delores glanced at him over her glasses. "Oh yes! Christmas took over Kringle a decade ago."

He gave the woman a curt nod, not knowing what the hell that meant. Sure, Kringle was synonymous with all things Christmas, but his last name was Rudolph, and that didn't mean he was a fan of the red-nosed reindeer. He started to tell her this when a rhythmic beep from the kitchen cut him off. He glanced over at Tanner Baker, who popped another gummy into his mouth, oblivious to the sound.

Did anyone get annoyed in this town?

"Dear, I think your brownies are done," Delores remarked.

"You do?" the kid asked.

"Yes, the timer's going off," Bridget added with a touch of irritation to her tone.

He could tell that his wedding planning, schedule-making, one-night vixen was itching to turn it off.

A little Type A?

Well, he couldn't fault her on that. He was a workaholic himself. The only time he ever took off was when he was with Tom and the Abbotts.

Tanner cocked his head to the side. "I thought it was aliens sending me a message."

What the hell?

He stared at the guy who definitely didn't seem to be the sharpest knife in the drawer and was blown away to think that he could hold down two jobs as well as dabble in farming.

"No, dear, it's the oven," Delores answered, sweet as pie, or fruitcake, or whatever Christmas crap people ate around here.

"Right on," the kid replied, still not moving as the timer continued to beep.

What would this guy do if the fire alarm went off? He'd be toast or a glop of smoldering gummy bears. He certainly could put away the sugary snack.

"Tanner, could you show our guests around the kitchen and offer them a sandwich? I need to run into town," Delores said, removing her purse from a hook on the wall.

"Sure thing, Mrs. D. But could you wait a few minutes? I could use a ride into the village."

"I'll wait for you in the car, dear," Delores said. She started for the door, then turned. "I almost forgot. Breakfast is served from seven to nine. Lunchtime is twelve to one, and we keep the condoms inside Frosty," she added, gesturing to a ceramic snowman.

"The what?" Bridget stuttered.

"Condoms, you know, for sex," Delores answered before walking out the door as if she didn't drop a Frosty the Snowman condom bomb. What the hell kind of place was this?

"Follow me," Tanner said, unfazed by the old lady condom drop and waved them into the kitchen.

The guy set his bag of gummy bears on a table in the center of the room, then leaned against the counter as the timer continued to beep.

Did he not notice the irksome sound?

"Let me get that for you," Bridget offered.

She dropped her purse onto a chair in the corner of the room and jumped into action, turning off the incessant beeping, then donning oven mitts to remove the tray of brownies from the oven.

"Thanks, bird lady," the guy replied with an easy grin.

Bridget held out the tray and cringed. "Your brownies look a little green."

Tanner slid his shades down and assessed the baked goods. "No worries! I'm playing around with a new recipe."

"I see. And you help prepare food here at Kringle Mountain House?" she asked with a nervous lilt to her question.

Truth be told, he wasn't all that crazy about eating anything this guy touched either.

"Yep, and at Kringle Acres. But don't worry. I don't experiment with food for the guests, if you know what I mean. Oh, yeah! Let me get you those sandwiches!" he exclaimed and pulled a platter out of the refrigerator.

Bridget's plastic smile said she absolutely didn't know what he meant, but she nodded politely.

Tanner set the platter on the center table. "Mrs. D. made these for lunch while I was busy experimenting with a new recipe."

Thank Christ, this kid didn't have a hand in preparing lunch.

Soren took one look at the platter, piled high with deli-style sandwiches, and his stomach released a monstrous growl. He swiped a turkey slider off the plate and ate it in two bites.

"You're one hungry dude!" Tanner remarked.

He wiped a crumb from the corner of his mouth and caught Bridget's eye. "I had quite a workout last night. I need to build up my strength."

His one-night vixen huffed as she buzzed around the kitchen, collecting ingredients when a horn beeped, and Tanner didn't move.

Did this kid have selective hearing loss?

He took another sandwich from the platter. This time, opting for a delectable looking ham and cheese. "That's prob-ably Delores, wanting you to join her in the car," he said through a bite.

"Yeah, good thinking," the pseudo-Santa-surfer replied.

"I think she's trying to tell you that she's ready to go," Bridget added, wrapping the tray of brownies in a dish towel and handing them to the clueless man.

"Right! Catch ya later." With the tray in one hand, he grabbed a sandwich with the other, then disappeared out the kitchen's side door.

Okay, what did he know so far?

They were in a strange mountain town that really got into Christmas and had the best fucking sandwiches on the planet. He took another one, switching back to the turkey, and watched as Bridget twisted her hair into a bun, snagged an apron, then went to the sink to wash her hands.

"Aren't you going to eat first?" he asked, working on his third sandwich.

She glanced at her watch. "There's no time."

He leaned against the counter. "What do you mean there's no time?"

"I mean, we have to get to work."

He raised an eyebrow. "We?"

"Um, yeah! You know, doing maid of honor and best man duties," she answered, rocketing around the kitchen like a petite baking ninja.

He popped the last bite of the sandwich into his mouth. "I tried to exercise my best man duties. I sent strippers, but your sister didn't seem to like that."

"Neither did your best friend," she shot back, now operating a giant mixer.

She was like the Energizer Bunny of bakers.

"Don't you need a recipe?" he asked as the distinct scent of peanut butter filled the room.

She tapped her head, and he couldn't help but notice the strands of dark hair that had broken free of her bun and brushed past her chin.

"It's all in here, Scooter. Don't you worry," she offered, piling on a nice helping of condescension.

This woman!

"What are you making?" he inquired, maintaining a neutral demeanor as the memories came flooding back.

"*We* are baking peanut butter blossoms, and *you* need to unwrap all the chocolate kisses. Wash your hands, then get started. The bag is on the counter," she instructed, then gestured with her chin to the bag containing a hell of a lot of the foil-wrapped Hershey's chocolate kisses.

He eyed the bag. "Are these the peanut butter cookies where you have to plop the kiss on top right after they're done baking?"

She glanced up from making the dough balls and smiled at him—a real smile this time. Baking clearly made her more amenable.

"Yes, they are. They were a Christmas staple at my grandmother's house. Have you made them before?"

Had he made them before?

That would be a yes.

Crammed into Janine's cozy kitchen, the day before his mother fired his favorite nanny, he'd helped Janine's sons unwrap the tiny chocolate treats. 'Open five kisses, and then you can eat one,' she'd said as he sat at the table, legs dangling, with the boys. And for the entire afternoon, he'd felt normal, like he was a part of something real.

"Yeah, I made them with Janine," he said over his shoulder as he turned on the sink to wash his hands.

"You call your mom Janine? That's a little bizarre," Bridget remarked with a thread of humor.

"Janine isn't my mother. She was my nanny. Well, one of many nannies," he answered, drying his hands on a dish towel.

"Many, huh?" she echoed, focused on her work.

He steadied himself. He sure as hell wasn't about to pour his heart out to Birdie Dasher and share his sad, lonely tale of his parents not giving a damn about him.

He needed to change the subject.

"Are you a lawyer, like your sister? Is baking your hobby? Is this how you de-stress, or do you prefer picking up strangers in hotel bars?" he pressed, throwing in a healthy dose of jackass as he unwrapped the chocolates.

And he was slightly curious. He didn't know a damn real-life thing about her.

Well, that wasn't exactly true.

To be fair, he did know a few things. Number one: she and her sister were a serious threat to his happiness. But he also knew other things, intimate things—like the way she bit her lip and released the sexiest of breathy moans before he made her come. And how, when she entwined her fingers into the hair at the nape of his neck, he damn near forgot his name. Just the thought already had him rock-hard.

He had to stop thinking of her like that!

He glanced at her and noticed a muscle tic on her cheek as she formed tiny balls of dough between her hands, then placed them delicately across a giant baking sheet.

"No, I didn't go to college. I've worked in bakeries since I was eighteen," she answered without taking her eyes off the task.

He barked out a little laugh. "I figured you were an Ivy Leaguer like your sister. Tom couldn't stop telling me Lori went to Harvard when they first got together." He tossed a wrapper into the trash. "Why didn't you go to college? You seem as tenacious as Lori."

Bridget set a ball of dough, rolled into a perfect sphere, onto the tray, then looked up and held his gaze. And a cold trickle worked its way down his spine. There was nothing playful in her eyes, but they blazed with a determined ferocity.

"I'm the oldest. I was Lori's guardian after my grandmother died, and somebody had to pay the bills to make sure she had everything she needed to get into a school like Harvard."

Between the scent of the cookies and the warmth emanating from the oven, a buzzy headiness came over him. Pain flashed in her eyes before she broke their connection and started in on another ball of dough.

He placed an unwrapped chocolate kiss on the counter next to the others and stared hard at the candy lining the wooden table. "I'm sorry. I forgot that Lori said you'd taken care of her after your grandmother passed away. I didn't put two and two together."

She gave him a sharp nod, acknowledging his half-assed apology but not really accepting it.

And for God knows what reason, that hurt. Unlike anyone he'd ever met, her fierce protective retort had elicited a response in him.

"That was a shitty thing for me to say. What can I do to make it up to you?"

Her hardened demeanor melted away as a decidedly mischievous smirk pulled at the corners of her lips, and immediately, he regretted his apology. She was cooking up—or baking up—a plan, and it didn't look good for him.

She placed the tray of cookies into the oven, dusted off her hands, then pulled her phone out of her bag.

"Are you setting your phone's timer?" he asked, working to keep the nervous edge out of his voice.

Why did she make him nervous?

He didn't know. But she did.

"Well, Mr. Rudolph, to make it up to me, I've got a job for you," she said, tapping away on her phone.

"What's that? More chocolate to unwrap?"

Jesus! Was it getting hot in here? It had to be the oven.

She glanced at the mound of chocolate kisses. "Nope, that's enough."

He unzipped his coat and hung it on the back of the kitchen chair. "Then what?"

With one last tap to her cell, music played and a deep voice crooning "White Christmas" filled the peanut butter scented air.

She plucked a gummy bear from the bag Tanner had left on the counter and popped it into her mouth as her mischievous smirk morphed into a full-on shit-eating grin.

"You, *Scooter Rudolph*, are going to dance."

D ance?

"Are you out of your goddamn mind?" he shot back.

He glanced around the kitchen. They were alone in the mountain house, but there was no way he was about to break into a jig or whatever the hell she wanted him to do.

Bridget popped a few more gummy bears into her mouth, then swayed to the music. He recognized the tune—he wasn't a complete Grinch. It was Bing Crosby. Janine had played the very same holiday album in her kitchen all those years ago. The guy had a deep voice and, to a ten-year-old, sounded pretty corny. He'd giggled with Janine's sons at the sound of it. But there was a soothing, calming quality to the music he'd never forgotten.

Bridget sashayed around the room, tidying up as the heady scent of the baking cookies mingled with the pile of unwrapped chocolates. His mouth watered, and he wasn't sure if he craved her or the sweets.

And speaking of sweets, when was the last time he'd indulged in baked goods? He couldn't even remember. Those cupcakes Mr. and Mrs. Angel had left at his office smelled delectable, but he didn't eat that kind of junk. It took work to get abs like his.

Discipline.

Self-control.

Two important qualities his parents never possessed.

Entitled.

Selfish.

Thoughtless.

Careless.

Those were more emblematic words to describe his family if you could call it that.

He crossed his arms. "Why don't you eat a sandwich?" he said, going into scrooge mode.

"I'm good sticking with the gummy bears. They aren't half bad. They've got an earthy cinnamon flavor to them. I'll have to ask Tanner for the recipe," she answered, eating another, then doing a little twirl in front of him.

He frowned. "When was the last time you ate a real meal?"

She cocked her head to the side. "Define, a real meal."

"We know you didn't have dinner."

"Nope," she answered with another twirl.

His one-night vixen had mellowed out quite a bit.

He huffed an exasperated breath. "What are you doing, Bridget?"

"Dancing," she replied, enunciating the syllables slowly as if she were addressing an idiot, then took his hand and twirled underneath it. It was a bizarrely charming move.

He'd never met anyone like her.

"Why are you dancing?" he pressed as "White Christmas" ended, and Bing started in on "God Rest Ye Merry Gentleman."

She pointed at the oven. "It's for the cookies."

"You're dancing for lumps of sugar and peanut butter?"

"No, I'm injecting joyful Christmas spirit into them," she

answered, then swiped the oven mitt off the counter and threw it at him.

He snapped it out of the air with one hand. "Are you on something?"

She frowned with her hands on her hips. "No, I've never done drugs in my entire life. I barely drink. But I do dance for anything I bake."

He walked across the kitchen and set the mitt on the counter. "Is this why you got fired? Did you freak out the people in the bakery with your prancing and dancing?"

She beckoned with her index finger for him to come closer.

"I know what you're doing," she whispered with a sly hint of a grin.

He schooled his features. "Yeah, what's that?"

"You're trying to scrooge your way out of dancing. But I'm not about to let you get your *bah humbug* vibe into my cookies."

"Your cookies didn't mind my *bah humbug* vibe last night," he replied, pretty damn pleased with that retort.

Unfazed, she wagged her finger at him and clucked her tongue. "See, you're trying to upset me. You think that if you act like a real scrooge, I won't make you dance."

He swallowed, surprised to find his throat had gone dry. "How do you know I'm not a real scrooge?"

He'd never thought of himself in stupid Christmas terms— except the damn Rudolph part, which, thanks to his last name, he couldn't escape.

But was he a *real* scrooge? He did prioritize earning money. He didn't give a shit about the companies he decimated. Not only that, he'd screwed every air-headed Manhattan socialite and Page Six party girl and never had nor wanted the hassle of a relationship.

On those fronts, he wasn't winning any sappy save the world points.

But he did have one redeeming quality. For whatever reason, the Abbotts cared about him. And that one thing meant everything.

Without them, he was a scrooge—a scrooge able to bench three-fifty and built like a brick house. But on the inside, in the dark corners of his heart, he was an empty, lonely soul.

Bridget screwed her face into a puckered, curious expression. "You might be a real scrooge. Lori did say that you've made buckets of money destroying people's livelihoods."

He squared his jaw. This is why he couldn't allow Tom to marry Lori. He'd only seen Tom once in the last five months—and that was when his best friend invited him to lunch to meet his new fiancée. Granted, he'd ignored her and then left early to go bang a waitress. But he'd known instantly that a Tom, Soren, and Lori triad wouldn't work. And after seeing Lori with the Abbotts today, it was only a matter of time before she'd poison the well with Tom's family.

A dropped comment here.

A subtle observation there.

And then a five-month stretch without seeing his friend would extend to six months, then eight months, and then, when the holidays rolled around, would they even remember to include him? Would sixteen years of happy holiday memories revert to the solitary Christmases he'd endured as a boy?

He swallowed past the lump in his throat.

"Soren?" Bridget said, her voice pulling him out of an anguishing spiral.

He turned away from her and opened the refrigerator, searching for something to drink. He pulled out a bottle of water, took a sip, then pulled himself together. Bridget Dasher had a way of turning everything upside down, and then with just one word, bringing him back from the brink.

He set the half-drained bottle on the counter.

"The money part is right, but the notion that I've had a hand in ruining anyone's business is wrong," he replied, maintaining an even tone.

Good! He was in corporate raider mode. All he had to do was stay in this callous groove, and he'd be immune to her charms.

She tucked an errant lock of chestnut hair behind her ear, and he had to ball his hands into fists to keep from sweeping the strands back himself.

Get some control, Rudolph!

She watched him closely. "Explain it to me."

He maintained his muted expression. "I run a private equity firm. My company invests in businesses. If they aren't profitable, I sell off the assets to recoup any losses."

She nodded, taking in his succinct explanation. "Let me get this right. You give a little money to a business that needs help. Then you wait for it to fail, fire everyone, and squeeze every dime out of it that you can?"

She was a quick study.

He shrugged. "If they don't become profitable, essentially, yes."

Bridget tilted her head to the side. "How do you know if a business is really failing?"

That was easy.

"The numbers," he answered.

That damn adorable crinkle in her forehead was back.

She watched him closely. "That's it? Just a bunch of numbers?"

"What more is there?" he replied with another shrug.

She smiled up at him as if he made up the sun, moon, and stars. And if he wasn't such an ass, he might have admitted that he didn't mind that one bit.

"What?" he barked instead.

She shimmied around him. "If you haven't noticed, Mr. Scrooge, you're dancing."

What?

He looked down to find his feet tapping to the beat as he swayed side to side along with her.

When the hell did he start doing this?

She raised her hands in a couples' dance position. "Let's do this right. Do you want me to be the guy, or do you want to be the guy?"

Still swaying to the beat of Bing's holiday serenade, he stared at her for a second, then two.

She shook her head. "Sorry, I used to do this with my grandma Dasher or Lori, and somebody had to dance the guy part."

He took her hand, then pressed his palm to the small of her back, drawing her into his embrace. And that buzz was back. The feeling he had the moment he'd laid eyes on her back at the hotel bar, which seemed like eons ago.

"I can handle being the guy," he said, his voice taking on a gravelly edge as he pulled her in a fraction closer.

She rested her hand on his shoulder and gazed up at him as they swayed to the slow rhythm of Bing's rich baritone.

"Do you have any moves?" she asked, rosy-cheeked with those dark chestnut tendrils framing her face.

He leaned in, allowing his lips to hover a breath away from her earlobe. "You know, I do."

She blushed, and all that blood she had rushing to her cheeks, in his body, surged due south, straight to his cock.

"I mean on the dance floor," she countered.

He suppressed a grin, then brought her flush against him as the hard planes of his chiseled body merged with her petite curves. He stared down at her petal-soft kissable lips and slid his hand down from the small of her back to allow his fingertips to graze the curve of her ass. Her eyes went wide, and just before she was about to protest, he spun her out of his arms only to catch her hand and reel her back in.

She gasped. "Holy moly! You can dance!" she replied, using the same stupidly adorable exclamation she'd used the night he'd brought her to his hotel suite. He'd known that she wasn't a one-night stand kind of girl, and still, he'd pursued her.

Why? Why was he breaking all his rules?

He pushed the thought out of his mind.

"You can thank the Manhattan cotillion," he answered, finally finding a use for the ridiculous dance and etiquette training he'd tolerated until he'd gone off to boarding school.

She scrunched her face in confusion. "I don't know what that is. But if that's fancy talk for dance lessons, then I'm all for it."

He chuckled as she reached past him and snapped up a chocolate kiss from the table.

"Do you want one? My grandma used to always let me have one before the cookies were done baking."

He glanced away. "I don't do sweets."

With Bing belting out "Silver Bells," he was ready to change the lyrics to *silver balls,* or more like, *blue balls.*

He rubbed slow circles on the small of her back, his body aching for her as Bridget held the tiny bite of chocolate to her mouth. But she didn't eat it right away. Instead, she drew the kiss across her bottom lip.

It was too much to bear, and Bridget Dasher was enemy number one. He should not kiss her—again.

A muscle ticked in his jaw. "Just eat it, *Birdie.*"

"Not yet, *Scooter,*" she purred.

"What are you waiting for?"

"I can only have one. It's my grandma's rule, and I want to make it last."

With his hand on her back, he gripped her blouse, bunching the fabric in a feeble attempt to calm the hell down.

"If you don't eat that damn piece of candy right now, I can't be responsible for what I might do."

She closed her eyes as the tip of her tongue brushed across the base of the kiss. "Too bad. I want to wait."

A maddening spark snaked through his veins, prickling and taunting him. This woman made him, Soren Christopher Traeger Rudolph, the manwhore of Manhattan, fucking crazy.

"I'm done waiting," he hissed.

In the space of a breath, he plucked the chocolate from her grip. "Open your mouth."

Surrounded by holiday music and driven damn near insane from the chocolate peanut butter scented air laced with this infuriating woman's cinnamon vanilla scent, she held his gaze, and without a word in protest, complied.

He slid the kiss past her lips, and she closed her eyes, humming a deliciously sexy sound that went straight to his raging hard-on.

"Want more?" he pressed.

Brimming with confidence and just the right amount of mischief, her lips curled into her one-night vixen smile. "I told you, I'm only allowed to have one, or do you want me to be bad and indulge in two?"

Sweet Christ! He was ready to indulge, and it had nothing to do with chocolate.

He gripped her hips and lifted her onto the wooden table.

"If you thought that first chocolate kiss was good, you won't know what hit you with the second."

She rested her hands on his shoulders. "Why do you say that?"

"Because your second kiss is coming from me," he rasped, taking her face in his hands.

Their lips came together in a chocolate cinnamon explosion of desire. The spicy heat of the cinnamon and the lush richness of the chocolate lingered on her tongue. It was like kissing the X-rated version of Mrs. Claus. And not only did he want more, he wanted everything, all of her. She sighed into his mouth, and he pulled her forward, her ass teetering on the edge of the counter as their bodies came together. Instinctively, her legs wrapped around him as his hard length strained against the confines of his jeans and pressed between her thighs.

They were like horny teenagers, hands exploring, bodies rocking, hips thrusting. Each lick, each caress, every sensual slide of his lips across hers sent him spiraling out of control.

"I've never met anyone like you," he bit out between heated kisses.

Yes, it was a cheesy as hell line, but he meant it. And he'd never said anything like this to a woman.

For him, sex was sex. He didn't have the time or the desire to get to know a woman beyond how fast he could get her on her knees with his cock in his mouth. He should hate the one-night vixen currently wrapped in his embrace. He should be plotting his and Tom's escape from this bumble-fuck nowhere mountain town. But when he kissed Bridget Dasher, he entered an alternate universe, and another Soren Rudolph emerged. A Soren who only wanted this one-night vixen's kisses.

Bridget pulled back, and her mahogany gaze had grown darker and more resonant.

"And I've never—" she began, then stilled when a shrill beep cut through the kitchen's Christmas cookie-scented make-out haze.

He stared at her, unable to look away from her wild mane of hair. In the throes of cookie-scented dry-humping, he must have released her makeshift bun. With her kiss-swollen lips and heaving chest, she was an angel and a vixen, all tied up into one irresistibly beautiful woman.

Irresistibly beautiful woman?

What was wrong with him! He didn't think about shit like that!

He took a step back, coming to his senses.

This had to stop. He was a strong man—strong in body and mind. Bridget was an attractive woman. Who wouldn't want her? But from this moment on, this kissy-face bullshit had to end.

Bridget pressed her fingertips to her lips, then shook her head with a woozy swivel before glancing from the oven to the pile of chocolate.

"I need more kisses." She shook her head again. "I mean, the chocolate kisses, for the cookies. You should unwrap a few more."

He nodded. Good, they were back on track. She was the maid of honor baking cookies, and he was the best man, helping while sporting a raging hard-on.

Dammit!

He blew out a tight breath. "Why don't you get the cookies, and I'll be ready with the kisses for your cookie. No, strike that! I'll unwrap a few more *chocolates,* then put the damn things on the peanut butter balls."

Christ! He was not a bumbling idiot—ever—except, it seemed, when it came to Bridget Dasher.

"They're blossoms now. They're not balls anymore," she answered, remarkably straight-faced considering the relatively humorous nature of all this ball and blossom talk.

Cookies, kisses, and balls! This had to stop or else he'd have no choice but to bend her over the counter and take her hard and fast like he did the first time they'd made love.

He pinched the bridge of his nose as every cell in his brain seemed to be going haywire.

"Whatever they are, I'll *de-blossom* them with a kiss," he answered.

She cocked her head to the side. "*De-what*?"

God help him!

"Get the cookies out of the oven. I understand what I have to do."

She glanced around the kitchen as if she just realized she was in a kitchen.

She popped another gummy bear into her mouth. "I better get the cookies. I think that's the timer."

He watched her closely. "I literally just told you to do that."

What was going on with her?

Luckily, the baking part of her brain kicked in, and she sprang into action. She removed the tray of cookies from the oven, then slid them onto a baking rack with one hand.

"Kiss time," she called.

Without thinking, he pulled the strap of her apron and twirled her into his arms. A slick as hell move until the surprise on her face clued him in that she meant for him to put the chocolate kisses onto the peanut butter blossoms.

She stroked his cheek. "I like your scruff. It feels like kitty cat kisses."

"Kitty cat kisses?" he repeated. This was getting weird.

"Yeah, but since you're so cantankerous, we can call it kitty cat cantankerous kisses," she replied, then giggled.

Was she losing her mind?

"I better get to the chocolate."

She glanced at the pile. "Yes, they're ready."

He looked at the mound of Hershey's kisses. "You dance for cookies and commune with chocolate?"

Her eyes went wide. "I've never talked to chocolate before today. This is something new."

This was getting weirder by the second.

"Why don't you find something to put the cookies in and then we should probably go."

She nodded, then started opening and closing the cabinets as he plopped chocolate kisses on the center of a few dozen cookies.

"Got it!" she called, carrying over a large picnic basket.

"Really?" he asked.

"It's a picnic basket. How fun, right?"

She found a clean dish towel, lined the bottom, then placed each cookie into the basket while humming "Rudolph, the Red-Nosed Reindeer."

This gave him some time to observe his curious vixen. She looked like the same woman, but this behavior went well beyond injecting Christmas juju into baked goods.

"Are you okay?"

She held up the last cookie and gazed lovingly at it before placing it into the basket. "I am more than okay because the chocolate is happy. It's happy to be united with the peanut butter blossom."

"You take your baking seriously," he remarked, trying to figure out this chick.

She closed the basket, then switched out her apron for her coat.

"I'm keeping these with me. They're great to snack on," she said, ignoring him and pocketing the baggie with considerably fewer cinnamon gummy bears left inside.

"Are you ready to go?" he asked.

She stared at him blankly. "Go where?"

"To Kringle Acres. The retirement community where we're throwing a spaghetti dinner."

She gasped. "That's tonight?"

"Yeah, you made the schedule."

Bridget glanced around wildly. "Well, then we have to go!"

Was she messing with him?

"Have you forgotten to take your meds or something?" he asked, not kidding in the least.

That perplexed crinkle returned to her forehead. "Like vitamins? I took my multi-vitamin this morning."

He shook his head, giving up. If she wanted to play some bizarro game, he was not going to bite.

"Let's go. You probably need a little air."

They settled themselves inside the pickup truck. He had to get through this bullshit spaghetti thing, and then, he'd find a moment to talk with Tom and make his case.

He got the keys from the visor and started the car as Bridget bounced on the seat like a toddler in a bouncy house.

"It's jiggly in here, like Jell-O," she said with a wide grin.

"Can you try and focus? We need to figure out how to get to Kringle Acres," he said as he shifted the vehicle into gear and headed down the snow-packed road.

She opened the glove box, then gasped.

"What?" he shot back. Terrified as to what she might have found. Who knows what crazy shit people living in the sticks kept in their cars!

And it wasn't like he could get a good look. With hairpin twists and turns, the drive down Kringle Mountain was not for the faint of heart.

"It's a map! A map will tell us where to go!" she exclaimed as if she'd stumbled upon the Holy Grail.

"Yeah, that's exactly what a map is for, Bridget."

She spread it across the dash and tapped her finger on the crinkled paper. "Okay, take Mountain House Drive to Mistletoe Avenue, then turn right."

"That's the name?" he asked. "Mistletoe Avenue?"

This place really did milk the Christmas themes.

"Yeah! And look! There's even a reindeer crossing sign on the map!" she said, pointing to, yep, a bright yellow reindeer crossing sign.

"Why don't you roll down the window and get some fresh air," he suggested.

She clapped her hands. "Good idea! We can find out what the town smells like."

He glanced at her again. As the sun hung low in the sky, Bridget tilted her head and pointed her nose out the window, smelling the town like a golden retriever.

She was a relatively normal person a few hours ago. Was she still screwing with his head? Was this her baking persona? This flighty, head-in-the-clouds attitude? She'd gone toe to toe with him in the snarky banter department. He'd say something asinine, and she'd throw it right back at him. But this Bridget was not so much the vixen or the type A maid of honor. No, this Bridget was—

He caught a movement in his peripheral vision. "What are you doing now?"

She had her hand stretched in front of her face with her nose pressed to her palm.

"Hands do so many things, Soren," she answered.

"Yeah, they're your hands. They're supposed to do things."

"But so, so many things," she replied, then ate another bite-sized gummy bear as a grizzly bear-sized realization hit him.

Oh shit! This was not good!

He turned onto Mistletoe Avenue. With shops donning Christmas wreaths and candy cane decorations, the place looked like a holiday movie set.

"Are we in Santa's Village in the North Pole? This is just how I'd imagined it! Do you think we're going to see a real Christmas fairy here?" Bridget trilled.

"No, we're still in Kringle, Colorado," he answered, trying to figure out what the hell to do as the sign for the Kringle Acres

Retirement Community came into view. But when he went to turn into the parking area, two men, each with a white beard, raised their hands and signaled for them to stop.

He rolled down the driver's side window. "What's going on?"

"We're moving the cats around," a Santa lookalike replied as Soren did a double take.

Did he know this Santa?

Bridget leaned over to get a better look. "Kitty cats?"

Jesus! Not kitty cats again!

He gave the somewhat familiar man another look.

Could they have met?

No, there was no way he'd be acquainted with anyone in this damned place.

The other bearded man chuckled. "No, snowcats. You know, what you use to groom all that snow for the skiers on Kringle Mountain. The retired residents here take care of grooming the slopes and doing basic maintenance on the snowcats, right here, in the parking lot. We're moving Rudolph to the front. He's the snowcat with the big red light on top."

"Rudolph is a big cantankerous cat," Bridget exclaimed, then ate yet another gummy bear.

Soren pointed to her bag of candy. "Can I see that?"

She handed it over, and he leaned in and lowered his voice.

"I need you to act normal."

"I am normal," she whispered back, which, when whispered, sounded the exact opposite of normal.

He cleared his throat and turned back to the snowcat Santas. "Where should I park? We're here with the cookies and to help with the spaghetti dinner."

The man pointed down the road. "Over there, on the street! Just head inside. Tanner's in the kitchen now. He can show you around. You're the first volunteers to arrive."

Deck the goddamn halls! Thank God! And this Tanner was

going to have some explaining to do if his hunch about these freaking gummy bears was right.

He parked the truck, and Bridget bounced out the door with the basket of cookies.

"Hey! Wait for me!" he called.

She turned in circles as she walked, taking in the snowy, festive scenery.

"It's magical here. It wasn't like this when I was a kid. Look at all the decorations and lights. They're everywhere!"

"It is Christmas," he grumped.

"But this is like..." she trailed off, her words infused with wonder.

"Christmas on steroids?" he offered, taking in the town's decked out Main Street.

She shook her head. "No, I was going to say it's like Christmas on steroids."

Shit! The more she talked, the more certain he became.

They entered Kringle Acres to find the main vestibule empty —a godsend because if his hunch was right, she'd only be getting loopier.

"Bridget, remember, you need to act normal," he said, scanning the space.

"I told you, I am normal," she whispered again, which didn't make it sound any less *not-normal.*

"Hey, dude! Over here! I need to ask you something."

Soren looked up to find Tanner waving to them from the other side of the room. He took Bridget's hand and hurried toward the kid.

"I need to ask you something, too," he replied sternly.

"Come on. Let's get to the kitchen," Tanner said with a nervous cringe as he led them down a hallway that opened up into the retirement community's spacious kitchen.

The kid shifted his weight from foot to foot. "I was

wondering if I left something in the mountain house kitchen. Something I was working on."

Soren pulled the bag of gummy bears from his pocket. "These?"

Tanner's eyes went wide. "Where'd they all go?"

Bridget did another twirl. "I ate them. I was so hungry, and they were so delicious, and then the chocolate started talking to me. Oh, and I'm a normal person, right, Soren?"

Oh, for fuck's sake!

The kid's jaw dropped. "You let her eat all of those?"

He shook the bag in the guy's face. "I thought they were candy!"

"They are. Candy with a decent amount of THC mixed in."

Dammit! That was exactly what he'd feared when he'd smelled them.

"These are marijuana gummy bears?" he hissed, lowering his voice, then glanced over to find Bridget tapping a row of hanging pots, telling each cooking utensil that she was a normal person.

Heat rose to his cheeks. He'd been the only one with Bridget all day. If her sister saw her like this, God knows what she and the rest of the Abbotts would think. After the stripper incident, he was already walking a thin line with Tom and, if he wasn't careful, he was in jeopardy of damaging their relationship. He needed to be stealthy in his tactics. If anyone thought he'd had a hand in Bridget's stoned-out-of-her-mind condition, he'd be screwed.

He pinned the kid with his gaze. "Is she going to be okay?"

Tanner gave him an exceptionally hesitant shrug. "I mean technically, yes. Everything she ingested is organic. She's just had a lot. Like...a lot, a lot."

He blew out a tight breath, then checked on his baked vixen. She wasn't upset or in pain. She was just talking to a spatula.

He paced the length of the kitchen. "Should I take her to the hospital?"

"Take who to the hospital?"

Ah, shit! He recognized that haughty Harvard lilt.

Lori, Tom, and the rest of the Abbotts filed into the kitchen, with Bridget's sister sporting a scowl.

"Birdie, is everything okay?" she called.

Bridget looked up, and his heart jumped into his throat.

She grinned at the group. "Hey, everyone! I have hands, and I'm a normal person."

"What?" Denise asked, her gaze pinballing from Bridget to him.

Just as he'd expected! If they thought anything was wrong with Bridget, the blame would fall squarely on him.

"Are you feeling all right, dear?" Grace pressed.

Bridget set down the spatula. "I think I can smell color."

Grace shared a perplexed look with Scott.

"Hey, you all remember me. I'm Tanner from the kitchen at the mountain house," the kid said, breaking into the conversation and taking the attention off the baked bridesmaid.

"Living in the mountains of Colorado, I've seen people act like this before. I think this lady has altitude sickness. She probably needs some rest. Like, six to eight hours of solid rest," Tanner added, catching his eye.

He gave the guy a minute nod. What the hell was he supposed to do with her for six to eight hours?

"Scooter, you and Birdie have been together all afternoon. Has she been like this the whole time?" Lori asked, sounding very lawyerly. But the worried glance she shared with Tom was decidedly more concerned than upset.

"It just came on. I think she's exhausted. She didn't get much rest last night," he answered with a wave of his hand, going for casual as Bridget bent down and smelled a rolling pin.

"How would you know that?" Tom asked, sharing another look with his fiancée.

"Know what?"

"That she didn't get much rest," Tom pressed.

He parted his lips, wondering what verbal vomit would spew out of him when Bridget raised her hand like she was in third grade.

"I can answer that!" she chimed. "It's because—"

"Because you told me that you were a little sleepy when we were baking cookies," he interrupted, then turned to Lori. "I think your sister needs a little air and some rest."

Lori squeezed his hand as the mistrust in her eyes morphed into worry. "Thank you for keeping an eye on my sister, Scooter. I think you're right. Birdie, do you want us to take you back to the mountain house?"

Anxiety welled in his chest. He had to get Bridget out of there and away from these people. It was only a matter of time before somebody figured out that she wasn't suffering from altitude sickness.

He plastered on a grin and turned up the wattage. "There's no need for everyone to go. I've got the truck, and I know how important it is, especially to your sister, for you to put on the spaghetti dinner. Here are Bridget's cookies. I de-blossomed her, I mean, them—the cookies. I added the chocolate kisses to the peanut butter blossoms," he blathered, handing over the basket when Cole and Carly ran into the kitchen with Dan on their heels.

"Scooter! Birdie! There's a room full of Santa's helpers out there!" Carly called.

A grin stretched across Cole's face. "No Christmas fairies that I could see, but lots of Santas. Want to take a look? They're right outside!"

Crap! He didn't need more people seeing Bridget like this!

"That sounds really cool, but I'm going to take Birdie home because—"

"Because she's talking to an egg?" Carly interrupted, cocking her head to the side.

He looked over his shoulder to see that, yes, Bridget had found an egg and was, in fact, talking to it.

He crouched down to the kids' level. "Birdie's very tired, and she's acting a little loopy because we're up so high."

"High is right," Tanner muttered.

"What was that, son?" the judge asked, pinning the kid with his watchful gaze.

"I meant high, like elevation. Your bird lady has an elevation high," Tanner backtracked.

"You mean altitude sickness, right Tanner?" he corrected, hoping the guy caught the hint of urgency in his tone.

"Right! Totally! This is absolutely not chemically induced," Tanner chimed with a resolute nod.

Sweet burning sleigh bells. He was so screwed!

"I think I would like some air," Bridget said—to the fucking egg.

He went to her side and patted her arm. "Nobody needs to worry. I'll take care of Birdie and get her back to the mountain house—best man duties and all," he added, taking the egg from the baked bridesmaid and placing it back in the bowl with the others.

He pressed his hand to the small of her back, praying she didn't fall on her ass or bid goodbye to the cooking utensils. They'd made it a few steps before he glanced over his shoulder to see every Abbott, plus Lori, watching them in stunned silence.

"Please try and act normal," he whispered.

Bridget stopped in her tracks and looked back at the group. "Where are my manners! Goodbye, everyone! And don't worry, I'm totally normal."

"Let's get started making the spaghetti," Tanner called with a clap of his hands, blessedly shifting gears.

"We're not having spaghetti?" Bridget asked as they left the kitchen.

"No, not tonight."

She made a sad little puppy sound. "I told the egg that I'd make him a plate."

"The egg will be fine," he answered, taking her hand as they entered the main area, no longer empty and now occupied with about a dozen Santa-looking dudes.

"Holy Father Christmas!" Bridget exclaimed as he led her through the mass of white-bearded men.

How many obstacles could they encounter tonight?

"Is this where Christmas goes to die?" he mumbled.

"No, young man! It's where Christmas goes to retire. We're former members of the Fraternal Order of Real Bearded Santas," a Santa in a plaid shirt replied.

He looked around, taking in the sea of white beards and rosy cheeks.

That explained a hell of a lot—and who knew there was a Santa frat?

A naughty grin bloomed on Bridget's lips. "Santas, there's something you should know. This guy, right here—his name is Rudolph. But don't be fooled. He's no sweet red-nosed reindeer. He's been very, very naughty."

A Santa in a red turtleneck nodded. "Oh, we know. He's definitely on the naughty list."

"I am?" he blurted, taken aback.

Okay, there was no such thing as an omnipresent, all-knowing Santa. He knew this. But confronted by a gaggle of them left him off balance. He ran his hands through his hair, then blew out an exasperated breath when a cool rush of air washed over him, and the door to Kringle Acres slammed shut.

He glanced around.

Where was his stoner maid of honor?

A short Santa chuckled. "You better go find her, young fella."

The turtleneck Santa nodded. "Yep, that young lady is as high as a kite, and there's no telling the trouble she could get into in Kringle."

"How do you know?" he exclaimed.

"We're Santas. We know things," the short Santa replied and tapped his head.

"And her pupils are the size of papayas," the plaid shirt Santa added.

"Shit, I mean shoot! You're right! I need to find her," he answered, snapping out of the Santa haze.

He busted out the door and looked up and down the street. Thank Christ, she hadn't gone far. He jogged half a block and found her staring into a darkened storefront.

"There's nothing sadder than an empty bakery," she said with her nose pressed to the glass.

"Yeah, it's too bad," he answered, trying to get his bearings, then nearly fell onto his ass when he saw the awning for the Cupid Bakery.

Sweet Christmas cupcakes!

Undoubtedly, this was one of the Cupid Bakeries he was in the process of liquidating.

He crossed his arms. "We should get going. The car's back the other way."

But Bridget wasn't listening. She gasped and pointed down the street.

"No, Soren, we can't. I just saw one," she exclaimed, breaking into a run.

He trailed behind her. Weren't stoners supposed to be chill? Whatever Tanner put in those gummy bears had his vixen raring to go.

"What did you see?" he called as they came upon the town square.

Surrounded by evergreens and twinkling lights, Bridget skidded to a halt.

"Soren, just look! It's a gathering of Christmas fairies."

It was easy to mistake what they'd happened upon as a gathering of fairies. Children stood together holding sparklers, and in the darkness, the glittering light created a shimmering, ethereal halo, like something out of a fanciful fairy tale.

Bridget leaned against him. "My dad used to tell us that the snow fairies traveled around as tiny balls of light. It's too bad we left the egg behind. He would have loved to have seen this."

"Is that right?" he asked, using all his strength not to wrap his arm around her.

"It's magical," she said, staring up at him.

He stared at this beautiful enigma of a woman. "It is."

She stroked his cheek, and he closed his eyes. Could this be a dream? Or perhaps his sandwich was laced with something, and he was on a psychedelic trip right alongside her. Whatever it was, he was losing control.

"What's that smell?" she asked, breaking their connection.

He inhaled. Whatever it was, it smelled amazing.

"Soren, it's funnel cake," she exclaimed with more enthusiasm than funnel cake deserved.

And then it was back to the running business.

Bridget took off like a shot toward a table teeming with the sweet treat, then swiped a funnel cake and kept moving like the Grinch pilfering Whoville.

"Hey! That's five dollars," called a lady manning the table.

He pulled out his wallet. "Sorry, my friend is a big fan of funnel cake." He glanced over to find Bridget covered in a white floury substance and going to town on the sugar-covered dough.

The woman gasped and pressed her hand to her chest.

He stared at his vixen, feeling an odd sense of pride. "Yeah, she's a really big fan of funnel cakes. She's also suffering from altitude sickness."

The woman raised an eyebrow. "Is that so?"

He shrugged and shook his head. "No, she's baked out of her mind, but that's the story we're sticking with tonight," he said as Bridget waved him over, and the funnel cake lady's jaw dropped.

"Take a bite. It's like eating happiness," she said, ripping off a piece and holding it to his lips.

"I don't know," he answered.

"Just one bite," she tempted, eyes twinkling.

He opened his mouth, powerless to say no. Granted, she was completely out of it, but no one had ever looked at him the way she did—like she saw him.

"Bridget, we need to get back to the mountain house," he said, swallowing the bite as well as the emotions rising to the surface.

"Not yet! Look! There's a photo booth. Let's take a picture, and then we can leave Christmas Fairy Land. Deal?" she replied, then crammed the last bit of funnel cake into her mouth with the gusto of a truck driver.

He bit back a grin. "With charm like that, how can a guy say no?" he replied as she took his hand as if it was second nature, then pulled him into the snug booth.

She stared at the instructions pinned to the wall. "It takes three pictures. We can do surprised faces, happy faces, then one more. But I'm not sure what the last picture should be. Ready?" she asked, pressing the button to start their photo session.

The screen counted down with a ping.

Three.

Two.

One.

"Surprised faces!" she chimed, and yes, he made a stupid surprised face.

The camera flashed, and she leaned into him.

"Okay, happy faces next. Get ready!"

She looked up at him and grinned that sun, moon, and stars smile as the camera flashed, but frowned as soon as the timer for the last photo started counting down.

"Last one. What should we do?"

The timer pinged.

Three.

He held her gaze.

Two.

Unable to stop, he cupped her cheek in his hand.

One.

His heart took over, and he pressed his lips to hers. For a fraction of a second, he'd feared that she'd pull away. But relief flooded his system when she hummed a sweet, sated sound as he deepened the kiss. The pop of the flash and the mechanical whirr of the booth printing their pictures buzzed in the background. This was risky. No, not risky. It was damned stupid to lock lips with Bridget Dasher, but he couldn't resist. Her cinnamon vanilla scent entranced him into a dreamlike holiday haze. It transported him. It altered him. Warm and soothing, her kisses tasted like sunshine and s'mores. She stroked his cheek, then pulled back slowly and stared into his eyes.

"Soren," she whispered. The silly, playfulness in her tone was gone and replaced with an air of haunting seriousness.

"Yes."

She glanced away. "Do I seem stuck to you?"

"What do you mean?"

"Like, stuck in my life."

"I don't know much about your life," he replied, hating that he wished he did.

She nodded, then reached down and removed the photo strip from the tray.

"When you kiss me, it feels like you know everything," she remarked softly as she stared at the pictures.

"You're tired, Bridget. That's all."

But it wasn't. Not even close.

"Garrett said that I'm stuck—that I'm not living a real life. But I made a promise and promises matter. You believe that, don't you?"

He thought of his parents and all their empty promises, then caressed her cheek, reveling in her honesty.

"They should matter."

She handed him the photo strip. "Can you hold on to this? I feel a little woozy."

He folded it carefully, making sure not to crease any of the photos, then slid it into his wallet.

She stared up at the ceiling of the booth. "I just don't think he saw me. He'd look at me, of course, but maybe there wasn't anything to see. The Abbotts, they see you, don't they, Soren?"

This got deep quick.

"We should go, Bridget."

They did see him, but so did she.

She just didn't know it.

And he couldn't let her know, not now. Not ever. Because if things went the way he wanted, after this time in Kringle, he'd never see her again.

And, despite the knot in his stomach at the thought of that prospect, he needed to start acting like it.

BRIDGET

*B*ridget pulled the pillow over her eyes and groaned. Her head pounded. Her mouth tasted like she'd binged on straw and powdered sugar like some kind of Candy Land farm animal. Blindly, she reached over to the side table to grab her phone to check the time when her wrist bumped a plate.

But she didn't have a plate on her bedside table—at home.

"Be careful! You'll get crumbs everywhere!" came a familiar, irritable warning.

She shot up and immediately regretted the move as the pounding intensified. Cradling her head in her hands, she brushed back her bangs and cracked open her eyes.

"Good afternoon, Birdie," purred the last person in the entire world she wanted to see moments after waking with bed head and morning breath.

But, of course, there was no escaping Soren "Scooter" Traeger Rudolph.

She tried to orient herself. Her memories of last night were foggy at best. What was the last thing she remembered? She racked her brain, but all she got was a jumble of disjointed images like a half-completed puzzle. She wasn't even sure she was awake. This could be another dream.

"It's afternoon? And what are you doing here?" she replied with raspy morning, or in this case, afternoon voice.

"We're sharing a room," he replied without an ounce of emotion.

A room? The last clear memory she'd had was the two of them leaving the mountain house.

She looked around wildly. "Where are we?"

"Where else? The place on Kringle mountain."

"When did we get here?" she pressed as the sleep haze lifted.

Soren paced across the room. "I brought you back last night. You weren't feeling well."

She shook her head, hoping the pieces of last night would fall into place. But it didn't work. She glanced around to assess the situation.

She was in bed, and Soren was with her.

Oh no!

Did she sleep with him again?

She scrambled to pull the covers over her body in a flash of misplaced modesty.

"You're wearing pajamas, Bridget. You don't have to do that," he said, all trademark dark and moody.

She glanced down at her Christmas pajamas, covered in prancing reindeer and smiling Santas. Her cheeks burned with embarrassment.

Welp, Soren got the whole package today: bed head, bad breath, and a ridiculous sleep-set. She glanced at the red-nosed reindeer on her left boob. These pajamas looked like something a toddler would wear.

And hello, holiday pajama fail—so much for being not the average vixen!

"For your information, I bought these pajamas for the trip as a joke," she said, going for indignant.

Soren cocked a skeptical eyebrow. "That's your story?"

She rolled her eyes. "I don't remember much of anything that happened last night." She ran her hands through her tangle of dark hair as snippets from the evening flashed in a confusing cluster of events. "We made cookies, and then there were Santas, and fairies, and cake? Is that right? And what happened at the spaghetti dinner?"

Soren started to speak, but she raised her hand and stopped him.

"You said it's afternoon, right?"

"Yes," he answered, raising an eyebrow.

Dammit! With all the wedding prep still left to do, she didn't have a second to lose!

She sprang out of bed, another poor choice, especially with the sheet wrapped around her leg. Wobbling forward, she put out her hands to break her fall when Soren caught her.

"You need to slow down and eat something with a modicum of nutrition." He helped her stand, then lifted the lid off a plate revealing scrambled eggs, toast, and bacon. And next to it, a giant glass of orange juice.

Her stomach growled something ferocious as she snapped up the fork and went at it like a starved animal.

"Sorry, I'm so hungry," she said between bites of egg and toast.

He waved her off. "That's nothing compared to what you did to a funnel cake last night."

She took a bite of bacon. "There was really a funnel cake?"

"Yep."

The food jumpstarted her brain, and she glanced at her ridiculous pajamas. "I don't remember changing into these."

His gaze flicked to the plate. "You didn't."

"Lori helped me?" she asked, but the knot in her belly indicated that while her mind was fuzzy, her body was pretty sure that her sister had nothing to do with her outfit change.

A muscle ticked on Soren's perfect chiseled face. "No."

"You did this?" she blurted.

"Who else, Bridget?" he threw back.

She gasped and pointed at him with the piece of bacon. "You saw me naked?"

He cocked his head to the side with a smug quirk of his lips.

The creep! He was supposed to be her one-night stand—her one night to frolic in the land of *Vixenhood*. Instead, he'd become her roommate.

She took an angry bite of bacon. "Never mind. Do not answer that."

What was going on with this guy anyway? More Jekyll and Hyde hijinks. When they were making cookies, he'd seemed different. He'd danced. He'd held her in his arms and kissed her.

And holy sleigh bells, when their lips met, she'd felt weightless, like a snowflake drifting in the air.

The heat in his gaze had burned through her. The intensity of those green cat-like eyes had left her stunned and drowning in another Birdie and Scooter lip lock free-for-all.

And that was yet another mistake.

She had to get it together when it came to this guy. He wasn't her friend, even though, in the strangest of ways, they'd connected in a confusing, convoluted alternate universe kind of way.

Is it normal to hate a guy but want to tear off his clothes and ride him until you're cross-eyed from multiple orgasms?

"Swallow, Bridget."

Her eyes popped open.

"The bacon, in your mouth. You've been chewing it the whole time you've been spacing out," he added.

Bacon?

She swallowed, but not because he told her to do it. "I didn't space out."

"You did."

Maybe she did. But she wasn't about to admit that she'd daydreamed about screwing his brains out.

Because that wasn't going to happen...again.

"I have to take a shower. I need to get to that bakery in the village and start making the wedding cake. I'm already behind," she said, shifting gears.

From this point on, there would be no time spent on silly Soren sexual fantasies. Lori's wedding was in three days. That was the priority.

"Tom and Lori left this morning to get started on the cakes," he commented.

She frowned. "They did?"

"Yeah, Lori said she knows your grandmother's recipe for the red velvet cake, and Tom insisted on helping," he finished with a scowl.

But she didn't have time to dwell on his Tom obsession. Shame tore through her chest. All her planning for the perfect wedding and, somehow, she was still getting it wrong. She'd promised Lori that she'd take care of everything, just like her grandma Dasher would have wanted.

Instead, Lori was baking her own cake!

Add another failure to the Birdie life scoreboard.

She chugged down the glass of orange juice, then searched the space for the bathroom. Just as she'd remembered when she'd come here as a girl, the rooms were tidy little suites with rustic furnishings, characteristic of a mountain getaway. She spied the tub and shower combo past an opened door and peeled off her top, then shrieked and covered her breasts.

"I forgot you were here!" she blurted.

Soren resurrected his scowl. "How? We're having a damn conversation."

"I have a lot on my mind," she replied, adjusting her arms to hide her bare breasts.

That muscle in his jaw ticked again as his gaze slid down the length of her body. "Do you want some privacy?"

She shook her head, ignoring the crackle of sexual tension between them. She cleared her throat as his wandering eyes migrated to meet her gaze.

Bridget Dasher, forget the tingles and figure out what happened last night!

"I need answers, and I need them now. You're coming with me," she commanded as best as one commands half-naked.

His jaw dropped. "Into the shower?"

Shirtless, she shimmied past him. "Of course not! Just stand outside the door with your back turned."

"You're kidding! You know I've seen everything—and tasted most everything," he replied with a hint of that wolfish grin that had made her toes curl the night she'd met him.

Truth time. Did she want him to leave?

Yes?

No?

Definitely, yes! But she needed answers. He had to stay, *not* because she liked the way his eyes devoured her body. No, he needed to remain in the room only because she required basic information.

Nothing more. That tingling sensation was not a sexual reaction. It was chills. There must be a draft in the room.

She cleared her throat, going all business. "I need to know exactly what happened last night, and you're going to tell me. Now, turn around and let me get in the shower."

"Fine," he grumbled.

She kicked out of her pajama bottoms, then leaped into the tub and pulled the shower curtain closed.

"Okay, I'm in. Shut your eyes."

"My back is to you. Why do I need to close my eyes?"

"Because you do!" she huffed as she turned on the water, then screamed as a frigid spray peppered her body.

The shower curtain flew back, and Soren peered in. "Are you okay? Are you hurt?"

She grabbed the curtain. "Get out! It's only cold water."

"Then don't scream!" he griped, all Grinch meets Scrooge.

He was especially cantankerous today.

And where did she come up with *cantankerous*? Who used that word?

She fiddled with the temperature control, and the water went from icy cold to toasty warm. "I need you to start from the beginning. I can't remember anything about the spaghetti dinner."

"That makes sense. You weren't there."

She pulled back the curtain. "Why was I *not* there?"

"Can I turn around?" he asked, irritation pricking each word.

"Yes, tell me what's going on!"

The twitch on his cheek made him look like he wanted to laugh, but he'd gone all broody sex god.

No, not sex god! Broody creep who wanted to derail Lori's wedding.

No. More. Sex. Thoughts.

"Well, Birdie. I won't mince words," he began with a nice helping of jackass.

"Just tell me what happened, Scooter!"

"Fine. Here's the short version. You were stoned out of your mind last night."

She dropped the curtain, then recovered, and tugged it back into place. "I was not!"

"You were. Remember those gummy bears?"

"Yeah."

"They weren't just sugar and whatever the hell you use to make gummy candy. They were Tanner's special recipe made with, in my opinion, way too much THC. You know what that is, don't you? It's what produces the high in cannabis."

THC? Cannabis?

"Like, pot?" she questioned.

"That's right. Think of it this way. Now, you can change your nickname from Birdie to Maryjane."

She closed the curtain, then opened a travel-sized shampoo and started in on washing her hair.

Stoned?

She could barely believe it. Those gummy bears did have an interesting flavor to them. Still, never in a million years would she have thought they were laced with psychoactive compounds.

She stood under the spray as the bubbles from the shampoo pooled at her feet. "Why was there THC in the gummy bears?"

"I don't know. It's legal here in Colorado," he huffed.

"But why didn't Tanner tell us?" she asked, popping open the conditioner with a bit more force than necessary. She was damned angry.

"I'm guessing that even though it's legal, he keeps it on the down-low."

She shook her head. "Dabbles in agriculture, my ass."

"And you had a lot. You ate almost the entire bag. The kid was a little freaked out when we got to Kringle Acres," Soren added.

She tore back the curtain. "So, we did make it there?"

"Oh yeah."

She closed the curtain, then shut her eyes, thinking.

"I remember seeing my sister, Tom, and his entire family... and a whole bunch of Santas. Is that right?"

"That is correct. And you sniffed a rolling pin, talked to an egg, and stole a funnel cake," Soren continued.

She stared at the mini water tornado spiraling down the drain, pathetically apropos of her life, as the fuzzy pieces of the night came back to her.

A camera.

Dots of sparkling lights dancing in the darkness.

Fairies.

And...oh crap!

A spasm of anxiety rippled through her chest like a bomb hitting a pool of water. "The Abbotts must hate me! Lori must be livid!" she said, lowering herself to sit in the tub under the spray.

Footsteps caught her attention as Soren entered the bathroom, his outline visible through the shower curtain.

"Nobody knows you were baked. At least, I don't think they do. Tanner told them you were suffering from altitude sickness, and then I got you out of there," he said, his voice taking on a gentler note.

She rested her head on her knees. "Do people with altitude sickness talk to eggs and steal cake?"

"That would be funnel cake, which you wolfed down like a champ. And no, people stoned out of their minds talk to food and engage in petty theft."

She glanced at his form on the curtain. "Why did you help me?"

He ran his hands through his hair. "What do you mean?"

She sighed as rivulets of water trailed down her body. "Isn't this what you wanted—for the Abbotts to hate the Dasher sisters, and cast us off, so you can run off with your best friend and a gaggle of bimbos?"

Soren didn't reply right away, and she glanced up to see the man's outline had slumped a fraction.

"I want Tom to know that he doesn't have to make any rash decisions," he answered with a somber edge.

"By ruining his wedding?" she shot back.

He straightened. "By whatever means possible."

She stood and wiped the water out of her eyes as another piece of last night's puzzle came to her. "You kissed me yesterday."

"Yes, but only because you were molesting a Hershey kiss, and I had to make you stop," he grumbled but not as grumbly as usual.

She shook her head, her gaze locked on his form. "No, I remember that kiss. There was another one."

She closed her eyes as a flash and a pop echoed through her mind.

"We also kissed in a photo booth," he conceded.

"That's where we were," she said as the evening came into focus.

"It was a lapse in judgment," he answered, still without the usual bite.

She stared down at the swirling water. "We seem to have a lot of those lapses."

He touched the shower curtain. "We do."

There he was—the man who'd made love to her with such tenderness, who'd held her in his arms and twisted her hair between his fingers before she'd fallen asleep.

She slid her fingertip up the shower curtain but stopped just below where his index finger rested. Beads of water ran down the slick surface as they stood inches apart. She should detest the man on the other side of the curtain. And she did hate his intentions when it came to Tom and Lori's wedding, but there had to be more.

Or not.

The knot in her belly twisted.

Was there more to Garrett or even Gaston? Hadn't she hoped that her connection to them was real, or at least, based on mutual respect, only to learn, that in both cases, she was just some *nice girl* who didn't make the cut?

Why did she always assume there was more to others and never more to herself?

You're the most stifled, stuck person I know. I feel sorry for you, Bridget.

Jagged and rough, Garrett's words cut through her.

But now was not the time to dwell on her failings, on all the missed opportunities and forgotten dreams—all the should haves and could haves.

This was who she was and perhaps all she'd ever be.

But one thing was certain. She needed to stick to the plan and make Lori's wedding a success. Grandma Dasher had entrusted her with her little sister's welfare, and she couldn't fail the woman who had taken them in when there was no one else.

She drew back her hand, then turned off the water. With newfound resolve coursing through her veins, she was ready to do whatever it took to get the job done when a ping rang out in the bedroom.

"Is that my phone?" she called.

"No, it's mine. And it's a text from Tom."

She wiped the water from her eyes.

Game on.

"*W*hat does the text say?" she asked, doing her best to keep her tone light and breezy.

She could *not* let on that anytime these two communicated, it set her pulse racing.

"Tom says to tell you that the cakes are in the freezer. Do you know what that means? Are you making ice cream cakes or funnel cakes that require refrigeration? Why the hell would you need a freezer for a cake?" Soren grumbled.

A cake question? That's it?

Score a point for Team Dasher!

She released a relieved breath, ignored his *Scroogyness*, and reached for a towel. "It's easier to frost a cake when it's cool. Lori knows almost as much as I do when it comes to baking."

"Is that what you're doing today? Frosting cakes?" he called from the bedroom.

She towel-dried her hair, then twisted it into a damp bun. "It's what *we're* doing today," she answered, making sure to add a touch of vixen to her tone.

"We?" he bit out.

"Yes, Mr. Best Man, my sister and the Abbotts are spending

the day in the village. There's ice skating and all sorts of activities to do there while *we* work on the wedding cake."

He groaned. "The wedding isn't until Christmas Eve. That's three days away!"

"Right, and I need to make sure the cake is ready. Plus, I'm preparing a croquembouche for the rehearsal dinner, and that's no small feat. So, we have to get the wedding cake done a couple of days early," she answered, wrapping a towel around her body.

"*Croak-um-what*?" he exclaimed.

"It's a French dessert, and it's on the schedule. Now, open my bag and hand me my bra, a pair of panties, my black leggings, and the red flannel shirt dress."

"You want mé to get into your bag?" he griped.

Touchy, touchy!

"What else are you doing?" she threw back.

"Fine!" he huffed.

She tightened the towel and peeked out the half-opened door and found him holding up two of her G-strings, one black and one red.

"What are you doing with my underwear?"

"I'm deciding which ones match the bra," he answered.

"Just pick a pair!" she snapped.

"I don't spend a lot of time picking out women's undergarments. I'm more of a rip-them-off kind of guy."

She knew that.

"Go with the black," she said, waving for him to hurry the hell up.

"No, red," he countered, gathering the items she'd requested.

She pinned him with her gaze. "Are we going to fight about everything?"

"Don't you like fighting with me?" he answered, handing her the pile of clothing.

She channeled her make-believe vixen. "I'd like it if you got on board with *this wedding*."

"What have I actually done to hamper *this wedding*?" he threw back.

That was easy.

She narrowed her gaze. "Hookers."

His lips curled into an amused, surly expression. "They were dancers. What besides that?"

She racked her brain. "Nothing I can think of off the top of my head. And that's how it's going to stay because—"

"Because you're not letting me out of your sight," he finished.

She dressed, then left the bathroom to find her boots. "Exactly."

"You look nice," he said, then crossed his arms then looked away as if he regretted paying her a compliment.

She tucked a damp lock of hair behind her ear, suddenly feeling exposed—no, not exposed, seen.

"Thank you."

Whatever this was, it boomeranged between loathing, tenderness, and straight-up animal attraction. The buzz from going toe to toe with him made her head spin. It gave her a feisty sharpness as if she really were a vixen.

But she wasn't. A lifetime of settling and playing it safe proved that.

She had to endure him for a few days, and then what? There wasn't a future for them.

A knock on their suite door knocked her back into reality.

She put on her coat and grabbed her bag as Soren opened the door. He glanced back at her, then hurried into the hall to speak to whoever was there.

She followed him out. "What's going on?"

"Hey, bird lady, I wanted to check on you and apologize about the gummies."

Ah, Tanner, the drug dealer.

"You can't leave those things lying around like that. What if one of the children found them?" she chided.

He hung his head with a sad, puppy dog nod. "You're right."

"Who eats those things around here anyway?" she asked as the trio walked down the hall and entered the main room.

"The retired Santas and Mrs. Clauses," he announced proudly.

"They do?"

"Totally! Imagine spending like forty years of your life being a Santa and Mrs. Claus at a mall in Sheboygan. You'd want to chill out in retirement, too."

Soren met her gaze. "The kid's got a point."

"So, Kringle is now a town with a bunch of stoned Mr. and Mrs. Clauses?" she queried.

"No, they don't get blitzed and go all mental like you did. They eat one or two to take the edge off."

Blitzed like you? How about unintentionally drugged?

She rubbed her temples. The shower had helped quell her pounding head, but talking to Tanner reignited her throbbing frontal lobe.

"Is there something you needed? We're on our way out," Soren said as he put on his coat.

"I was coming to tidy up and pick up your plate."

Bridget reached for the doorknob, then froze. "Did you make my breakfast, Tanner?"

"Sure did," the guy answered, back to all grins.

"You didn't do anything to it, did you?" She turned to Soren. "Am I going to be stoned all day? I have way too much to do to be talking to eggs and stealing baked goods."

Tanner put up his hands defensively. "Don't worry, bird lady! I didn't add any special ingredients to your food."

Soren's smirk was back. "Looks like you get to spend the day with me stone-cold sober," he teased as they left the mountain house and headed toward the truck.

This man! Full disclosure. If he wasn't such a wedding wrecking prick, she would have laughed. He was a curmudgeon, but he wasn't totally without a sense of humor.

He opened her door, and she got in the truck. It was a sweet gesture, old-fashioned chivalry like something her grandpa Dasher used to do.

Did she like it?

It didn't matter.

She pulled her planner and a pen from her bag as Soren started the truck, and they headed toward the village.

To Do:

Finish the wedding cake

That was a must! Her plan was to recreate their parents' three-tiered red velvet cake with buttercream frosting. It wasn't a technically difficult recipe. She'd created far more intricate designs at the pâtisserie. But she had to get it right. She and Lori had made red velvet cake dozens of times with their grandmother in the two years after their parents had died. Baking had become a way to remember the good times. The simple act of mixing, combining, and creating had allowed her to funnel her despair, anger, and sadness into something sweet, beautiful, and delicious.

She might have been very much alone since Lori went to college, but she was never lonely when she baked.

"We're here," Soren said, cutting the ignition.

"Already?" she asked, sliding the planner into her bag.

"Yeah, you hum to yourself when you're concentrating," he added.

For a detached jerk, he noticed quite a bit.

"I must have gotten lost in my thoughts," she replied, then glanced out the window at the bakery and gasped.

"What?" Soren asked.

"It's a Cupid Bakery. The one in Dallas closed not too long ago. Gaston was elated."

"Who's Gaston? Another boyfriend?" Soren asked, his words taking on an irritated inflection.

"No way! He's my ex-boss—a real pompous jackass. You two would get along great," she added as butterflies fluttered in her belly, waiting for Soren's pithy retort. Except he wasn't biting.

"If it's where we're stuck today, we might as well get to it," he muttered under his breath.

A gal could get whiplash reacting to his mood swings.

She got out of the truck and spied Lori and Tom inside the bakery. Her sister had her arms around Tom's neck while his encircled her waist. They were the picture of happiness when, as if on cue, Tom leaned in and pressed a kiss to her sister's lips.

Bridget sighed as a contented warmth spread through her body.

Tom loved her sister. From the first minute she'd met him, she couldn't help noticing that he looked at Lori the same adoring way her father used to look at her mother.

She glanced at Soren and found him glowering in full-on sourpuss mode. If he couldn't be happy for them, then that was his issue.

She opened the door to the bakery as a bell on the hinge rang out their arrival.

The couple pulled apart, their cheeks growing pink.

"I hope you did a little dancing along with all that kissing for the red velvet cakes," she teased as she and Soren entered the quaint shop.

Lori's blush deepened. "Yes, Birdie, I make Tom dance with me no matter what we bake."

"And it always turns out delicious," Tom added with a kiss to Lori's temple.

"Speaking of delicious," Lori went on. "What did you do to those peanut butter blossoms?"

Bridget stiffened. "What do you mean?"

"They're always good. But last night, they were absolutely divine. I've never seen people scarf down cookies as fast as they did at Kringle Acres," Lori continued.

"My entire family was raving about them," Tom added.

Oh no!

She didn't add any special gummy bears to the batter, did she?

"I followed Grandma's recipe. But I can tell you that there was absolutely no substance that would cause a psychotropic response in those cookies." She looked to Soren. "Was there?"

He dropped the jackass vibe. "No, those cookies were plain old cookies."

"But you danced when you baked them, right?" Lori pressed.

Bridget nodded, really hoping the peanut butter wasn't pot butter if that was even a thing.

"We did."

"We?" her sister questioned.

"Yeah, me and Soren."

Tom's eyes went wide. "You got Scooter to dance?"

Her gaze bounced between Lori and her fiancé. The last thing she wanted was for them to think anything was going on between her and the worst best man.

"Yes, we danced. And that's all we did. Just dancing. Nothing else. No hanky-panky. Nothing even remotely close to hanky-panky."

Why was she saying hanky-panky so many times? She pressed her lips together, vowing to never repeat the words again.

"Why would there be any *hanky-panky*? And who says that?" Lori replied, sharing a puzzled look with Tom.

She needed to do some damage control...and fast.

"Not me, and certainly, not him. Soren, Scooter...whatever you want to call this cantankerous man. He doesn't use the word or participate in hanky-panky either," she answered, unable to stop the rush of verbal vomit.

Soren stared down at her. "Are you okay? Did you get into the gummy bears again?"

"Birdie, are you feeling better today?" Tom asked, blessedly changing the conversation's trajectory.

She plastered on a grin. "I feel much better today. Thanks for asking."

"We looked in on you last night, but you were fast asleep," Lori added, then turned to Soren. "And thank you for keeping an eye on my sister. Did you get the cookies? We left a few for you on a plate."

Soren glanced away. "Yeah, I got them."

That's what that plate was doing on the bedside table!

"You ate my cookies?" she asked Mr. You-Don't-Get-Abs-Like-These-Eating-Baked-Goods.

"There wasn't much else to do," he mumbled.

"Scooter pulled up a chair next to the bed and fell asleep watching over you," Tom said with the hint of a grin.

She pinned her Grinch with her gaze. "You did?"

"Don't you need to frost a cake?" he replied, keeping his features infuriatingly neutral.

This indifferent jackass business wasn't working on her anymore. She'd seen his passionate side. He was capable of so much more. Why did he fall into this cavalier asshat groove?

"The cakes are ready to go, Birdie. And I want to record as you frost them. You're like a magician with that spatula," Lori said, cutting short her little staring contest with Soren.

Bridget frowned. "Why would you want to do that?"

"I follow these baking blogs, and, Birdie, you're better than all of them."

Bridget waved her off. "You may be biased, little sister."

"I'm not! Tom and I watch those baking shows and—"

"And Lori is constantly saying that you can do it better," Tom replied, finishing Lori's sentence.

Soren stared at his BFF like the guy had ten heads. "You watch baking shows?"

"It's crazy relaxing, man. You should try it," Tom replied, wrapping his arm around Lori.

Lori leaned into her fiancé. "I still can't believe you haven't opened up your own shop. Birdie, you'd be amazing."

Bridget went over to the sink, washed her hands, then plucked an apron from a hook on the wall, ignoring the comment.

Amazing?

No, she didn't have what it took to be amazing. Amazing meant taking risks and putting it all on the line. And that...that wasn't who she was. She'd been tasked with Lori's welfare since she was a teenager, and that's when her dreams had moved to the back burner.

Dreams wouldn't pay the rent.

No, she played it safe.

"Hypothetically, what would you do if you had your own bakery?"

Soren had posed the question—surprisingly enough.

She mulled it over as she put on the apron, then opened the large refrigerator. It was stocked with butter, eggs, and heavy whipping cream. Dan and Delores had delivered on making sure she had everything she needed, plus a whole lot more.

"The butter's out and softened," her sister said, taking out her phone.

Bridget nodded as she gathered the rest of the ingredients to make the buttercream frosting, and suddenly, she wasn't worried about the brooding Soren or pulling off the perfect wedding. No, here, with her ingredients and the scent of cake in the air, the answer to Soren's question came together in her mind.

She glanced around the cozy shop. It was a shame Cupid Bakery was going out of business. Anyone could tell the equipment and space were in good shape. The bakery chain wasn't going under due to lack of care or cutting corners, and the couple who started the business were legends in the baking world.

But what did they do wrong?

Combining sugar and water, she prepared a simple syrup on the stove as she chewed on this question. Her best ideas came when she was baking. She went to the mixer and added the butter, watching carefully to get it smooth, like her grandma Dasher had taught her, before incorporating the powdered sugar, vanilla, and heavy whipping cream to create the perfect buttercream frosting.

She picked up a wooden spoon and gave the fluffy mixture a stir to feel for the correct texture. Satisfied with the consistency, she fell into the familiar routine of assembling a wedding cake, then glanced up to find Soren watching her.

"Well, what would you do?" he prodded. He was still in grouch mode, but curiosity flashed in those cat-like eyes of his.

"If I had my own bakery," she began. "I'd make sure to be dialed into the community. That's important, but it's not all you need. Word of mouth can only get you so far. You'd want to have a signature dessert available year-round, as well as new creations to pique continuous interest. And in this day and age, a vibrant social media presence is required. The bakery should become an extension of the bakers, and that personality should shine through. And I'd make sure to have a robust online sales presence. That's what Cupid Bakery did wrong."

She was in the zone as she gathered the dowels that would hold the three stacked layers in place as well as the cake turntable, an offset spatula, and a bench scraper to keep the frosting even and smooth. She barely registered Tom's presence as he set the cooled bottom layer of red velvet cake next to her. Carefully, she removed it from the cake pan, cut off the top to level the layer, set the deep red slab of red velvet onto the cake turntable, then applied the simple syrup with a pastry brush.

With her tools assembled and her mind focused, she went to work frosting the bottom layer.

"What do you mean when you say, 'that's what Cupid Bakery did wrong'?"

Soren again.

She kept her gaze locked on the cake as she spun the turntable and evenly applied the crumb layer of frosting. "I mean, they were a great bakery, but they only had one stream of revenue—in-store purchases. To be profitable, you need multiple streams. You should branch out."

Tom brought her the cooled center and then the top layer. She glanced over to find Lori with her phone out, filming her. And as she worked, she began explaining what she was doing and why she was doing it just like her grandmother.

Always use a simple syrup to lock in moisture, especially if you're making your cake a few days in advance.

Apply a crumb layer of frosting to create a smooth, even surface.

Be generous with your frosting—for many, it's their favorite part.

Use that freezer! The cooler the cake, the easier the frosting application.

The tips and tricks she'd learned from her grandmother flowed from her lips, and muscle memory took over. It was as if Grandma Dasher was standing next to her, humming a holiday tune, and looking on as she assembled Lori's wedding cake. Every flick of her wrist and each swipe of the spatula moved her closer to confectionary perfection as the cake table rotated in a mesmerizing twirl of buttercream-covered precision.

"Wow! That looks so good, Birdie! I want to eat it right now!"

Bridget blinked as a child's voice pulled her from her buttercream-scented trance. She glanced up to find Tom's entire family watching her.

"When did you all get here?"

"About twenty minutes ago," Denise answered.

"Watching you work is like observing a sculptor," Grace remarked as Scott nodded.

The children scurried across the shop and over to the worktable.

"We went ice skating in the village, and I got to see Santa, like fifty of them! But not one Christmas fairy," Cole reported with a little frown.

"They are very mysterious and usually don't like big crowds," Lori offered.

"Do they come out at night?" Cole asked, perking up.

Bridget shared a furtive glance with her sister. "I think that's the time they like the best, especially when there's not a lot of people around."

"Got it!" Cole replied with a resolute nod.

"It's quite exciting in the village today. There were many families out and about," the judge added.

"It sounds like you all had a great afternoon!" Bridget said, tossing the group a quick nod as she checked each cake layer.

Russell sauntered behind the counter, glanced at the cake, then shot a quick look at her breasts. "The town is all right. Not the best singles scene, if you know what I mean," the guy remarked, then pointed at Soren. "Since you and I are the swinging bachelors in the group, we should check out the nightlife here in Kringle. I did meet a couple of lovely ladies who said they're in town on business for the next few nights."

"We'll see, Russ," Soren answered, sharing a look with Tom.

Ugh!

It was bad enough keeping Soren in check. She did not need the handsy uncle making trouble, too.

Carly tugged on her apron. "How did you make that big wedding cake, Birdie?"

She pointed to each tier. "It's just three different sized layers all stacked up. It takes practice and a lot of patience. Do you want to help me add a little more frosting?"

The little girl chewed her lip. "What if I mess up Aunt Lori and Uncle Tom's cake?"

She handed Carly the spatula. "That's the great thing about frosting. You can always add a little more because it all smooths out, and in the end, it just gets sweeter."

"Our grandma Dasher used to say that," Lori added.

Could that be what Soren needed—a little or a hell of a lot more frosting?

"Here's what we'll do. I'll rotate the turntable, and you can hold the spatula just like this, and then the cake will be done," she instructed.

"I get to finish the cake?" Carly asked, eyes wide.

Bridget nodded. "You arrived at the perfect time. Are you ready?"

The little girl glanced at Soren. "Are you watching, Uncle Scooter?"

Her surly wolf's expression softened. "I wouldn't miss it for the world, kiddo."

The tenderness in his voice sent a shiver down her spine, and she exhaled a shaky breath.

Focus!

"Here we go," she said, swiveling the turntable as Carly applied another thin layer to the bottom tier.

"I'm doing it!" the girl exclaimed just as the door to the bakery flew open.

"Thank goodness, you're not closed!" a panic-stricken woman cried, pressing her hand to her heart.

"I'm sorry, but the bakery isn't open. The shop went out of business. We're only using the space temporarily," she answered as Carly handed over the spatula.

"Could you use the space temporarily to help the Kringle Cares Foundation?" the distraught woman asked.

"I'm sorry, but I don't know what that is?" she answered.

"We work with children with special needs, and today is our holiday celebration. We have dozens of families here to take part in the activities in the town square. This year, with the Cupid Bakery closing, we ordered sugar cookies from another bakery in Denver, but I just learned that they lost our order, and now we don't have any cookies to share with the families."

How awful!

"I'm so sorry to hear that," Bridget offered.

"We're in a bind. It's not Christmas in Kringle without sugar cookies. What do you say? Can you help us out?" the woman asked, her eyes pleading for assistance.

Could she pull it off?

"How many cookies do you need?" she asked.

"At least twelve dozen sugar cookies—and we need them in less than an hour. The kids look forward to them every year."

One hundred forty-four cookies in under an hour!

Bridget swallowed past the lump in her throat. "That's a lot cookies to make in a short amount of time."

"The children look forward to eating cookies after they go ice skating, and I hate to disappoint them and their families," the woman added.

Bridget twisted the tie on her apron.

In all honesty, she'd never been totally in charge. There was always a safety net. If something awful came out of Gaston's bakery, he would have been the one to take the brunt of the criticism. Sure, he would have let her have it, too, but until this moment, the buck had never officially stopped with her.

She glanced around the bakery, calculating exactly what she needed to pull off prepping and baking one hundred and forty-four cookies in less than an hour. Her pulse kicked up. Flour, sugar, baking powder, salt, eggs, butter, milk, vanilla extract. Everything she needed was there.

And instantly, so was the spirit of her grandmother.

What would Grandma Dasher do if she were here?

The answer was clear.

Her parents and grandmother believed in volunteerism and charity. And above all else, extending a helping hand to those in need.

Yes, they would have been proud of how she'd provided for Lori. But had Garrett been right? Had she twisted her situation into an excuse to shy away from her dreams and hide behind the guise of sacrifice?

Was there more to the lowly assistant baker and the girl who'd never pushed past her limits?

It was time to find out.

Bridget lifted her chin. "We can do it. Let your group know that they'll have their cookies in *less* than an hour."

The woman clapped her hands. "Thank you! And can you deliver them to the pavilion in the Kringle Square?"

"Absolutely," she replied as a heady rush of resolve coursed through her veins.

The woman released a sigh of relief. "You're an angel! Thank you! I can't wait to let everyone know," she said, then hurried out of the shop.

The door slammed closed, and Bridget felt all eyes fall on her.

"How will you make all those cookies?" Lori asked.

Bridget brushed her hands together, removing the bits of dried frosting.

It was vixen baker time.

"It's going to take all of us to get this done in under an hour. Who's in?" she asked, surveying the group.

"Me, me, me!" Cole and Carly chimed as Lori and every Abbott raised their hands.

"What about you?" she said, eyeing Soren.

"What about me?" he asked with a cocky grin that, God help her, made her toes curl inside her boots.

"Are you in?"

"Do I have a choice?"

The air crackled between them. The banter was back.

"No, sir, you do not have a choice. Take out your phone. We need holiday music, STAT."

Soren bit back a grin but followed orders like a good soldier, and she took on the role of cookie captain.

There was no going back now. It was cookies or bust time!

Soren tapped on his cell as Bing's voice rang out, and she started calling out orders.

"The wedding cake goes in the refrigerator. Russell, that's you, and then you're on dish duty."

Better to keep the handsy uncle busy.

"Yes, ma'am!" the man called, snapping to it.

There was no time to lose.

She and Lori whipped up the royal icing and the cookie dough as the Abbotts, plus her sexy scrooge washed up. When the group was ready to go, she assigned them to teams. There were Abbotts rocking rolling pins, Abbotts cracking with the cookie cutters, and Abbotts icing and applying sprinkles.

Like a finely tuned machine, the cookie assembly line hummed as everyone sang and swayed to the beat.

"Cole and Carly! Let's see your dance moves. We need to add plenty of good holiday vibes to our cookies," she called as she applied a dollop of frosting.

The kids busted out their moves as the adults chuckled.

"We're running low on sprinkles," the judge called, shaking a near-empty container of the tiny multicolored balls.

"Let me see what I can find," she replied as she wiped her hands on her apron.

She searched the shelves and spied a canister up high near the back of the shop. Stretching to reach it, she pushed onto her tiptoes but stilled when a presence came up behind her, and a tingle ran down her spine. She'd know this energy anywhere.

"Allow me," came the sexy rasp of the man she could not figure out.

He'd joined in the cookie assembly as if he actually cared—and maybe he did, or perhaps he was pretending, playing the dutiful best man in front of the Abbotts. Either way, she had to keep her guard up. The highs and lows with this cat-eyed Romeo could give a gal whiplash.

She glanced over her shoulder. That Soren sex tractor beam was downright irresistible—especially when he was wearing an apron.

"Sprinkles," she breathed, because that was all her sex mushed brain could come up with.

"Sprinkles," he replied.

Perfect! They had one word between the two of them. That would get weird fast.

She parted her lips, not sure what would come out. Perhaps, she'd repeat *sprinkles* when Carly giggled.

"What is it, honey?" Grace asked her granddaughter.

"Uncle Scooter and Birdie have to kiss," the little girl chimed.

"Why would you say that?" Soren asked, his cheeks growing pink.

Carly pointed to the ceiling. "You're under the mistletoe."

She glanced up and, yep, there was mistletoe.

"It looks fake," Soren said with an uncharacteristic hoarseness to his voice.

Was he nervous?

"Fake or real, if you get caught under the mistletoe, you have to kiss. It's Christmas rules," the judge offered with the hint of a grin as the rest of the Abbotts egged them on to offer up a kiss.

"I didn't see the mistletoe. That's not why I came over to help you," Soren said without a smirk or a glare.

"I didn't notice it either," she whispered back.

"Go on, Birdie! Tame the beast!" Tom teased.

"I could take your place, Scooter," Russ offered, throwing her a leisure suit Larry leer.

"No, you couldn't," Soren said softly, for only her to hear, as his breath tickled her lips.

Her pulse hammered. Her heart felt too large for her chest. His nearness sent her body into overdrive.

Just one kiss.

One little peck.

That's it.

Nothing more.

She could restrain herself. For Pete's sake, there were children in the room!

The bakery faded away as his sandalwood scent mingled with the cookies, carrying her off into holiday horniness. She fluttered her eyes closed, so ready to have his lips pressed to hers, if only for a moment when the door chime cut through the pre-kiss mistletoe haze and a Santa and Mrs. Claus lookalike combo entered the bakery.

The man looked around the space as if he'd come upon an old friend, then wrapped his arm around the woman.

"It's a Christmas miracle, Agnes!" he exclaimed.

Bridget stared at them. The pair seemed oddly familiar. Maybe she'd seen them last night when she was baked—and not in the good cookie way. Or perhaps, they were interested in purchasing baked goods.

But those notions vanished when she glanced back at Soren.

Wide-eyed, the color had drained from his cheeks. The man looked as if he'd seen a ghost as a prickle spider-crawled its way down her spine; and she was sure of one thing.

There was more to this couple than two people on the prowl for sugar cookies.

*N*o!

It couldn't be!

Had he lost his mind?

It sure as hell felt like it.

Bridget Dasher and those damned brown eyes of hers were driving him insane. That had to be it. The pendulum swinging between wanting to throttle her while simultaneously having every cell in his body screaming to hold her in his arms and never let her go had turned out to be the precursor to a one-way ticket straight to a padded cell.

His gaze bounced between her petal-soft lips and the couple who sauntered in off the street, like ghosts of his not-so-distant past.

He blinked. At least he had control of his eyelids.

Had he accidentally eaten those damned pot gummy bears?

Was he straight-up stoned? Was he about to start conversing with eggs like his baked vixen had last night?

No, he'd thrown the gummy bears into the trash after they'd returned to the mountain house. As of right now, aside from feeling drunk off a misplaced Bridget Dasher momentary fascination, he was completely sober. And that's never a good thing when you're ninety-nine percent sure you're hallucinating.

"Wait a second," Bridget said as she broke away from him and headed toward the couple. "I recognize you two. It's an honor to meet you," she added, hurrying around the counter to the front of the shop to greet the couple.

Not just any couple.

Agnes and Ernie Angel, whose acquaintance he'd made only a handful of days ago when he'd thought more about banging their attorney than bailing out their business.

The couple whose livelihood he was in the process of liquidating.

And then it hit him.

He owned Cupid Bakery.

He'd never thought of his acquisitions as anything more than assets. It never occurred to him to visit or even think about a purchase as something tangible. To him, they were simply line items on a spreadsheet.

But through some insane Christmas plot twist, the Angels had landed literally on his doorstep.

"Everyone, these lovely people are Agnes and Ernie Angel. They're the owners of the Cupid Bakery chain—the bakery we're making cookies in right now," Bridget said to the group with a wide grin.

Ernie shook his head. "That's not quite accurate, miss."

Bridget frowned. "It's not?"

"No, dear, that gentleman over there in the apron owns the bakeries now," Agnes said, throwing him the sweetest of smiles as she pointed a gloved finger at him.

"What are they talking about, Scooter?" Scott asked.

Soren scanned the room and found all eyes on him.

"About that," he began, only to have Tom's sister cut him off.

"You must be mistaken. Scooter's a businessman. He doesn't

own a string of bakeries, do you?" Denise asked, pinning him with her hawkish gaze.

He cleared his throat as he descended into holiday-scented hell.

"That's a complicated question," he answered as Denise raised an eyebrow—not for a second falling for his legalese.

"This is your bakery, Uncle Scooter?" Carly asked, coming to his side.

What was he supposed to do? Lie to her?

Shit!

And what was he supposed to say? These two sweet old people didn't keep up with the times and couldn't maintain the financial demands of their life's work?

He patted Carly's shoulder. "Technically, I own Cupid Bakery along with Ernie and Agnes Angel. I, however, have a larger stake and can act unilaterally."

"*Uni-what*?" the little girl replied.

He started to give her some bullshit answer when Bridget's jaw dropped.

"You're kidding? This has got to be a joke!" she said, clearly having put the pieces together.

He loosened his collar. Damn, it had gotten hot in here.

Feeling his cheeks heat, he held Bridget's gaze. Sure, she'd given him side-eye, rolled eyes, and glared at him more times than he could count. He'd liked all that—their usual tête-à-tête, toe to toe, Birdie versus Scooter battle of wills. But this look, this look made him want to crumple up into a ball. Yes, she was angry, but he could deal with anger. This look cut straight to the bone. Visceral disgust burned in her eyes like nothing he'd ever seen—or felt.

Aside from his connection to the Abbotts, he hadn't felt all that much in many, many years.

And this was why he didn't allow business to become personal.

He squared his jaw.

He'd spent a lifetime closing off his heart and muting his emotions.

She would not get to him. He simply wouldn't allow it.

"It's no joke at all, young lady. I'm surprised to see you here, Mr. Rudolph," Agnes said, still smiling as if she weren't about to lose everything.

Bridget gasped. "You make them call you, Mr. Rudolph?"

He threw up his hands. "That's just what they call me! I don't make anyone do anything!"

"Besides buy their business out from under them to make a buck," she threw back.

Holy holly and the ivy hell! The mittens were coming off this vixen!

"We know of your bakeries. There used to be one by us in Boston," Lori said, throwing a worried glance at her sister.

If he didn't want her to marry his best friend, he'd be grateful she'd taken the microscope off of him—at least for the moment.

Tom nodded. "We wondered what happened when it closed suddenly."

Soren glanced at the ovens. Maybe it was cooler in there because it had become blisteringly hot in this shop.

"I run an outreach center for homeless teens, and Cupid Bakery always donated baked goods to our center," Denise added.

What he wouldn't give for about two hundred of Tanner's "special recipe" gummy bears. And even that probably wouldn't be enough to improve this shit show.

He'd never had the different parts of his life intersect like this in one giant cookie-infused cluster fuck.

He'd done a damn good job compartmentalizing his life. His parents existed in a box. A box he tried like hell never to open. His work occupied another. His friendship with Tom and his relationship with the Abbotts were completely separate from those realms. He'd incorporated a very specific set of behaviors for work and shutting out his parents—the two places where he couldn't let his guard slip, not even for a second.

It wasn't that hard.

Not anymore.

Not with Fiona Traeger and Palmer Rudolph.

The divide between himself and his mother and father had happened gradually, like a crack in the ice. Slowly, one year of no contact turned into two, and two into four. And then, when he'd graduated from college only to look out into the crowd and see Grace, Scott, the judge, Russell, and Denise clapping as he received his diploma, he'd realized that the separation from his parents was complete. The unwanted child was no longer a child. He was an island unto himself, and this reality was mutually accepted by all parties.

It boiled down to this: Soren Christopher Traeger Rudolph was a ruthless man. But with the Abbotts, he was Scooter. The gangly kid they'd known since he was fourteen.

But who was he to Bridget? What box did she fit into?

She was supposed to be a fling, a fleeting romance on the periphery of his life. Instead, she straddled both worlds.

Soren or Scooter, she knew them both.

No one had ever bridged that divide.

And no one ever could because it would never work, would it?

All eyes were back on him. He needed to say something.

"What brings you to Kringle, Colorado? I thought you lived in Vermont," he asked coolly.

If this wasn't a Santa-sized mind fuck, he didn't know what

was. But he couldn't reveal how affected he was by this twilight zone situation.

"I'm not sure if you know this, Mr. Rudolph, but Ernie is a member of the Fraternal Order of Bearded Santas. We have many friends who reside in Kringle now," Agnes answered.

Of—freaking—course, Ernie was a member!

Was every dude with a real white beard part of this club?

"We had a little extra time on our hands this holiday season, and our friends invited us to stay with them in Kringle. We're here through Christmas Day, and then we'll head back to Vermont to see our children and grandchildren," Ernie finished.

Agnes closed her eyes and inhaled. "What's that I smell?"

Bridget's cheeks grew rosy. "I'm so sorry. You're probably wondering what we're doing here."

"No, no, Delores told me that she had a guest who needed to use the space. We're always happy to help if we can, and it's so nice to see the shop humming with holiday activity."

Bridget squeezed the woman's hand. "I'm very grateful. This morning we made a wedding cake here—a three-tiered red velvet cake frosted in buttercream, and then you're also smelling the—"

"Sugar cookies!" Ernie exclaimed, rubbing his paunch of a Santa belly.

"Please, try one," Bridget said, throwing eye daggers at Soren as she came behind the counter, then handed the Angels each a cookie.

"We all helped make them!" Carly chimed.

Cole walked up to Ernie. "Are you the real Santa?"

Ernie chuckled. "No, dear boy, I'm one of his helpers."

"Have you seen a Christmas fairy?" the boy asked earnestly.

"Not recently," the man replied warmly.

Cole blew out a frustrated breath as the Angels each took a bite of their cookie.

"Divine!" Ernie remarked through his bite as few sprinkles settled in the white of his beard.

"Perfect crunch on the outside and moist and delicious on the inside. Just the right amount of frosting. Well done," Agnes said, complimenting the group.

"It's our grandma Dasher's recipe," Bridget added.

"Dasher, you say?" Agnes asked.

"Yes, I'm Bridget Dasher, but everyone calls me Birdie. And that's my sister, Lori Dasher."

Ernie glanced around the room. "Dasher sisters and new friends, thank you for breathing Christmas spirit into our Kringle Cupid Bakery location."

"You're not out of business yet," he blurted, like an idiot.

And again, everyone stared at him.

"The Angels have until the day after Christmas before we begin liquidation," he added, knowing instantly that little tidbit didn't make him look any less scrooge-like.

"That's not even a week, Scooter," Grace said with a crease to her brow.

"Well, it's..." he began, but Ernie Angel cut him off.

"Oh, it's plenty of time."

He stared at the man. "It is?"

"We've seen a holiday miracle or two in our day, haven't we, Agnes?"

Soren gave the couple a forced grin and a curt nod. This wasn't some Christmas Story with a happy ending for the lovely old bakers.

That didn't happen in the real world.

Short of Santa dropping off a sack full of millions and a bold operating plan, there was largely nothing that could save their business. Hell, only a handful of locations were even open at this point.

"We should be getting back to our friends. Merry Christmas

to all!" Ernie said with the finesse of the real Santa as he opened the door for Agnes and the Angels left the bakery.

No one spoke. Cole didn't even ask him about Christmas fairies for the fifty billionth time.

"Scooter, how very sad. Is there nothing you can do to help those lovely people?" Grace asked, shaking her head when a kitchen timer cut through the heaviness that had overtaken the bakery.

Nancy turned it off. "Sorry, I forgot that I set the timer, so we'd know when to leave to deliver the cookies to the Kringle town square. We should head out now if we want to get to the Kringle Cares group in time."

Bridget manufactured a grin, but he could see that, beneath her faux pleasant demeanor, she was seething.

"Why don't you each take a box and head out. I'll get the last batch ready to go. *Scooter*, would you mind staying behind to help out?"

Fucking festive fruitcake! She was gearing up for a fight when he needed everything to go back to normal—or whatever normal he'd stumbled into after falling into bed with her.

No, the normal he needed would only return the minute the Dasher sisters were out of the picture.

That's what he wanted, right?

That's what it had to be. It was the only damn way he could go on.

"Sure thing, *Birdie*," he answered, manufacturing a plastic grin of his own, as the rest of the group left the shop and headed for the square.

Bridget closed the last box, then pinned him with her gaze. "Why didn't you say anything about owning the Cupid Bakeries?"

He took off his apron and put on his coat. "It's none of your business."

"I'm baking in their shop. Well, your shop. Who knew you were a baker?" she added with a nice helping of go-fuck-yourself infused into her reply.

"I'm not a baker. I'm a—"

"A businessman. A cold-hearted businessman. Yes, I got that part," she replied, still laying it on thick.

Who was she to judge him?

"I'm a meticulous businessman, and in business, it's all about profit. I don't go out of my way to hurt anyone."

"You don't?" she threw back along with a few more eye daggers.

"No," he hissed, but that wasn't the whole truth.

He'd never turned the tables and put himself in the shoes of the person whose business he'd taken over.

She huffed an unconvinced breath as she put on her coat and gloves, then picked up the last box.

"Let me carry it," he said, gesturing for her to hand it over.

"No," she answered, balancing the box between her arm and her hip, then opened the door.

"Bridget, let me help. I'm not going to walk alongside you, doing nothing, while you carry that giant box."

"I don't need your help, *Scooter*, the fancy bakery owning businessman."

Dammit! Now he had to piss her off.

"I do own everything you're carrying. I could demand you return my property," he parried back, pretty sure that would rile her up.

"Wow! Just wow!" she murmured, then thrust the cookies into his arms.

He took a step back, nearly falling over. He'd forgotten about her freakish baker strength.

She charged down the sidewalk, mumbling something—

most likely cursing him. He stayed a step behind as they walked, no, not walked, dashed toward the town square.

She could really move when she wasn't stoned.

He blew out a tight breath, and since she wasn't about to shoot the shit with him, he did the only thing he could and took in Kringle Village. It lived up to its Christmassy name. Shrouded in fresh snow, twinkling lights outlined every shop, and no door was without a wreath, decked with bows, berries, and ornaments. With its Bavarian Alpine ski-lodge feel, it did have a certain charm. Even a Grinch like himself could see that.

He turned his attention to the brunette beauty leading the way. The sound of laughter and children hooting and hollering grew louder, and it wasn't long before they arrived at the square, and he spied the photo booth.

The location of another kiss that had left him, Mr. Manhattan Womanizer, besotted like a lovesick teenager.

That kiss in the snug space seemed like it happened a lifetime ago.

He stared at the festively decorated photo booth as a couple ducked in to have their picture taken.

He glanced at Bridget. Last night, that was them.

And last night was another first for him—or rather—another Bridget Dasher first.

After their night of funnel cake thievery and photo booth fawning, she'd fallen asleep in the truck on the drive back with her head resting on his shoulder. He'd carried her inside and got her ready for bed. And then, he'd pulled up a chair, removed the photo strip from his wallet, and stared at the pictures. He couldn't help himself. He looked so damn happy in them. And that kiss—that kiss would be forever captured in the last frame. She'd smiled when he kissed her, and the photo also caught his hint of a grin the moment their lips met.

He'd be lying if he said his fascination with her ended with the pictures.

Once he'd tucked the photo strip back into his wallet, for the second night in a row, completely enchanted yet again, he'd watched her sleep.

Yes, he wanted to make sure she didn't fall into a psychotropic coma or whatever could happen after ingesting enough THC to subdue an elephant. But that didn't stop him from twisting a lock of her hair around his finger, just as he did when they were strangers sharing a night of passion in a hotel suite.

"Soren, what are you doing?"

Bridget's words pulled him from his daze.

She glanced at the photo booth. "Is that it?"

He nodded.

"I don't remember a whole lot," she said, but she was a terrible liar. The tremble to her bottom lip gave away that she remembered just as much as he did.

"It's better that way. It wasn't a big deal," he replied, luckily a good enough liar for them both.

A storm brewed in her eyes. Part anger and part outright confusion; she stared at him.

Seeing him—all of him.

A chill passed through his body that had nothing to do with the temperature, and all he wanted to do was confess like the sinner he was. Confess everything about his parents, his lonely childhood, how he hated who he'd become, and what the Abbotts meant to him. Like a tidal wave forming in the depths of the ocean, poised to crash upon the shore in a fury of sound and energy, he wanted to let everything out as if she possessed some special power to tame the tumultuous sea of longing and loathing he'd lived with for as long as he could remember.

But why her? Why did she have to get to him? Why couldn't

she have been nothing but a quick fuck in a hotel room? How had she gotten under his skin in so little time?

"Bridget, I—"

"What?" she asked, the storm in her eyes intensifying.

"I'll take those cookies!"

He and Bridget startled as the Kringle Care's woman hurried up to them.

"Thank you so very much! You truly are an angel," she said, taking the box out of his hands and carrying it over to the families gathered near the frozen lake covered with ice skaters.

"Did you have something to say?" she asked, concern edging out the anger.

But he didn't want her pity.

"I was going to ask if this place looked different to you—you know, now that you're not completely blitzed out of your mind."

"Unbelievable," she bit out with a shake of her head, but before she could lay into him, Carly called out to them.

"Birdie! Uncle Scooter! Over here!"

"We're doing a snowball fight competition," Cole called excitedly.

"Boys versus girls," Carly added, taking his hand as Cole took Bridget's.

Cole pushed up his red glasses. "It's like capture the flag with snowballs. If you get hit, you're out."

"The boys are the green team, and the girls are the red team," Carly added.

The children pulled them over toward the west side of the square that backed up to thick snow-covered foliage dotted with evergreens and willowy white wisps of leafless aspens.

"Doesn't this look fun, Scooter!" Grace said as the snowball attendant handed her something that looked like large salad tongs with ice cream scoopers on the ends.

"What's that for?"

"It's a snowball maker," Tom answered, grinning ear to ear as he formed a snowball, then chucked it at his head.

Soren veered out of the way just in time.

"Isn't it great!" Cole exclaimed, making a snowball, then handing it to the judge.

"Not too shabby," the man said, pretending to assess the weight of his great-grandson's ball of ice.

Another Santa lookalike clapped his hands. "Gather around, folks. Welcome to Kringle's version of capture the flag. We're losing daylight, so you'll be the last group to go out today."

All these retired St. Nicks in one place was getting to be a bit much.

"All right, snow warriors, here are the rules. Each team gets five minutes to hide their flag. It must be visible from all directions," the man continued.

"No hiding it under the snow?" Cole asked.

"That's right. You've got to be able to see it. Now, after the five minutes have passed, you'll hear me ring the bell, and then, the competition begins. The first team to steal the opposing team's flag and carry it over to their side of the course wins. I'll ring the bell again to let you know when the game is over."

Soren glanced at Bridget as she stood with the women, carefully inspecting her snowball maker like a James Bond weapons specialist.

No matter.

He could roll with this. Fresh air and some fun with snowballs would be an excellent reset to get everyone's minds off the whole *cold-hearted corporate raider fleecing the nice bakers' business* business.

He stole another look at Bridget, who threw a fresh batch of eye daggers at him.

So much for a little fresh air changing anything with that vixen.

Russ handed him a green snowball maker. "Birdie's got some spunk to her—a real take-charge woman," the man said, lowering his voice.

"I guess," he mumbled.

"Do you think she'd go for me? I know I'm a few years older."

Soren pegged the guy with his gaze. "A few?"

"You should have seen the ladies that I was talking to yesterday. They were around the same age as Birdie, and they were really into me," Russ replied with a triumphant glint in his clueless eyes.

"Yep, I'm sure they were," he answered.

He'd heard all the bullshit *Russ is smooth with the ladies* stories. They never bothered him. In fact, he'd gotten a kick out of them until the lady in question was Bridget.

"Stay away from her, Russ."

The man frowned. "Why? Do you like her, Scooter?"

"I—"

Dammit! Did he like her?

"Let's focus on the snowball competition," he said, hoping Russ got the message.

"Right, right! Always out for the kill, huh, Scooter," Russ replied with a slap to his shoulder.

Was he always out for the kill? Is that all he'd become? And did that make him as myopic as his parents?

No, he ran a business, and there was no room for pussyfooting around when it came to managing hundreds of millions of dollars in assets and hundreds of people on the payroll. His parents lived off their trusts and only thought of themselves. But was he any different? Without the Abbotts, maybe not.

Nine times out of ten, he didn't give his mother and father a second thought. But with Christmas, even with the good times he'd had with the Abbotts, he couldn't erase what had happened when he was thirteen. The last Christmas he'd spent in Manhattan.

The attendant held up a bell, attracting everyone's attention and, blessedly, pulling him from the past.

"Here we go! On your mark, get set, go!" the man cried as the clang of the bell rang out.

The women were off like a shot, clustered together as they ran into the wooded area, and he watched Bridget disappear behind a veil of evergreens.

"Come on, men!" Scott called, waving for them to follow as Cole rushed ahead.

Tom and Russ jogged to catch up with the boy, and he was about to join them when he felt a tap to his shoulder and glanced over to find Tom's grandfather.

"Hey, Judge," he said, gaze bouncing between the man and the others running into the woods.

"Walk with me," the judge replied.

"What about the game?" he asked, gesturing to the others.

"Just for a moment, then we'll catch up. There are a few things I'd like to say to you."

He nodded and did his best not to appear rattled.

While the judge was a kind and impartial man, he wasn't one to mince words either.

Whatever he had to say to him in private would *not* be good.

*H*e gave the man the once-over. Maybe he was overreacting. The judge was in his eighties. He probably wanted someone to walk with and shoot the breeze. But the elder Abbott's neutral expression didn't give away anything.

"Are you feeling okay? Would you like to sit down, Judge?" He pointed to a tree lying across the snow. It wasn't that cold out. There was a nip in the air, but it wasn't frigid.

The judge patted his arm again. "No, no, Scooter, I've got at least a few more years left in me. But let's hang back for a moment."

The muscles in Soren's body tensed. "Sure, we can do that."

He and the judge passed a cluster of sturdy evergreens as the sound of the men hunting for a spot for the flag grew farther and farther off.

"Curious happenings at the bakery," the man continued.

Dammit! He should have known that this was coming.

He didn't talk to the Abbotts about his work. Not really. Of course, they knew what he did, but when they were together, it didn't come up that often. And in the off chance it did, he'd become a master at guiding the conversation in another direction, which was damn near impossible today when his work life, his personal life, and his Abbott life collided like three submarines headed straight for each other, full speed ahead.

"What a coincidence, right? It's too bad about Mr. and Mrs. Angel," he replied, surprised that he actually did feel bad about it. He shook off the emotion.

"Meeting the Angels was interesting, but I was talking about Birdie," the man corrected.

"Birdie? What about her?"

The ghost of a grin pulled at the corners of the judge's lips. "She's quite something."

Russ and now the judge! Was every unattached male Abbott into this woman?

"Yep, she sure is *something*."

Infuriating. Hard-headed. A taskmaster in the kitchen. A vixen in the bedroom. Heaven in his arms.

No, he could not go there!

"She reminds me of Alice," the judge said, his blue eyes growing a touch glassy.

Soren stopped in his tracks "Your Alice? Your wife?"

"Oh, yes, there was only ever one Alice. She was magnificent from the first moment I saw her. And would you like to know something else?"

"Sure."

"I've never told anyone this, not even my sons, but Alice despised me when we met," the judge said with an amused chuckle.

Soren's jaw dropped. That was not the story he'd been told countless times at Abbott family gatherings. He'd known the judge as an unbiased, reflective, ethical, and steady-tempered man.

Who would hate that?

"I thought you guys were madly in love?" he pressed.

"We got there eventually. But I'll have you know that I was quite a Casanova in my day."

Soren bit back a grin. "Is that so?"

"I know what you're thinking, and I may not look it now. But when I was your age, I was also a bit of a scoundrel," the judge added, that hint of a smile blooming into an ear to ear grin.

"Oh, really?" he asked, fascinated by the admission.

"That was before I was appointed to the bench. I was a hot-headed prosecutor and a real man about town...until Alice. I thought I knew it all back then. Luckily, Alice showed me that I didn't. I didn't know a damn thing about love. I asked her out thirty-seven times before she agreed to have dinner with me. And then when she relented, she still had a condition."

"What was it?" he asked as a light snow began to fall.

"She told me I had to be myself on our date—not the cocky litigator or the dirty dog of a womanizer—those were her words, mind you, but she wasn't off the mark. She said she wasn't interested in that husk of a man. And you know, I wasn't that interested in being him either," the judge finished.

Soren nodded, unable to speak. He knew a thing or two about putting on a facade.

"You see, Scooter, Alice made me work, and she helped me see that the best kind of love is the kind you have to fight for, the kind that shows you who you really are. Real love makes you want to do better—be better—and not for yourself. You do it because life isn't about taking. It's about giving. And, good heavens, did Alice make me work."

The judge gestured for them to start walking as Soren felt a tightness clench his heart.

What kind of man was Soren Christopher Traeger Rudolph?

Not the kind the judge would be proud of—not if he saw the empty life he lived when he was away from the Abbotts.

"Why are you telling me this, Judge?" he asked, his voice barely a rasp.

"I've known you a long time, Scooter, and I think you could use an Alice."

Soren released a bark of a laugh. "I'm not really the Alice type."

"No?" the judge replied with the ghost of a smirk.

"No, there's no Alice out there for me," he replied, the words tasting of regret.

The judge nodded. "Perhaps not, or maybe you haven't met your Alice. But I hope you know, no matter what happens, my family has always treasured our time with you."

What was this past tense "treasured" talk?

"Judge, what are you saying?" he asked as a bell rang out in the distance.

"I found a spot!" Cole cried from beyond a smattering of Aspens. "Let's put the flag here."

"Dad, Scooter! It's go time!" Scott called, jogging toward them with Cole and the others close behind.

"Scooter, take the south side," Tom said, pointing off in the distance. "I'll go north with Uncle Russ. Everyone else, guard the flag."

"Let the games begin!" the judge said, taking Cole's hand and heading off with the rest of the team.

And then he was alone.

"What the fuck was that?" he whispered.

He'd had countless conversations with the judge over the years, and none of them had gone anything like that.

He trudged through the snow, his head spinning.

He could barely tell up from down at this point as the far-off squeals and shrieks peppered the air in the distance. His thoughts were all over the place. The Angels, Bridget, Tom's damned wedding, and this godforsaken town were starting to take a toll on him. He kept walking, grateful for the quiet, when something small and white whizzed past his head. He looked around, but he couldn't see anyone. The light was fading fast, and in the shade of a grove of towering blue spruce, he looked for the person who'd thrown the snowball that had passed only inches from his head but didn't see a soul.

"Hello?" he called, shielding his eyes from the falling snow.

No reply...until...*smack!*

Smack, smack, smack, crack!

Five snowballs hit him in rapid succession—two to the head and three to the shoulder.

He raised his hand defensively.

"Who is that?" he called, bending down and scrambling to make a snowball with the damn ice scoop salad tongs.

He stilled as movement flashed in his peripheral vision.

Then a crack.

A crunch.

And...*pow, pow, pow, pow!*

Another round of blistering snowballs hit him square in the head.

Again!

This must be what it's like to live inside a Slurpee machine!

Cold snow slid down his face, and he dropped the snowball maker. Stumbling back a few feet, he lost his footing and toppled over.

Fucking fantastic! With his luck, Carly was his assailant, and he could add having an eight-year-old little girl knock him flat on his ass. If this day wasn't already a giant shit show, this would be the icing on the cake.

He ran his hand down his shivering, wet face, but before he could reach for his snowball maker to retaliate, Bridget, not Carly, appeared. She jumped out from behind a tree and pinned him back onto the ground.

"What the hell are you doing? I'm already down! You got me with four hundred snowballs! Are you crazy?"

That storm he'd seen in her eyes now raged. "Am I crazy? No, Scooter, I'm furious."

"With me?"

"Of course, with you!"

"What did I do now?"

She'd been stewing since the Angels came by the shop, and that exercise and fresh air he'd hoped would have helped her move on, clearly hadn't. Unfortunately for him, she looked more pissed off.

She held a snowball in her hand, poised to nail him in the chest like a baker phenomenon turned snowball ninja. "How can you do it? How can you go out of your way to hurt so many people? I let a lot go, Scooter. I didn't even yell at my boyfriend when I caught him in bed with a woman who was wearing my lingerie. I let Gaston take advantage of me. He paid me nothing to do the job of three bakers and a store manager. But you, you take the cake. Literally. You don't want to help Cupid Bakery or for Tom and Lori to get married. You are a matrimonial meddler and the killer of cake all wrapped into one!"

Matrimonial meddler? Killer of cake?

He'd been called a lot of things in his day, and perhaps she had him on the meddling, but killer of cake wasn't something he'd ever imagined anyone would call him in a million years.

He needed to get her talking like a normal human.

He glanced at the perfectly formed snowball clutched in her gloved hand. "I'm not saying this to piss you off, but I don't know what the hell you're talking about with the whole lingerie and Gaston rant?"

She shook her head and released a frustrated sigh. "I should apologize for that part. That stuff doesn't have anything to do with you. There's just a lot making me mad right about now—

and I'm not the kind of person who gets mad. Somehow, you've turned me into a lunatic!"

"I've turned you into a lunatic?" he threw back, exasperation woven into each syllable.

"Absolutely," she replied, eyes blazing. "What you're doing to the Angels and Cupid Bakery is pure *scroogery*. You get the chance to save the day with your work, to help people who dedicated their lives to creating a bakery that brought joy to its customers and community, and you do nothing. You're no Rudolph."

"It's who I am," he answered, a little, no, a lot more truthfully than he'd expected.

"It doesn't have to be, Soren," she whispered as her words hung in the chilly air.

Chests heaving and the breath hot between them, they stared at each other.

"You mentioned lingerie," he said, needing more than anything to change the trajectory of a conversation that was hitting too damn close to home.

She glanced away and released a wry bark of a laugh. "It wasn't officially my lingerie. I saw it in a bag at my ex-boyfriend's house. I assumed it was a gift for me. But we're not talking about me. We're talking about you."

"You're the one who said it," he replied with a cocky twist to his lips.

"Soren!" she chided.

He dropped the arrogant facade. "I'm sorry you caught your boyfriend cheating on you."

She set the snowball on the ground. "I should have known it wasn't a relationship that was going anywhere. He'd never kissed me like..."

"Like what?" He stared into her truthful eyes, allowing him to see her very soul.

"Like, how you kiss me. Like, I'm all you're thinking about."

Christ! How true that was.

"I shouldn't have said that," she replied with a slight shudder.

He pulled off his glove and cupped her cheek in his hand, his heart hammering in his chest. "You're cold."

She gave him an adorable cringe of a grin as she brushed a bit of snow from his hair. "You've got to be colder. I got you pretty good."

That was the understatement of the century.

He sat up but didn't release her from his lap. "I'm not cold when I'm with you, Bridget."

He didn't mean temperature-wise. He wasn't the cold-hearted man he despised when he was with her. She was light and warmth and gooey-delicious goodness, and he wanted to bask in her beauty and indulge in her honey-sweet radiance. He wanted her spirit to overtake his lonely soul and replace it with nights tangled together on the cusp of ecstasy and days when all he had to do was look up to find her smiling at him.

"You're not?" she asked, twisting one of his dark curls between her fingers.

He ran his thumb across her bottom lip, then leaned in, powerless to fight the forces that drew them together.

"What is this, Soren? What's going on with us?" she whispered, her breath warm against his cheek as the words went straight to the darkest part of his heart, threatening to let in the light.

But he couldn't let her in there—not where the damaged little boy dwelled.

He pulled back a fraction. "It's nothing."

"Nothing?" she repeated with such sorrow in her eyes, he had to look away.

He shook his head. "No, it's—"

"Over. The game is over," Tom said, walking over with the judge, then glanced at them on the ground. "What are you two doing?"

"Nothing," Bridget answered, borrowing his word, her voice void of warmth as she scrambled to her feet. "I hit Scooter a few times with the snowballs. I was making sure he was okay."

Tom reached out his hand and helped her up, then his friend turned to him.

"What would you think of you and I breaking off from the group and grabbing dinner in the Village? We can call Dan when we're ready to head back to the mountain house. I feel like I've barely gotten to see you, Scooter. It's a pretty low-key night. Right, Birdie?" Tom asked, meeting Bridget's gaze with his trademark good guy grin.

Bridget glanced between the men, and he knew exactly what she was thinking. There was no way in hell the wedding Hun wanted him out of her sight. But what was she to say? Tom was the one initiating this guys' night.

Perhaps not all was lost.

"Walk with me, Birdie. The ladies won, and Carly is demanding ice cream up at the mountain house to celebrate," Judge said, offering her his arm.

Bridget glanced over her shoulder at them as the judge led her toward the course's exit.

And then, it was the two of them—Scooter and Tommy—just like it had been all through high school, college, and grad school. And life felt...off, as if something had whittled its way into their usual rhythm.

He shook off the strange feeling. It was nothing. He was still recovering from a Bridget Dasher encounter. That could make any man question his sanity. After a couple burgers and many beers, he'd be right as rain, or snow in this place.

"Lori didn't have any objections?" he asked as they entered

the town square which only looked more North Pole-ish to see it freshly kissed with a dusting of snow.

"Not at all. I told you, Scooter, she's amazing."

"Right, sure," he answered in a tone that screamed, I call bullshit.

Tom pointed toward a Swiss chalet two-story structure with Kringle Tavern illuminated in white lights. Like everything else in this town, the place looked like it was straight out of Santaville.

"Russ says the Kringle Tavern is the happening place in town," Tom said as they crossed the square and entered the dark, yet mindbogglingly wholesome-feeling tavern.

They grabbed a booth looking out onto the square. He stared out the window at the goddamn photo booth as Tom asked the waitress to bring them a couple of burgers and two pints of beer. He'd been in this town no more than two days, and Bridget Dasher was already everywhere.

"I need to ask you something, man," Tom said, leaning onto his elbows.

"Shoot."

"Is everything okay with Birdie?"

Oh, for fuck's sake! He couldn't escape her.

"What do you mean?"

Tom shrugged. "I don't know. It seems like there's something weird between you two."

Weird was an understatement, but he'd barely had a moment to talk with Tom away from a Dasher sister and wasn't about to waste it.

"Maybe the weirdness you're feeling is your own?" he tossed back, playing devil's advocate like they used to do in law school.

"This again?" Tom said with a sigh as the waitress set two giant steins of beer on the table.

Soren took a sip. "Think about it. You've never been one to

rush into anything—and now you're going balls to the wall toward something as huge as marriage?"

"I'm not rushing."

"You're making a decision without all the facts."

"What facts are more important than love and..."

"And nothing," he interrupted. "I'm not saying there's anything wrong with love. Fall in love ten times over. I don't give a damn. It's marriage. It's a big deal, and as your best friend, I'm telling you, I think you should wait. You don't want to make a mistake that would hurt Lori, would you?"

"Two Dasher burgers, boys," the waitress said, setting the platters teeming with fries and burgers on the table.

"You're kidding?" he said, staring at Tom, but the waitress answered instead.

"Nope, I'm not kidding. It's Dasher night here at the tavern. All our burgers are named after Santa's reindeer. Dasher's a little spicy. Watch out for those jalapeños!"

"But there are eight reindeer: Dasher, Dancer, Prancer, and Vixen. Comet, and Cupid, Donner, and Blitzen. Well, nine with Rudolph," Tom replied.

"We had to nix Blitzen. Too many folks came in to get *blitzed* on Blitzen night. You've never seen unruly until you've seen a herd of drunk Santas."

Soren bit back a grin and shared an amused look with Tom. "I can imagine."

There! They were back—sharing inside jokes and shooting the shit!

"And the Rudolph burger is only available on Christmas Eve, of course," the woman answered before heading off to check on another table.

"Your namesake's got a burger," Tom joked, but his smile didn't reach his eyes.

Something was on the guy's mind. Soren nodded, giving his friend space to talk.

Tom tapped the table pensively. "Listen, Scooter, I want to tell you something that I haven't told anyone."

This was it. He could see it in Tom's expression. Despite all the *Lori's the one* talk, he wasn't completely sure.

"You can trust me with anything," he replied.

Tom nodded, then drained his beer stein in one long gulp.

This had to be big. Soren leaned forward.

Tom set the empty glass on the table and stared at it as if he were rehearsing something in his mind.

"I'm just going to say it. Not even Birdie knows this."

"Just say it, Tommy. You know I'm behind you no matter what."

Tom released a slow breath. "I hoped you'd say that."

"Well, what's weighing so heavy?" he pressed.

"Lori's pregnant. I'm going to be a dad. I had to share it with you, Soren. And I could use a night of getting hammered with my best friend," he revealed with a glazed, dumbfounded grin.

"Pregnant?" Soren repeated as the blood in his veins went ice cold.

No fucking wonder he was marrying her, and no wonder Tom wanted to knock back a few.

"Life will never be the same," Tom added, shaking his head.

Soren stared at the man. No shit!

Now, it was his turn to chug the beer. What the hell was he supposed to do now?

The waitress stopped at their tables and assessed the empty steins. "You boys must be thirsty. Can I get you two another round?"

Was this their last round? Had the judge figured out what was going on with Tom and Lori? Was that why he'd gotten the *treasured moments* speech?

Soren pulled his credit card from his wallet and set it on the table. "Open up a tab and keep the rounds coming. We're drinking until we can't see straight," he said, doing his best to keep his tone even.

"I'm in!" Tom replied, slapping the table.

The sound reverberated like a door slamming shut.

And that door was the one that led to the only place he'd ever felt whole. He looked at Tom and wondered if that's what his father had looked like when his mother had dropped the news of her surprise pregnancy.

A pregnancy neither wanted, producing a bundled burden they were wholly unprepared to meet.

He let the ice coursing through his body temper his reaction.

Tonight, they'd get hammered. He'd allow the alcohol to numb the searing pain tearing through his chest.

Because tomorrow he damn well needed to figure out his next move—and it had to be something big.

"*B*irdie, it's just like the pictures."

Bridget tied a white satin bow to the end of a wooden bench and glanced up to find Lori gazing around the cozy chapel.

She stood and tucked a wayward lock of hair behind her ear. Two days before the wedding, today was the day she'd given herself to decorate the quaint Kringle Chapel and to make the decadent croquembouche dessert for the rehearsal dinner tomorrow night. She'd arranged for the wedding party to spend the day on the slopes, and then the adults would spend the evening attending a holiday music concert while she babysat Cole and Carly and finished up her wedding to-do list.

And she needed to keep busy, not only because she had a decent amount to do to prep for the rehearsal dinner and the nuptials, but because she also needed to keep her mind off her brooding worst best man.

She was all over the place when it came to him and the revelations from yesterday.

The man owned—at least for the meanwhile, before he sold it off piece by piece—the Cupid Bakery chain and hadn't said a word about it until the Angels walked in out of the blue and outed him.

One minute, she wanted to drop kick the guy off the top of Kringle Mountain. And the next, she'd find that she'd wasted the better part of an hour lost in a cloud of lust, her body tingling at the thought of his touch, his kiss, and the way he'd hold her in his arms as if she'd finally found a place where she belonged.

It wasn't like she was trying to think about him, but her treacherous mind kept replaying the moments of when they couldn't seem to take their eyes—and hands and lips—off each other like a soundtrack stuck on repeat.

The night they shared as strangers, cocooned in orgasmic bliss.

Their kiss in the car when they'd arrived at Kringle Mountain House.

Their almost kiss two minutes later on the front porch.

The kiss in the mountain house kitchen, laced with chocolate and the scent of peanut butter, that made her dizzy with desire.

Not to mention, the shower, the bakery under the mistletoe, and when she'd taken him out in the snowball version of capture the flag.

A shiver ran down her spine at the thought of his green, cat-like eyes devouring her in one titillating glance.

It was honestly a miracle she'd gotten anything done for this wedding with all the kissing and almost kissing the two of them had done in the last forty-eight hours.

He and Tom had rolled in well past one in the morning and must have really tied one on last night. She'd heard Soren enter the room, but before she could get out of bed and confront him, she'd found him snoring and out like a light, sprawled across the suite's sleeper sofa with his phone still in his hand. And that's where she'd left him this morning, still asleep and smelling like he'd ingested a distillery.

Bridget straightened the bow and came to her feet, grateful for the distraction. "I didn't hear you come in."

Lori ran her hand along a garland made of fragrant evergreen branches. "I had to come to see for myself before the big day. Birdie, it's everything I dreamed it would be. But I wish you'd let me help you put it all together."

Bridget took a few steps back and stood at the altar as Lori came to her side, and the sisters took in the simple splendor of the Kringle Chapel. Reached only by a lone gondola, on the outside, the chapel appeared to be a modest stone structure with a pitched roof in keeping with the town's Bavarian architecture. But once inside, the secrets of the petite sanctuary were instantly revealed. With four polished oak benches flanking each side of the aisle, the real beauty came from the view. Beyond that altar, a giant window framed the awe-inspiring snow-covered peaks and valleys of the majestic mountains that exacted their tranquil beauty from every angle. It was an extraordinary place that, while remote and set apart, wove its solitude together with kinship and a deep connection to all those who had set foot in the fairylike space.

A thick blanket of clouds had rolled in, and the gentle sprinkling of snow that began last night had continued throughout the day. It cast the space in a hazy blue glow, and while two antler chandeliers that mirrored the ones in the mountain house lit the space in pools of golden light, they flickered each time the wind whipped up.

Bridget squeezed her sister's hand. "You know there's no way I'd let you do that. It's your wedding. This is my gift to you—and you know Grandma Dasher would have agreed. She was all about taking care of others, especially on special occasions. Plus, Dan and Delores have been great. They made sure everything I needed was up here. So, it wasn't like I had to lug anything up and down the gondola."

She'd ordered candles, garland, and white satin bows to decorate the chapel to look just as it had when their parents wed here nearly three decades ago.

And she'd succeeded.

Lori sighed, a deep contemplative sound.

Bridget bumped her sister's shoulder playfully. "What is it?"

"This," Lori answered as she walked over to the front row bench, sat down, then picked up one of the many photos scattered across the oak seat.

As if it required a moment of silence, the women stared at the picture of their parents, dressed in their wedding attire and standing less than six feet away from where they now sat.

"It's hard to believe we're here again," Bridget said as she joined her sister.

Lori glanced up, her eyes growing glassy. "I miss them, Birdie."

"So do I."

Bridget stared at the image of their parents. The couple wasn't looking at the camera. No, the photo captured the newlyweds staring into each other's eyes. Bridget had seen her mother and father do this, hundreds, maybe thousands of times. She also couldn't count how many times, as a young girl, she'd rolled her eyes at her lovey-dovey parents. But frozen in time, it was impossible to look away, and there was no eye-rolling employed now. No, she'd give anything to see them gazing at each other again.

Gently, she took the photo from her sister and turned it over to reveal *Delilah and Roger, Wedding Day at Kringle Mountain*, scrolled in Grandma Dasher's handwriting on the back.

Lori ran her finger over the inscription. "I wish they could be here."

Bridget nodded. "Me too."

She lifted her gaze from the picture, then stared at the place where her parents once stood—where they'd all once stood together many times over the years when they used to come here as a family.

"But you know, Lori, I think they are here. Can't you picture them? Standing there and holding hands as if it were their wedding day all over again?"

Lori threaded their arms together. "I can. I can also hear Mom telling us to stop standing on the benches."

Bridget blinked back tears as she laughed. "You were good at jumping across the aisle."

Lori cocked her head to the side. "Why didn't you ever try, Birdie? I can't remember you ever doing it?"

"I guess I was too scared to make the leap."

Just as the words left her lips, a heaviness settled in her chest.

That was true even today in nearly every aspect of her life.

She'd always thought that her parents and Grandma Dasher would be proud of how she'd cared for Lori—how she'd been a part of securing her sister's success. But what now? This wedding marked the end of the part of her who'd become more like a mother than a big sister. Lori was starting a new life with Tom. She had a partner. She'd found her soul mate.

Where did that leave her? She'd put her sister first in her mind for so long; what came next?

They sat there, each staring at the spot on the altar where their parents had stood when a whoosh of wind made the lights flicker, and the women gasped and clutched each other, startled and laughing until something sharp dug into her side.

"Ow! What have you got in your pocket?"

Lori patted her coat. "I almost forgot. Tom said a courier

delivered it to the mountain house for you," she replied, pulling a small box from her pocket.

"Tom's awake?" she asked carefully.

"Yes, he's been up for hours. But I haven't seen Scooter. Tom said he and Scooter had quite a night—a real nostalgia-fest. They talked about their boarding school days, college conquests, and stupid pranks they'd pulled on each other over the years."

"Really? That's all?" Bridget replied, going for casual.

What did she care?

But the uptick in her pulse betrayed her attempt at nonchalance.

"He also said Scooter drank about twice as much as he did, which Tom also said isn't like the guy. Why do you ask? Is there something going on with you and Scooter?" Lori added, eyeing her closely.

"No, of course not!"

Shoot! She couldn't have Lori thinking that she...what? Thought about Soren? Cared about Soren?

Did she care about Soren?

No, she was there to run defense and keep an eye on the man. And so far, she'd succeeded, that is, until last night when Tom intervened and requested a guys' night.

What was she supposed to do? Steal a Santa costume to go all *Kringle incognito*, search the village until she found them, then eavesdrop on the pair? No, once they'd all gotten back to the mountain house, *sans* the groom and the best man, Cole and Carly had kept her busy answering questions about Christmas fairies. There was no way she could have snuck back into the village.

She gathered a few stray pine needles from the bench. "So, that's all they talked about—old times?"

"I think so. Why?"

Why?

Bridget twisted the pine needles into a zig-zagged bunch, then crossed and uncrossed her legs.

She was the absolute worst at faking calm and collected.

The *why* rattling inside her head was because as much as she hated to admit it, she wanted to know if she'd gotten to Soren the way he'd gotten to her. And if he were to confide in anyone, it would be Tom.

And one thing was certain when it came to her and the worst best man.

Something happened to the two of them when they were within arm's reach of each other—and it had nothing to do with whatever Tanner had put in those gummy bears.

What had started out as pure wanton attraction the night they'd met in that darkened hotel bar had changed into this strange reality. Now, she couldn't remember what life was like just a week before when she was blissfully dating a cheating creep of a boyfriend and busting her ass for a tiny French pastry tyrant.

"You don't think Scooter dragged Tom to a strip joint or whatever the equivalent of that is in Kringle?" she asked.

Lori pressed her hand to her belly and chuckled. "No, Tom would have mentioned that."

She stared at her sister, surprised by her lack of concern.

"But you were so worried about Scooter's influence over Tom. Did something change?"

Lori glanced down and blew out a breath.

Bridget shook her head, feeling awful. "I'm sorry. I don't want you to think that I'd ever assumed Tom would do anything to hurt you. It's just that you were worried when we talked on the phone before I got here."

Now Lori was the one shaking her head. "No, I've had a lot on my mind with the wedding and—"

"And I get it," Bridget said, cutting her sister off. "This is an emotional time. I can't imagine how you're feeling. How about we change the subject, and I open that gift, so we can see what's inside?"

"Sure, let's take a look," Lori said, but something was on her sister's mind. She could sense it. Still, she didn't want to upset the woman. The fact that this was the first time they'd visited the Kringle Chapel without their parents was emotional enough.

She opened the box, then set it on her lap and removed the card.

"Who's it from, Birdie? Do you have a secret admirer in Kringle?" her sister teased, sounding more like herself.

Did she have an admirer? Could it be from Soren?

She slid the card from the slim envelope, anticipation building. But instantly, disappointment panged in her chest when she'd read the note.

"It's from the Kringle Cares organization. It says they wanted to share a token of their appreciation. They didn't have to get me anything," she replied, hating herself for hoping that Soren had sent the gift.

Her sister bumped her shoulder. "You did solve their cookie conundrum."

She pushed all thoughts of that man aside. The day he gave her a gift would be the day reindeer flew over Kringle Mountain with Rudolph leading the pack.

"It was nothing."

"You must know that it wasn't, Birdie," Lori said, and she could almost hear her grandmother in her sister's voice.

"It was sugar cookies."

"Yeah, a delicious snack for children and their families to enjoy at an event that they look forward to all year. And you pulled it off by mobilizing a group of people to help you bake a gazillion cookies in forty-five minutes. I think you sell yourself short. You could run your own shop."

She waved off her sister. "Let's see what they sent," she answered, ignoring the whole *start your own business* cheerleader routine Lori fell into any time they discussed baking.

She lifted away the tissue to reveal a necklace.

"Look, it's got an angel pendant. I saw these at a shop in the village. It's lovely, Birdie!"

Bridget traced a tiny wing with her index finger. "It is, isn't it?"

Lori took the box and carefully removed the necklace, then stood. "Let's get this on and see how it looks."

Bridget rose to her feet and gathered the wisps of hair that had broken free of her bun as Lori draped the chain around her neck.

"Shoot, Birdie! I'm terrible at these clasps," her sister said, fiddling with the necklace when a rush of cold air hissed through the snug space.

The heavy wooden doors slammed shut as Soren entered the chapel.

"I guess he's not the devil," Lori whispered into her ear.

Bridget bit back a grin. "Why are you here?"

She stared at the man. He hadn't shaved, and when he pulled off his hat, his hair was a sexy disarray of dark curls.

Of course, this Adonis of a man would look good, even hungover.

Soren took a few more steps inside the sanctuary. "I was told to be here."

"By who?"

"The judge. He said you were up here doing wedding *things*," he replied, stuffing his hands into his pockets as if that maneuver would protect him from the *wedding things* going on in the snug space.

He turned his attention to Lori and watched her a beat.

"Did you have something to tell me, Scooter?" her sister asked.

He glanced away. "Tom says you should probably head down to the mountain house. Everyone is getting ready to leave."

Bridget gasped. "That's right! You need to get back, so you're ready to leave for the concert on time."

"We're not going?" Soren asked.

She crossed her fingers behind her back. "No, you were so late to RSVP, I wasn't able to get you a ticket."

Honestly, she'd totally forgotten about looking into getting him a ticket. But it was better this way. Thank the stars, the Scooter and Tom bro-fest last night didn't sway Tom into calling off the wedding or doing something crazy that would upset her sister.

Still, the man had sent strippers—a ballsy move with everyone staying in the same location.

She cleared her throat. "And you wouldn't be able to go even if there was an extra ticket. You have best man duties, and you'll need to attend to me all night."

Soren and her sister stared at her.

She twisted an errant lock of hair. "I meant that you have best man duties to attend to, with me. Duties that include helping me in the kitchen and other wedding-only related tasks that require us to be fully clothed. All wedding preparations and no holiday hanky-panky," she finished, feeling her cheeks heat as she dug herself deeper into the hole.

Why did she let this man turn her brain into scrambled eggs?

"There you are, using that *hanky-panky* again. What's up with you?" Lori asked with a crinkle to her brow.

Ah, crap!

Bridget pressed her hand to Lori's back and guided her

toward the door. "It's a catchy little phrase. But never mind. You need to get yourself on that gondola, little sis. I'm going to tidy up in here, and then we'll be down to get the kids ready for bed."

"We're babysitting, too?" Soren blurted.

She put her hand on her hip and cocked her head to the side, channeling a little vixen into this exchange. "Yes, see what fun it is to be a *responsible* best man?"

"Be good, you two," Lori said, tossing her a confused glance, before continuing down the aisle, but she stopped when she got to Soren. "Could you help Birdie with this? I'm terrible with clasps," she added, dropping the necklace into his hand.

The rush of mountain air entered the space as Lori left, and then it was just the two of them.

She crossed her arms, dredging up a little more vixen sass. "Rough night, *Scooter*?"

He started toward her, his long strides eating the hardwood.

Why did his walk have to be so sexy?

He was awful. He was about to kill off Cupid Bakery. He didn't want Tom to marry Lori. If only the cavewoman inside her could get the memo and stop getting all tingly whenever he was within ten feet of her.

"I've had rougher. Turn around."

She sucked in an audible breath. "Why?"

It was happening again. She could feel the rational part of her brain turning into oatmeal raisin cookie dough.

Something hard and dark flashed in the man's eyes. "So I can bend you over that bench and have my way with you."

She parted her lips, but not even the vixen part of her had a response for that.

A mirthless smirk twisted his lips. "I'm kidding, Bridget. It's so I can help you with your damn necklace," he answered, holding the delicate chain in front of her face as if he were preparing to hypnotize her.

"Right, yeah," she swiveled around and waited, biting her lip to get herself under some semblance of control.

"Where'd you get this?" he asked, his voice gruff.

"The Kringle Cares group sent it as a thank you," she replied as his fingers trailed across the base of her neck.

"That lady did call you her angel."

She steadied herself. "It was no big deal. I was happy to help."

"Always, the helper. There, it's on," he said, stepping away from her as heat again bloomed on her cheeks. But this time, she wasn't embarrassed. No, she was angry. What kind of Grinch was against helping others?

"Yes, I like to help when I can. You should try it for once," she countered.

He scoffed. "It's not who I am."

"No kidding," she huffed under her breath.

She had to remember that this was who he was to her—a grade A jerk intent on keeping the Abbotts a Dasher-free zone.

He ran his hands through his hair. "Listen, Bridget, I'm here. What do you want me to do?"

She glanced around the chapel. All the decorations and greenery were in place. Once the candles were lit, the sanctuary would glow, bathed in the warm light. There was really nothing left to do but clean up. She spied the broom in the corner and pointed to it.

"You can sweep up the loose pine needles."

He frowned. "You want me to sweep?"

She stared up at the wooden beams. "Please don't tell me that you've never used a broom."

A muscle ticked on his jaw. "I know how to use a broom," he shot back, plucking the old thing from the corner.

She gave him a screw-you grin. "Congratulations, now get to work."

No matter if they were in a hotel suite, kitchen, or chapel, this man brought out the fire in her—the vixen she never knew dwelled beneath the surface. Was that a good thing? Being a bitch was never a good thing, but with Soren, it worked. She glanced over to find him doing a damn good job sweeping up every loose pine needle.

Maybe he was good for something other than supplying her with multiple orgasms.

Ugh! Focus!

She pushed the idea out of her head and went to the bench to collect the items she'd brought to decorate when Soren's voice cut through the swish of the broom.

"What were you and Lori talking about?"

She brushed a few bits of trimmed ribbon into her hand. "Just now?"

"Yeah," he replied, not making eye contact.

She held up one of the photos. "Our parents' wedding. This is where they got married."

Soren propped the broom against the wall, then came to her side. "They look happy."

"They were very much in love, like Lori and Tom," she replied, getting in a little dig.

But his eyes revealed nothing.

"Lori didn't have any big news?" he asked, expressionless.

What was he after?

"Soren, what are you talking about?"

He shook his head. "Nothing."

Just great! They were back to Soren, the stone man.

"Is there something I should know?" she pressed.

Had Tom mentioned something?

That muscle on Soren's cheek ticked again. "No."

Tired of playing games, the vixen inside her took over.

"Is this how you act when you're hungover? A cretin who grunts and responds with one word?" she questioned.

"I wish like hell this was just a bad hangover." He looked around. "Are you done?"

Now, on top of being a Grinch of a curmudgeon, he was also an enigma!

"Yeah, let's head down to the mountain house," she replied, keeping him in her peripheral vision as she put on her coat, then collected the photographs.

He looked like the same man—a little rougher around the edges—but there was something different about him today.

He opened the door and held it for her as they crunched through the snow over to the waiting gondola. She entered the enclosed space and rubbed her hands together. Soren took no notice of her as he closed the door and hit the button to start the lift, and slowly, the gondola began its descent down the mountain.

She touched the glass. "It's like being in a snow globe, isn't it?" she offered, staring out at the flurry of white circling around them.

She'd extended the olive branch. Would he take it?

The answer: a colossal no.

Nothing. The man couldn't even agree on something as trivial as snow acting like...snow.

She turned to him, ready to lay into him yet again for excessive *bah humbug* behavior when the gondola lurched, and she fell forward into his arms.

Suspended in time, they stared at each other.

"Dan said that the gondola's been acting up," he said, their noses touching as he held her in his firm grip.

"Oh," she replied, capable of nothing else.

She stared into his eyes and again saw that flash of searing pain. And heaven help her, her heart literally ached, wanting to quell whatever storms raged inside him. Because no matter how hard he tried to put up an icy front, she knew firsthand that the man was capable of fiery passion and all-encompassing desire. But before she could say another word, he morphed back into aloof curmudgeon mode.

He set her back on her side of the gondola. "You need to stay over there to keep the weight even. Do you think you can do that?"

She bit her tongue and ignored him.

How would she get through the night with this Grinch?

Luckily, they'd be with Cole and Carly, but that would only be for a little while. She'd put him to work. That's what she'd do. After the kids were in bed, she had to assemble the croquembouche. A labor-intensive endeavor, the French dessert consisted of several ping-pong ball-sized profiteroles, a pastry similar to cream puffs, stacked into a tree-shaped tower that's held together by drizzled caramel. She'd made the many profiteroles this morning, but the real work was in constructing the tower and making sure it held its cone-like Christmas tree shape before decorating it with sugar and almonds.

She'd put him on caramel duty or make him hold the cone that held the dessert in place.

"What do you want me to do with a cone?"

She blinked. "Did you say something?"

He frowned. "No, you said something. You're doing that thing again where you talk out loud without realizing it."

She huffed her disbelief. "I do not do that!"

"You just said you wanted my balls in a cone," he answered without the hint of emotion.

Dammit!

Screw him! No, not screw him!

To hell with him!

She lifted her chin. "I don't want your balls, *Scooter*. I was thinking about all the things I needed to get done tonight. You're going to help me put together a dessert made of many ball-shaped pastries that requires a cone."

He cocked his head to the side. "Street cones? Like the ones they put on the road? What the hell type of dessert requires diverting traffic?"

She laughed. She couldn't help it. He may be all Mr. Surly, but he didn't know a damn thing about baking.

"It's a pastry cone used to shape the dessert and hold it in place. And no, it's not made with an orange traffic cone."

He sat back and watched her. "You know a decent amount about baking."

Bridget stared at the man. "Is that a question or a statement?"

"Question."

She sighed and glanced at the mountain. "I know enough."

She could feel his eyes on her, taking it all in as if he were weighing her worth.

This had to stop.

She cleared her throat. "Tonight, we need to get the kids to bed and then finish up a few things for the rehearsal dinner. After that, you can do whatever you want."

He nodded as the gondola came to a stop, and the Kringle Mountain House glowed against the mountain backdrop as the darkening skies crept in.

"Whatever," he mumbled.

The light snow continued to fall as the wind kicked up, swirling snow across the mountain. They headed to the house only to have Delores open the door as they stepped onto the porch.

"Good! You're back. The children were asking for you," she said, ushering them in out of the cold.

Smoldering logs crackled and popped in the roaring fireplace as they entered the main room to find it quite altered. The sofas and loveseats sat bare of their padding, and the cushions and throw pillows littered the ground.

"The floor is lava!" Cole called, adjusting his candy apple red glasses as he hopped from pillow to pillow.

Bridget searched the room. "Where is everyone?"

"Dan wanted to leave a little early on account of the snow," Delores replied.

Bridget checked her watch. "I'm sorry. I didn't think they were leaving for another half hour."

"It's no trouble. I was happy to spend some time with the youngsters. I'll be in my cabin if you need anything. And don't forget about Frosty. Safety first," the woman answered with a singsong trill as she headed out the side door that led to the cabins.

What was up with Delores and safe sex?

"Uncle Scooter, your feet are in the lava!" Carly cried, bless-edly calling attention away from the condom filled snowman as she leaped from a chair to a couch cushion.

"Save yourself!" Cole cried.

Bridget chuckled, but when she looked at Soren, his green eyes again flashed that deep, agonizing pain. He glanced at her, then back at the kids. He smiled at them, but it wasn't his Uncle Scooter smile. That grin brimmed with affection and excite-ment. This one showed a hint of melancholy.

He kicked off his snow boots and jumped onto the pillow next to Cole.

"Birdie, you're not going to make it. Help her, Uncle Scooter!" Carly directed.

"Can't she get on her own cushion?" he asked.

"They're not cushions! They're rocks!" Cole corrected, getting into it.

"And they're the only things keeping us from getting burnt to a crisp!" his sister added, not to be outdone by her little brother.

"The floor is lava!" the children cried in unison.

Reluctantly, Soren reached toward her. "You better play along. If you haven't noticed, Carly and Cole don't mess around with this game."

"Remember last Christmas when you jumped over the coffee table to get to the couch, and Uncle Tom balanced on one foot until we threw him another pillow?"

Soren ruffled the boy's hair. "Yeah, I remember."

"Hurry, Birdie! Hurry!" Carly chided.

Bridget took off her boots, then reached toward Soren. He took her hand, and the electricity they could not seem to escape crackled between them as he pulled her onto the cushion.

She inhaled. He no longer smelled like the inside of a whiskey bottle. No, now the tantalizing sandalwood scent she remembered from their first night sent her reeling. She rocked back, but he caught her.

"You need to be careful. Someone might not always be there to catch you," he said, looking as shellshocked as she felt.

She nodded. She knew that better than anyone. For the last ten years, she'd had only herself to rely on.

"Jump over to me, Birdie!" Carly beckoned.

"Yeah, let her go, Uncle Scooter," Cole added.

Soren stared at her a beat before dropping his hands from her waist.

She shook her head, clearing the Soren-inspired cobwebs, then glanced between the kids.

"I'm going to jump, and then you two are going to get into your pajamas," she said in her best big sister voice.

"Aw, Birdie," the siblings whined in unison.

"Don't you, 'aw, Birdie, me,'" she teased. "Your moms want you in bed a little early. We've got a lot going on tomorrow, and we don't want you falling asleep while we're eating all the desserts that I'm making for the rehearsal dinner."

"Desserts!" the kids yelled, then hightailed it from cushion to cushion before they jumped over the couch and headed down the hall that led to their room.

She watched the kids scamper away. "That was easy."

"Denise and Nancy don't let them indulge in sweets all that often. If you mention dessert, you can pretty much get them to do whatever you want," he said, picking up a couple cushions, then tossing them back onto the couch.

She followed suit, gathering the throw pillows. "Good to know."

The pendulum swung, and the man she'd pegged as a creep again proved her wrong—at least when it came to Cole and Carly.

With the room back in order, silently, they walked side by side down the hall. Giggles met their arrival as they entered the kids' room and found them already under the covers.

"Did you brush your teeth?" Soren asked in quite the paternal tone.

"Yes!" the kids answered, squirming under the covers next to each other in the queen-sized bed.

"Did you use the bathroom? Cole, I'm talking to you," Soren continued.

The boy groaned. "Yes, Uncle Scooter, I'm empty."

Carly sat up. "Birdie, what are you wearing? Is that a new necklace?"

Bridget touched the angel pendant. "Yes, it is. Remember the nice people we helped when we made all those sugar cookies?"

"Yeah."

"They sent me this as a thank you present," she finished, sitting on the bed to give the girl a closer look.

"It's an angel," Carly said, leaning in.

Cole crawled across the bed to take a look. "Is it a snow angel? Did a Christmas fairy make it?"

Bridget chuckled. "Maybe."

"Will you tell us more about Christmas fairies?" Cole asked, sinking into the pillows.

She tapped her chin theatrically. "You already know that they love to make snow angels, and that they're shy, extremely hard to catch in the act, and can also offer you a Christmas wish."

"Yes, we've been looking all over for them," Carly replied.

"Has my sister told you about the time when a Christmas fairy left us a present?" she asked as Soren settled himself on the other side of the bed next to Cole.

The little boy gasped. "No, Aunt Lori didn't say anything about presents."

Soren's expression grew a touch sour at the mention of *Aunt Lori*—no surprise there!

She waved the children in. "Well, a few days before Christmas, when my sister and I weren't much older than the two of you, Lori and I went looking for snow angels. And guess what?"

"What?" Carly asked on a bated breath.

"We found one."

"You did?" Cole whispered as Soren gave a skeptical harrumph. But she ignored his *bah humbuggery*.

"We didn't see the fairy when we found the snow angel. We were too late. But she'd left us something."

"What was it?" Carly asked, twisting the covers in anticipation.

Bridget lowered her voice. "Two candy canes. One on each wing."

"One for you and one for Aunt Lori?" Carly asked.

"Yes, and they were the sweetest, most pepperminty candy canes we'd ever tasted."

"Wow!" Cole breathed, grinning ear to ear.

A warmth filled her chest, imagining her mother and father making the snow angel, leaving the treats, then using a shovel to smooth out the tracks around the make-believe fairy's creation.

She tapped Carly's nose, then Cole's. "And with that, it's bedtime. Sweet dreams."

"Will you make me a Scooter burrito?" Carly asked, reaching out to the somber man on the other side of the bed.

Soren glanced at her, then to the girl. "Sure, Carly. One Scooter burrito coming up."

"With the sound effects, please," Carly requested, wiggling with excitement.

The man shook his head as the hint of a smile appeared on his lips. "You got it."

Soren vroomed as he tucked the blanket around the little girl like a race car or, in his case, a scooter. It was sweet—a counter to the gruff, growly man who'd met her at the chapel.

"Cole, do you want a Scooter burrito tuck-in, too?" he asked, patting the boy's leg.

"Not tonight," the child answered, adjusting his glasses.

"Would you like me to set those on the side table for you?" she asked.

Cole stopped playing with his bright red glasses. "No, I'll do it by myself in a minute. I have one more question about fairies, though."

"Sure, what is it?"

"Is a pixie a fairy," he asked with a serious expression.

She nodded. "Yes, a pixie is very much like a fairy."

"All right, Abbott kids. Eyes closed," Soren said, ending the fairy talk and switching off the light.

She went to the door and stood next to him. "We'll be in the kitchen if you need anything."

"Okay, Aunt Birdie. I mean, just Birdie," Carly said through a yawn.

She glanced at Soren, expecting to find the silly, sweet uncle who just made vroom sounds, but found him frowning. The Aunt Birdie slip of the tongue most likely the culprit. They stepped into the hall but left the door to the children's room open a crack.

"Let's get this over with," he said, striding down the corridor a step ahead of her.

She followed him into the kitchen about done with his lightning-fast personality shifts.

He glanced around the kitchen. "Where are the cones and the balls?"

She barked out a laugh. "There will be no cones or balls until we get something straight."

"What's that?" he asked, as if he couldn't care in the least.

"I don't understand what's going on with you, Soren. Do you hate me, or do you like me?"

He rubbed his hands down his face. "Bridget, stop."

She paced the length of the kitchen. "No, I'm tired of this. I'm sick of the back and forth. I'm exhausted from trying to decipher if you truly are an awful person or if there's more to you."

"More to me?" he repeated, condescension coating the words.

"Yes, there are times I think that maybe..."

"Let me stop you there, *Birdie*," he interjected. "You want to know what's going on? I hate that I can't hate you. How about that!"

"That makes no sense," she replied, turning away from him when two strong hands gripped her hips, spun her around, and pressed her back to the wall.

Soren cupped her cheek in his hand as his chest heaved, and lust and anguish burned in his eyes. "How about this for making sense, *Bridget Dasher*. My entire life made sense before you and your sister ruined the only part that mattered."

She clutched his biceps as his body pressed against hers, pinning her in place. But she didn't try to move—didn't attempt to escape. She'd be lying if she said she didn't like his hard angles cutting into her soft curves.

She steadied herself. "My sister has been nothing but kind to you, and I—"

He leaned in. "And you, with those damned hauntingly beautiful eyes that draw me in. And those perfect lips that make me want to kiss you and never stop are making me crazy. You smell like cookies and sunshine and lazy Sunday mornings. I don't know what a worse punishment would be—knowing what it's like to hold you close and make your body tremble with desire or never knowing. Never touching you. Never kissing you. Never knowing what it feels like to fucking feel anything."

She inhaled a sharp breath. "What happened, Soren? What changed? You're different—something is different. I've never seen you look so lost."

His gaze hardened. "I had everything under control until you. You turned my world upside down. Now, I can't go a damn hour, let alone a minute without thinking of you."

"Is that so terrible?" she whispered, her body trembling.

He ran his thumb across her bottom lip and tilted her chin up. "It's excruciating."

His lips grazed the corner of her mouth. But before they lost themselves, a little voice cut through the lust-charged haze.

"Uncle Scooter?"

In the space of a breath, she and Soren pulled apart.

"What is it, Carly? Did you have a bad dream?" he asked, doing his best to recover, but the slight shake to his voice gave away that he was just as stunned by their overpowering attraction as she was.

The little girl rubbed her eyes. "No, Cole's gone."

"Could he have gone to the bathroom?" Soren asked, his voice still a tight rasp.

"No, he's not there, Uncle Scooter. I think he went to look for a Christmas fairy."

A Christmas fairy?

Bridget stiffened as an ominous chill prickled down her spine.

"Now?" she asked, her voice going up an octave.

The temperature had to be well below freezing, and a blustery wind blew swirling pellets of snow against the window.

"His coat and boots are gone, Birdie," Carly replied.

She met Soren's eye and saw the same alarm she was sure was mirrored in her eyes.

"Hello? Are you in here?" Delores called from outside the kitchen.

Bridget ran into the main room with Soren on her heels.

"The back door was open, and I wanted to make sure everyone was okay," the caretaker said, concern marring her features.

Bridget's heart hammered in her chest. Panic flooded her system. She didn't want to frighten the little girl, but there was no time to waste. She grabbed her boots and threw on her coat.

"Would you mind helping Carly back to bed, Delores? I think Cole wandered outside. I have to find him," she said, working to keep her voice even.

Delores frowned, then glanced out the window. "In this weather?"

Bridget's stomach twisted into a sickening knot.

"Don't worry, I'll find him," she said over her shoulder as she hurried toward the door that led out to the cabins dotting the rugged mountain terrain.

The icy air stung her cheeks the moment she left the warmth

of the mountain house, but she pressed on, glancing wildly between the dark towering evergreens that seemed to be closing in at every angle.

"Bridget! Wait!"

She glanced back as a light bobbed in the darkness.

"Delores is calling Dan to let Denise and Nancy know what's going on," Soren said, coming to her side.

"We have to find him, Soren. It's so cold, and he won't last long on his own. It's my fault he's out there. I'm the one who filled his head with all those Christmas fairy stories," she said, her nerves getting the best of her as she trekked into the darkness.

He took her hand. "We'll find him. He couldn't have gotten far."

She gathered her wits. She had to be smart and keep her cool.

Step one: figure out which way Cole had ventured.

"Shine the light and check for tracks. The snow couldn't have covered them yet," she instructed.

Soren panned the golden beam across the dark expanse of snow, revealing pint-sized boot prints. They ran, following the tracks until Soren stopped.

"Bridget, look!"

"Do you see him?" Relief washed over her until a fleck of red caught her eye, dashing her hopes.

Soren plucked the item from the snow. "It's Cole's glasses. He can barely see without them."

She glanced around wildly, shielding her eyes from the biting wind whirling with frigid snow.

What chance did a five-year-old have out here on his own? And how could she ever forgive herself if anything happened to the little boy?

14

*S*oren stared at the tiny red spectacles, and his heart leaped into his throat.

"Oh my God!" Bridget said, her gaze trained on the child-sized frames.

On the one hand, finding Cole's glasses was a sure sign they were on the right track.

On the other, between the snow and the darkness, it was confirmation that the boy was unquestionably lost in the wilderness.

They didn't have a moment to lose.

"Cole, where are you? Call out to us!" he cried as he and Bridget dodged tree branches and trudged through drifts of snow.

"Cole, let us know where you are!" Bridget yelled.

They stopped to listen. The wind howled. It whipped their cheeks with unrelenting icy lashes.

"Cole, sweetheart, where are you?" Bridget tried again, her voice straining against the wind.

They needed a plan. Every minute that ticked by was another minute the young boy wandered farther away from the mountain house. And even worse, the snow, that had once revealed the boy's boot prints, now covered the ground in a pristine blanket of white, muting his path.

He took Bridget's hand. "Where do you think he'd go? Is there a spot he'd mentioned to you?"

She shook her head, then stilled. "Wait, I might know where he's headed."

"Where?" he pressed. This might be their only shot.

"When we first arrived at the mountain house, Cole talked about the cabins—the ones Dan had mentioned. There are several scattered along the mountainside, but they're summer and fall rentals and not equipped for the frigid winter temperatures."

He nodded. It was a start.

"Do you know where they are? You've been here before. You came here many times as a girl, right?"

She glanced into the darkness. "Yes, they're along the trails. Lori and I used to go snowshoeing on them with our parents. There are posts that mark which trail you're on. See," she said, pointing the light at a tall wooden pillar and something clicked in his mind—a snippet of a conversation he'd overheard.

"That's what Scott and Grace did with the kids today. I heard them telling Denise and Nancy about it before I left for the chapel. How many trails are there?"

"Several and they veer off and wind around. They traverse the mountain," she answered, then gasped.

"What is it?"

"Pixies!" she cried, shielding her face from a gust of icy wind.

He pulled her in to protect her from the arctic blast, allowing his back to bear the brunt of the cold.

"What do pixies have to do with finding Cole?" he asked, rubbing his hands on her arms to keep her warm. She'd grabbed her coat and gloves, but she had to be freezing in only leggings and a flannel beneath.

"Each cabin has a name. There's one called Pixie Rock Cottage. Lori and I loved it as children because of the name. And remember, Cole asked us about pixies when we were putting the kids to bed. He wanted to know—"

"If a pixie was the same thing as a fairy," he finished, putting it together.

Cole was after a Christmas fairy.

Determination edged out the anxiety welling in his chest. That had to be it. Despite pulling this late-night stunt, Cole was a bright kid. There had to be a reason for him taking a chance like this.

"Do you know how to get there?" he asked, shining the light into the trees.

"It's the furthest cabin from here—a tiny cottage nestled into the mountain." She took the flashlight and shined it into the inky darkness. The beam landed on a post fifty feet off in the distance. "It's that way. We have to follow the poles with red caps."

"That's got to be where he's headed," he said, about to set off when Bridget grabbed his arm.

"He did! Look!" she cried, shining the light on the hint of a print, dusted over with a smattering of fresh snow.

Before he could even acknowledge the discovery, she took off like a shot. Adrenaline coursed through his body as he caught up to her, pushing branches out of the way as they followed the snowshoeing path.

"We have to find him, Soren," she called, her voice a ragged scrape, but underneath the fear, steely resolve wove through her words.

The flashlight slipped in her hand, momentarily illuminating her face. She might be a petite thing, but dogged determination gleamed in her eyes—that heady vixen spark he'd seen the night he'd met her. He recognized the intense focus and the unwavering set of her jaw.

She might not know it, but she was a force to be reckoned with.

And the two of them would move heaven and earth to find Cole.

"We'll find him!" he answered, praying he was right.

"Cole!" Bridget shouted as they passed another red-capped post, but the child didn't respond.

The wind whistled through the thick clusters of evergreens, a stark reminder of the harsh terrain.

As much as he and Bridget were hellbent on finding the boy, the dangers that lurked in the darkness couldn't be discounted.

No, he could not let his mind go there.

He kept moving, straining his eyes to focus on the slim light cutting through the darkness. Bridget tightened her grip on his coat sleeve. Her audible breaths were the only sound he could hear over the wind until the faint hint of a child's voice passed by like a thread drifting on a current of icy air.

"Is that you, Christmas fairy?"

He wrapped his arm around Bridget and forced her to stop. "I think that's Cole!"

They stood stock-still, straining to listen above the rustle of the wind through the imposing foliage.

"Christmas fairy, where are you?" came Cole's trembling voice.

Bridget wiped the swirling snow from her eyes, then shined the light over a wide swath of white drifts. "He has to be by the cabin. We're not far. If I remember right, Pixie Rock is past the next post."

He took the flashlight from her and shined it into the distance, catching the tip of a wooden pillar.

"Cole, it's Uncle Scooter and Birdie! Can you hear me? Tell us where you are!" he called at the top of his lungs as they headed toward the cabin.

"I'm here! I'm here! I'm cold, and I'm scared!" the boy cried.

"We're coming! Don't move! Stay right where you are!" he shouted, working to keep the shake of frantic relief out of his voice while his heart shattered into a million pieces. He was damned grateful to hear Cole's voice but terrified he'd be hurt or suffering from frostbite.

He shared a look with Bridget, and his fears were reflected in her worried gaze.

"He's in one piece. He'll be okay," he said, more to himself than to her, but he had to say the words.

Then, as if out of thin air, the flashlight's beam hit the side of a cabin. He waved it around carefully, taking in the structure, and paying special attention to a pair of windows framing a stone chimney.

They'd made it! Now, with the minutes ticking away and the temperature dropping, they had to find the boy.

"Cole!" he bellowed.

"I'm here, Uncle Scooter!"

"The porch. He's on the porch," Bridget exclaimed, taking off as they rounded the curve and arrived at the front of the cabin.

Cole sat on the bottom step—a tiny ball in the darkness, his arms clutching his knees.

Bridget sank to the ground and hugged the child. "We're so glad we found you!"

He joined her and gathered the two of them into his strong embrace. "Are you okay, buddy? Did you get hurt?"

"My mommies are going to be so mad," the boy whimpered, his little body shaking.

"No, you're not in any trouble. I'm sure they'll be so happy that you're okay," Bridget replied, stroking Cole's cheek.

The child's body swayed as the boy went limp. "I'm really cold and so, so sleepy."

Shit! That wasn't good!

Bridget met his eye, and a fresh surge of adrenaline coursed through his veins.

They couldn't let him fall asleep. Not until he'd warmed up, and they could assess his condition.

There was no time to get him back to the mountain house. They needed shelter now. He glanced around, shining the beam of light across the front of the cabin, and spied half a dozen logs piled next to the front door.

"We need to get him inside and start a fire," he said, coming to his feet.

"I don't think the cabins are open in the winter," she replied, glancing at the imposing door.

He took off his coat and wrapped it around Cole, then tried the doorknob. Bridget was right. The damn thing wouldn't budge.

He stepped back and stared at the barrier that separated them from shelter.

It was time to see what two hours a day in the gym pumping iron could do.

He reared back, and with all the force he could muster, he charged the door with his shoulder. His body pounded into the hard wood, the force reverberating through his flesh and bones. But he felt no pain as the creak of metal buckling and the scrape of wood on wood cut through the gusts of icy wind. The hinges whined in protest as the door gave way; no match for his strength and determination. Losing no time, he scooped up as much wood as he could carry.

"Come on. We need to get him out of the cold," he said, ushering them inside.

Bridget lifted Cole into her arms and hurried inside.

He headed straight for the stone hearth, arranged a trio of logs in the fireplace, and then shined the beam around the space. Sparsely furnished, the simple one-room cabin would be their refuge until they could make sure Cole was okay. He ran his hand along the mantle, then thanked the Pixie Rock fairies when a box of matches slid into his palm.

Bridget grabbed a blanket slung over a chair and wrapped it around the boy as the two sat on the floor a few feet away.

He glanced over his shoulder. "Do you have anything in your pockets that we can use as kindling?"

Bridget cradled Cole in her arms. "No, I don't think so."

He set the matches down and pulled his wallet from his back pocket.

"Hold the light," he said, handing Bridget the flashlight as he opened his billfold and pulled out the cash—the only paper he could think of.

But he wasn't prepared for what else was tucked away between the bills.

With a red border and a festive stocking printed above three distinct images, the photo strip sat prominently on top. Two images of them, all silly smiles. The final shot captured them kissing—looking as if they were made for each other. He'd forgotten he'd tucked the evidence from their time in the photo booth away in his wallet. Clumsily, he slid the strip to the bottom of the pile, but Bridget's sharp intake of breath signaled her surprise and recognition.

"I remember the sound of the flashbulb," she whispered, and the vice grip that held his heart captive loosened a fraction.

But this wasn't the time to unpack the cluster of competing emotions that boiled to the surface at the thought of Bridget Dasher. More than that, he had no time to worry about looking like some sucker who'd saved her picture. Working quickly, he set a few bills on the floor, then returned the picture and the rest of the money to his wallet.

He struck a match, lit the first bill on fire, then held it near the logs. Thank Christ, the covered porch had kept the wood dry. He stared at the flame, dancing in the darkness as the lapping orange glow took hold and the top log began to burn.

His muscles trembling from the frigid temperatures, and the adrenaline tapering off, he sat back as the small fire crackled and took hold in the hearth.

"Mommy said you were rich, Uncle Scooter. But I didn't know you were so rich that you could light money on fire."

There was that pint-sized spitfire of a five-year-old.

Lit by the glow of the burning logs, he couldn't hold back a relieved, grateful grin. "I don't usually like to burn money, Cole. But this was a unique situation."

"Here, you've got to be cold," Bridget said, handing him his coat.

He slipped it on. "Did you check Cole? Is anything broken, or are there any signs of frostbite?

She patted the boy's shoulder. "I'm no doctor but, he looks okay to me. He had on his gloves, and he can still move his fingers and toes."

"Are you warming up, buddy?" he asked.

Cole nuzzled into Bridget's lap, pulled the blanket over his head, and let out a heart-wrenching sob.

Bridget uncovered the child's face. "What is it, honey? Does something hurt?"

The boy shook his head as tears streamed down his cheeks. "My glasses! I lost my glasses, looking for the Christmas fairy. I was running and running because I thought this would be the perfect place to see a fairy. It's far away from anyone, and it's got a fairy name," the boy whimpered.

He patted Cole's leg. "Lucky for you, Uncle Scooter and Aunt

Birdie found them," he said, pulling the frames from his pocket and handing them over.

"It's not Aunt Birdie. It's just Birdie, Uncle Scooter," Cole corrected, slipping on the red frames.

"Right, just Birdie." He glanced at Bridget, who looked at him with such tenderness that the breath caught in his throat. "Sorry, you know what I meant," he finished, sounding nothing like a sharp-witted corporate raider and everything like a tongue-tied enamored teenager.

They stared at each other. The flickering glow of the fire sent shadows across her face. She was so hauntingly beautiful it was almost too much. He'd seen plenty of attractive women. Models and socialites dolled themselves up for a chance to spend the evening on his arm. But those women couldn't hold a candle to Bridget Dasher. Completely disheveled, with wild dark tendrils framing her face, he'd never seen anything quite as exquisite as this radiant woman. And again, like each time before, he couldn't ignore the pull between them.

"You're staring," she said softly with the trace of a sweet smile.

He pretended to check the fire. "I wanted to make sure you were all right, that's all."

"Do you want to kiss Birdie, Uncle Scooter?" Cole asked, perking up.

His mouth opened and closed like a confused goldfish. "No, why would you even think that?"

"Because you're looking at her real, real hard. Like she's a cookie, and you want to eat her. But you can't eat a person. So, I thought you really, really, really wanted to taste Birdie, and the only way to do that is to kiss her."

Holy hell! This kid was way more observant than any kinder-gartner should be.

"Well," he began when a sharp ping cut through the crackle of the fire.

"Is that your phone?" he asked, directing the question to the pink-cheeked Bridget.

"No, it's Cole," she replied, peeling back the blanket.

"It's my tracker," the boy answered with a nonchalant wave of his little hand.

"Your what?" he asked.

"My tracker for skiing. Mommy put it on my coat and one on Carly's coat, too. We have them so she can find us if we got separated on the mountain," Cole answered, showing them the circular fob attached to the zipper of his jacket.

"Delores must have gotten word to everyone," Bridget said when a grinding, mechanical rumble thundered over the crackle of the fire.

"What could that be?" he asked as the fob continued to beep.

"It sounds like a snowcat," Bridget answered, coming to her feet.

The grind of an engine ceased, and within seconds, Cole's tracker stopped beeping, and voices cried out.

"Cole! Scooter!"

He caught Bridget's eye. "It's Denise."

"Your moms are here, Cole," Bridget said, smoothing the boy's hair across his forehead.

Nancy was the first inside the cabin. "Honey, what happened?" she asked, falling to her knees and gathering the boy into her arms.

At the sight of his mother, tears trailed down his cheeks. "I wanted to see a Christmas fairy. I wanted to make a Christmas wish. Am I in trouble?"

"Oh, Cole," she replied, her voice a cascade of nerves and relief.

Denise stood in the doorway with her hand pressed to her

heart, then turned and called out toward two beams of light tinged with red. "He's here! Scooter and Birdie are with him."

Nancy glanced up. "Thank you for finding my little boy. I'm so sorry you had to venture out into this awful weather!"

Bridget shook her head. "No, I'm the one who should be sorry. I told Cole all about the fairies. If it wasn't for me..." she trailed off, anguish written all over her face.

"If it wasn't for you, this evening could have ended far worse," Denise answered as she entered the cabin, then sank to her knees to embrace her son.

"The tracker was a good call," he said, working to smooth out the shake in his voice as the true magnitude of the evening sank in.

Denise sighed and wiped her cheek. "Kids. They make you crazy, but I couldn't imagine a life without this pint-sized knuck-lehead," she finished with a teary chuckle as she ruffled her son's hair.

"I didn't lose my glasses, right, Uncle Scooter? See, they're still on my face. So, I probably shouldn't be in big, big trouble," Cole added, tossing him an uneasy glance.

Soren bit back a grin. He wasn't about to fill in the details of how the kid got his frames back. In fact, he was impressed. Cole's negotiation skills were on par with all the legal eagles in his family.

"Yep, your glasses are safe and sound, just like you, buddy."

Denise released a slow breath, and the woman he admired, who'd nicknamed him Scooter all those years ago, held her son's gaze, going into social worker mode.

"While we're so relieved that you're all right, you could have gotten hurt, son. It's never okay to go out alone without telling anyone, especially into the wilderness."

"But the Christmas fairies, Mommy! They would have

protected me," Cole answered with the trusting innocence of a child.

"Fairies didn't rescue you tonight, Cole. Guardian angels did," Nancy said, glancing between himself and Bridget.

He looked over at his guardian angel counterpart. She smiled and nodded, but he'd caught the flash of guilt in her eyes.

She didn't see herself as an angel. No, she blamed herself.

Nancy lifted Cole into her arms. "It's been quite a night, kiddo. Everyone's back at the mountain house, and we should get going. Dan's friend from Kringle Acres took us up in a snow-cat, and we don't want to keep him out late either."

"You got to ride in a snowcat?" Cole exclaimed, clearly catching his second wind.

"Yep, there's too much snow to get here in a car, so we came up along one of the ski runs," Nancy answered.

Cole gasped excitedly. "Do I get to ride in the snowcat, too?"

"You do. The nice man even let us take the snowcat they call Rudolph. It's got a red light on top just like—"

"Rudolph, the Red-nosed Reindeer! Let's go!" Cole cried, pumping his little fist—another sign that the child was no worse for wear.

With Cole in her arms, Nancy headed for the door.

"Come on, Birdie and Uncle Scooter!" Cole chimed.

"Honey, they'll have to wait," Nancy replied.

Cole frowned through a yawn. "Why?"

Denise turned to them. "It's a tight fit in the snowcat. Rudolph's operator said he could come back for the two of you."

Bridget shook her head, then resurrected a plastic expression, but he could see right through it.

"No, you don't have to do that. I know the way back. I'll stay behind and put out the fire," she replied as she twisted the cuff of her coat.

"Are you sure?" Denise asked, eyeing them warily.

"Yes, I'll stay with Birdie to help with the fire and secure the door. We made it here just fine, and there looks to be a break in the snow," he added, glancing out the window. The brutal pellets that had battered the cabin had tapered off since they'd arrived.

And he wouldn't let her stay behind on her own. But there was something else lurking beneath the surface of her placating expression. They walked to the porch with Denise, and the sharp scent of diesel from the snowcat idling hung in the air as two golden beams sandwiched a red flashing light, painting the darkness in a holiday glow.

"I'm riding in Rudolph," Cole called, waving from the snowcat as Nancy helped the boy inside the cab.

Denise descended the porch steps but stilled before heading to the waiting vehicle. "Nancy's right. Tonight, you two truly were Cole's guardian angels."

He waved her off. "We're just glad he's okay. We'll see you back at the mountain house."

The wind had died down, and he and Bridget stood side by side as the beams of light from the purring snowcat faded into the darkness. He glanced over his shoulder at the hearth. The three logs crackled as the fire burned through the wood.

"You know, we don't have to stay. The fire will burn itself out in a half-hour or so," he said, following her back into the cabin.

Bridget stared into the waning firelight. "I know."

He stood a step behind her, wanting more than anything to touch her—to reach out and take her into his arms but stifled the impulse.

"I know what you're thinking," he said instead.

"And what's that?" she asked.

"That you're to blame."

She took the poker that rested against the side of the fireplace, then prodded the logs, separating them to allow the remaining flames to peter out.

"I am to blame. I had a feeling Cole was up to something. But I never thought he'd sneak out on his own. And we only knew he was gone because Carly came into the kitchen and found us..."

Found us.

Found them engrossed in the dance that had become like second nature when passions flared, and every impulse drove him to her like a ship lost at sea, finally catching a glimmer of light from a safe harbor.

"You're not to blame, Bridget. Cole's headstrong, and once he gets an idea, there's no stopping him. Last Christmas, I gave him a one-thousand-piece puzzle. He wouldn't stop working on it until he had it finished. It took the whole family, but we got it done. It was the longest five hours of my life, and Cole never left the table. He's tenacious like that."

Bridget poked the logs once more and smoldering embers replaced the expiring flames. A cocoon of misty darkness surrounded them as they stood there in silence for what seemed like ages before Bridget glanced over her shoulder at him.

"You're not a horrible person, Soren."

He chuckled, not expecting that. "That's what you have to say after all we've been through tonight?"

Her eyes full of questions as the moonlight streaming in from the window framed her features in a blue glow. "I don't understand you. I don't know how someone can be so cold and cruel and then be so kind and tender."

With the scent of the burnt cedar logs suspended in the air, a tiny crack formed in the impenetrable walls he'd constructed around his heart. Like a sinner on the cusp of confession, he closed his eyes.

"It's how I survive."

Survival. That's what his life consisted of when he wasn't with the Abbotts.

She took a step toward him. "What do you mean?"

He shook his head, trying to hold back the words. But he couldn't. Not with her.

"My parents didn't want me. Neither wanted to have a child. I was a mistake. An inconvenience."

She blinked, giving nothing away.

And just like that—he'd revealed his cards to the one person who could ruin everything.

15

SOREN

*H*e'd heard the words. He'd said them, for Christ's sake! But he didn't expect that this admission would come with such succinct clarity.

Tom knew the gist of his story. His best friend knew about his parents' careless disregard for their only child. But he'd never spoken the words aloud to anyone. He'd never laid it out in black and white.

"Soren," Bridget said, the two syllables like a salve to his heart.

He held her gaze, unable to look away. "It's not like I grew up in squalor—quite the opposite. I never went without. Both my mother and father come from money. Old money. I went to the best schools, lived in expensive homes, but neither of my parents had the drive or the desire to be anything more than ornaments on the social scene. A child threw a wrench into their lives. There was a forced marriage, followed by a bitter divorce before I'd even taken my first steps. The wealth allowed my parents to hire people to care for me. Well, the word care is a stretch, but I did have one kind nanny—Janine. She's my secretary now. She tries to keep me in line when I'm not with..."

"Tom and his family?" Bridget supplied.

"Yeah."

"Do you see your parents very often?"

He stared into the darkness. How long had it been since he'd heard his mother's moneyed trill of a laugh or caught one of his father's blasé remarks?

Years.

A message on his phone the day he'd graduated from college.

He'd invited them to come to Boston.

A mistake.

When he'd looked out into the crowd, he'd only seen the Abbotts and the two empty chairs Grace had saved for his absent mother and father.

Something's come up, and I won't be able to make it, Soren.

That something? A party on a yacht docked in St. Croix.

At least the son of a bitch had called. His mother had blown the day off entirely. He'd come to learn she'd been shopping in Monte Carlo.

"No, I barely saw my parents when I was growing up. The divorce gave them shared parental rights, but that only meant that I was shuttled from one penthouse to another. But they were never there. They'd timed their travels perfectly to avoid me. Once I was sent to boarding school, I was truly out of sight and out of mind. During those years, I had more contact with the court and the law firm that oversaw my finances. Once I graduated from law school, I stopped taking their money and built my own private equity firm."

"Why didn't you practice law?"

The vice clamped around his heart tightened. "I decided to use the knowledge I'd gained in school to start my company. I wanted to make money—a lot of money and do it quickly."

And he wanted the power to tear this world apart the way

his soul had been shredded by the two people who should have nurtured it. He'd funneled that ruthless energy into any company that didn't make the cut. But he wasn't about to admit that.

"It must have been very lonely," she said, her voice barely a whisper.

"It was."

Here in this abandoned cabin, he revealed himself to her—this woman who he'd known for less than a week. She'd worked her way into his psyche. By sharing this slice of his tortured past with her, it unburdened his heart and loosened the hold of the anger and disappointment he'd harbored for so many years. But he couldn't share the darkest part—the kernel of torment that never left. Even in the best of times, it nudged and cajoled him. It whispered in his ear before he succumbed to slumber each night.

You are a Traeger Rudolph.

Cut from the same cloth as your parents.

The brutal truth?

If not for the Abbotts, he'd be no different from his mother and father.

But he couldn't reveal that. No, that fear had woven itself around his heart so tightly that it had become part and parcel of who he was in the depth of his soul. And while he felt a strange relief sharing his past with this enigma of a vixen, he couldn't reveal this part to her or to anyone.

His most ruinous flaw.

"Do you mind if I ask what happened to your mom and dad?" he said, needing desperately to change the subject.

Bridget stared into the hearth's dying light. "They were on their way to celebrate their anniversary. They'd booked two nights at a hotel downtown. It was a big deal. I remember my mother putting on lipstick. She never wore all that much makeup, so I knew this little getaway was a big deal. My parents were college professors, so we didn't grow up with a lot of money, but we always made do. Lori and I were staying with my grandma Dasher for the weekend. We'd only been at her house a few hours before there was a knock at the door, and we found two police officers standing on my grandmother's porch."

He watched her closely. "What happened?"

"They were there to tell us that our parents had been in an accident. That's when we learned that my mother and father had died like they lived—helping people."

"What do you mean—helping people?"

"A woman was on the side of the road trying to change a flat tire, and they stopped to help her put on the spare when a drunk driver plowed into them. From what the officer told us, it happened very quickly. They were both gone by the time the ambulance had gotten them to the hospital. After that, Lori and I lived with my grandmother until she was taken by cancer almost two years later. Thankfully, she didn't suffer too badly, and just like that, we'd lost them all."

He knew she was strong—but what she'd endured would crush the spirit of most people.

But not her.

"Jesus, I'm sorry, Bridget. I don't know what to say. I had no idea."

Of course, he didn't because he hadn't taken a lick of interest in Tom's fiancée and her family—or lack thereof.

"You don't have to be sorry. I only had my parents and my grandma Dasher, but Lori and I grew up surrounded by love." She shook her head. "That was insensitive of me! I didn't mean to sound so thoughtless."

He took a step toward her. His eyes had adjusted to the darkness, and in the moonlight that came and went as the clouds lumbered across the night sky, hiding and revealing the curve of her cheek and the set of her chin, he twisted a lock of her hair between his fingers before tucking it behind her ear.

"You're not thoughtless, Bridget. You're..."

Luminous.

Truly good-hearted.

Extraordinarily devoted to others.

"You're smart and focused. I don't think there's anything you can't do. You assembled an army of mostly lawyers to bake a shit ton of delicious cookies for charity, and you don't give an inch when it comes to your family. Your work ethic is almost as insane as mine. Hell, I'd hire you," he said instead, chickening out.

He wasn't lying. He'd spoken the truth—just not the whole truth.

She huffed an amused laugh. "I'm not qualified to work for you. I'm barely an assistant baker. My only credentials are my grandmother's seal of baking approval and a few online courses."

"I think you underestimate yourself," he countered.

She stared at the ground. "You don't know me."

"I know you've dedicated your life to making sure that your sister had what she needed to succeed."

"That was my grandma Dasher's dying wish. Both Lori and I spoke to her alone before she passed."

"What did she say to you?"

He wanted to know everything.

"She asked me to watch out for Lori. I was the oldest—still only eighteen, but the oldest. And we got by once it was just the two of us. I had to put college on hold. I got a job at a bakery, and Lori worked her butt off at school and earned a full-ride scholarship to Harvard. She would have made my parents and grandmother so proud."

"What about you?" he asked, growing more in awe of this woman by the second.

She gave a sad little chuckle. "I'm not sure. Currently, I'm unemployed and recently dumped. Maybe it's time to start looking for something more."

He traced the line of her jaw with his fingertip, unable to stop himself from touching her.

"What's that *more* look like for you?"

She rested her hands on his chest and pushed onto her tiptoes. His arms encircled her waist, and he drew her in.

"Tell me, Bridget?" he coaxed, completely enthralled and powerless to resist.

She gripped the fabric of his coat. "I honestly don't know. I've never let myself dream. I've never taken the leap and just gone for it."

The leap. The letting go. Putting it all on the line and rolling the dice.

He'd never allowed himself that luxury either.

But none of that seemed to matter when she was locked in his embrace.

All the bullshit faded away, muting the grating pain that dwelled deep in his heart.

He inhaled her vanilla scent as their breaths mingled together. They inhabited this space, this place where time stood still. The anticipation grew palpable—the air buzzing with a delicious expectancy.

"Who are you, Bridget? The angel or the vixen?" he whispered.

She trembled in his arms. "I—" she breathed as the sharp ping of an incoming text sliced through the cabin, severing their connection.

She sank from her tiptoe position, then took a step back, and broke free of his embrace.

She pulled her cell phone from her pocket. "It's a text from Lori. Everyone's wondering where we are." She glanced up at him as the light from her smartphone illuminated her face. "I'll tell her not to worry and that we're on our way."

He took a step back as well and ran his hands down his scruffy jaw. "Yeah, we should get going."

They threw snow on the last of the dying embers, extinguishing the last glimmers of orange light, and he propped the door closed with a few logs. With the intimacy of their exchange interrupted, a heavy silence stretched between them.

Did she regret sharing her past with him?

Bridget held the flashlight as they followed their boot prints, passing evergreen after evergreen, neither uttering a word. His mind spun with not only the events of the evening but the events of the last four days.

Four days!

He'd known this woman for ninety-six hours, give or take, and he could not for the life of him remember who he was before he'd fallen victim to her infuriating charms.

They entered the mountain house to find the main gathering room empty. Lit only by the Christmas trees twinkling in the corners, he followed Bridget down the hallway toward their room. She reached for the doorknob when another door a few rooms down swung open, and Lori poked her head out into the darkened corridor.

"Are you guys okay?" she whispered.

He stared at her. This was the first time he'd seen Bridget's sister since Tom dropped the pregnancy news, and all he felt was emptiness.

"We're fine. Is Cole okay?" Bridget asked.

Tom joined Lori in the doorway. "Yeah, he's fine. He was out like a light the minute Denise put him in bed, then everyone decided to call it a night."

Bridget's shoulders slumped a fraction. "I'm so glad he's safe, but I'm sorry for ruining your evening. I should have kept a better eye on him."

Tom wrapped his arm around Lori. "Don't sweat it, Birdie. Everyone's fine. That's what matters, right, Scooter?"

He nodded in a daze. "Yeah."

It was like living in some strange alternate universe. There was his best friend. They'd been inseparable for years, and now, they were on the cusp of the ultimate separation. Lori had replaced him, and a child would further widen the gulf.

"Is everything okay, Scooter?"

He blinked to find Lori staring at him.

"What do you mean?"

The woman cocked her head to the side. "You have a strange look on your face."

He glanced away. "I'm tired. It's been a long night—that's all."

Bridget turned the knob and opened the door to their room. "We should all get some rest. Tomorrow's a big day. We've got the rehearsal and then—"

"Then, I plan on eating as many of those little ball éclair thingies as I can. Lori says it's one of your signature desserts," Tom replied with a grin, and he barely recognized the man.

They'd summited Everest, went skydiving in New Zealand, and had picked up women all over the globe.

Now, the guy was jazzed about balls of dough.

"He can't wait for the croquembouche!" Lori added, patting Tom's cheek.

"Well, good night," Bridget said, throwing a pointed glance his way.

Christ! What did he do now?

He closed the door behind them and turned on a lamp just as she spun on her heels to face him.

"You can't even summon up a sliver of kindness toward my sister, can you?" she snapped, eyes flashing.

He took off his coat and slung it onto the sleeper bed. "What are you talking about?"

Color rose to her cheeks as she paced in front of him. "Just now! The contempt in your eyes! It makes me want to..."

"Makes you want to do what?" he asked, gripping her elbows and holding her in place.

Her eyes glittered with that damned determination that made him want to shut her up with a kiss that left them both breathless.

She lifted her chin. "It makes me want to hate you, but I can't."

"Why not? Why can't you hate me? You can see that I don't want Tom to marry your sister."

There! Now, the gloves were off. But just as quickly as she'd switched into the take no prisoners vixen, her gaze softened.

"I don't think my sister is the only issue you have with this wedding."

"*Issue*?" he repeated, incredulity coating the word.

"Can't we call a truce? Can't you see what's right in front of you?" Bridget pleaded.

Oh, he saw it. His friend might be playing the happy groom, but the man had been railroaded into marriage by the oldest trick in the book. And Bridget didn't even know, which gave more credence to his conclusion.

Tom was trapped.

"I don't want a truce, Bridget."

She huffed an exasperated breath. "There's nothing left to do. This wedding is happening."

He tightened his hold on her. "You don't think I know that. You don't even know the half of it."

"Then tell me why you're so against Tom marrying my sister."

A muscle ticked in his jaw. "It's complicated."

"Then tell me what's happening between us," she said, her voice barely a whisper.

"Do you really want to know?"

She lifted her chin, challenging him. "Yes."

He leaned in. "You make me insane, Bridget Dasher. You're in my damn head. And when I look into your eyes, I'm lost, and I'm found. And I can't escape this idea that, with you, I could be different. I could be whole."

"Then why won't you agree to a truce?" she asked.

He stared into her eyes as he grew more and more bewitched by the second.

"Because I don't want a truce. I want you."

"You do?" she whispered.

Her goodness shined in her eyes, and in it, he saw the possibility of a better version of himself. A version that didn't leave him alone and toiling in a pit of emptiness.

Maybe he could have her, and she could fill the emptiness in his heart?

He released a ragged breath. "You know, I do. From the moment I saw you, I wanted you all for myself."

A hopeful glint sparked in her eyes. "I want you, too. But I need you to promise me something."

At the mention of a promise, all he could think of was the wreckage of his childhood, littered with unkept promises.

I promise I'll come to your baseball game.

I promise we'll spend time together next week.

"Promise me that I don't have to worry about you doing anything crazy with this wedding," she said, cutting through his cluttered mind.

He stared at her—at this woman whose word meant everything. Brimming with integrity, she was the kind of person who'd move heaven and earth to help a stranger.

He'd observed her doing just that.

"How do you do it?" he rasped.

She was almost too good to be true.

Bridget cocked her head to the side. "Do what?"

"Always put others ahead of yourself?"

"I told you. If I make a promise, I keep it. Now, I need you to make one," she replied gently.

He'd never promised anything to anyone. He'd never wanted to risk following in his parents' footsteps. And he'd never actually had the inclination to give his word.

And as far as promises go, it wasn't like many people had asked him to pledge his honor.

Tom never asked for promises. They were buds. Best friends. They hung out. They spent the holidays together. There was, at least, an unsaid code between them—but never a promise.

Was Soren Christopher Traeger Rudolph even capable of such an oath?

But with his world tumbling out of control and his emotions calling the shots, he knew what had to be done.

"I do."

She grinned up at him, and God help him, if having her meant he had to give his word, he was all in. Or perhaps, he'd been mesmerized. Whatever it was, her presence quieted the gnawing voices in his head. It dared him to believe that maybe, just maybe, he was worthy of someone like her.

Her sweet expression morphed into a naughty twist of her lips. "Now that we've got that business out of the way, I've got a proposal for you."

He stared at her lips. "What's that?"

"I propose you kiss me and don't stop," she answered through her lashes.

"There's the vixen," he replied, peeling off her coat as lust edged out the emotional turmoil that had rocked his body since he'd laid eyes on her.

She would be his salvation. He would take her kindness and her beautiful light and use it to ward off the darkness that consumed his soul. Cupping her face in his hands, their lips crashed together as a spark ignited between them. She hummed as he deepened the kiss, the sound going straight to his hard length.

He wanted to remember everything about this night—every kiss, every touch, every sweet moan.

Lifting her into his arms, he carried her to the bed, then gently set her down. He removed her boots, then worked his way up her body. Slowly, he trailed his hands under her flannel dress. Bridget inhaled sharply as he stripped off her tights and unbuttoned her shirt dress, revealing her creamy skin and lickable curves.

In a white lace bra and matching panties with the pendant twinkling in the dim light between her breasts, Bridget Dasher was the dirty angel he desired. He kicked off his boots, then whipped off his shirt and jeans. Her plump red lips parted as he slid her panties down her toned legs. Bathed in the glow of the lamp, he devoured her body with his gaze.

"You're beautiful. You're the most beautiful thing I've ever seen," he confessed.

She sat up, unhooked her bra, and dropped it onto the floor.

Her confidence was intoxicating. When she let the vixen out, there was no holding this woman back. Staring up at him, she held the angel pendant between her fingers, toying with it, just like she was toying with him.

And he fucking loved it.

She shook her hair out of her makeshift bun, and her dark chocolate locks fell around her shoulders.

"I like the way you look at me, Mr. Rudolph," she purred.

He prowled up the length of her body.

"Then you're going to love the way I make you come, Ms. Dasher," he growled, carnal desire taking over.

His hard body met her soft, smooth curves as he kissed a line up her abdomen. Settling himself between her thighs, their mouths met in a scorching kiss. Their tongues clashed in a frenzy of need as she rocked her hips and ran her nails down his back, sending a fierce surge of lust rocketing through his body.

He'd never lost himself the way he did when he was with her. That veneer of control he'd worked so hard to construct crumbled with every sweet sigh that escaped her kiss-swollen lips. She trembled beneath him as he diverted his kisses from her lips to her neck before taking her earlobe between his teeth.

"Soren," she gasped as he palmed her ass, needing more of her. All of her.

He was a man on the brink of starvation, who had found himself at a decadent feast.

And everything was his to devour.

Teasing her slick entrance, his cock wept with desire. He nudged forward, entering barely an inch. Near delirious with the need to feel her, fill her, and pump and thrust until they didn't know the difference between up and down or night and day. Their mouths met in a desperate kiss, and her chest heaved as sweet anticipation lingered in the air, peppered with the slap and grind of their bodies finding a sensual rhythm.

"Soren," she whispered between kisses.

"Yes," he rasped, barely able to speak.

"Do you have protection?" she bit out between hot exhales.

And sweet Christ! He'd never forgotten to use protection.

"Hold on."

He left the warmth of the bed, found his jeans, retrieved his wallet, then removed a condom.

The last condom.

He held it up. "I've got one left. My supply took a significant hit back in Denver."

Bridget put out her hand, and he set the foil packet on her palm. "Then we'll have to make it count," she replied, ripping the condom open before coming onto her knees. And, like the vixen she was, she took him in her hand and rolled the condom down the length of his cock.

"Do you know how damned captivating you are?" he asked.

She stared at his cock, licked her lips, then flicked her glittering gaze to meet his eye. "I think you're about to show me, but..."

"What?"

She glanced at the door. "We have to be quiet."

He joined her on the bed, and she straddled him as he sat, looking him in the eye.

He bit back a grin. "We both know I can be quiet. You, on the other hand—"

But when he expected her to throw a zinger right back, she wrapped her arms around his neck and rested her forehead against his.

"Soren, did you mean what you said?" she asked, her voice quivering.

He stroked the back of her head. "About what?"

The breath caught in his throat. What was she asking? Was it about the promise?

Yes, he'd promised her he wouldn't meddle with the wedding—well, he didn't explicitly say the words *I promise*, but he'd implied it.

She pulled back. "About me underestimating myself?"

Relief washed over him. This was a topic that gave him no pause.

He tucked a lock of hair behind her ear and allowed his thumb to linger and caress her cheek.

"You're extraordinary. I've never met anyone like you. And I don't think there's anything you couldn't do. You're a force to be reckoned with, Bridget Dasher. And you're everything I never thought I deserved."

She pulled back and captured him with her mahogany gaze. "You deserve to be happy. You deserve to be loved."

Loved?

The word strung with divine, beautiful pain as if he'd been convicted and pardoned at the same time.

He'd never considered finding love.

Not until her.

His heart hammered in his chest. "How do you do it? How do you make it seem so easy?"

She stroked his cheek. "I told you back in Denver, I'm not your average vixen."

"There is nothing average about you," he whispered against her lips as he thrust inside her.

Bridget gasped and tightened her grip as she welcomed his hard length, and he kissed her with the burning intensity of a man on the brink of redemption. Their bodies came together in a torrent of need and desire. Thrusting and bucking, the friction between them awakened a need deep within—primal and raw. He flipped her onto her back, taking complete control, just as he was on the edge of losing total control.

"Open your eyes," he bit out between long, deep thrusts.

She complied, and he gazed into the pools of deep mahogany. And a realization struck.

He'd never had a real home—never had a place where he truly belonged. But here, in her eyes, he could see forever.

"I see you, Soren," she whispered, her words like grains of magical fairy dust floating in the air.

He worked her body, changing the angle of penetration to go deeper, to make her feel everything. And that's when he lost himself. There was no telling where his pleasure started, and her pleasure ended. They were one body, one soul. He increased his pace, and she tightened around him. Meeting her release and writhing in ecstasy beneath him, she dug her nails into his back as he swallowed her wild cries and kissed away her lusty moans. And then, he couldn't hold back. Suspended in a place where only he and this extraordinary woman existed, he surrendered to wanton oblivion, flying over the edge. The power of his release sent tremors through his body. Wave after wave, they rode the tumultuous sea of mutual satisfaction until, in a tangle of sweaty limbs, their bodies stilled.

He cradled her face in his hand. "I don't want to let go of you."

Had he heard any other man utter something so goddamn sappy, he would have laughed his ass off.

But here, with her, he meant every corny word.

She hummed a satisfied little sound. "You don't have to. At least, not yet. But you will need to leave this bed."

His eyes went wide. "Why? I thought that we had something."

Jesus! Had he read her wrong? He'd transformed himself into a pool of sappy bullshit for this woman!

She covered his mouth and chuckled. "Because you need to raid the Frosty jar."

"The Frosty jar? Are you talking about the condom-filled Frosty the Snowman?" All those stupid nerves dissolved into a naughty grin of his own.

She raised a teasing eyebrow. "Don't forget. I know exactly what you're capable of, Soren Rudolph. And that was only round one."

He kissed her forehead, then her cheek, then the tip of her nose, completely enamored.

"Bridget Dasher, you are part angel, part vixen, and all mine. And all I can say is one more thing."

She smiled up at him. "What's that?"

He gave her a wicked grin. "Good old Frosty better be stocked."

"*W*hen you said you wanted to play with my balls, this is not what I was expecting."

Bridget gasped, almost knocking over the croquembouche and nearly spackling the kitchen in the hot caramel used to hold the dessert together.

Thanks to the events of Cole's unscheduled Christmas fairy expedition last night coupled with an evening—and a few early morning hours—spent tangled in Soren's embrace, making love like they were born to do nothing else and depleting the Frosty filled condom receptacle, she'd failed to assemble the croquembouche until now.

And even that was up for debate thanks to her sexy as sin baking assistant.

"Shh! They'll hear you," she whisper-shouted, glancing toward the other side of the kitchen where Delores and Tanner were prepping the Cornish hens for the rehearsal dinner.

This was it. Tonight, they'd have the wedding rehearsal, and then tomorrow, like her parents did thirty years ago, Lori and Tom would recite their wedding vows inside the Kringle Chapel on Christmas Eve.

All her planning and organizing had come to fruition along with something she'd never expected.

And what was that crazy revelation?

Soren Christopher Traeger Rudolph, the good old super player, uber-creep, stupidly nicknamed Scooter, was no longer her mortal marital adversary.

Now, the thought of the man sent her pulse racing—and not in the God, I hate you way, but in the Oh, God! Oh, God! Don't stop way.

They hadn't talked nuts and bolts or any long-term relationship plan. And honestly, between all the sexytimes and all the wedding preparations she'd already tackled today, there wasn't a moment to spare. Not to mention, they'd been around everyone, and there was no way she would take the spotlight off Lori and Tom by announcing that she was possibly dating the former worst, now, truly best man.

But after last night, she knew that, whatever they had, it was real.

Between hating him and lusting after him, and then hating him a little more, she couldn't deny that somewhere between screwing him and screaming at him, she'd fallen for him.

Her once curmudgeon of a baking assistant was now positively the devil of baking—in the best and naughtiest of ways.

She held Soren's gaze, those cat-like eyes glittering with mischief. "You must have misheard me, *Scooter*. I said that I needed your assistance stacking the profiteroles into a cone shape."

The mischief factor in his eyes dialed up another notch. "And then I said, 'What are profiteroles?' And then that little line appeared on your forehead, and you made that face like you're pissed off at me. But you're not. And then you said, and I remember this quite clearly, 'I need your balls.'"

She bit back a grin. "That is not at all how that conversation went, and you know it!"

"Ah, semantics! It must be the law school in me," he teased.

She dipped her wooden spoon into the warm caramel and drizzled it over the decadent dessert, putting on the final touch.

She did her best to disregard his provocation, but the man was hard to ignore.

She cleared her throat. "If you can't tell, I'm engaged in some serious caramel application, mister. You do not want to upset a woman wielding a spoonful of hot, sticky deliciousness."

He leaned in, all cat-eyes and chiseled cheekbones. "Bridget Dasher, you make baking a real turn on."

She felt her cheeks heat as he moved in a fraction closer. She'd never look at caramel the same again.

"If you're not going to play with my balls, then you have to let me kiss you," he said, his voice a low, sexy whisper.

She threw another glance at Delores and Tanner. They weren't even twenty feet away!

"Right now? Right here?"

This man made her a tingly, lip biting mess. Again—a dangerous thing to be while working with hot, sticky deliciousness.

Gah! She had to nix the hot, sticky, delicious thoughts, or else she might not be able to stop herself from doing a lot more than just kissing this baking scoundrel.

His gaze flicked to their kitchen companions. "They won't even notice. Look, Delores is in the zone with those little chickens."

"Cornish hens," she corrected with a giggle.

Soren shrugged. "Cole calls them little chickens, so that's what I'm sticking with. And we both know there's a good chance Tanner's hit the gummy bears today. He wouldn't notice if Santa's sleigh plowed through this place."

She stifled another laugh and shook her head. "I'll have you know that Tanner is stone-cold sober. He promised that he wouldn't bring any of his special *medicinal* treats to the mountain house. I think I freaked him out that night I ate half the bag."

Soren blew out an exaggerated breath. "Yeah, you freaked out a lot of people that night. If it wasn't for me, you probably would have ended up in the Kringle detox unit."

She lowered her voice. "I was not that bad, and I highly doubt there's a Kringle detox unit."

He eyed her skeptically. "You had a conversation with an egg, Bridget."

She rested the spoon in the copper pot and leaned against the counter. "I've never met an egg I didn't like."

He picked up a dish towel and draped it over a carton of eggs sitting on the counter.

"Why did you do that?" she asked as he carefully covered the entire container.

He leaned in, and his breath tickled her ear, sending a charge of heat through her body. "So, we can agree that nobody, not even your little egg friends, are going to catch us."

She swallowed hard. More of his sexy voice, and she'd be the one ransacking Frosty for another six condoms.

Yep, they'd been busy last night.

"I can see why you're so successful. You're hard to turn down," she replied.

"It's my specialty," he rasped.

Holy hot sticky caramel surprise!

That voice would be her demise.

She threw another glance at Tanner and Delores. Soren was right. The cooks were busy with the meal prep and not paying a lick of attention to them. And while she and Soren hadn't discussed the future, they had adopted an unspoken no PDA rule. In front of the Abbotts, the mountain house staff, and her sister, they'd continue on as Birdie and Scooter, cordial combatants—not Bridget and Soren, the vixen and the sex god. She'd tell Lori everything after the wedding. But until then, the maid of honor best man cliché hookup scenario would stay on the down-low.

"All right, I will agree to a kiss. But first, you have to agree to my terms."

That cat-like glint was back in his green eyes. "The vixen's playing hardball. I like it. Shoot."

Before he scrambled her brain with a toe-curling lip-lock session, she needed to relay the schedule.

This wedding wasn't over yet.

She poked him in his chest. "You cannot let me forget to pick up the wedding cake after dinner. We've got a lot going on this evening. There's the rehearsal up at the chapel, then the big meal at the mountain house after. And then, you and I need to take the truck and go get the cake. It'll be fine to sit out overnight." She glanced out the window as snow fell at a steady clip. "And who knows what the weather will be like tomorrow. I cannot stress this enough. There's going to be so much to do. No matter what happens tonight, we positively must remember to drive down to..." she trailed off as a thread of anger wove through her heart.

She couldn't help it, and Soren noticed the shift.

"To the Cupid Bakery. And yes, I know that you're not happy with me regarding their fate but, it's the way it is sometimes," he said, reading her mind.

She adjusted one of the profiteroles at the base of the croquembouche that did not require adjusting. "Yeah, I understand that."

She could make peace with it, right? This is what he did. But that nagging voice in the back of her head still wasn't totally sold with it being okay.

He tilted her chin up. "And just think what we can do in the front seat of that old Ford F150."

He was trying. She could see it in his hesitant expression. And this wasn't a man who hesitated. She pushed her disappointment over Cupid Bakery's demise out of her mind—or at least tried to.

"The seats are rather bouncy if I remember correctly," she replied, giving him the hint of a grin.

They could figure this out. They each had a life outside of this mountain wedding bubble. They'd find a rhythm. They could do that.

The muscles in his shoulders relaxed as the unease receded from his beautiful face.

"They are quite bouncy," he affirmed, looking more like the man who'd rocked her world all night long.

She'd figured him out, or at least, she was pretty sure she had.

He wasn't an awful person.

He just didn't like change. And who could blame him after the childhood he'd endured. She could relate to being underestimated and underappreciated. Thanks to Gaston and a string of lackluster boyfriends, she'd earned a Ph.D. in those *uns*.

But she'd never been *unwanted* or *unloved*.

She'd grown up surrounded by love. From baking and singing in the kitchen to cuddly bedtime stories to the reassuring comfort of listening to her mom and dad talk about their day in hushed voices as she drifted off to sleep as a child. Her parents and her grandma Dasher never missed a moment to show her and Lori how much they cared. Sure, she'd been the timid sister, never one to take a risk. But that was changing.

Perhaps, she would look into opening her own business or

maybe apply to culinary school. Soren had awakened her inner vixen, and what once seemed impossible now appeared strangely possible.

"What's going on inside that head of yours?" he asked.

She gave him her best vixen pout. "I'm deciding which part of my body I want you to kiss."

He twisted the tie of her apron around his fingers, sending sparks right to her lady parts. If he kept looking at her like she was tonight's dessert, she'd be lucky to make it out of that kitchen with anything left underneath her apron.

He stroked her bottom lip with the pad of his thumb. "How about we start here and see where it takes us?"

"It takes us all the way up to the top of the mountain, Uncle Scooter!"

As if they'd been shocked by a cattle prod, she and her devil of an assistant baker pulled apart.

Soren cleared his throat before addressing the pint-sized kiss crasher. "Hey, Cole! What's going on?"

"It's time to go! Everyone is getting in the gondolas," the boy said, taking a few more steps into the kitchen, then frowned.

"What is it, bud?" Soren asked.

"It's Birdie's eyeball again," the boy answered, watching her closely.

She stole a glance at Soren, but all he gave her was a hell-if-I-know expression.

"My what?" she asked.

Cole pointed to his eyes. "When you got here, Birdie, Uncle Scooter was helping you get dirt or an eyelash out of your eye. Don't you remember? Your hair was all messy, and Uncle Scooter's pants were too tight."

She shared another perplexed look with Soren.

"My pants fit fine, Cole," Soren said, glancing at the pair he had on.

The child adjusted his glasses. "They looked a little small below your belly that day."

She bit her lip to keep from laughing as Soren turned as red as Rudolph's nose.

"I must have had something in my pocket. That's all," he replied, clearly going for nonchalant, but Cole's frown said he wasn't buying it.

"A really big banana? I didn't see you eating a banana," the child replied as Soren's blush deepened.

She could watch Cole take this man to task all day.

But as much as she'd love to watch the man squirm a bit more, they were on a schedule.

She clapped her hands, taking control of this conversation on the brink of completely flying off the rails. "Cole, could you tell everyone to start heading up to the chapel. Your uncle Scooter and I need to put the croquembouche in a safe spot, and then we'll catch the next gondola."

"Do the pants you have on today fit, Uncle Scooter?" Cole asked, not moving on.

Now it was Soren biting back a grin. "They do now, buddy. We'll see you up there."

"Okay," the boy chimed over his shoulder as he skipped out of the kitchen.

She chuckled. "There's never a dull moment with Cole."

"Never," he agreed, dusting off his hands.

She set the croquembouche in the center of the worktable, then removed her apron.

"He's great. All the Abbotts are."

The teasing glimmer in Soren's eyes dimmed. "Yeah, they are. They're the best. I'll get our jackets. It's really starting to come down out there."

"Sure, I'll be right out," she replied, pretending not to notice that the muted man had returned.

Breathe, Bridget.

The guy's best friend was getting married. A new Abbott, well, a Dasher-Abbott would be joining the mix. That had to be what had him on edge. She'd already Psych 101-ed him on that, and by now, he had to see that Tom and Lori were not only a good match but madly in love.

Tidying up her workspace, she checked in with Delores and Tanner. The savory scent of the Cornish hens baking away in the oven combined with the aromatic cranberry stuffing—the same meal her parents had dined on thirty years ago—already had her mouth watering. The dinner was coming along nicely, and everything would be good to go once they returned from the chapel.

They were on schedule.

No lost children.

No baking catastrophes.

All was good.

But she didn't feel *all good.* A shiver that had nothing to do with the dropping temperatures and thickening blanket of snow covering the mountain spider-crawled down her spine.

Stop overthinking it.

She smoothed her dress and joined Soren at the door. Robotically, he helped her with her coat.

"Are you okay?" she asked over her shoulder.

"I'm fine," he answered, sounding the exact opposite.

Maybe marriage made him uncomfortable. That would also fit into his narrative. Crummy parents, who didn't love him or each other? That could put a dent in anyone's perception of vowing to love and honor someone for all the days of your life, right?

"What about my perception?" he asked.

Dammit! She was doing it again.

She waved him off. "I'm just running through all the *preparations* that need to be done before tomorrow. That's all."

He nodded. She was a terrible liar, and she expected him to call her out. But his mind was somewhere else.

They stood on the porch and waited for the gondola to make its way to the bottom, then hurried through the swirl of falling snow to enter the enclosed space.

"We're the last ones up," she said with a touch too much enthusiasm as she took the seat across from him, unable to think of anything else to say.

He must have sensed her apprehension because just as she was about to drop the upbeat Birdie persona and go full vixen and demand he explain exactly what had turned him back into the Tin Man, he leaned forward and took her hands into his. "Sorry, I'm just—"

"No, you don't have to apologize," she interrupted.

She needed to give him a break. He hadn't done one damn thing to endanger this wedding. Strike that. He did send strippers, but that was before. Yes, he'd been a killjoy and had mentioned to Tom his concerns about the wedding, but he hadn't acted on his fears. Not really. She'd prepared to go to war with the worst best man. She'd expected for him to try to undermine her at every turn. Instead, he'd helped her. In his curmudgeon way, he'd taken care of her.

She entwined her fingers with his. "You don't have to explain anything. I get it."

That had to be it. A terrible childhood plus a warped view of marriage would equal trepidation when witnessing one's best friend's nuptials.

But what did that mean for them?

Was he against marriage? Did he detest the entire institution?

Did she want to marry him?

Stop!

Their chemistry was off the charts, but they'd known each other for five days.

They hadn't even had the boyfriend-girlfriend talk. It was hard to say much of anything after six orgasms.

She leaned forward, ready to shift gears and cash in on that missed promised kitchen kiss, when the gondola lurched. She gasped as the steel cables whined under the weight of the now swaying structure. The gondola rocked from side to side at the mercy of the wind as it dangled above the mountain.

"This just keeps happening! What are we going to do?" she cried, flying over to his side, weight distribution be damned.

He chuckled and wrapped his arm around her. "It's all right. Dan said the gondola gets testy with the weather. Just wait a second."

"Okay, one. That's one second," she counted.

"Wait twenty seconds," he countered.

She raised her index finger. "One, two—"

"Are you going to count it out all the way to twenty?"

She balked at him. Of course, she was going to count.

"We cannot have the gondola out of commission. It's the only way to the chapel. And I have a rehearsal dinner to put on and cake to retrieve and—"

The mechanical hum cut off her rant as the wobbly gondola continued its ascent.

"See, it's fine. No crazy wedding lady counting necessary," he said, biting back a grin.

She leaned against him, savoring his comforting warmth, and sighed. "I'm a little tense."

"A little?" he teased, but his tone was gentle.

"I want everything to be perfect for Lori and Tom. And I would want my parents and grandmother to think I did a good job. I know it sounds silly. But being here makes me feel closer to them."

"It's not silly, Bridget," he answered with a touch of longing to his words.

She stroked his cheek. "Thank you."

He glanced down at her. "For what?"

"For not being the worst best man after all," she replied, craning her neck to give him a peck on the lips.

But he was in no mood for gondola kissing.

"Is that what you called me?"

She lifted her chin with mock haughtiness. "Among other things, yes."

He chuckled and pressed a kiss to the crown of her head as they sat back and watched the chapel come into view. Falling snow framed the structure, and the windows glowed with the soft light of the chandeliers as forms moved past the two windows flanking the entrance. Tomorrow, she'd have the candles going, which, her parents had said, gave the space a beautiful, ethereal feel when they'd wed.

A grateful ease set in. It was all coming together.

Soren opened the door, and they hurried into the chapel, entering the sanctuary in a bluster of icy wind and a rush of snowflakes.

"Ah, good, you're both here," the judge said, waving them in from where he stood at the altar next to Tom and Lori.

"Cole and Carly just practiced their flower girl and ring bearer duties," Grace said from where she sat in the front row with Scott and Russ.

"I pretended to throw the flower petals. Watch!" Carly chimed, mimicking the motion.

"Very well done," Bridget replied, taking in the scene. "But don't you want to practice from the beginning with all of us?"

Her sister shared a look with the judge. What was going on between the two of them?

"Tom and I had another thought for the rehearsal," Lori said, now sharing a glance with her fiancé.

The judge patted Lori's shoulder. "Because this is such a small gathering, Tom and Lori asked me to say a few words, and then they wanted to address everyone here in the chapel."

"You don't mind, Birdie, do you? There are a few things we need to say to you and Scooter in front of everyone," Lori finished.

She couldn't deny her sister's request! It was the woman's wedding, for Pete's sake. She scanned the cozy space. Everyone had a curious expression. Even the kids seemed to be in on whatever this was.

Had her sister and Tom figured out that she and Soren were...

Were what?

A thing.

Or worse!

Did someone see Soren tiptoeing out to the Frosty jar five times last night?

Were they about to get called out in front of everyone?

She glanced back at the door. There was no turning back now.

There was nowhere to go, and no way to get out of whatever was about to go down.

*B*ridget put on her best fake Birdie grin.

The one she used in real times of panic.

"I don't mind at all. The judge is right. There isn't much to practice with such a small group, and if you have something else that you'd like to do here, I'm all for it," she replied with a touch too much go, team, go to her tone.

"Excellent, because we'd like for you and Scooter to join us at the altar," the judge said. With Tom and Lori to his left, he gestured for her and Soren to stand at his right.

She glanced up at her wedding party counterpart to find him opening and closing his mouth like a fish out of water.

At least she wasn't the only one caught off guard.

They took their places at the front of the chapel, and Lori threw her a strange little wink. But before she could give her sister a what-is-going-on look, the judge addressed the group.

"First, I want to speak for all the Abbotts when I say that we are thrilled to have Lori joining our family."

"Here, here!" Denise called, as the others rang out in agreement with claps and hoots.

"Thank goodness! Just run-of-the-mill wedding-family

stuff," she cried with a relieved sigh that brought on an awkward silence.

"Of course, it's wedding stuff, Birdie. Why else do you think we'd want you two up here?" Lori asked.

She glanced at Soren, but the man gave her nothing.

"Please, Judge, go on," she said, stretching her crazy lady smile another few millimeters.

"Thank you, Birdie," the man answered with a curious glint in his eyes before reverting back to judge mode. "Now, I think it's safe to say that Lori has not only made her way into Tom's heart but into all of our hearts. We only wish that your parents and grandmother could be here. But I'm sure they are in spirit."

At the mention of her parents and grandmother, a lump formed in her throat. She stared at an empty bench. They could be there, sitting, smiling, basking in Lori's bridal radiance. Her sister was the embodiment of the modern glowing bride.

"Thank you, Judge. And thank you, everyone. It's an honor to join your family," Lori replied softly, brushing a tear from her cheek.

The judge glanced at Soren, then turned his attention to the others. "We Abbotts also have someone who we wish could be here. I know my late wife Alice would have adored you, Lori. She was a straight talker, tough as nails, and the love of my life. And when I see Tom look at you, dear, I'm reminded of how I used to look at Alice."

Bridget blinked back tears. This is just what her family would have wanted.

The judge turned to Lori and Tom. "Love is many things. It's joy, and it's sacrifice. But more than that, it's a promise. A promise to love, to cherish, and to fiercely protect another's heart."

Soren went rigid. She could sense his body tightening,

retracting, pulling away. A muscle ticked in his jaw. The man looked ready to crack a molar.

"Now, I don't want to go on for too long. I need to save up some good bits for the actual wedding ceremony," the judge added with a chuckle. "So, with our warmest wishes and thoughts of Lori's family, I'd like to turn it over to Tom and Lori, who requested to address the maid of honor and the best man here in the chapel."

"Us?" Bridget asked. Her emotions were all over the place. She was happy for her sister. She longed for her parents and grandmother. But overriding all that was the fear that something awful was going on inside the best man's head.

Her heart hammered in her chest, but she had to keep it together.

"Birdie and Scooter," Tom began, breaking into her thoughts, "Lori and I wanted to thank you both, here, in a place that means so much to us all now, and we have something special for you."

She stole another glance at Soren, who remained stone-faced.

"You go first, honey," Lori said, handing Tom a gift bag.

"Is this going to get sappy?" Soren asked.

"Yeah, pretty sappy. Deal with it, dude," Tom answered with a playful clap to his best friend's shoulder before handing him the bag.

Soren held the item awkwardly.

"Open it!" Cole and Carly cried.

"Yeah, okay," he answered, lost in a fog.

Slowly, he removed a picture frame from the bag, and his expression softened.

"I didn't know you had this," Soren said, staring intently at the frame.

She glanced over, expecting to see a photograph. Instead, a

worn metal plate with the numbers twelve twenty-four engraved in the muted silver sat mounted in the center.

"What is it?" she asked.

For a fraction of a second, she would have sworn she'd seen Soren's lip quiver. He held out the frame for everyone to see. "It's a doorplate for a dorm room."

"Thomas, did you steal that from boarding school?" Grace asked, a mix of incredulity and humor in her question.

Tom gave his mother a good-natured grin. "Steal is such a polarizing word. Hypothetically, if one jammed a ruler underneath a doorplate until it popped right off the wall, that wouldn't actually be stealing. It would be revealing a design flaw."

"Always the lawyer," Russ called as everyone except Soren chuckled.

"Why did you take it? And why didn't you mention it to me?" he asked, looking truly mystified.

"It was our first room together, and our first year at boarding school. I felt like I wanted to keep a part of it, and I was pretty sure if I told you that back then, you would have called me a p—"

"Tom! Kids," Denise said, cutting off her brother.

Tom gave a quick salute to his sister, then turned back to Soren. "Here's the kid-friendly version: it was the place where I met my best friend, and I wanted to remember it."

Soren nodded, clearly moved by the gift. "Thank you, Tommy. This brings back a lot of good memories."

"I'm glad you like it, Scooter. But I can't take all the credit. It was Lori's idea to frame it and give it to you. She's thoughtful like that. You know that if it was completely up to me to get you a gift, I'd probably pick out a beer koozie," Tom replied with another clap to Soren's arm.

"This was your idea?" Soren asked her sister.

Lori waved off Tom's praises. "Tom and I were going through

some of his old boxes, and we found some of your old boarding school things in it. I thought it might make a perfect best man's gift. That's all," Lori replied as that muscle on Soren's cheek ticked again.

"It's a very thoughtful gift. Thank you," he answered, barely able to crack a smile.

What in the world was going on with him? Could it be the attention?

"And, Birdie, I have something for you that I've held on to for a long time, and now feels like the right time to give it to you," her sister said, retrieving an envelope from the front bench.

"What is it?" she asked, but there was something vaguely familiar about it.

"Look at the handwriting," her sister instructed.

Bridget turned the envelope over, and the breath caught in her throat at the sight of Grandma Dasher's delicate cursive handwriting.

She ran her finger over the wrinkled surface. "But it's addressed to you."

"It is. But there's a part in it that's meant for you, Birdie."

Her hands trembling, Bridget pressed her lips together, trying to hold back the emotion as a tear slid down her cheek. The letter her grandmother had left her didn't have a special message for Lori in it. They'd never read each other's letters either. But Lori had never mentioned that her letter contained a separate message.

She lifted the flap cautiously as if this letter were a portal to one last conversation with her grandmother. One last dance around the kitchen. One last offering of wisdom. She had no idea what her grandmother could want to convey all these years later.

She released a shaky breath, feeling all eyes on her when Cole's shriek of a yelp sliced through the heavy silence.

"Pee! I have to pee so bad, Mommy! I can't hold it much longer!" Cole cried.

Bridget blinked, pulled from the trance of the unexpected envelope, and slid the letter into the pocket of her coat as she went into crisis mode.

The tiny chapel didn't have running water, let alone a working toilet.

"You didn't pee before we left?" Denise asked.

The boy stood in the aisle, hopping from foot to foot. "No, I went to tell Uncle Scooter and Birdie it was time to leave. But Uncle Scooter was fixing Birdie's eye again. He was looking at her real close like when you have to fish an eyelash out of my eyeball. And then we talked about bananas and pants, and I forgot to go potty."

"There was flour in your eye?" Lori questioned.

Oh no!

"Yes, I must have gotten some flour in my eye, and Scooter was just..." she began, flailing like the awful fibber she was.

"Getting it out," he finished.

"Yes, that's right! Getting it out! Just like that." she answered, like a moron.

"Sounds pretty crazy! Next time you have a flour emergency, you can call me, little lady," Russ said, most likely in an attempt to be funny.

"Will do," she replied, again with way too much go, team, go infused into her reply.

Score one point for the creepy uncle coming in handy.

"Mommies!" Cole yelled, clutching his crotch.

Denise patted her son's back. "I'm sorry, everyone. We better go. Cole did drink a small cup of cocoa before we left, but I didn't think it would do this."

"And then he drank mine," Carly added.

"And mine," Scott chimed.

Denise eyed her son. "How much cocoa did you drink?"

"A lot!" the boy bit out, squinting his eyes, tightening every muscle in his little body.

Bridget checked her watch. "Everyone should go. The gondola seats ten. Scooter and I will stay behind and close up."

"Are you sure?" Lori asked.

"We'll be right behind you, and dinner should be ready any minute."

"I'm going to pee an entire lake, and then I'm going to eat a little chicken!" Cole said as Nancy zipped the boy's coat, and everyone quickly filed out to the waiting gondola.

The door banged shut, and she took a moment to pull herself together.

"Leave it to Cole to have a potty emergency," she said, but Soren didn't answer.

He stared at the framed doorplate.

"It's a touching gift. I can see it means a lot to you," she said gently.

He swallowed hard, the muscles of his neck straining. "I know what I need to do for Tom."

She wasn't expecting that. After his somber demeanor at the wedding rehearsal, she couldn't read him.

"What do you need to do?"

He pulled his gaze from the door plate and caught her eye, then gave her the saddest smile she'd ever seen. "What a best friend should do."

This must be him coming to peace with Lori and Tom's marriage. A warmth settled in her chest.

"I should double-check that everything I need for tomorrow is in the storage closet," she said, heading down the aisle to give him a moment.

He nodded as his gaze slid back to the framed plate.

There honestly wasn't much to do. She straightened the

garlands and arranged the candles. After a few minutes, she felt a rush of cool air and glanced at the door.

Soren stood at the entrance. "It's a big night. We should head down. I can see the gondola making its way back."

Look at him! Ready for a big night. She'd give him an even bigger night once all the festivities were over.

She joined him, and they rode down the mountain in a peaceful, easy silence, staring out at the winter wonderland all around them. Life had never felt so full of promise. A new man combined with the newfound desire to take a leap of faith with her career had left her giddy.

"What are you thinking about with that big smile on your face?" he asked.

The mountain house came into view, and she sat back.

What was she thinking?

How her once predictably empty existence now felt new and exciting?

Yes, that was it, exactly.

"I'm thinking about..." she began, then stopped and cocked her head to the side.

"Yes," he coaxed, but she couldn't focus on his question.

The front door to the mountain house was wide open and flashing neon lights extended out onto the porch.

There was nothing about neon lights in her rehearsal dinner plan.

The gondola came to a stop, and she hurried toward the house. In the short amount of time they'd been up at the chapel, at least another few inches of snow had fallen. She lumbered through it, kicking up the white powder with Soren on her heels as music streamed out the door.

"Do you know what this is all about?" she asked, then stopped dead in her tracks as they took in the scene.

She glanced up at Soren and watched as the color drained

from his cheeks.

Her sister and the Abbotts stood slack-jawed along with Delores, Dan, and Tanner while four young women, dressed in nothing but skimpy lingerie, gyrated and flashed cleavage as they danced around the Christmas trees. A neon strobe light flashed, and music boomed as Nancy, looking as shell-shocked as the rest of the group, scooped up Cole, then took Carly by the hand and ushered the children down the hall to their suite.

It looked like the rustic version of a seedy holiday gentleman's club.

Bridget waved wildly to Dan and Delores. "What is this?"

Delores shook her head. "I don't understand it at all. These ladies said they were paid to come here for the bachelor party. I told them they had to have gotten it wrong. But the dancer in the red number over there said they'd already been paid double to be here tonight for Tom."

For Tom?

Bridget grabbed Soren's coat sleeve as Tom pulled the cord to the strobe light, then turned off the stereo, and the room went dead quiet for a beat.

"Hey, these are the gals I met in the village!" Russ said with a stupid grin, waving to two of the scantily clad women.

"Russ, go help Denise and Nancy with the kids," Tom said, his voice a tight, forceful whisper.

"Sure, Tom," the man replied, confusion written on his face, but he complied.

"We'll go and help with the kids, too. Come on, Scott," Grace said, taking her shocked husband by the hand and heading to the room.

"I don't know why you're so upset, mister," the dancer in red said with a pout as she sauntered up to Tom. "This is your bachelor party."

Tom took a step back from the woman. "I'm upset because

my fiancée and I asked you and your friend not to come back. And now you're here with two more people."

The woman released an annoyed groan before grabbing a bag off the floor and pulling out a cell phone. "I know you told us not to come back, and we were going to leave this little town yesterday, but then, we got this text two nights ago from a Soren Traeger Rudolph."

Bridget's stomach twisted into a knot.

"He's the guy paying us so much. We talked to his secretary. She's the one who set everything up for him. Not a super nice lady—real testy on the phone. But the money went through, and that's all that matters," the woman finished with a flick of her hair.

"You got a text from Soren two nights ago?" Tom repeated, his face awash in shock.

Two nights ago, Soren and Tom had the bro-fest night on the town. An image of the worst best man passed out on the sleeper sofa with his phone clutched in his hand flashed through her mind.

He wouldn't. This had to be a mistake.

"See, I've got the text right here. It says, SOS! Send reinforcements. Bring as many entertainers. By the way, I love that you call us entertainers. Stripper is so 2002," the woman crooned, oblivious to the firestorm she and her *entertainer* friends' presence had caused. "Anyway, SOS! Send reinforcements. I need extra ladies because the groom requires an over-the-top bachelor party. He was railroaded into this wedding by his pregnant girlfriend, and now he has to marry her. Spare no expense! Bring extra body glitter." She held out her phone. "And then there are about fifty vomit face emojis."

"I don't remember sending that," Soren said, shaking his head.

Now, the quartet of strippers was no longer the biggest surprise of the night.

She went to her sister. "You're pregnant? Why didn't you say something?"

Lori took her hand. "I was going to. We were going to tell everyone. We only found out the night we got here. I was a few days late and decided to pick up a test at the drug store in town. That's when we found out."

"The night you got here?" Soren interrupted, his voice a hoarse crack. "You didn't tell me you just found out about this," he said, turning to his best friend.

Tom glared at Soren, then went to Lori. "Babe, I'm sorry. I shared the news with Scooter because I was excited—because I've shared everything with him since I was a kid. I thought he'd be happy for me—for us. I thought it would help him with all the changes. I should have talked to you first. But I never in a million years thought he'd do anything as cruel and selfish as this."

Lori stared at Soren. "How could you?"

Soren paced the length of the room. "I don't remember texting these women."

Tom put out his hand. "Give me your phone."

Soren stilled. "What?"

"Give me your phone, Scooter," Tom bit out, and Soren handed it over.

Tom's cheeks bloomed crimson as he scrolled through Soren's messages. "You bastard! I wondered what the hell you were doing on your phone."

"What? I've barely looked at the thing," Soren said, swiping the phone from Tom.

"You texted Janine and asked for the strippers' contact information. Then you texted the strippers. The evidence is right there. Thank God you went into business. You would have made a shit lawyer."

"Not stripper—dancers or entertainers," the head dancer chimed.

Tom turned to Dan. "Could you drive these *dancers* down to the village and help them find their way home. I'll pick up the cost of whatever it takes to get them out of here."

Tanner perked up. "I can take them down. It's no problem."

"Let me cover the cost, Tom. It's the least I can do," Soren offered.

Tom barked out a laugh. "No, you've done enough."

Soren took a step toward his friend. "Tommy, I didn't know what I was doing. I'd had way too much to drink that night."

"Clearly not too much to text Janine and the strippers!" Tom threw back.

"Dancers," the woman said again from the other side of the room where the ladies were zipping into their coats.

"Let's head out the back," Tanner said, waving the dancers out through the side door.

"Tommy, I didn't—" Soren began, but Tom stopped him.

"It's time to set the record straight. Lori didn't railroad me into anything. I love her. I want to marry her, and I want to have a family with her. Yeah, we were thrown for a loop to find out she was pregnant. But I want her and our baby. They are the most important things in my life."

"I must have misunderstood the situation," Soren replied, stone-faced.

Tom shook his head and stared up at the ceiling. "No, that's not an answer, Scooter. You didn't misunderstand. I'd hoped you'd be flexible. No, not flexible—supportive of me and stand behind my choice to get married. But you didn't. Your first impulse was to maintain the status quo at whatever cost. You told me that you thought I wasn't ready for marriage. But it's you, Scooter. You're the one who can't see that I'm the happiest I've ever been. I've always been a friend to you. But you've crossed a line. I love Lori. I'm marrying Lori, and it's not because we're expecting a baby. And I'm so damned disappointed in you for thinking so little of me as a man. Not everyone who gets married ends up like your parents. After spending sixteen years with my family, I thought you understood that."

Soren met his friend's eye. "Is that all?"

Tom shook his head. "No, I have one more thing to say to you. You think you love this family, but you don't. Your happiness stems from when it serves you to be a part of us."

"Tom, honey," Lori said, coming to her fiancé's side. "That's enough."

Soren shook his head. "No, Tom's right. I've been fooling myself all these years—thinking I was some adopted Abbott. I'm not. I'm a Traeger Rudolph through and through. Nothing will change that."

"I think you should go. This friendship is over," Tom said with his angry gaze trained on the door.

Bridget stood stock-still, hardly able to believe the scene that played out before her.

"This has to be a misunderstanding. Was this supposed to be a joke—a terribly inappropriate joke?" she asked, her words coming out in a tumble when a steadying hand pressed against her back.

She blinked away tears to find the judge standing next to her.

"Scooter, let's go. I'll drive you down to the village," the man said, his calm voice vibrating through the frenzied energy of the night's revelations.

At the judge's words, Lori led Tom away from the group, and the two sat on a sofa in the far corner of the room. Their heads bent close together as they spoke in hushed whispers.

Bridget scanned the room—the room that should be hosting a lovely rehearsal dinner. They were supposed to dance and share stories late into the night, just as her parents had done the night before they wed.

Soren couldn't have done this on purpose—could he?

"Are you okay, Birdie?" the judge asked.

She nodded, unable to speak.

"Come on, Scooter. I'll wait in the truck," the older man said as Dan handed him the keys to the vehicle as the judge walked out the front door.

For what could have been five seconds or five days, she felt Soren's gaze bore into her. But she couldn't look up—couldn't meet his eye. His heavy footfalls reverberated through the hardwood floor—each step a dagger slicing into her heart—before the door slammed shut behind him.

She released a pained breath.

He was gone.

"Birdie, are you okay?" Lori called from the couch.

"I...I'm..." she tried.

But she couldn't let him go.

Not yet.

"I'll be right back," she called over her shoulder as she flung open the door and ran into the swirling snowstorm.

She cupped her hands over her eyes, shielding them from the cold, heavy flakes, then spotted Soren as he walked across the snowy drive, lit only by the truck's headlights.

"Wait!" she cried, taking the porch steps two at a time.

He stood, expressionless, bathed in the golden beams.

"This has to be a misunderstanding. Don't go. Let's figure this out," she pleaded, her heart in her throat.

But Soren didn't budge. Instead, he crossed his arms.

"Tom saw the texts. He's right. I set this up because I didn't want him to marry your sister."

Why was he acting like a heartless robot? This wasn't him! This couldn't be him!

She shook her head. Maybe he was ready to give up and accept defeat, but she wasn't. She'd seen the good man in him. There had to be a way to make this right.

"No, you promised me that you were done with that—that you wouldn't do anything to jeopardize the wedding."

The light caught the rigid set of his jaw.

"I never said that I promised, Bridget. I just agreed."

"It's the same thing," she threw back.

He leaned in, and the cold tip of his nose brushed against hers. "It's not the same," he answered, the words coated in ice.

She reached to touch his cheek, but he took a step away from her, and her heart shattered.

It was like watching a building collapse in on itself.

"Why are you doing this, Soren? Why are you throwing everything away?"

In the space of a breath, he was millimeters away from her. He gripped her elbows, and his eyes, those green cat-like eyes she loved, shone hard and empty in the truck's headlights. "Because, Birdie, this is who I am. You can't add a glop of frosting to me and smooth out all the bad parts. I am the bad parts. Selfish and self-serving, I used you like I used the Abbotts."

His words hit like a punch to the gut, but she stood firm. "I don't believe that."

"Believe this. There won't be any Christmas miracles happening for me. No Christmas fairy wish can change what I am. There's nothing here for me, and there was never anything more than sex between us."

"You're a liar," she bit out, willing herself not to cry. She would not give him the satisfaction.

A smug expression ripe with contempt and condescension

graced his dark features. "You're a little slow on the uptake, but now you seem to get it, *Birdie*. I am a liar. Better you learn that now," he replied. His words, colder than the frigid snow, sliced through the broken pieces of her heart.

Soren left her side and slammed the truck's door shut.

But she couldn't move. She couldn't go back inside. She could only stand there, tears frozen on her cheeks, and watch as the truck disappeared into the darkness.

18

SOREN

*S*oren attempted to bend his neck, but a sharp kink in the muscles had another agenda. He groaned and cracked an eyelid, then immediately shut his eye at the blast of bright light. And it wasn't just his neck that wasn't pleased with him. Cottonmouthed, he tried to swallow, and instead, tasted whiskey and gingerbread—a terrible combination. But when the judge brought him to Kringle Acres of all places to crash last night, he'd fallen in with a few retired Santas who were partaking in drinks and cookies while playing poker in the main gathering area.

And at this point in his clusterfuck of a life, he was sure of three things.

One, a contingent of the retired fraternal order of bearded Santas really knew how to hustle a guy out of his hard-earned cash.

Two, he'd completely decimated a sixteen-year friendship.

And three, Soren Christopher Traeger Rudolph was wholly unworthy of love.

Yes, he'd been a wreck after Tom shared that Lori was pregnant.

Yes, he'd jumped to the conclusion that Tom's only motivation to wed was tied to the obligation he owed to the child.

And yes, while he did contact the strippers, he hadn't remembered doing it. That was the God's honest truth. But he wasn't surprised he'd done it. He'd already been out of sorts about the wedding—not to mention his yo-yoing emotions when it came to the maid of honor. Tom's baby bomb had thrown him for a loop, and a big stripper blowout seemed like the only card he had to play. It was a stupid, drunken decision. But he'd done it, and he had to own it because that was who he was at his core.

Just like his mother.

Just like his father.

Selfish and self-serving.

He'd used the Abbotts' acceptance as a mask—a way to play the part of a good person. If they cared for him, he couldn't be all bad, right?

Wrong.

He'd held on to that false prophecy for far too long.

There was a reason he didn't practice law after graduating from law school—a reason why he chose to build a business that made money hand over fist tearing other companies apart. It was his true nature. He was a taker. He took and took until there was nothing left but what fell into his greedy hands.

He'd taken Tom's friendship and fed it to a shredder. He'd taken the Abbotts' affection and turned a blowtorch to it.

No more Uncle Scooter. No more holidays circled around the kitchen table playing scrabble or putting together one of the kids' LEGO sets.

He'd come full circle. From this point on, during the holidays, he'd sit alone in a room surrounded by expensive things. At least when he was a kid, he'd spent those dreary holidays with a maid or a nanny. Now, he'd have only his own miserable company.

And what of her? Bridget Dasher, not your average vixen. Not by a long shot.

He had to hurt her—had to sever the connection between them. It was his only choice after seeing the heart-wrenching pain in her eyes. She cared for him deeply—more than he ever deserved. For a beautiful moment, he thought he could be hers. He believed that he could shed the Traeger Rudolph heartlessness and shield her from the part of him that dwelled in darkness.

Had he told her that he wanted to change, that he wanted to make it right with Tom and Lori, she would have stood by his side. She would have vouched for him, had he asked.

That was the heartbreaking beauty of her soul. That was her radiant goodness. He'd seen it the first night they spent together in the hotel, cocooned in anonymity, far away from the truth of who he was.

She was all sweet chocolatey kisses and bright twinkling eyes.

He was one-night stands, power suits, and bank statements.

A soulless Grinch of a scoundrel.

He squeezed his eyes shut in an attempt to keep out the world and give himself one more moment of tortured solitude before he had to put together the pieces of what came next.

"Is he awake, or is he talking in his sleep?" a man asked as the sound of clinking silverware and the clank of plates being stacked dialed up in his hazy, half-awake state.

"Let him rest! You all swindled the poor thing at poker last night. The least you could do is allow him to sleep."

"It's nearly three in the afternoon, and he's the one who finished off the whiskey, then ate the gingerbread house."

"He ate it? That gingerbread house was for decoration. I'm

pretty sure one of Frank's grandchildren made it with glue," the woman replied.

What the hell was going on out there?

Soren swallowed again. Yep, glue would explain the severe cottonmouth.

This is what hitting rock bottom looked like. A man who'd wolfed down an ornamental gingerbread house sprawled out on a couch in a retirement community populated by ex Santas in the middle of nowhere, Colorado.

Could he just sleep until the new year?

"Should we give him the Kringle drunk tank treatment?" a man asked as a rush of frigid air whooshed into the room.

"The what?" he exclaimed, bolting upright, hangover be damned.

The only thing that could make this situation more pathetic was spending Christmas Eve in a cell cooped up with a bunch of hungover Santas.

"Good morning, Scooter!" came a cheery voice as someone shoved a glass into his hand.

He stared down at the orange liquid. "Is this juice?"

"See, he's sober enough to recognize orange juice. I don't think he needs the drunk tank treatment," another woman remarked.

"You didn't watch him eat the glued-on gumdrops off the gingerbread house. Don't you worry! This naughty lister will thank me for this."

"Naughty what?" he mumbled, but before anyone could answer, a snowball hit him square in the forehead.

Forgetting the juice in his hand, he flung his arms up to protect his face. The liquid splashed across his cheeks—another rude wake-up call. Sticky and wet, he blinked and assessed his surroundings.

A group of white-bearded, red-cheeked, slightly pot-bellied

older men stood alongside women donning frilly aprons and warm grins while several other very Santa-like couples sat nearby, drinking from steaming mugs and reading the newspaper.

"Now that's one way to make an orange smoothie," a shorter Santa remarked to a taller Mrs. Claus doppelgänger.

"Here, dear, let's try a nice glass of milk this time," another apron-clad, sweet little grandma-looking lady offered with a smile.

He handed over his empty cup to whoever the hell this drinks lady was, then accepted the tall glass of milk. He swallowed it down in two big gulps, grateful to get the taste of gingerbread, glue, and hard alcohol off his tongue.

"Look who finally decided to join the living."

Soren perked up. He recognized this voice and saw the judge coming toward him with a dish towel in hand.

"Here, Scooter, clean yourself up."

Soren patted his face. "I figured you went back to the mountain house, Judge."

The man took a seat next to him. "No, I told you somewhere between your ninth or tenth shot of whiskey that the people at Kringle Acres had offered to put us up for the night due to the late hour. They had two spare rooms, but it appears you never made it to yours."

The aftermath of his life blowing up had been almost as surreal as walking into a cozy Christmas mountain house teeming with strippers. The judge had driven him to Kringle Acres. The man had made several friends there over the last few days, and the kind residents had assured him that they could put him up for the night. He'd wanted to go straight to the airport and get the hell out of town, but the roads were terrible. The truck had slipped and skidded down the icy, snow-packed street that led from the mountain house to the village.

He rubbed his hands across his scruffy cheeks. He had to look like a Christmas zombie.

"Let me get cleaned up a bit, and then I'll call for a cab."

"No, you won't be doing that. Not yet," the judge answered in his firm judge voice.

Soren propped his elbows on his knees and ran his hands through his tangled, sticky hair. "Why is that?"

The Santa and Mrs. Claus crew pulled some chairs over and sat down, observing him closely.

A burly Santa cleared his throat. "You're on the naughty list, son. And we're here to help."

"There's a naughty list for adults? What do you do? Check people's web browsers and see who's been watching porn?" he joked.

A petite Mrs. Claus raised an eyebrow. "Do you look at naughty pictures on the computer, young man?"

He sat up, ramrod straight. "No, ma'am."

The woman narrowed her gaze.

He glanced around, wishing like hell the drinks lady would bring him another glass of milk so he could slowly sip it and buy some time to figure out how to extricate himself from this Christmas catastrophe.

He shifted on the couch. "Maybe I've accidentally seen a few naughty things on the internet. But not a lot. A normal amount. A normal adult man amount."

Fuck.

You've never known shame until three Santa couples stared you down like the deviant you were.

"Scooter, last night, while we were kicking your ass at poker, you shared a few things with us," the burly Santa continued.

Why were they calling him Scooter? That life was over.

He rubbed his temples as the events of last night came back to him. They'd entered Kringle Acres, and the bearded men had waved them over, then dealt himself and the judge into the game before he'd had a chance to decline the offer to play. To his surprise, it had been the perfect surreal escape. The Santas didn't say much, and as one drink became five, it gave him the opportunity to confess his transgressions.

The whiskey probably helped, too.

What did it matter? He knew he'd be gone in a matter of hours.

He set the dish towel on a side table and addressed the North Pole contingent. "I appreciate your hospitality and thank you for letting me get a few things off my chest. But I've come to realize that there's not much hope for someone on the naughty list, is there?"

The Mrs. Claus, who'd given him the stink eye for the naughty internet browser history, softened her expression. "That's not how it works, dear. You're not bad, but you've made some unfortunate choices."

"Oh, I'm bad, Mrs. Claus. Ask the judge. I ruined his grandson's—and my now ex-best friend's—wedding because I didn't want anything to change. I didn't want to lose the only thing that mattered. I was selfish and greedy. A real-life scrooge," he finished, leaving out how he'd also stomped on the heart of the only woman he'd ever loved.

Loved?

He pictured Bridget's face, the curve of her neck, the way she could go from angel to vixen in a split second.

He'd loved her from the moment he saw her.

He rubbed his bleary eyes. "I can see why I spilled my guts to you last night. It's remarkably easy to talk to all of you."

"Well, we get quite a bit of practice talking to youngsters," a Mrs. Claus offered.

"And you're also a chatty drunk," the short Santa, who'd won fifty bucks off him last night, chimed.

Great! He was not only hitting rock-bottom—he was living out the holiday edition of hitting rock-bottom.

"Scooter, does the name Lawrence Duncan sound familiar?" the judge asked, blessedly shifting gears, but he didn't know of any Lawrence Duncan.

Or did he? The name had a strange familiarity.

"I don't think so."

A quiet Santa who hadn't swindled him at cards raised his hand. "I'm Lawrence Duncan."

Soren stared at the man. "You're one of the Santas I talked to a few days ago when we'd come for the spaghetti dinner. You were fixing the snowcats."

"That's right," the man replied with a twitch of a grin hidden in his white beard.

But there was something else familiar about him. He'd thought it that day as well.

The judge sat back. "Larry's an old friend from law school. We'd lost touch over the years after we each retired from the bench. I was quite pleased to run into him again, here, in Kringle."

Soren stared at the Santa judge. "You can be both a judge and a Santa?"

Larry chuckled. "What do you think we did for the rest of the year?"

Soren glanced around the group. "Make toys?" he answered, knowing he sounded like an idiot as Team Ho-Ho-Ho broke out into laughter.

"I never get tired of that response," the burly Santa crooned, slapping his leg in delight.

"Larry was a judge for the family courts in Manhattan," the judge offered with a curious glint in his eye.

Soren nodded to this retired judge, Lawrence Duncan, trying to place him. "Okay."

"You see, Scooter, Larry came to me with a perplexing case many years ago. He was charged with overseeing a very contentious custody battle."

Larry Duncan nodded. "But this was different from most custody battles I'd presided over. In this case, despite being exorbitantly wealthy, neither parent wanted custody of the shared child."

Soren froze, unable to move. His heart hammered in his chest as the name Lawrence Duncan clicked into place.

"Larry came to me for advice when it was time for the minor child to go to high school," the judge continued.

Larry leaned forward. "The parents finally agreed on something. They each advocated for boarding school. I knew that Frank here had a grandson the same age as this minor, so I asked for his advice on possible schools."

Soren looked from Judge Lawrence Duncan to Judge Franklin Abbott, before his gaze settled on the man who had taught him how to fish. "You suggested that I go to the same school as Tom, didn't you?"

The judge nodded. "And that you share a dorm room."

Soren sank back into the couch cushions, unable to believe that there had been those looking after his welfare as a child. Not just Janine for the short time she'd been his nanny, but Judge Lawrence Duncan and Judge Franklin Abbott. A man who knew he'd been unwanted from the start.

He shook his head to clear the stupefied haze. "Why didn't you ever say anything, Judge? All this time I thought..."

"That you'd just gotten lucky?" the man supplied.

Soren nodded.

"We spoke about the decision. I believe one of your nannies had brought you to meet with me. Do you remember what you said when I'd told you the news?" Lawrence asked gently.

Soren nodded. Judge Lawrence Duncan's beard wasn't white

when they'd met years ago in that Manhattan courthouse. But there was no doubt that he was sitting across from the man who'd changed the trajectory of his life.

Larry Duncan shared a look with the judge. "You hugged me, right there in my chambers, son. And you told me how excited you were to have a place that could be a real home. I knew right then and there that you were a good kid. And that you deserved to find a place where people cared about you."

"And I knew you and Tom would hit it off," the judge added.

Crushing guilt weighed heavy on his heart. All that kindness, and he'd never learned from it. He'd never thought to incorporate all he'd learned from the Abbotts into his life.

He slumped forward. "Judge, I ruined everything."

"Well, you may have outdone yourself in upsetting Tom, but I think you and my grandson can work it out."

He exhaled a shaky breath. "I would love to believe that."

"Now, what about your *Alice*," the man pressed.

He searched the judge's eyes. "My Alice?"

"This fell out of your wallet when we were bleeding you dry at the poker table," the short Santa said as he handed over the photo strip.

"You don't have to be like your parents, Mr. Rudolph. Your birth doesn't determine who you are. You and you alone are responsible for your choices. And I know that the grateful young man I'd met in my chambers is wholly capable of forging a new path," Larry Duncan offered.

"And wholly capable of dedicating himself to his friends and to the love of his life," the judge added.

"You know about Bridget?" he asked.

"Oh, kid! We could all tell that you were crazy about that stoned young lady the night you brought us those peanut butter blossoms," the burly Santa answered.

The judge bit back a grin. "I've spent a lot of time with

couples over the years. Overseeing marriages, divorces, and everything in between, you start to get a knack for reading between the lines when it comes to love."

Soren turned to the Santa crew. "And she's not actually a stoner. She accidentally ate a bunch of Tanner's gummy bears without knowing the special ingredient," he replied, remembering that wild, wonderful night.

"I don't think that there's anyone here who hasn't indulged in Tanner's treats. Just make sure she only eats a few next time. Unless she's spent the day with hundreds of screaming toddlers. In that case, give her the bag," a Mrs. Claus replied as the Santa contingent nodded in agreement.

He stared down at the photos. "As much as I wished it were true, I don't think that there will be a next time with her. And more than that, I don't deserve her."

"What kind of person deserves her, Scooter?" the judge asked.

Soren sat back and pictured the life he wanted for the woman he loved.

A sad smile pulled at the corners of his mouth. "A man who puts her first. A man who sees how lucky he is to have her every day of his life. A man devoid of selfishness and greed. A man capable of keeping a promise," he answered, tracing his finger over the image of their photo booth kiss.

The judge patted his leg. "How about a man who grew up without love but found it through friendship and an adopted family? How about a man who desperately needs to give himself a gift?"

Soren released a sad little chuckle. "Judge, I have more money than God. What gift do I need to give to myself?"

"Trust," the man replied.

The word hung in the air.

"Trust?" he questioned. What could he mean by that?

"The gift of trusting yourself not to be like your parents. The gift of taking a leap and promising to protect another's heart. The gift of trusting in the goodness of your own heart," the man answered.

Trust. That was it. He'd trusted himself with the Abbotts because he believed that they had made him good. And in that slice of his life, up until completely jacking up Tom's wedding, he had been good, loyal, and trustworthy. The qualities he'd learned from the people who called him Scooter. Still, a thread of doubt wove its way through his heart.

"But what if I fail, Judge?"

The man he'd known since he was fourteen held his gaze. "What if you don't?"

What if you don't?

Like the Grinch himself, his heart swelled with love. He had two promises to make. Two promises he'd spend his life honoring.

"Now, if you still want to go to the airport, Scooter, I'll call you a cab. It's your decision to make," the judge said.

Soren stared at the picture of Bridget. "There's somewhere I need to go. But it's not the airport," he replied, voice brimming with conviction. He pressed the photo to his heart and closed his eyes as a sense of peace washed over him. But he wasn't expecting for something to poke him in the chest.

He unzipped his coat. Yes, he'd passed out wearing his jacket. It happens when drinking with ex Santas. But when he reached into his breast pocket, he couldn't believe what he'd found.

A black velvet pouch.

"The rings! Judge, I forgot I had them in here. Tom gave them to me the day Bridget and I arrived at Kringle Mountain and..." He glanced at the clock. They still had a little time before the Christmas Eve wedding festivities would start. "And you, Judge! We have to get you back to the mountain house. You're the one who's supposed to officiate the wedding. We have to go!"

With determination flooding his system, he rose to his feet.

"I'm putting it all on the line! It's time to take the leap. Whether I'm forgiven or not, I need to get to Kringle Mountain and speak my peace. I'm hoping for a Christmas miracle," he said, a man on the verge of redemption.

The North Pole contingent clapped and cheered as Judge Lawrence Duncan tossed him a little wink.

"Go get 'em, Soren Christopher Traeger Rudolph!"

"Excuse me, but I don't think anyone is going anywhere. Have you looked outside?" another Santa-looking man said, cutting short the celebration as he pulled off a snow-covered cap and propped a snow shovel against the wall.

Soren stared at the man. "What do you mean?"

"The roads are treacherous. They even closed the highway. Not to mention, it looks like Kringle Mountain has lost power," the man added, stomping the snow off his boots.

"But we have to get to the Kringle Mountain House. I've got a wedding to save, and I need to tell Bridget that I love her."

"Sit tight, young fella. They usually get the power back in a day or two. Dan and Delores know what to do. They've got a generator and are always stocked up this time of year."

"What about the gondola to get to the Kringle Chapel," he pressed.

The man scratched his head. "Kringle Chapel has a fireplace, so if you could get there, you'd be able to keep warm. But if the mountain's lost power, the gondola to the chapel won't be running."

No, no, no! Not when he was so close!

Soren paced the length of the gathering area, staring out the large windows into the parking lot, covered in drifts of snow.

He'd give anything if Cole were right, and Christmas fairies did exist.

He knew exactly what he'd wish for.

He rested his head on the cold windowpane when the answer to his dilemma looked him square in the eye.

He turned to the Santa contingent. "Those three snowcats—they could make it up Kringle Mountain, right?"

The bearded men joined him at the window along with the man who'd been out shoveling snow.

"You mean Rudolph, Vixen, and Dasher."

"Who?"

"The snowcats," one of the Mrs. Clauses called. "They're named after our reindeer."

"Santa's reindeer," he corrected.

"Yes, *our* reindeer," the honorable Lawrence Duncan, retired judge and part-time Santa, replied with another sly wink.

"And the three snowcats you've got here just happen to be Rudolph, Vixen, and Dasher?"

"That's right," the burly Santa replied.

Soren stared at the snowcats, feeling more determined than ever, as something else caught his eye. "What's that, over there?"

"That would be a snow angel," the shoveling man replied.

Holy Christmas fairies!

"Did you make it?" he asked excitedly.

The man chuckled as he brushed the snow off his coat. "No, son. My snow angel making days are well behind me."

It had to be a sign!

He turned to the Santas. "I need your help. The judge and I must get to the Kringle Mountain House, and then the wedding party will need a ride up to the chapel. Can Rudolph, Vixen, and Dasher handle that?"

"There's not much that Rudolph, Vixen, and Dasher can't handle," the burly Santa replied.

Soren grinned. No, there wasn't!

"Then, we need to go. There's no time to lose. Judge, are you ready?" he asked, glancing around the room.

Judge Franklin Abbott clapped him on the shoulder. "You bet I am, Scooter."

The Santa snowcat squad sprang into action, putting on their coats and gloves.

Soren glanced at the velvet bag containing the rings and the picture strip, lying safe in the palm of his hand when an idea so perfect and so Christmas-complete sparked in his mind.

"Wait!" he cried.

"What is it?" the judge asked, buttoning up his jacket.

Soren scanned the room. "Do any of you know how I could get into contact with Agnes and Ernie Angel, the owners of the Cupid Bakeries? They'd said they'd be here, in Kringle, visiting friends through Christmas Day. I need to speak with them before we go anywhere."

The Santas all grinned at him.

"What?" he asked, not sure why they were smiling.

"Look behind you," Lawrence Duncan offered, then shared a knowing look with the judge.

Soren turned just as Ernie and Agnes Angel lowered the newspapers that had hidden their faces.

He shook his head in grateful disbelief, then checked the clock on the wall, ticking away precious time.

If this worked, he had a fighting chance.

"Mr. and Mrs. Angel, I have a business proposition for you. But I'm going to need your answer in the next thirty seconds."

"There, that's the last one. It fits like a glove."

Bridget fastened the top button on the back of Lori's dress. Her little sister was the picture of a winter bride in their mother's timeless satin wedding gown. With an elegant boat neckline that revealed the hint of her sister's shoulders as the three-quarter sleeves hit just below her elbows, Lori was the mirror image of their mother on her wedding day thirty years ago.

She tucked a curl behind her sister's ear as the women stared at each other in the mirror. How quickly time passed. It seemed like only yesterday she was braiding Lori's hair in the tiny apartment they shared when it was just the two of them, barely getting by. And now, here they were—back at Kringle Mountain.

This should be one of the happiest days of her life, but a cloud of chaos had come in with the winter storm thanks to Soren's actions. This morning at breakfast and then again at lunch, no one had spoken of what happened last night. Not even Cole or Carly mentioned it. Everyone had put on a brave face and tried to keep it light. It was Christmas Eve and Lori and Tom's wedding day, for goodness' sake. But nobody seemed to know how to navigate the conversation around the missing best man. So, understandably, much of the day had passed in a heavy silence.

No matter. She and Lori had endured the loss of those they loved best. They knew how to press on. And the Abbotts were good people who loved her sister. It would all work out. It had to.

Bridget couldn't let her guard down. She was determined to get the wedding back on track. But she kept catching glimpses of Soren's things, lying about inside their room.

No, not *their* room. Her room.

She still couldn't make sense of what happened last night—still couldn't understand why Soren hadn't even tried to make it right with his best friend. And his words, his cruel and callous words, had shattered her heart.

Why had he reverted to his old ways?

Old ways!

She was fooling herself.

Those weren't his old ways. Those were *his ways*. His self-imposed *modus operandi*.

Yes, he had monstrous parents who planted the idea in his mind that he was unlovable and that there was a part of him that would always be like them. That alone broke her heart. But she had to come to terms with the fact that, as much as she saw the good in him, he didn't see it. And that would be his greatest downfall.

But that hadn't kept her from crying herself to sleep last night with the hint of his sandalwood scent in the air. This man, who a week ago meant nothing to her, now invaded her every thought. And as much as she wanted to, she couldn't forget his touch, his kisses, or the way the breath would catch in her throat and butterflies would erupt in her belly when he said her name.

Bridget Dasher, you're part angel, part vixen, and all mine.

And she was.

Despite knowing he'd lied when he said that she'd meant nothing to him, she had to put him out of her head. She needed the gift of distance.

And he'd given it to her.

By now, he was most likely long gone.

She'd buried her parents. She'd buried her grandmother. She'd raised her little sister. She had the strength to get over Soren. She had no other choice.

The lights in the room flickered, and she glanced out the window at the falling snow.

"I'm glad Dan was able to pick up the wedding cake last night. It's really coming down out there."

Best man or not, this wedding was going to happen. She'd veered from her focus thanks to his beguiling eyes that drank her in with each look. And there was no denying the overpowering attraction that crackled between them whenever they were together.

Stop!

He was gone. He'd made his choice.

Putting on a brave face, she adjusted the neckline of the wedding dress as Lori ran her hands down her abdomen.

"It won't be long before I look like I've eaten an entire wedding cake," Lori said, resting her hand on her belly.

The strippers couldn't hold a candle to the shock of learning that Lori and Tom were expecting.

Bridget placed her hand on top of her sister's as they stared into the mirror. "You'll be an amazing mother."

Lori grinned, her eyes growing teary. "Can you believe it? Me, a mom?"

"I can. You'll be just as loving as Mom and Grandma."

Lori turned to face her. "And you! Don't forget, you had a hand in raising me. You were almost worse than Mom and Dad.

You'd check my homework. You never let me date, and you still signed us up for community service projects," she finished as her expression grew somber.

"What is it, Lori?" she pressed.

Her sister blew out a slow breath. "I'm sorry I didn't tell you about the pregnancy right away. It was such a shock. It didn't even seem possible. I had Tom run down to the village to buy another test. And after that one came back positive, there was no denying it. I was going to tell you after the wedding. I know how much work you've put into it, and I didn't want that huge announcement weighing on you while you were busting your ass to replicate Mom and Dad's big day."

Bridget waved her off. "I understand. But were you guys trying to conceive?"

Lori shook her head. "No, I'd switched birth control pills and must have started the new pack at the wrong time. But to be honest with you, I don't know what happened, but I'm over the moon about it. I'm so in love with Tom, and despite what Scooter thought, he's excited to become a dad. He loves being an uncle. Sure, we're terrified of taking the leap into parenthood, but we're in it together."

At the mention of Soren, her body stiffened as a sharp pain, both icy and searing, sliced through her chest.

How many times could a heart break?

She'd stopped counting.

"Birdie, have you read the letter yet?" Lori asked gently.

Bridget frowned. "What letter?"

"The one from Grandma Dasher."

How had she forgotten?

Well, that was a stupid question. After she'd lost the man who she foolishly believed could be the one, she hadn't even thought of what her sister had given her at the chapel.

Flustered, Bridget rose from the bed. "I think it's still in my coat pocket."

"We have some time now, Birdie. I would like you to read it. You need to know what's in the letter."

Bridget eyed her sister warily. "You keep saying that."

"It's very important. Let's read it while it's just the two of us."

Bridget resurrected her placating expression. In all fairness, she didn't know if she could handle another jolt of shocking information. From Soren's deception to the strippers to Lori's pregnancy, a message from the past felt eerily ominous.

But if it was important to Lori, she'd do it.

She found her jacket hanging over the side of the couch and retrieved the envelope from the pocket. Again, she was met with Grandma Dasher's handwriting. How many times had she watched her grandmother jot a note in a cookbook or write down an order from a client? She loved how her grandmother wrote the *D* in *Dasher* when she signed her name—the gentle loops reminding her of a snowflake dancing in the air.

The sisters settled themselves on the end of the bed as Bridget slid the stationery out of the envelope.

Before unfolding the paper, she met her sister's gaze. "My letter from gram was about what I needed to do to take care of you. I tried to do everything she'd asked."

Lori touched the corner of the stationary. "And my letter has a part about taking care of you, Birdie."

That didn't make sense.

"Of me? You were only a kid."

"Grandma knew that. Just read the last paragraph, Birdie," Lori said, brushing a tear from her cheek.

Bridget willed her hands not to shake. In her grandmother's last hours, she'd sat with the woman, holding her hand, staying strong and steady. Even at eighteen, she'd understood the circumstances. She was responsible for her sister and didn't have the luxury of falling apart.

And she hadn't fallen apart.

But at this moment, she feared the words written on the page might be her undoing.

Carefully, she unfolded the letter and skimmed the words her grandmother had written to Lori.

Work hard.

Listen to Birdie.

You are meant for great things.

I am so proud of you.

But her heart nearly stopped when she came to the last paragraph.

Lori, we both know that Birdie is going to make sure that you're safe and loved. But here is something you might not know about your sister. She will do all these things to the detriment of herself. She will give and give and never stop. After you're older and can understand what I'm telling you, it's up to you to give Birdie permission to let go. My dear Lori, I know with all my heart that you will find love, happiness, and success. But Birdie won't take the leap to reach for those things for herself until she knows that, without a doubt, you no longer need her as a guardian but are ready to walk beside her as a sister and a friend.

Now, for you, sweet Birdie, when you read these words, please know that it's time for you to spread your angel wings, set your own course in this world, and soar.

I, along with your mother and father, will always be with you both.

Bridget stared at her grandmother's message until the blue ballpoint pen loops and lines blurred together.

"Birdie?" Lori said, her voice barely a whisper.

With the weight of her grandmother's words, Bridget had to come clean to her sister about Soren.

"There's something I've been keeping from you. And you might be disappointed in me."

Lori took her hand. "You can tell me anything, and there's nothing you could do to disappoint me."

"Do you remember that night when I had to stay over in Denver at the hotel?" she began.

Lori gave her a strange look as her brows knit together. "Of course."

"You should know that the man at the bar—my hotel hottie —the one that I spent the night with."

Lori leaned in. "Yes, I remember."

Bridget swallowed hard. It was now or never.

"It was Scooter," she confessed.

Her sister's jaw nearly hit the floor. "You're kidding?"

"I wish I was."

Or did she? Did she regret that night?

Her head said she should, but her treacherous heart couldn't let him go.

"Why didn't you say anything, Birdie?"

Bridget shook her head in frustration. "I didn't know what to say. The guy had been an absolute creep to you, but we had this amazing night together. I didn't know it was him at the time. We didn't share any personal information. He only knew me as Bridget, and I only knew him as Soren."

Lori gasped. "I never told you that Soren was Scooter's real name, did I?"

"No, and he only knew of me as Birdie. That is, until the next morning, when Dan picked us up at the hotel, and we put it together."

Her sister chuckled. "Well, it all makes sense now."

Bridget reared back. "What are you talking about?"

"I was telling Tom that half of the time, you guys looked as if you wanted to tear each other apart. But the other half of the time, you guys looked more like you wanted to tear each other's clothes off," Lori added with the hint of a mischievous grin.

Oh no! Had everyone gotten that vibe off of them?

Bridget held Lori's gaze. "I never wanted to complicate anything. I didn't know what to say to you about him. I thought that, once Soren and I figured things out, I'd tell you that I..."

"That you like him?" Lori offered perceptively.

Bridget blew out an exasperated breath. "Something like that. But now, after what he did, I feel so foolish for falling for him."

That wasn't a lie, but there was so much more to what she was feeling. Even when they were going at each other, she'd found such comfort in his presence. And not only that, he'd pushed her. She'd never had a real adversary—never had to fight so hard for what she believed in.

Thanks to this curmudgeon of a man, she'd learned that she wasn't the doormat Dasher sister. She possessed a backbone of steel, and it was time to put her tenacity to the test in her own life.

He'd brought out the vixen in her. There was no denying it.

There was also no denying that she wasn't the only one he'd hurt.

"How's Tom holding up?" she asked.

While the man had maintained his kind, positive persona throughout the day, she'd seen sadness in his eyes when he didn't think anyone was looking.

Lori released a pained sigh. "He's crushed. Tom sees the best in everyone, so it hit him especially hard."

Bridget nodded. Despite only knowing Soren for a handful of days, she understood Tom's pain.

"You really like Scooter, don't you?" Lori asked without even an ounce of judgment.

Bridget glanced at the bed where she'd slept in Soren's arms and dreamed of a forever with him.

A forever that would never come.

She smoothed her dress, needing to work out her nervous energy. "I don't know. Maybe," she lied.

Lori caught her eye in the mirror. "I'm so sorry, Birdie. But if it's meant to be, it'll work out."

"But he's awful. He tried to stop Tom from marrying you. How can you say that? Don't you hate him?" she shot back.

Lori's expression softened. "No, I don't hate him. I feel sorry for him."

"Why?" Bridget asked, stunned by her sister's response.

"Because now I understand. He doesn't know that he's surrounded by love, and that's the saddest part. That's Scooter's greatest tragedy."

Bridget stared out the window at the falling snow. Her sister was right.

"Birdie, look at me," Lori coaxed gently.

She blinked back tears, then turned to meet her sister's gaze.

Lori took her hand and gave it a squeeze. "We're Dasher girls. We're made of tough stuff. Look at where you are in your life. Now, you can do whatever you want. The sky's the limit for you, Birdie. You don't have to stay in Texas. You could move to Boston and be close to me and the Abbotts. You could even open a shop there. Look at everything you've done just this week!"

Her first impulse was to say no, but then, she remembered Grandma Dasher's words.

Spread your angel wings, set your own course in this world, and soar.

She felt for the angel pendant around her neck.

Lori and her grandmother were right. It was time to take a leap.

She was no longer the Dasher sister who was afraid to jump.

She'd embrace the vixen.

"When did you get so smart?" she teased her sister through her tears.

Lori smiled as her gaze reflected deep gratitude. "I learned by watching my big sister. You see, she's a remarkable woman. She cared for me. She worked two jobs to make sure I could focus on my studies. She cheered me on every step of the way. She's the reason why I am the woman I am today. And more than that, she's my hero."

Lori's words danced in the air like magical fairy dust, and Bridget could feel the shift in their connection.

She'd kept her promise to her grandmother. And while she knew her family would be grateful for her sacrifice, she couldn't deny that she'd used the promise as an excuse for something less noble. A guise that masked her fear of reaching for the stars and living a full life.

That ended today.

Lori's words set her free.

It was time for this Birdie to fly.

Bridget slid Grandma Dasher's letter back into its envelope. "I could do with a change of scenery, and I like the thought of living on the East Coast. After working for Gaston and running his shop for years, I know what it takes to maintain a successful bakery. I'm ready for the challenge."

"I'm thrilled to hear you say that," Lori exclaimed.

Bridget wrapped her arms around her sister, not seeing her as the little girl she had to protect, but a capable woman. A confidant. A best friend. An equal.

Bridget Dasher was no longer stifled or stuck. It was time to believe in herself. And, lucky for her, she had three angels to guide the way.

The lights flickered again when a knock at the door caught their attention.

"Aunt Lori, Birdie, it's me, Cole! I think I saw a Christmas fairy! Come quick!"

Bridget shared a look with her sister. "At least he didn't leave the house this time."

The women started down the hall, but Grace, Denise, and Nancy met them before they'd entered the main room.

"I'm afraid there's some bad news," Grace said, worry written all over her face.

"Cole just missed the Christmas fairy?" Lori asked.

Nancy shook her head. "No, I wish it were something as innocent as that. It's the gondola. It's not working."

Denise nodded. "The main power to the mountain is out. You might have noticed the flickering lights. Delores told us that was the generator kicking on. Dan's been trying to run power to the gondola, but the generator isn't powerful enough. We didn't want to worry you, but it looks like we may need to make alternative plans."

"We know how much you wanted to get married at the chapel, Lori, but I'm not sure what can be done," Grace said, squeezing her sister's hand.

Bridget paced a few steps back and forth in the corridor.

Not the gondola!

She'd worried this could happen.

Think, Bridget! Think!

"Has anyone checked the weather report? Is the snow supposed to taper off soon?" she asked.

Scott joined them in the hall. "No, in fact, it looks like another eight to ten inches could fall before tomorrow. And there's something else."

Lori threw the man a nervous glance. "What else?"

"The judge isn't here. He left me a message last night that he was going to spend the night in the village at Kringle Acres. I thought that he'd returned early and just went to take a nap, but Russ says he hasn't seen him all day."

"The snow. He's probably stuck there because of the weather," Bridget replied, leaning against the wall.

No gondola to the chapel.

No judge to marry Lori and Tom.

"And the rings," Tom called from the main room.

"The rings?" Lori repeated, her voice going up an octave.

"I'm sorry, honey. I gave them to Scooter for safekeeping. He put them in his pocket, and I don't think he ever took them out."

"Oh no!" Lori cried on a tight breath.

Bridget's heart hammered in her chest.

Had Soren kept the rings on purpose?

Anger, coupled with intense disappointment, burned in her veins.

"I'll run to the room and see if the rings are there," she said, breaking from the group.

Had this been his plan all along?

She blinked back hot tears as she went through his things, throwing his clothes onto the floor, and found nothing.

She set her sights on the chest of drawers. One after another, she rifled through the extra towels and sheets but found most of the drawers empty. She slammed the last one closed, then banged her fist on the top of the dresser.

How many more things could go wrong?

At the end of her rope, she rested her head against the wall.

"What now? How do I fix this? What would you do?" she whispered to her grandmother. But instead of hearing a voice from the great beyond, a five-year-old called out.

"Hurry, Birdie! It's coming up the mountain!" Cole cried from the main room.

She wiped a tear from her cheek and released an exhausted

huff of a laugh. Another near Christmas fairy sighting, she presumed. Add it to the list of disasters and near misses.

She could sure use a little Christmas fairy magic right about now!

"It's Rudolph!" the boy cried, waving her over.

Rudolph?

"Birdie, you've got to see this," Lori said with a bewildered expression.

"What is it?"

She found Tom and Lori standing together, staring out the front window with the rest of the Abbotts. What in the world could have made the bride reveal herself to the groom and break wedding protocols? It had to be something big.

Fortunately, she didn't have to wait long for the answer.

The floor vibrated, and a low rumble grew louder as a red flashing light projected onto the snow.

"See, Birdie! It's Rudolph! The same Rudolph that I got to ride in," Cole said, tapping the glass as Rudolph and two other snowcats lumbered up the mountain, easily traversing the heavy drifts of snow.

"What are they doing here?" Carly chimed.

Bridget stared wide-eyed as the snowcats came to a stop in front of the mountain house. The door on the Rudolph snowcat opened, and a man climbed down from the humming vehicle.

"It's the judge!" Cole called, giving a play-by-play to the stunned adults.

Bridget gasped, hardly able to believe her eyes. But when the door to the mountain house swung open, the judge entered.

"Now, that's a way to make an entrance," he said, smiling as Cole and Carly hugged him around the waist, peppering him with questions about riding in Rudolph.

The rest of the family gathered around the elderly gentleman, making quite a fuss, but he waved them off.

"I'm fine. I'm fine. Now, the snowcats are here to take us all up to the chapel, and I've got the rings," the man said, holding up the velvet bag.

Bridget wrapped her arms around the judge and gave him a grateful hug.

"Thank you! You've saved the day," she said as the tension melted from her body.

The man chuckled. "I didn't save the day. None of this was my idea."

"Then whose idea was it?" Tom asked.

The judge opened the door and waved to the snowcat, and a second man emerged from the purring vehicle.

Bridget stared in disbelief. "It's..." she trailed off, feeling weak in the knees. She'd know those dark curls and that large, muscular frame anywhere.

Soren hadn't left Kringle.

Not only that, he was here.

Her heart hammered in her chest.

Did she want to kiss him or throttle him? Both seemed like reasonable options.

"It's Scooter, and I'd like you all to hear what he has to say," the judge said, then came to her side and offered her his arm. Gratefully, she took it.

And before anyone could object, the door to the mountain house swung open again, and Soren appeared.

Red-cheeked, he scanned the room, then his eyes fell on her.

"Hi," he said with a nervous grin.

She swallowed past the lump in her throat. "Hi."

He held her gaze, and those cat-like eyes sparkled with an intriguing hopefulness. He looked like a new man.

"I need to talk to your sister first, but then there's something I'd like to ask you."

"Okay," she replied, limited to one-word utterances.

What was he doing here?

"Don't even think of upsetting my fiancée," Tom said as he wrapped his arm around Lori protectively.

Soren took another tentative step into the room. "Tom, I know that I betrayed your trust and that you're furious with me."

The man huffed an incredulous bark of a laugh. "Furious? Furious doesn't even come close to how I feel."

Soren put up his hands defensively. "I understand that, Tom. I owe you and everyone in your family an apology. I'm not making any excuses for my behavior. I did come to this wedding to stop it. That's the truth, but it's not as simple as that."

"Enlighten us," Tom said, but there was more hurt than anger in his tone.

Soren looked around the room. "I thought I was on the brink of losing everything that was good in my life. I allowed my fear of losing all of you to bring out the worst in me. I convinced myself that you weren't ready for marriage, Tom. But it wasn't you who wasn't ready. The minute I saw you with Lori all those months ago at the restaurant, I knew you loved her. And I could see how much she cared for you. I just couldn't admit that to myself."

"What did you think was going to happen?" Tom asked as pain and confusion flashed in his eyes.

Soren held the man's gaze. "I thought that if you got married, you'd move on without me. No more Abbott family holidays, and no more Scooter. When I'm Scooter, I'm whole. I'm kind. I'm the person I want to be. But this is where I made a mistake."

"And what's that?" Tom asked, his voice softening.

"I used to think that I never learned how to love because of my parents. I focused so hard on that and couldn't see that I'd spent the last sixteen years surrounded by love. From Grace and Scott, to Denise and Nancy, and then to Cole and Carly, and now, from you and Lori, I've seen firsthand what love is. Tom, you've been my best friend for most of my life. You taught me acceptance and loyalty, but fear kept me from understanding that Scooter and Soren could be the same man. And that's why I want to make a promise to Lori," he finished, turning to her sister.

"To me?" Lori asked, sharing a perplexed look with Tom.

"Well, to you and to your baby. Will you hear me out?" Soren pleaded.

Lori's lips parted once, then twice, before she finally nodded.

Soren blew out a shaky breath. "I was nothing but sullen and cruel, and you met my horrendous behavior with nothing but kindness. I promise that from this day forward, I'm on your side. I promise to always be there for you, Tom, and your child. You've made my best friend happier than I have ever seen him, and I'm grateful to you. But you don't have to take me up on this promise. I know my relationship with Tom, and everyone here may be beyond repair. And if none of you want to see me again, I understand. But I give you my word that, from this moment on, I'm going to live my life in a way that would make you proud," he said, looking as if the weight of the world had been lifted from his shoulders.

Lori glanced up at Tom, who nodded with tears in his eyes.

"We accept, Scooter," Lori replied, then embraced the man.

But Bridget wasn't convinced. Not yet. Not after what he'd said and what he'd done.

"You don't make promises," she said as her voice, sharp and strong, sliced through the room.

He met her gaze head-on with conviction written all over his face. "I do now because I understand what it means."

"What does it mean to you?" she challenged.

Her senses heightened as he walked toward her—each of his footfalls vibrating through her body.

"It means something like this," he replied, unzipping his coat and retrieving a folded packet of papers from his breast pocket. He handed them over to her, and she stared at the first few lines.

Bridget Dasher

Owner

Cupid Bakery Corporation

She glanced at the judge and then back to Soren.

"You're giving me a company? When did you have time to put this together?" she asked, dumbfounded.

The hint of a boyish grin bloomed on his lips. "Kringle Acres has a remarkably robust business center, and Mr. and Mrs. Angel just happened to be in the lobby, so I asked them if this was a workable solution to their company's situation."

Workable situation?

She kept reading. "It says here that Mr. and Mrs. Angel only want to remain involved in an advisory capacity."

"Yes, no one in their family is interested in taking over the business. They're ready to retire, and after sampling your cookies and seeing how you jumped at the chance to help the Kringle Cares group without a second thought, they feel the company would be in good hands with you at the helm."

"Oh," she answered, back to one-syllable utterances.

Not ten minutes ago, she was ready to forge ahead and open her own shop. Never, in a million years, did she see herself in charge of hundreds of bakeries across the country.

"All it takes is a signature, and it's yours if you want it. But there's a condition," he said.

She schooled her features and stared him down. "Of course, there is. What is it? The second I lose a penny, the company gets sliced and diced for profits?"

"No, you would be in complete control of the company. Rudolph Holdings will provide a healthy injection of cash to implement whatever changes and upgrades you choose to make. Rest assured, I'll have no say in what happens after that. If you choose to sell the business or decide you only want to specialize in making those *croque-whatever* ball desserts, it's all up to you."

Holy Christmas surprise!

In her hands, she held the chance to save a company that cared about its employees and its community. But that wasn't all she held.

This was a chance to save herself—to take the leap. But could she trust Soren?

She turned to the judge. "Is this for real?"

The man nodded. "It is, Birdie. And Mr. and Mrs. Angel expressed quite passionately that they very much want you to take over."

She stared at the contract in disbelief. "But they hardly know me?"

"They know your character, and they also know that you've always been on the nice list," the judge replied, cracking a grin.

She frowned. This was getting stranger by the second. "The nice list? That's really a thing?"

"And," the judge continued, "Ernie Angel would also like you to bake him a dozen sugar cookies. Not to mention, the residents of Kringle Acres also requested more of your peanut butter blossoms. It seems your baking skills have impressed even the most highly acclaimed cookie enthusiasts. If anyone knows good baking, it's a bunch of retired Santas, wouldn't you agree?"

It seemed too good to be true.

"Birdie, think of what Grandma Dasher wrote," Lori said from the other side of the room.

She met her sister's gaze, then looked around the room. All eyes were on her.

She lifted her chin a fraction and focused on the man in front of her. She wasn't sold yet.

"What's the condition?"

"That's the second promise I need to make today," Soren replied, his eyes burning with determination.

She watched him closely. "The condition is a promise?"

"Yes, but don't worry. Cupid Bakery is yours whether you choose to believe what I'm about to promise or not. But I hope you do."

"Are you two a thing?" Russ asked, scratching his head as Denise gave the man *duh* eyes.

"So, you were the ones who raided Frosty," Delores added, biting back a grin.

Oh boy! She'd almost forgotten they had an audience.

"Russ, Bridget and I met the day before we arrived at the Kringle Mountain House, and from that moment on, I haven't been the same," Soren answered.

"Do you mean that?" she asked.

"Every word. You've challenged everything I thought I knew about myself. You took me to task, and you never gave an inch. I didn't believe that someone like me deserved someone like you. I didn't trust myself. I thought I was destined to follow in my parents' footsteps. But I was wrong. I don't have to be like them. I get to choose the kind of man I want to be. And I choose to be someone worthy of you, Bridget. I'm sorry for all the terrible things I said last night. None of them were true. But here's what is. I choose you over everything else. I promise I will guard your heart and never be reckless with it again," he said, taking her trembling hand.

"You do?" she whispered.

He stroked his thumb across her knuckles. "I want to be with you. I want to dance with you while you bake. I want all your chocolate kisses. I want to watch you eat funnel cake. I want to kiss you under the mistletoe. If you let me, I want to spend my life proving to you that I'm worthy of your heart. I know I can be that man for you. I know because I've learned from the best," he said, first, meeting the judge's eye, and then, glancing over his shoulder at the Abbotts.

Who was this man?

"What happened to you?"

She had to ask.

He chuckled. "A bunch of Santas kicked my butt in poker last night, then they sat me down this morning and helped me get off the naughty list."

"The naughty list?" she repeated, unable to hold back the ghost of a smile.

"Let's just say that they helped me see the person I need to be for my friends and for the woman I love."

The breath caught in her throat. "You love me?"

He cupped her cheek in his hand. "You know, I do. I was just too stupid and too blinded by my fears to admit it. And that's the promise. Right here, right now, I promise to love you and protect your heart every day for the rest of my life."

Time moved slowly. She could see the edge and feel the pull to follow her grandmother's advice and take the leap.

But not yet.

"Your best friend is marrying my sister. You could have just pretended to like me if you wanted to be around them."

"I never thought of that," he replied, those cat-like eyes glittering with mischief.

She cocked her head to the side. "It might have been an easier solution than professing your undying love and giving me a multi-million-dollar company."

His jaw dropped, and she laughed.

"I'm just giving you a hard time," she added with a vixen smirk.

"She's a real Alice, this one, isn't she?" the judge said, clapping Soren on the shoulder.

"She sure is, Judge," Soren answered with sweet devotion coating each word.

"Tell me if I've got this right," she said, unable to hold back a grin. "You want to give me a company. You love me, and you promise to always protect my heart."

"And I'm not going to be a giant creep to your sister anymore. Don't forget that part," he added with a playful wink.

"Thanks, man! We appreciate it," Tom teased with his good-natured grin back in place.

Bridget shook her head and laughed. "I can see why the Santas beat you at poker. It looks like I'm holding all the cards, and you're supposed to be the big-time businessman. From where I'm standing, it appears I'm getting all the perks in this deal."

Soren's expression grew serious. "That's where you're wrong. If you say yes, then I'll have closed the best, most consequential deal I've ever made. From the first time I held you in my arms, I knew that I didn't want to be without you. Tell me you feel it, too."

She stared at his beautiful face as a memory bubbled to the surface. She was seven or maybe eight as she watched Lori leap from bench to bench in the Kringle Chapel.

Now, with her guardian angels watching over her, it was time for her to jump.

She blinked back tears. "I agree to your terms, Mr. Rudolph."

"All of them? Me and the bakery?" he asked, his gaze growing glassy.

"As long as you also promise you'll always hold the pastry cone when I make a croquembouche, then my answer is yes."

"Somebody, get me that damned cone," he replied, gathering her into his arms.

She melted into his embrace. Who would have thought that

this wild journey from anonymous lovers to mortal enemies would end with them as soul mates?

"A deal should be sealed with a kiss," the judge said and pointed to the ceiling.

She and Soren glanced up and found a sprig of mistletoe hanging from one of the rafters.

"When did that get there?" she asked.

"The Christmas fairy must have done it!" Cole answered,

"I think you're right, buddy," Soren replied, holding her gaze. In it, she saw nights spent warm in his embrace, gatherings with family and friends, and Christmases to come filled with love and joy.

The life she'd always wanted.

"I love you," she said, hardly able to believe that this man was hers.

He leaned in, a breath away from kissing her, and whispered against her lips. "And I love every part of you, Bridget Dasher, not your average vixen."

EPILOGUE
SOREN

"I love when you test a new recipe," he growled, wrapping Bridget's dark locks around his hand and pulling—hard—as he thrust into her from behind.

"It's a lot of trial and error," she answered with a gasp, welcoming his hard length as he drove into her, watching their bodies rock and writhe in the mirror.

If someone had told him that whenever the love of his life, Bridget "the eternal vixen" Dasher, had perfected a recipe that she'd instantly want him to rock her world in bed to celebrate her culinary conquest, he'd have declared his adoration the moment he'd met her.

But some things were worth the wait.

And that's where they were. A year after he'd handed her his heart and promised to protect hers, he could not imagine a life without this petite brunette beauty by his side.

"Soren, don't stop!" she cried, arching her back as he gripped her hips, taking her hard and fast.

He could never get enough of his angel-eyed vixen.

Life had moved fast after he'd put it all on the line and

professed his love in front of Dan, Delores, and the entire Abbott clan.

A little recap:

Tom and Lori's wedding went off without a hitch.

Thanks to the snowcats, Rudolph, Vixen, and Dasher, everyone made it to the Kringle Chapel. Lit by candlelight, Tom and Lori had wed surrounded by the people who loved them the most. Cole had been an incredible ring bearer, and Carly had scattered petals like she was born to be a flower girl.

They'd celebrated at the mountain house, drinking good wine, eating Bridget's delicious wedding cake, and dancing the night away to the sweet crooning of Bing Crosby, singing their Christmas favorites.

It was a night to remember. The first night he didn't straddle the line between Soren and Scooter, and the first night when he trusted his heart to lead the way. And as he laughed with Bridget by his side, watching Tom smash red velvet cake into Lori's mouth, he understood the real meaning of family.

Thanks to the kindness of Lawrence Duncan, a bunch of retired Santas, and the judge, he'd shed the chains that tethered him to his childhood and had risen to become the man he was supposed to be. A man who didn't focus on the sorrows of the past but set his sights squarely on the possibilities of the future.

"Do you know how sexy you are?" he asked, catching her eye in the mirror.

"Show me," she purred, then bit her bottom lip.

Holy holly and the ivy! That vixen drove him the best kind of crazy!

He pulled out and had her on her back in the space of a breath. Covering her body with his, he held her wrists above her head with one hand while positioning himself at her entrance with the other. But before he thrust inside, he kissed a trail down her jawline and inhaled her cinnamon vanilla scent that sent his pulse racing. She hummed her pleasure, a dirty little sound that went straight to his hard length, and it took everything he had to hold himself back. He wanted one moment, this moment, to lose himself in her deep mahogany eyes, and his best friend's words had never rung truer.

I wish you could understand what it's like when you lock eyes with someone, and you know that your life will never be the same.

When Tom had first dropped this sappy love bullshit on him, he'd balked.

Now he understood completely. His raven-haired beauty had captured his heart the first time he met her gaze.

So much had changed this past year. He'd met with all his employees once he'd returned to New York and shared a new vision for the company. A vision where Rudolph Holdings wasn't a predatory firm that snapped up weak businesses ripe to be pillaged and sold off piece by piece.

No, his revelation in Kringle, Colorado, had changed him, heart and soul.

With a resounding nod of approval from Janine, Rudolph Holdings became a consulting firm that provided companies with a plan for improved profits and viability.

Did it make him the millions it used to?

Actually, yes.

Investing in struggling businesses and providing sustainable plans rather than standing by as they failed turned out to be highly lucrative. And it allowed him to go to bed each night knowing that instead of greedily taking, he'd given from the heart.

Take that, Scrooge!

And the truth was, he didn't even have to work if he didn't want to.

Why?

He had a sugar mama!

His sexy baker was making money hand over fist.

Bridget had taken over Cupid Bakeries, and with her innovations, she'd brought the mom and pop company into the twenty-first century. She'd also made a few acquisitions over the last year, purchasing struggling bakeries, and then converting them into Cupid Bakeries while simultaneously working with the staff to make them profitable.

Now, a certain French pâtisserie in Dallas belonged to the Cupid Bakery family.

That's right! His vixen was Gaston Francois' boss.

Boom!

And if that wasn't enough, she'd also become an internet baking sensation. Once Lori had posted the video of his vixen icing the wedding cake, the fanbase for Cupid Bakery's new owner and CEO went through the roof.

And there were even more changes.

Bridget no longer called Texas home, and he'd said goodbye to New York City. They'd made Boston their base, each opening an office in the area, and called a townhouse near Lori and Tom's Beacon Hill neighborhood home. He'd kept the NYC office open, with Janine running the show, but his life was here with Bridget and the Abbotts in Massachusetts.

He didn't need to compartmentalize anymore. He didn't have one persona that lived like a spoiled playboy while the other enjoyed the camaraderie of friendship and family. No, he'd integrated Soren and Scooter just as his girlfriend was both Bridget and Birdie.

"What are you waiting for?" Bridget asked with a tantalizing twist to her lips. Her dark tangle of hair fanned out over the pillow like a halo, framing her face. Sweet Christ! He could stare at her all day. But when his vixen rolled her hips, it was time to get down to business.

Tightening his grip on her wrists, he held her in place as he slid inside her wet heat and sucked in a tight breath. The sensation never dampened. Their connection never diminished. The magnetic pull between them only strengthened, and he made love to her with a frenzied ferocity. Pistons pumping, he drove in hard, grinding into her sweet bud while setting a pace that had Bridget purring.

He knew her body and could read all her tells. She was so close, hovering on the edge. Her eyelids fluttered open, and she was there, bucking and meeting him blow for delicious carnal blow. Lost in her eyes, he let go. Their mouths crashed together, swallowing each other's cries of delirious pleasure as the feverish pace slowed, and their bodies, warm and sated, gasped for breath in the glow of sweet release.

He let go of her wrists, and she cupped his face in her hands. "Have we depleted Frosty?"

He chuckled. "Just about."

They were back at Kringle Mountain to spend another Christmas together with the Abbotts. They'd decided to make it a tradition. But this year, they welcomed one more along for the festivities when a sharp knock at the door reminded them that they weren't alone in this house.

"Hey, Uncle Scooter and Birdie! When can we eat that giant Christmas tree you made with all those balls? I need those balls!"

Bridget pressed her lips together to stifle a chuckle.

"Give us a few minutes, Cole. We're checking the cookbook for another treat Birdie wants to make for you."

"More treats! I love Christmas! Oh, and Aunt Lori says she could use your help, Uncle Scooter."

"Let everyone know we'll be right there, buddy," he called as they listened to Cole skip down the hall toward the main room.

It was good to be back at Kringle Mountain.

"Checking the cookbook for another treat? You know I have all my recipes memorized," Bridget said, eyes twinkling.

"I had to go with something a bit more PG than we were screwing our brains out."

"Good call," she answered with a giggle. "But we better get out there. It sounds like the Scooter Whisperer is needed."

They dressed quickly, and as Bridget twisted her hair into a bun, he covertly slipped a little something into his breast pocket.

"Ready?" she asked.

He nodded.

She was about to find out just how ready he was.

They entered the main gathering area. The decorated trees twinkled in each corner, the fire roared, and holiday music played in the background as snow swirled, setting the scene for the perfect mountain Christmas when a sharp cry caught their attention.

"Scooter, can you help? Little Scooter only seems to settle with you," Lori said, handing over a tiny fussing baby, swaddled in a blanket covered in scooters.

He rocked the child in his arms and smiled down at Soren "Little Scooter" Abbott.

The boy stared up at him, and he ran his finger down the baby's cheek.

"Who knew you'd be so good with babies. What other Christmas surprises do you have in store for us?" Bridget teased.

He gazed at the people he loved most in this world. Everyone was here. This was the moment.

He handed the cooing baby back to Lori, then sank to his knee in front of Bridget, and removed a velvet pouch from his pocket.

He emptied the contents into his hand and smiled up at the woman who, every day, took his breath away.

"There's one more surprise, and we'll get to see if my

Christmas wish comes true." He held up a sparkling diamond ring. "Bridget Dasher, part angel, part vixen, will you be all mine until death do us part?"

"How did you know?" she asked, her mahogany eyes sparkling.

He cocked his head to the side. "Know what?"

"That this was my Christmas wish, too," she answered, extending her left hand.

With their family and friends looking on, he tossed Cole a little wink before sliding the ring on Bridget's finger. "A Christmas fairy must have told me."

Thank you for reading *Not Your Average Vixen*! Are you ready for more romance? Of course, you are!

If you're up for another romantic comedy, check out Krista Sandor's 3-book Bergen Brothers Series.

Want to add a little angst to the mix? Binge the 5-book Langley Park Series.

For updates on author appearances and new releases, visit www.KristaSandor.com

ALSO BY KRISTA SANDOR

Sign up for Krista's newsletter to get all the up-to-date Krista Sandor Romance news at www.KristaSandor.com

The Kiss Keeper

A sexy romance set on the coast of Maine

The Bergen Brothers Series

A steamy billionaire brothers romantic comedy series

Book One: Man Fast

Book Two: Man Feast

Book Three: Man Find

Bergen Brothers: The Complete Series+Bonus Short Story

The Langley Park Series

A suspenseful, sexy second-chance at love series

Book One: The Road Home

Book Two: The Sound of Home

Book Three: The Beginning of Home

Book Four: The Measure of Home

Book Five: The Story of Home

Own the Eights Series

A delightfully sexy enemies to lovers series

Book One: Own the Eights

Book Two: Own the Eights Gets Married

Book Three: Own the Eights Maybe Baby

Learn more at

www.KristaSandor.com

THE INSIDE SCOOP + PLAYLIST
NOT YOUR AVERAGE VIXEN: A CHRISTMAS ROMANCE

Back in 2018, I was asked to write a sexy short bedtime story for a romance site. I had three nights to share my tale, and I happened to get the three nights leading up to Christmas.

Hello, sexy holiday story!

Birdie and Scooter came to me immediately. I love silly nicknames and couldn't wait to put these two together! I can't even begin to tell you how hard it was to sit on their complete story. I'd spent the better part of 2019 and 2020 finishing the Langley Park Series and writing the Bergen Brothers. Then came the Own the Eights Series and my standalone, The Kiss Keeper. Finally, in July of 2020, it was time to write Birdie and Scooter's complete story.

To get into the holiday spirit in the middle of a hot Colorado summer, I asked my newsletter subscribers to send me the titles of their favorite holiday songs, and they delivered! From Bing Crosby to the Mannheim Steamroller, their suggestions got me feeling all the Christmas vibes. This was incredibly helpful because my husband and sons vetoed my request to put up the tree five months early!

To listen to the playlist on Spotify, go to Spotify and search for Not Your Average Vixen. Happy listening!

ACKNOWLEDGMENTS

NOT YOUR AVERAGE VIXEN: A CHRISTMAS ROMANCE

I don't know where I'd be without my team of editors, alpha-readers, and proofers. Tera, Marla, and Carrie are my eagle-eyed editing trifecta. This book was a beast coming in at over ninety-thousand words. These characters had a lot to say, and you checked each and every word. You will always have my heartfelt gratitude.

My cover designer, Marisa-rose Wesley of Cover Me Darling, crafted the perfect cover for Vixen before it was even written, and it became my inspiration. Then Emma Rider put together the book trailer. Thank you both for your creativity and kindness!

I have to thank the members of my Book Babes reader group and the women on my Advanced Reviewer Team. You guys are always behind me, cheering me on, posting reviews, and lighting up my life every day. I am grateful to know you and call you my friends.

Thank you to my author besties, Jessa York, Alley Ciz, and SE Rose, for helping me craft the perfect Vixen blurb. You guys are the best. Thank you for always making me laugh and keeping me sane!

And to you, dear reader, your support makes this all possible! Thank you!

ABOUT THE AUTHOR

If there's one thing USA Today Bestselling Author Krista Sandor knows for sure, it's that romance saved her.

After she was diagnosed with Multiple Sclerosis in 2015, her world turned upside down. During those difficult first days, her dear friend sent her a romance novel. That kind gesture provided the escape she needed and ignited her love of the genre.

Inspired by the strong heroines and happily ever afters, Krista decided to write her own romance novels.

Today, she's an MS warrior and living life to the fullest. When she's not writing, you can find her running 5Ks with her husband or chasing after her growing boys in Denver, Colorado.

Never miss a release, contest, or author event. Visit Krista's website and sign up to receive her exclusive newsletter.